I0653661

TO CURE THE

HUMANS!

Douglas Lewis

The characters and events portrayed in this book are
fictitious. Any similarity to real persons, living or dead, is
coincidental and not intended by the author.
Copyright © 2013 Douglas Lewis
All rights reserved.
ISBN-13: 978-0615900056
ISBN-10: 0615900054

Acknowledgements

This book would not have been possible without the efforts of a group of generous, wonderful, and talented individuals. Seriously, you should know these people. First and foremost, I would like to express my gratitude to my editor, Tammy Valentine, for her time and effort and skill, and for her patience with my many questions. I am also grateful for her understanding and forgiving nature – I'm counting on that understanding and forgiveness when she realizes that I didn't incorporate all of her editorial suggestions.

I would also like to thank Mike McNulty for reviewing my rough manuscript. His feedback, suggestions and support were invaluable. His recommendation to be consistent with serial commas was greatly appreciated (and yet ignored in the sentence preceding this one). Also thanks to Mark Card for taking the time to be a beta reader, but more importantly, for his support and encouragement. I am indebted to Michael Moebes for his technical assistance. It was a joy to work with David Simmer II, who is responsible for the awesome cover art and design. This book probably would not have been written and published if not for Robert Kroese. His success at writing and self-publishing guided and motivated me. He is a funny and gifted writer, and you should read his stuff.

Lastly, I thank my wife, Lori, for putting up with me for more than 400 pages and 30 years.

ONE

Overcorrected.

That was Benjamin Cotter's first thought after he turned his car's steering wheel by slinging his arms in a manner usually reserved for inattentive helmsmen surprised by large, sturdy icebergs. Seconds earlier, Dr. Cotter had been driving from Dallas to Hilldale, where he practiced ophthalmology. Though both cities were in Texas, the Dallas metropolitan area had as much in common with the town of Hilldale as the town of Hilldale had in common with a nice toaster over.

This probably won't end well.

Two weeks earlier, Ben had been following a gravel truck when errant gravel – distressed over its impending fate of being turned into turnpike concrete – leaped from the trailer. One of those pebbles struck Dr. Cotter's windshield, creating a crystalline spider-web fracture. "Yesss!" could be heard from the ricocheting gravel, had anyone been listening. The auto shop technician did a serviceable job of replacing Ben's windshield, but he ran out of glue at the critical step of rear-view mirror reattachment. In lieu of proper adhesive, he used a wad of chewed gum (probably his own) to secure the mirror to the windshield. When the rear-view mirror inevitably succumbed to gravity and fell to the passenger side floor, Ben reached for it and took his eyes off of the road.

With the mirror in hand, Ben turned his attention back to the road and noticed that he was driving on the left side – acceptable in some of your nicer European countries, but generally frowned upon in Texas. The oncoming red pickup truck created an even more frown-worthy situation. Benjamin slung the steering wheel to the right, the car pitched, and a tiny switch in his brain flipped - triggering a neurochemical cascade and altering his perception of time and space. Ben had sometimes performed experiments with this switch in college, unsupervised, alone in his dorm room.

Overcorrected thought Ben as the rear end of his car made a strong bid to overcome the front end of his car. As the pickup passed unscathed, Ben steered to the left in an attempt to correct his overcorrection. Then, for good measure, he steered to the right again culminating in an over-overcorrection.

This probably won't end well announced Ben's inner dialogue over the sound of plastic on metal as his front bumper scraped across a guardrail (dutifully protecting large cylinders of hay) like young knees across pavement. With the apparent slowing of time, Dr. Cotter's panic dissolved and his mind drifted to more mundane matters. He reminded himself to replace that broken coffee maker. He wondered why soccer never really caught on in America. And – in light of his current circumstances – he congratulated himself for not getting suckered into purchasing the optional undercoating. When the pinballing stopped, Ben realized that his car had spun a complete 360 degrees. He held up the rear-view mirror, still ensconced in his trembling hand, and watched the pickup truck continuing down the road behind him.

"Probably Mr. Daugherty," he said out loud with a hint of exasperation.

Ben guessed that the other driver was Vernon Daugherty. Mr. Daugherty wasn't mean spirited or incurious, but he *was* legally blind – he probably never saw Ben's car. Mr. Daugherty suffered from dense cataracts, but had refused surgical intervention. Instead, he opted to use "cataract reversal" eye drops imported from Estonia. That decision was heavily influenced by Mr. Daugherty's unfortunate possession of both gullibility and internet access. As Vernon's vision deteriorated from 20/20 to "should not be allowed to vote or use a microwave oven," Dr. Cotter made it a point to recognize Vernon's pickup truck.

Ben turned the ignition, but the car refused to start. He tried again, this time glaring harder at the "check engine" light. Still no luck. Unlatching the seat belt and stepping out of the car, Ben felt the sting of a seat belt burn to his torso, but all body parts seemed to be in working order. The car was a different matter. The front bumper appeared to have been fed into a wood chipper, and one wheel was tilted at an embarrassing angle. For a split second the image of a tower in Italy flashed in Ben's brain. Because of Ben's extensive medical training, he could only conclude that the engine would not start because it was "out of whack." He took the cell phone out of his pocket.

Great. No signal. He walked several yards behind the car to retrieve his origamied front license plate, returned to the car, and threw it onto the driver's seat. Turning the steering wheel to the right, Ben pushed the car as far off of the road as possible. Odds were Mr. Daugherty would be heading back this way.

Ben started walking. His plan seemed straightforward. He would walk to a convenience store and use their pay phone – because the Convenience Corner was less than three miles away and still in the 1950s. He would call a wrecker to retrieve his car and tow it to a shop in Dallas. Then he would call Wendy – his receptionist in Hilldale – to pick him up and drive him to the office.

Despite being thirty-something and paunchier than he had planned to be at this age, Dr. Cotter was more annoyed than daunted by the thought of walking three miles. Texas summers have the bothersome habit of lingering well into October, and soon after Ben started his trek beads of sweat drizzled from his forehead to his bushy brows. The afternoon sun revealed some premature gray and reflected off of his thickish wire-framed glasses, glasses that made a statement – that statement being "I sat too close to the TV as a youngster."

He saw an expanse of dead grass to his right with a line of trees at the far end. To make time he decided to take a shortcut across the field. Halfway across, inspired by heat and dust and inappropriate footwear, Ben again took the cell phone out of his pocket.

Still no service. He trudged onward, expecting to find the highway after getting past the trees. Instead he found a grassy clearing surrounded by post oaks, and at the edge of the clearing stood what appeared to be an implausibly large Samsonite suitcase. The suitcase appeared to be about three stories high, taupe, with a chrome handle attached to the top, and two bulky rubber feet on the bottom. Ben attempted to visualize the dimensions of the overhead bin required to house this oversized piece of luggage, and concluded that there was not an airline in the world that would accept it as carry-on without a great deal of carrying on.

Ben crept toward the object. He felt compelled to investigate. If nothing else, he would at least have something to talk about at the office instead of his sketchy driving skills. The closer he got to the unlikely monolith the more he felt drawn to it – like a moth drawn to a really nice moth hotel with an ocean view, great room service, and a check-out clerk who doesn't bat an eye when totaling up the in-room movie charges. Reaching the object, Ben heard the sound of flowing water coming from the opposite side; it was less than one might expect from a mountain stream, but more than one would expect to hear from luggage of any size. The sound stopped, and Ben froze. There was some rustling of grass and a wiry man with stringy hair and a thick black belt appeared from behind the structure.

"*What* are you doing here?" said the man, sounding more irritated than surprised.

"I was just taking a shortcut. I wrecked my -"

"How much have you seen?" asked the man.

"Just this here," Ben said, looking up at the suitcase. "That's all. And you, of course...but not till just now!" Ben was trying to assuage the stranger, in case he suspected that Ben was surreptitiously attempting to watch him take a whiz. Ben was prepared to reassure him that his curiosity regarding all things related to urine had been sated by the end of his second week of medical school.

"Arrrghhh," said the man. "You have already seen too much." He paced, head down, hands behind his back. Dr. Cotter scoured his memory of cocktail parties to unearth an excuse to leave. He considered "The hospital called," but that seemed to lack credibility here in the middle of nowhere. The thought of a waiting room filled with patients at the Hilldale office hadn't quite worked its way into Ben's consciousness when the man stopped and pointed a finger at him. It was a finger lacking a fingernail.

"What is your name?" said the man.

"Ben. Dr. Ben Cotter."

"Well, Dr. Ben Cotter. In less than six minutes you have turned my covert operation here on Earth into an un-covert operation. Well done!"

Hearing the word "covert," Ben first thought that he had stumbled upon a secret military project (which would make the suitcase khaki rather than taupe.) When "here on Earth" was spoken, he entertained the absurd possibility that the stranger in front of him was an extraterrestrial visitor. But when the stranger finished with "Well done!" Ben concluded that no alien being – however advanced – could master the subtleties of sarcasm in English in only six minutes.

Nut job, thought Ben. He took stock of the stranger's peculiar appearance. His shoulder-length hair was offset by a generous hairline originating near the crown of his head, and he sported a green paisley shirt that – if life was fair – should have come with a coupon for motion-sickness pills.

"I'm sorry. I really need to get going. I've got a waiting room full of patients who are by now being more unpleasant than usual," Ben said.

"My name is Cyril. And you're a doctor? Hmmm...might prove useful. Although it doesn't really matter. I can't have you running around willy-nilly telling everyone what you've seen here, can I?

So you will be coming with me – at least until my work here is done. And please don't be a whiner. I *hate* that." Cyril grinned as he removed the tin foil from a stick of gum, then he popped the gum into his mouth.

"No, thanks anyway. My schedule is really booked. And I'm not much of a talker anyway, I promise," Ben said. He made a zipping motion across pursed lips that he hoped was convincing.

Benjamin turned and started making his way across the clearing and away from Cyril. After four or five steps, Ben gave what turned out to be a premature sigh of relief. Cyril took the chewed gum from his mouth, rolled it into a ball between his palms, and threw it like a second-grade spitball ninja, striking Ben on the back of his neck with a *splitch.*

*Well, if that's the worst you can do...*was the thought Ben's brain generated, but he only managed to get out "well" before he felt tingling at the site of impact. By the time he said "if" Ben noticed two things. One – the tingling in his neck had exploded into excruciating pain, coursing through his body like shamelessness through a politician. And, two – he was unable to notice anything other than the excruciating pain. It hurt to move. It hurt to breathe. It hurt to think, so he tried not to while his body took a vote with Ben in absentia and decided in a landslide victory that lying flat on the ground might be a very good thing to do.

Feels like white-hot microscopic shards of broken glass soaked in rubbing alcohol and Karaoke ripping through every neuron and capillary in my body, Ben thought before his consciousness winked out.

Blutaark is a smallish planet orbiting a white star in the M81 galaxy, the largest galaxy in the M81 group, a fact Blutaarkians never fail to mention at posh intergalactic parties while hemming and hawing when asked about the size of their home planet. They are similar to humans in many respects, but by banning reality television and real estate agents, they evolved a vastly superior civilization and pioneered advances such as boson-complex communication, inflation-based space travel, and respectful teenagers. They are generally regarded as the brightest life forms in the M81 galaxy, but behind their backs they are relentlessly teased about their spaceships, most of which bear an uncanny resemblance to the hard-side Samsonite luggage sold on Earth circa 1970.

Teasing them to their faces is almost unheard of, since Blutaarkian saliva is one of the most potent pain-producing neurotoxins in the universe. Though fatalities are rare and the pain short-lived, many victims develop Blutaarkian Toxin Stress Disorder (BTSD). Sequelae of BTSD include an inability to maintain gainful employment and an intense fear or Saint Bernards. The upshot of this is that any species with a nervous system is on its very best behavior when within spitting distance of a Blutaarkian. That distance is approximately two feet. A wad of well-chewed gum increases the range to several yards, as Dr. Ben Cotter discovered on Earth one Wednesday afternoon in October.

Benjamin opened his eyes. His initial euphoria at experiencing pain-free blinking faded into profound disappointment when he realized Cyril still existed. They were seated in a long, narrow cabin with Ben belted into a molded plastic seat in the rear of the compartment. He reached into his pocket for his cell phone, but got nothing but pocket lint. Cyril was seated in a large black seat in the front, hovering over what looked to be an audio mixing board.

"Great," Ben said. "First I get tased, now you're going to torture me by playing some original music. Or worse, Celine Dion."

"Feeling better?" Cyril said. He manipulated switches and dials.

"No," Ben said. "How long will I have to listen to your mix tape before you let me go?"

"Shut up," barked Cyril. "We'll be taking off presently. Make sure you're buckled securely."

"We're taking off in a giant suitcase?" Ben said as he peered through a small porthole window.

"All right. Alllriiight. You just had to go there, didn't you?" Cyril said. "Like I haven't heard that a million times before. It's always 'Where did you find that, on the astro-port luggage carousel?' or 'It must take you *forever* to pack.' Believe you me, most Blutaarkians are sick and tired of the ridicule."

Ben took Cyril's rant as an opportunity to notice the unfortunate absence of an emergency exit door, air sickness bags, or decent reading material.

"It's jealousy, pure jealousy," Cyril said. "The *Rev 9* may not look like much, but she's fast and reliable. And then there's the resale value – she's easily worth twice as much as the same model year *Bevelmopgus II*. And *they* always upcharge for that pointless undercoating."

Ben had a strong suspicion that the passenger seats in the *Bevelmopgus II* were exponentially more comfortable than those in the *Rev 9*, but kept it to himself. Cyril's attention returned to the mixing board. Ben immediately felt his body being sucked into the increasingly uncomfortable seat as the tree trunks in the little round window turned into blue sky.

"Would a countdown been too much to ask?" shrieked Ben. The craft accelerated vertically, then rolled enough to allow him to see the trees below shrinking away like bacon in a frying pan – if you were watching a frying pan full of bacon from a spaceship approaching escape velocity. "Where are you taking me?" he shouted, despite the conspicuous absence of screaming babies and jet engines. "Some horrid, desolate alien planet?"

"No," Cyril said. "Alabama."

"Even worse," Ben said.

The *Rev 9* accelerated horizontally. Several thousand feet below a red pickup truck sideswiped a car abandoned on the side of a two-lane highway.

TWO

"Bummer." He glared at the "check engine" light. Peter relished life on the lam, but an unexpected failure of his *Rev 2*'s inflationary space drive threatened to end it. The *Rev 2* was moving fast enough to coast to the nearest solar system, but his landing options were limited. There was only one "Goldilocks" planet - one planet that wasn't so close to its sun that porridge would vaporize. One planet that wasn't so far from its sun that porridge would freeze solid. One planet with menacing bears.

To make matters worse, this planet had "anti-Goldilocks" technological development: advanced enough to annihilate itself in a matter of minutes, but not advanced enough to be able to repair a broken *Rev 2*. Peter entered the coordinates for Earth.

"Should engage the magnetic field brakes at the edge of the solar system, hit the retro rockets in the upper atmosphere," Peter said out loud. "Will be landing a skosh faster than the owner's manual recommends, but an uncontrolled landing is better than no landing at all."

No landing at all would mean coasting through intergalactic space until his sporty, single-seat dome-canopied *Rev 2* stopped dead. The annoying bounty hunter who had been pestering Peter for months would apprehend him and return him to Blutaark for a sizable reward. *Cyril*, thought Peter, shaking his head. *To be captured by him? How insulting.* He had shared a few classes with Cyril at Northern Blutaark U. Cyril would brazenly crib form Peter's notes during the day, and at night he'd track Peter down at one of the local pubs. There, he would attempt to engender a friendship with Peter by being disagreeable and alternating alcohol consumption with riding the mechanical looglack. (Although sometimes he attempted those simultaneously.)

Peter graduated before Cyril (Cyril's drinking and looglack - induced head trauma took its toll) and went to work for the Life Sciences Administration in the biological survey department. Cyril was rejected by the Blutaark Department of Defense, but he put his loud talking, excessive drinking, and indifference to head injuries to good use by becoming a bounty hunter.

"Here we go," Peter said. At this distance the sun was but a single white fleck on a black sweater belonging to a long-suffering dandruff victim. He engaged the magnetic field brakes and the *Rev 2* bucked like an ill-tempered looglack. Peter had never wondered what it would be like to have his head agitated by a pneumatic paint-can shaker, but now he knew. "Oh yeah," he said, remembering to disengage what was left of the inflationary drive. Fighting turbulence-induced tremors, he punched the glowing blue button and the *Rev 2* settled down. Later on his stomach did, too.

Will be coming in too fast for sure now. Peter realized that he would need to engage the retro rockets sooner than originally planned. He had narrowly escaped from Cyril on Gyllenhaal 6 and missed an opportunity to refuel. His *Rev 2* was low on propellant. Running out of rocket fuel was an ideal recipe for turning a perfectly good *Rev 2* into a large crater and spaceship dust. A water landing was out of the question; even if he survived the impact, walking away would be problematic. The sun was now the size of an aspirin tablet. He secured his backpack and put his helmet on.

Peter took a deep breath when the little blue dot appeared, and the *Rev 2*'s guidance system locked in an approach to Earth. He flipped a red toggle switch to activate the retro rockets, then tapped a button on the joystick to fire them. "Aces," he said, feeling the seat belt tense against his chest. The *Rev 2* ripped into the Earth's upper atmosphere. He depressed the joystick button, holding it a little longer this time. Peter felt the familiar strain against the seat belt and saw the fuel level sink faster than he expected. "Two of clubs."

Peter's spacecraft plummeted through wispy upper-level clouds, but a lower-level cloud deck was approaching like a hyper-caffeinated gray tsunami. Ship sensors detected solid ground below, approaching fast enough to elicit a cheery "Do please prepare for impact in sixty seconds" from Soledad, the onboard computer, like she was telling him to put his tray table in the upright and locked position.

"If it's all the same to you, I'd rather prepare to *avoid* impact, thank you," Peter said as he punched the joystick button and held it down. The *Rev 2*'s velocity decreased in lockstep with the shrinking green bar on the fuel indicator. It pierced the cloud deck and was enveloped in a gray fog – the only sound a reassuring roar from the retro rockets.

"Fuel levels dangerously low," chirped Soledad. The green bar was replaced by a flashing red light.

"Locate a service facility immediately."

"Why didn't I think of that?" Peter said. "Perhaps there will be one at the impact site."

"Prepare for impact in forty seconds."

"Thanks for the update. You're a doll." The muffled growl of the retro rockets stopped as the winking light froze solid red.

"Rocket fuel depleted. Calculations indicate that you will be crash landing in the United States, specifically - the state of Alabama. Prepare for impact in thirty, twenty-nine, twenty-eight..."

The *Rev 2* broke through the cloud deck. "Yee haw," Peter said. His left hand grasped a red-handled lever next to his seat.

"Twenty-five, twenty-four...I must say that it has truly been a pleasure working with you. Twenty..."

"Soledad – I was really hoping you'd give at least two weeks' notice," Peter said. He pulled the lever. Two red-and-white striped drogue chutes billowed behind the *Rev 2*. "Subtle," Peter said. The craft lurched upward before settling into a steady descent.

"Fifteen, fourteen...recalculating. Superb idea, using the emergency chutes," commented Soledad.

"Thanks."

"I wish I had thought of that. I hope this does not jeopardize our future working relationship."

"I doubt it," Peter said.

On a small farm outside of Liberal, Kansas (three-time winner of the "Most Ironically Named City in America") Carl Kenroy watched a strange object fall from the sky. He would later report that it deployed parachutes, and then landed without a sound behind his tool shed. A helmeted humanoid emerged from the vehicle, dragged Carl indoors by a black strap wrapped around Carl's ankles, made him listen to rap music, then tricked Carl and his wife Carlene into signing long-term gym membership contracts.

At the exact moment Carl Kenroy saw an object fall from the Kansas skies, Peter landed the *Rev 2* in an auto salvage yard on the outskirts of Birmingham, Alabama. Peter removed his helmet and placed it under the seat. He unbuckled, grabbed his backpack, popped the hatch, and scampered out.

"Buh-bye," Soledad said.

"Later, Soledad." Peter gathered up the chutes and stuffed them into the back of a '72 Ford Pinto. He leaned against the front-quarter panel, took a few deep breaths, and thought about his predicament. Now that he had avoided converting his spaceship from a three-dimensional object into a two-dimensional one, his focus returned to Cyril.

It had been a close call on Gyllenhaal 6, and now Peter was on the only habitable planet in the adjacent solar system. Even Cyril could figure that out. Eventually. With some prompting. Peter rifled through the items in his backpack: a couple of t-shirts, a pair of pants, one utility tool, a handful of snack bars, one travel brochure ("Fun Things To Do On Gyllenhaal 6"), an empty felt-lined box, two power modules, and at the bottom a cylindrical object – roughly the size of a large flashlight – with a brushed aluminum shell and a black matte handle. He took the last object out of his pack and inspected it. It was no worse for wear after a bumpy ride and rough landing. He pulled a power module from the backpack, plugged it into the bottom of the cylinder, and powered it up. The icy blue LCD screen reflected in Peter's eyes.

"Magnificent," Peter said. "All systems go." He

turned it off, disconnected the power module, and tucked both items into the bottom of his pack. He set the backpack down and scavenged from the flotsam of wrecked and abandoned cars. He cloaked the *Rev 2* with a mélange of loose body panels of varying shapes, colors, and rust content. Not a perfect disguise, but it looked enough like the other vehicles to ensure that no one would bother it – unless they happened to be looking for those particular car parts. Peter zipped his pack, lifted it to one shoulder, and trotted toward the chain-link fence.

"Are we there yet?" Ben said.

"Sure. Get out," Cyril said.

Ben looked out of the porthole. The cloud cover below made it impossible to see the ground or judge airspeed.

"Well, how long until we get there?"

"Stop whining," Cyril said.

"Not whining, just asking."

"Soon enough." Cyril's nail-less fingers turned some dials, depressed a couple of buttons, and flipped a few switches. Ben could feel the ship slowing to a stop. "We're directly over the landing site. Prepare for rapid vertical descent."

"How do I pre -" Ben would have finished his sentence, but at that moment the laws of physics decreed that his tongue be immobilized against the roof of his mouth as the *Rev 9* plunged toward the Earth. The cabin dimmed, then brightened as the ship passed into and out of the cloud deck.

On a small dairy farm outside of Yazoo City, Mississippi, Bertram Fowler looked up to see a small tan object against an overcast sky. The object grew larger, and at some point Bertram decided that it looked like a suitcase falling from the sky. According to witnesses, Bert stood transfixed, staring at the object until it was too late. His head was crushed by the tan Samsonite hard shell that had somehow managed to fall from Delta flight 1489 Atlanta-to-Houston.

At the exact moment that Bertram Fowler had become the first luggage-associated fatality in Mississippi in over eight years, Cyril landed the *Rev 9* in an auto salvage yard just outside of Birmingham, Alabama. Cyril bolted through the open hatch that appeared in the floor of the cabin. Ben unbuckled and followed Cyril down metal steps and out into the junkyard.

Peter had noticed the *Rev 9* breaking through the cloud cover right after he had noticed the concertina wire at the top of the fence. *Good thing I'm a fast healer.* The fence *clink clink clinked* as he scrambled to the top. Flinching, he pushed the razor wire down with his palms and forearms, grabbed the top rail of the fence, and flipped onto the ground. He ran across a dirt road that bordered the salvage yard. Peter was heading toward the woods beyond the road when Cyril emerged from the *Rev 9*.

"Halt, rapscallion!" Cyril said as he ran to the fence.

"No, thank you," Peter said, looking over his shoulder and flashing a mischievous grin. "Someone get a new thesaurus for his birthday?"

"Arrrghhh!" Cyril said. Cyril thrashed his shoulders from side-to-side, gathered himself, then pulled something from his belt and aimed it at the elusive figure. A luminous blue ping pong ball shot through the fence and crashed into the tree closest to Peter. It exploded, leaving a scintillating mess on the tree trunk and the smell of turpentine in the air.

"Recharging. Please wait," came a tiny voice from a speaker on Cyril's plasma immobilizer.

"Oh, perfect," Cyril said. He tapped his foot as Peter cut to the right and disappeared into the pines. Peter sprinted, knowing he could easily outrun Cyril, but he didn't know where he was running to. Cyril stood at the fence, then turned and shouted to Ben. "We're going after him."

"I'll go find a gate," Ben said, eyeing the razor-topped fence.

"No time. Come here and give me a boost."

Ben dashed to the fence, keen on the idea of having Cyril on the opposite side. But by the time he got there, Cyril was having second thoughts. He was looking at the top of the fence. He wasn't a fast healer.

"I can't go over the top," Cyril said. "I'll give you a boost."

"I can't. I'm a bleeder," Ben said, dragging out an excuse he had not used since high school gym class. "Besides, what would I do on the other side?"

"Good point," admitted Cyril. "Hand me your fence cutters."

"I don't know what you've heard about this planet," Ben said. "But we don't carry fence cutters with us all the time. Honestly, I don't know of anyone who even owns fence cutters. Besides, it would sort of defeat the purpose of having fences in the first place. I mean, if anyone could just go up to a fence and in a matter of seconds create an opening in it, then why bother?"

"Blast you," Cyril said. "Wait here." He stormed back to the *Rev 9*. Ben hoped that "blast" was a figure of speech. Cyril returned and set to work on the fence with what appeared to be electric fabric scissors, but probably weren't. The tool hummed and the chain links sparked and popped until there was a large opening cut into the fence that completely defeated its purpose.

"Come on!" Cyril said. He motioned to Ben through a crescent-shaped opening. "He couldn't have gotten far. Stay with me and keep your eyes open." They took off into the woods in pursuit of Peter.

Peter ran with abandon until he almost careened into a dry creek. He skidded down the bank and hunkered in the rocky creek bed. He held his hands in front of his face. Rivulets of blood flowed down his forearms. The punctures in his palms looked like stigmata. As his adrenaline ebbed Peter became aware of a scorching pain and the distinct smell of a burnt ham-and-cheese-and-gym sock sandwich emanating from his left elbow. *Plasma immobilizer must have grazed me.* He decided it was best not to look at it. His chest pounded and his temples throbbed. He held his breath and listened and thought he heard Cyril's voice in the distance. *Not sure.*

He yanked the aluminum cylinder and black module from his pack and snapped them together. The LCD screen glowed as it powered up. He held it at arm's length and pressed a button. An intense cobalt-blue light fanned from the device and traversed Peter's body from head-to-toe like a laser light bathing a stoner in the front row of a Pink Floyd concert. When the light went out he read the LCD screen:

Multiple punctures and lacerations of upper extremities
Second degree burn, extensor surface, left

extremity
Sinus tachycardia
Tension headache – moderate

He held the device at arm's length again. He pressed a different button. A white opalescent light engulfed his body, flickered, and then went out. Headache gone, he tossed the cylinder into his bag, clambered out of the creek bed and up the bank, and took off running.

Cyril and Ben searched the woods for almost two hours. Cyril searched methodically. He found a trail of blood droplets on the forest floor, but it petered out in a dry creek bed. Ben glanced up occasionally when he wasn't scanning the forest floor for snakes, ghastly insects, and poison ivy. At one point Ben found himself standing next to a narrow two-lane blacktop. He looked up in time to see an old white Chevy pickup disappear around a bend. But no sign of Peter. They trudged back to the salvage yard. Cyril stood by the *Rev 9*, stroked his chin and looked around.

"You know, I don't mean to be judgmental, but based on this parking lot – you humans are horrible drivers."

"It's not a parking lot. It's a junk yard. And yes, we are," Ben said.

"Vehicles," Cyril said, surveying the field of broken, twisted, and rusting metal. "He escaped on foot. His ship must be around here somewhere. Come with me." He darted to a row of junked cars. Ben followed, disappointed that Cyril hadn't seen him roll his eyes.

"Should I be looking for a trunk, or carry-on, or perhaps a cosmetic case?" Ben said, stopping himself when he remembered that this was sort of a touchy subject.

"Eureka!" Cyril said. Benjamin hoped this meant he would get to go home soon.

By the time Ben caught up to Cyril, he was pulling parts of cars off of the *Rev 2*. As the *Rev 2* was unveiled piecemeal, Ben decided that it had exponentially more aesthetic appeal than the *Rev 9*, but thought it best not to share this with Cyril.

"Hand me a pry bar," demanded Cyril.

"Sure. I've got it right here next to my fence cutters."

"Idiot! From my ship! Look in the locker next to the hatch." Ben returned with what looked the most like a pry bar to him and handed it to Cyril. Cyril wedged one end into the edge of the hatch and pried.

"I am sorry," Soledad said after Cyril popped the hatch. "You are not an authorized user."

"Shut up," Cyril said as he searched the cockpit.

"If you continue to trespass, I shall issue an even more stern verbal warning."

"Oh my. Sounds like somebody upgraded to the *deluxe* security system," Cyril said, stretching his sarcasm legs. Finding only an empty compartment behind the headrest, a glove box stuffed with unpaid parking tickets and snack bar wrappers, and a helmet under the seat, he slammed the hatch and threw the pry bar onto the ground.

"Buh-bye," Soledad said. Dejected, Cyril slumped against the *Rev 2*. Benjamin took his cue and leaned against a 1972 Pinto.

"So, what exactly are you looking for?" asked Ben.

THREE

Working in the archiving division of the Life Sciences Administration wasn't Peter's idea of a dream job, but the LSA did provide a company vehicle, a fuel stipend, and an almost irresponsible degree of latitude to its employees in archiving.

Blutaarkians were no strangers to criticism – sometimes because of their willingness to purchase vehicles that looked as if they were designed on a dare, and sometimes because of their potent salivary neurotoxin that made babysitting for them not worth the eight bunjits an hour. But planet Blutaark was beyond reproach when it came to its expertise in the arena of the biological sciences. They possessed a thorough understanding of all life forms on their home planet, they discovered cures for and treated all Blutaarkian illnesses (covered by insurance with reasonable monthly premiums and deductibles), and they were now attempting to identify, analyze, and catalog all life forms within reach of their inflationary space drive.

Peter was one of dozens of scouts in the archiving division, but he was already making a name for himself. He discovered a planet – Bletchley 4 – that had crossed the threshold from inert to living with its one and only life form. He documented two silicon-based species in the Alvaston system. And he cataloged every life form on planet Diss Beta in under nine days. Peter often used this last accomplishment to pad his résumé, neglecting to mention that a single day on Diss Beta is equivalent to three months on Blutaark.

After a four-month stint on Huull 4, Peter piloted the *Rev 2* back to Blutaark for routine maintenance. For his personal maintenance Peter planned a long weekend of local cuisine, cold Blutaarkian libations, and clubs where the women danced but he didn't have to.

"Might as well drop my BioScan off with tech support at LSA while I'm here," Peter said to the preoccupied garage mechanic with his head under the hood of the *Rev 2*.

(The BioScan is a hand-held device issued by the LSA to scouts in the archiving division. With the push of a button it can scan a life form, analyze it down to its genetic code, and document and store that information. Because it Scans, Analyzes, and Documents, it is often called *SAD* by the scouts. Upper management felt that *SAD* didn't convey a positive image and set about organizing a contest to allow the scouts to choose an official name. "BioScan" placed second in the voting after "that black-handled silver thing I'd like to use to crack the windpipes of the short-sighted meddlers in upper-management.")

"Uh huh," said the mechanic, not looking up.

"Could probably use a new power module and perhaps a software upgrade," Peter said.

"Mmhmm," hummed the mechanic.

"Or perhaps you could continue to make noises that could never be mistaken for actual words while I drive to your flat, have my way with your refrigerator, then tell your upstairs neighbor that you'd sleep better if they moved furniture around and practiced clogging all night," Peter said.

"Mmmkay."

Peter left the garage and strolled to the LSA complex. He found tech support in the basement of the Biotech annex. He pinched a slip from the "Take a number please" dispenser, read the number (3605), and sat on a bench that looked like it had done hard time outdoors before it was given clemency here at bureaucracy central. The clerk behind the counter stared at a monitor, touched the screen every few minutes, and blinked less frequently than that. Occasionally he would break up the monotony by turning his eyes toward the waiting area and announcing a number.

"Thirty-two fifty," said the clerk with an attitude honed by years of mediocre performance reviews. Peter noticed that customers thirty-two fifty through thirty-six oh-four had found three-hundred-and-fifty-five more interesting places to be.

"I'm thirty-six oh-five," Peter said.

"Uh huh," said the clerk, eyes glued to his monitor.

"Just dropping off this BioScan unit for a new power module and software upgrade," Peter said, laying the felt-lined case on the counter.

"Mmhmm."

"I'm heading back out in three days, so I really need to be able to pick this up first thing Monday morning," Peter said. "If it's not ready by then, I will be compelled to bind your ankles with your necktie, force you to listen to rap music, then drag you to a gym where I will force you to sign a long-term membership contract."

"Mmmkay," the clerk said. Peter put the box on

the counter and left. After a liver-boggling weekend, punctuated by a brief trip to the emergency room due to dehydration and an anaphylactic reaction to glitter, Peter schlepped back to the basement of the Biotech annex. He was greeted by the "Take a number please" dispenser, but no clerk.

"Too bad," Peter said to nobody there. "I was sort of looking forward to that dragging with the necktie thing." He spied the BioScan box on a shelf labeled "Completed Jobs" behind the counter. Peter was on a tight schedule, and he *had* given fair warning, so he took the liberty of lifting the hinged countertop door and retrieving the box. He stuffed it into his bag, and headed to the garage.

Peter entered the coordinates to Hillegom 2 and engaged the inflationary drive. Points of starlight burst into luminous rays streaming past the *Rev 2*'s window. Satisfied that everything was in order, he reached into the compartment behind his headrest and dragged his backpack onto his lap, then removed the black box and opened it.

"Impressive," Peter said. "Not just new software, but an entirely new hardware upgrade. Well played, LSA. Well, guess I'd better learn how to use this thing."

He plugged the instructional drive into the dashboard port and listened to the audio tutorial. In less than a minute Peter realized he was not in possession of a BioScan. This device was something else entirely. It was something astonishing. And wonderful. And dangerous.

Now that device was at the bottom of Peter's backpack, under some t-shirts and snack bars, as he hitched a ride from a man driving a white pickup truck through Alabama timberland.

"I'm Brooks," said the bald man in the driver's

seat. "I usually don't bother with hitchhikers, but you look like you've bathed this month."

"I'm Peter. And thanks for the ride, *and* the compliment," he said, climbing into the cab.

"Where you headed to?" Brooks said, wiping his mouth with his red flannel sleeve.

"Someplace safe, and far from here," Peter said.

"How's 'lanta sound?" Brooks said. "It's not too far – couple of hours. And as far as safe goes, well...it's not too far."

"Sounds good to me. Exactly how far is Lanta?" Peter said

"It's a ways," Brooks said. "About a hundred-and-fifty miles. I travel back-and-forth couple a times a month."

Peter reached into his backpack. "Snack bar?"

"No thanks," Brooks said. He watched Peter unwrap something that looked to him like a perfectly good candy bar had been melted and dipped in pencil shavings and sawdust. At first he thought that Peter might be pulling a weapon out of his bag, but Brooks found the snack bar even more unnerving than a knife or a gun.

"Thanks again for the ride," Peter said, licking his fingers.

Brooks, able to look in Peter's direction again, glanced up at Peter's striking hairline. "Combine?"

"Beg your pardon?" Peter said.

"You lose part of your scalp to a combine? Happened to a cousin of mine. Got too close to the harvester, and 'fore you know it he's getting skin grafts and picking wigs out of a catalog."

"Precisely. Got the tips of my fingers too, so I lost all of my fingernails," Peter said, in a preemptive effort to avoid further questioning regarding his appearance.

"Bet that smarted more'n moonshine on a razor burn," Brooks said.

"Indeed," Peter said. "Listen, I've had kind of a long day. You mind if I catch a few winks?"

"Be my guest," Brooks said. "We should make the interstate 'fore long. Smoother driving after that." Peter wadded a t-shirt between his head and the window and closed his eyes.

Cyril and Ben sat in the cabin of the *Rev 9*. Cyril was studying images on a monitor. Ben sat in the back, impressed that somehow his seat had managed to become even more uncomfortable. Cyril had been quiet since their return to the ship.

"You never told me what you were looking for back there," Ben said.

"Stolen goods," Cyril said. "Booty. Plunder. Contraband. Loot. Haul. Swag. Ill-gotten gains. Spoils. Makc." Benjamin thought that maybe the fugitive was right about the thesaurus.

"Thought maybe you could be more specific," Ben said.

"I cannot. It's classified. As a registered bounty hunter and affiliated agent of an auxiliary branch of a booster club supporting the Blutaarkian Police, I'm sworn to confidentiality," Cyril said.

"Ah, bounty hunter. So who's the guy we're chasing?"

"Peter," Cyril said, still staring at his monitor.

"So, do you want Peter?" Ben said. "Or just what he stole?"

"Both. There's a bounty on Peter's head. But if I return the BAT intact to the Blutaarkian government I can write my own check."

"Bat?" Ben said.

"BAT," Cyril said. "The Biolog – arrrghhh!

Stupid! Stupid! Stupid! Said too much again!" Cyril thrashed his shoulders. Ben imagined he felt the *Rev 9* swaying. He grinned for a second, picturing the absurd image of an unreasonably large suitcase falling over in a salvage yard, seemingly of its own accord. Just then a red pushpin of light appeared on the monitor. Cyril stopped and stared. "There. Right there – that's where he used the device last. Right where the trail of blood stopped."

"If this thing has sensors, then why couldn't we just search for him from the air?" Ben said.

"Too many trees. No place to land," Cyril said. "At some point the bounty hunter has got to put his boots on the ground, so-to-speak. Unless your prey is standing alone in the middle of a field, you just can't fire off your plasma immobilizer from altitude. You'll get collateral damage." Cyril winced at a brief unpleasant flashback of a bail jumper at a crowded outdoor wedding.

"Don't you have some kind of transporter beam?" Ben said.

"Oh, that's just brilliant," Cyril said. "The only advanced race with the computational power to drive a teleportation device is over 4,000 light-years away on the planet Amiplat. They're sort of busy using it, but even if they had a stroke of uncharacteristic generosity and let us borrow it, we would need something roughly the size of the land mass you call 'Australia' to put it on."

"Oh," Ben said.

"Besides, when they did experiment with a teleporter, it could only be used on lower life forms. Apparently species with nervous systems find disassembly off-putting," Cyril said. Hearing the words "off-putting" reminded Benjamin of the unplanned detour his day had taken.

"So what do you need me for anyway?" Ben said.

"Oh, so we're going to revisit that, are we?" said Cyril. "You can tell everybody about this when I'm gone. You'll just look unstable. But if I'm still around it could escalate to media involvement and international military misadventures. And nobody wants media involvement. Besides, since Peter left his ship here, I'm thinking it would be best just to track him on the ground. It will be easier to navigate this train wreck of a planet with your knowledge of the indigenous species."

"Oh," Ben said. He entertained the idea that being stuck with Cyril could end up lasting longer than most of his other relationships, but with roughly the same amount of unpleasantness. "But this doesn't really work for me. See, I've got my job to get back to, and my...my...I've got my job. People are depending on me. Besides, I'm a doctor so I'm really not very good with people. Maybe I could help you find someone better suited to –"

"Shut up!" Cyril said. "No whining." He sat up straight in his chair. Ben flinched as Cyril bolted for the hatch and raced down the steps. A few minutes later Cyril's head popped through the hatch in the floor. He tossed a brightly colored object to Ben and plopped back into his seat at the front of the cabin. "I pulled that out of his *Rev 2*. He won't be taking it anywhere now."

"What's this?" Ben said. He turned the object over in his hands. It was highlighter orange and resembled an 8-track tape. "Like a 'flux capacitor' or something?"

"Uh, we call it a 'starter,' " Cyril said. He turned back to his monitor.

"So what do we do now?" Ben said.

"We wait. The BAT Peter stole is registered, and

each one transmits a specific signal when it's switched on. Peter never leaves it on for long, but the next time he activates it I'll know where he is to the meter," Cyril said.

"So basically," Ben said, "we're waiting for the BAT signal."

FOUR

It was obvious that the Life Sciences Administration was the Blutaarkian government's favorite child, though the government would never come out and say that in front of the other departments. The LSA was given a mandate and obscene levels of funding to develop the Bio Analysis and Treatment (BAT) device.

The BAT shared some features with the BioScan. With the push of a button, both the BAT and the BioScan could analyze the anatomy, physiology and genetic makeup of any organism. What made the BAT interesting was its diagnostic capability. The same one-button scan that analyzed normal anatomy and physiology could also determine the presence of disease. But what made the BAT revolutionary was its therapeutic application. With the push of a second button it could cure almost any disease in any species.

After nine years of research, LSA scientists developed a working BAT and produced seven prototypes. The entire project was kept under wraps from conception through production, and was still considered classified when LSA officials started planning the official announcement. Upper-level managers pushed for a marketing blitz of press releases, a parade, and a commemorative postage stamp to publicize the unveiling of the BAT until someone in accounting mentioned that that might be a bad idea considering the far-reaching social, political, economic, and military ramifications of this extraordinary technology. She also pointed out that no one had used postage stamps for over 200 years. The accountant was pooh-poohed as "way boring" by the blond extroverts in marketing, so nothing changed except the accountant's unexpected transfer to Hillegom 2. Everything was going tickety-boo until one upper-level manager named Jerry decided that one of the technicians should take the seven BAT units home after work every day for safe-keeping until the big unveiling.

Ariadne was one of those technicians. She was a young, bright, and conscientious member of the BAT research and development team, though the general consensus was that she cut her own hair. Ariadne had few faults, but one of the most glaring ones was her inability to judge the roommate-worthiness of her fellow Blutaarkians. This resulted in her daily lunchtime litany of roommate horror stories told to an unenthusiastic yet captive audience in the LSA cafeteria. After Urso moved in with Ariadne, her verbosity turned to reticence. Some coworkers wondered if her luck had turned – although the smart money in the office pool said it hadn't.

It was Ariadne's week to take the BATs. At the end of the workday she packed the seven felt-lined black boxes into a duffel bag, threw the bag onto her back and walked to her bike. Seconds later she was slaloming through the rush hour traffic of Compote – the capital city of Blutaark. The duffel bag clung to her back like student loan debt as she darted between cars, taxis, and buses. Within minutes, she skidded to a stop in front of her apartment. She usually got home before Urso, who preferred to walk home after a stressful day of staring at a monitor in the basement of the Biotech annex.

Ariadne was surprised to find Urso home cooking. He had left work early because there were only three customers remaining in line in the tech support waiting area. He had promised Ariadne that he would be home in time to cook dinner, but in the past he had also promised to pay his half of the water bill, to pick up his comic books, and to stop referring to himself in the third person. She dropped the duffel bag next to her dresser and then went into the kitchen to investigate.

"Whatcha cooking?"

"Leg o'looglack," Urso said.

"It smells...unique," Ariadne said.

"Uh huh," Urso said. He stared at the skillet.

She spied an open box of "Looglack Helper" in the garbage can and rolled her eyes. "I've got some work to do."

"Mmkay," Urso said.

"Let me know when dinner's ready," she said.

"Urso will do that."

At 2 a.m. Ariadne awoke to two Blutaarkian rugby teams playing tug-of-war with her lower gastrointestinal tract. She spent most of the next few hours in the bathroom cursing Urso's lack of culinary competence. *Would be so easy to use the BAT,* thought Ariadne. *It's right there in the bedroom.* But she, like everyone else on the research and development team, had signed a contract that forbade unauthorized use. She didn't want to lose her job – just her current roommate. She felt no better by morning. The tug-of-war had turned into a full-fledged scrum. She had to call in sick.

"Urso!" she bellowed from the bathroom.

"Uh huh," he said. He rattled the bathroom doorknob.

"You don't need to come in! Listen, I'm sick. I just need you to take my bag and drop it off at the R&D office."

"Mmkay."

"Do not open it. And be careful. Can you do that?" she asked.

"Urso can do," Urso said.

A few minutes later, Urso walked out of the apartment with Ariadne's bag full of BATs in his left hand and his bag in the right. His bag contained seven BioScans in their individual boxes. Urso's supervisor had instructed him to take them home after work, because for some reason unfinished jobs were piling up in tech support. Urso didn't mind. He found it just as easy to ignore the BioScans at home as it was to ignore them at work.

On one of the nicest mornings anyone in Compote could remember, Urso lugged the bags to the sprawling Life Sciences Administration complex. He had been staring at "You are Here" on a sign in Building 1 for almost ten minutes when someone in a white coat escorted him to the R&D office. "Urso dropping off bag for Ariadne," he said. The bag in his right hand thudded to the floor next to the administrative assistant's desk. She smiled and nodded and felt for the pepper spray she kept on a shelf under her desk, putting it back after he was well down the hallway. Urso lumbered his way to tech support in the Biotech annex where he opened the remaining bag and placed seven black felt-lined boxes on the "Completed Jobs" shelf. He took his seat in front of the monitor, called out a random number that had just popped into his head (2951), and was happy when no one answered.

Of the seven BATs that were lost that day, three were returned promptly by LSA scouts who understood the gravity of the error. Two were returned immediately by scouts who had a low tolerance for change and thought that the BAT was just an updated version of the BioScan. One BAT was recovered from an unwitting scout who was chased down and stopped by interplanetary police soon after leaving Blutaark. The last BAT was in the possession of a scout who was well on his way to Hillegom 2 before anyone knew anything at all about the mix-up.

"Hillegom 2," Peter said. "Not really so interesting."

"I could not say," said the on-board computer. "Since I have never been there myself. But their vast quartz beaches are known galaxy-wide for their striking beauty."

"Yeah," Peter said. "Quartz beaches. I was thinking maybe someplace with multicellular sentient beings with opposable thumbs." Peter was fond of multicellular sentient beings with opposable thumbs, as they were often proficient at using single-celled organisms (with or without thumbs) to synthesize ingredients crucial for consciousness-altering beverages. Also, he found multicellular organisms to be better conversationalists than the single-celled variety in almost all cases.

"Where did you have in mind?" said the on-board.

"Huull 4."

"You have already been to Huull 4," said the on-board. "All variants of life scanned and cataloged. Did you forget your paperwork again? How many times have I reminded you to -"

"No, no. Not that," Peter said. "I just think we could do more good there than on Hillegom 2." He punched in the coordinates for Huull 4 and the *Rev 2* complied.

The Charpaqs of Huull 4 were known for their susceptibility to annoying (but rarely fatal) diseases – including (but not limited to) halitosis, acne, Huullian hoof rot, fetlock swelling, and idiopathic lisping. This, and their exceptionally long life spans, combined to create a population of complainers nonpareil. Despite this, Peter had enjoyed his work on Huull 4, mostly because the Charpaqs overcompensated for their chronic carping by producing sector-class stagecraft. Their production of Winifred Paisley's "Halitosis of a Salesman" received a gushing four-star review from the usually reserved theater critic at the Compote Sun-Times. "But it wasn't five stars" complained many, many Charpaqs.

After landing the *Rev 2* and clearing security at the spaceport, Peter stopped by the office of a local businessman he'd befriended on his first expedition to Huull 4.

"Maarsq!"

"Peter!" Maarsq said. "Good to shee you again. How've you been?"

"I'm well, thank you," Peter said. "You're looking good." He took a seat in front of Maarsq's desk. He knew this might take a while.

"Well, my fetlock ish acting up," Maarsq said. "My kidsh home with the mumpsh. And the shtarter jusht went out on my wife'sh *Bevelmopgush II*. They're trying to tell me that the warranty's exshpired. And I jusht had another accountant give two weeksh notish. You know how it is with thish younger generation – it'sh all about 'work-life' balansh. Whatta load. The good newsh is that I've got a lead on a Blutaarkian accountant who shomehow ended up on Hillegom 2. Go figure."

"Sounds promising," Peter said.

"Fingersh crosshed," Maarsq said. "Sho what bringsh you back sho shoon? You forget your paperwork again? How many timesh did I remind you?"

"No, no, not that," Peter said. "It's just that the LSA gave some of the scouts a BioScan upgrade, and I wanted to try it out here first – you know, to compare with the results from the old BioScan before I give it the 'thumbs up.' "

"Shounds good. You going to re-shcan the entire flora and fauna again?"

"Actshually," Peter said. "I'm sorry. Actually I don't scan the *entire* flora and fauna of a planet. Just representatives of each species. But I thought I'd just start by rescanning you, if you're not opposed to the idea."

"How long will it take?" Maarsq said. "I've got theesh performance reviewsh piling up..."

"Just a few seconds. Won't hurt a bit. Probably."

"Let'sh do it then," Maarsq said. "The shooner the better."

"Great," Peter said. "I'll just need you to stand. Sorry about the fetlock." He removed the box from his bag and set it on the desk. He opened it, removed the BAT, and held it with both hands.

Maarsq dislodged his girth from behind his desk and stood facing Peter. "Fire away."

"Might want to close your eyes," Peter said. "Here we go." He pushed a button and a beam of blue light – a blue that reminded him of the iridescent eyes of the Crested Spleen-Sucking Petrel of Dushku – fanned out from the BAT and swept Maarsq's body from head to hoof.

"That washn't sho bad," Maarsq said. "Pretty light." He had apparently kept his eyes open.

"Not done yet," Peter said. "One more step."

"Washn't the old BioScan jusht a one-shtep processh?" Maarsq said. "Typical R&D. They can't releash an upgrade without making it more complexsh." Peter read the LCD screen.

Swollen fetlock, left, moderate
Eczema, generalized
Idiopathic lisping (lateral)
Tennis elbow, right
Hemorrhoids

"Sit tight," Peter said. He paused. For a second he considered the possibility that this was all an elaborate practical joke concocted by some clever LSA manager with a good sense of humor – until he realized no such person existed. He pushed the second button. A sizzling white light burst from the BAT and somehow managed to encompass Maarsq's generous frame. Then it flickered and went out. Peter sat quietly for a few seconds, then finally said "Are you okay?"

"Yes," Maarsq said. "I'm fine. It's weird though. My fetlock doesn't hurt." He rolled up a sleeve. "And my eczema – it's gone." He flexed and extended his right arm. "My tennis elbow – gone. And my hem – hey, I'm not lisping, am I?"

"Not a sliver," Peter said. He'd already turned the BAT off, boxed it, and returned it to his backpack.

"How long is this gonna last?" asked Maarsq.

"Indefinitely, as far as I know."

Maarsq stood unmoving – awestruck, smiling and silent. And then he stopped the silent part.

"What can I possibly do to repay you?"

"I think I'm going to enjoy doing this," Peter said. "So I won't ask for much. Perhaps a place to sleep and a couple of squares a day while I'm here. I *did* see a playbill on the way over here. Any chance you could get us a couple of seats for 'A Chorus Segment' before I have to go?"

"Consider it done," Maarsq said. "How long are you staying?"

"Probably not long," Peter said. "I'm sort of working freelance here. Some might even characterize it as 'on the lam.' "

"Guess I'd better get to work on those tickets then. And if anyone asks, as far as I know you're on Hillegom 2. Anything else?" Maarsq asked.

"Sure," Peter said. "Let's say after we see if this thing works for the mumps, we find out how many other Charpaqs would like to get scanned."

FIVE

Peter spent twelve days curing sick Charpaqs. His efforts with the BAT made a considerable dent in the population of Charpaqs with health complaints (which was pretty much all of them), but a missive sent from the Blutaarkian Attorneys General Office to the Charpaq Department of State threatened to cut his endeavor short.

A search warrant was served for one "Peter, of Blutaark" and the Blutaarkian government informed the Charpaqs that a courteous and well-groomed yet armed and slightly miffed contingent from the Blutaarkian Police Force would be landing shortly.

Unfortunately for Peter, the Blutaarkian Police Force fleet came equipped with inflationary space drive, so the message sent from Blutaark arrived eighty years after the police landed on Huull 4 in search of Peter. Blutaarkian investigators had been tipped off by a night clerk at a pharmaceutical supply company who alerted the authorities after he noticed a suspicious drop off in orders of breath mints and skin cream from Huull 4.

The Charpaqs of Huull 4 saw Peter less as a threatening fugitive and more as a really nice guy who enabled them to sit comfortably for prolonged periods of time. When the Blutaarkian Police landed and commandeered the spaceport, a network of Charpaq conspirators quickly fell into place to protect Peter and to hasten his escape. At the spaceport police had booted Peter's *Rev 2*. One officer was stationed to guard the craft while the others dispersed to find and arrest Peter.

Maarsq and his cousin, Hutch, found Peter at the local high school where he was in the process of scanning a line of Charpaqs that snaked through the gymnasium.

"Peter," Maarsq said. "I'm sorry, you've got to stop what you're doing and come with us. Blutaark sent police. There's no time."

Peter finished the BAT scan in progress. "I'm so sorry," he said to Rachel, the next-in-line to be scanned. "I can't stay. I'll come back as soon as I'm able." He looked into Rachel's eyes which were red and weeping. His heart broke a little, although later he would learn that Rachel had chronic conjunctivitis. "Hold on. Let me try something." He took the BAT back out of the bag.

"Peter, *now*," insisted Maarsq.

"Get everyone together!" shouted Peter. "One bunch, in the middle of the room. This will just take a minute."

"One minute, that's all," Maarsq said. Maarsq and Hutch corralled the Charpaqs into the center of the gym while Peter took the BAT and scrambled to the top of the bleachers.

"Everybody, as close together as possible," shouted Peter. "Now try not to move." He held up the BAT and pointed it toward the crowd. "Now smile." Peter pushed the button. A blue light sprayed above the horde and descended until every Charpaq had been scanned. The gym floor seemed to snuff the light out as the beam passed underneath their hooves. Peter watched as a list of dozens of diagnoses scrolled down the LCD screen.

"Peter, it's been more than a minute," Maarsq said.

"Taking a little longer than expected," Peter said. "It's processing."

The gym doors that opened out to the schoolyard swung open, but were stopped with a *clank* by a chain looped through the inside handles. "Police!" came from outside the doors and then echoed through the gym. "Get the bolt cutters" was followed by the sound of footsteps.

"Peter!" Maarsq said.

"Done," Peter said. "Or rather, nearly almost done. Everyone stay put. Now say 'cheese.' " Peter hit the second button on the BAT. The huddled Charpaqs were doused with a white light that filled the gym like a quasar in a shoebox. The light flickered and went out. Peter shoved the BAT into his bag. A metallic *snap* echoed through the room and was followed by the clanging of chain links getting dragged through the handles as the gym doors flew open. He bounded down the bleachers and made for the doors to the hallway. Maarsq ran after.

"Everyone outside," shouted Hutch. He herded the flash-blinded crowd en masse toward the open doors at the far end of the gym.

"Police!" said officer Basingstoke. He charged into the gym followed by five armed officers. His straightforward plan to dash into the gym and apprehend Peter was quickly tabled in favor of an impromptu plan to not get trampled under the hooves of hundreds of blinded, stampeding Charpaqs. Hutch caught up with Maarsq and Peter in front of the school, and then all three dashed to

Maarsq's car.

"You'll be riding in the back, Peter," Maarsq said as they approached the car in the parking lot.

"I don't mind riding in coach," Peter said. "I'm just happy to have a getaway car."

"Sorry," Maarsq said. "Not coach. More like the luggage compartment." He opened the trunk and motioned Peter to get in. "Actually more like luggage itself. Sorry, but the footlocker is the best we could do on short notice."

"My apologies," Peter said. "Next time I'm planning an escape by the skin of my teeth I'll make reservations," he said as he climbed into the footlocker with his backpack. Maarsq closed the footlocker, latched it, then slammed the trunk. A muffled "It really seems more like coach" came from inside the trunk. Maarsq wedged into the front seat with Hutch.

"Hope you remembered everything. Bumper sticker?"

"Yep," Hutch said.

"You poke some air holes in that footlocker?"

"We'd better get going," Hutch said.

Maarsq started his red *Gran Neutrino*. He tore out of the parking lot leaving a wake of dust and gravel and police with hurt feelings and headed for the spaceport.

At the spaceport, Maarsq and Hutch loaded the footlocker onto a luggage trolley. Four whispered words (*Peter's in the footlocker*) and a cooperative baggage handler (who had been BAT-scanned three days earlier) was all it took to bypass security. The one remaining obstacle was the lone officer guarding Peter's *Rev 2*. They walked outside with Maarsq leading and Hutch pushing the trolley and headed for the long-term personal spacecraft lot.

"So where's he parked?" Maarsq said. They were halfway across the lot.

"I thought you knew," Hutch said. "Let's ask Peter."

"Brilliant idea," Maarsq said. "Nothing at all suspicious about two Charpaqs in a locked-down spaceport parking lot talking to a footlocker."

"What about his receipt?" Hutch asked. "Maybe he wrote his parking zone on it."

"I'm sure it's conveniently located in his backpack," Maarsq said. "You know, the one he has with him in the footlocker."

"You know whenever I park in public, when I'm leaving my vehicle I make a mental note to remember where I parked."

"As do I," Maarsq said. "But when a friend drops in from out-of-town, I'm not in the habit of asking them 'By the way, where exactly did you happen to leave your vehicle at the spaceport?' It's nosy at best, if not outright suspicious."

"Speaking of suspicious," Hutch said, "I find it odd that the same week you 'lost' my ticket to 'A Chorus Segment' Peter was somehow able to secure one."

"You're right," Maarsq said. "Standing here arguing looks suspicious. We should just keep moving."

"That's not what I sa -"

"Look!" Maarsq said. "Far end of this row on the right. Definitely a Blutaarkian Police officer. You remember the plan?"

"I do," Hutch said. "Just like I'll remember to bring up that theater ticket when this is all over."

Maarsq had already taken off. Hutch followed with the footlocker. Presently they were standing in front of a booted *Rev* 2 and a Blutaarkian officer wearing a name tag that said "Rhandull." Hutch parked the trolley and slowly made his way to the rear of the *Rev* 2 while Maarsq engaged the officer.

"Dear sir, what is the meaning of this?"

"I'm sorry?" Rhandull said. He was more confused than usual. No one at the academy had ever asked him to define a word, or how to proceed if someone did.

"The boot!" Maarsq said. "I met my friend here on his arrival last week, and I definitely recall that he purchased a long-term parking permit. If you ask me, forty-four bunjits is an outrageous fee to pay for uncovered parking. But that's how I remember that he purchased a permit."

Rhandull looked at Maarsq, then he looked at the *Rev 2*, then he looked at the bright yellow apparatus attached to it. "Oh, it's not for a parking violation," Rhandull said. "This vehicle belongs to a known fugitive. So it's been booted. I'm guarding it."

"Good thing you're guarding it, I suppose," Maarsq said. "We wouldn't want a booted *Rev 2* to go anywhere, would we?"

"No," was Rhandull's response to the hypothetical question. He had missed a lot of school because of frequent ear infections.

"Hutch," Maarsq said. "When did you become a known fugitive?" Hutch had made his way back to the front of the *Rev 2*.

"News to me," Hutch said. "I suppose I could be an unknown fugitive. But then how would anyone know I was a fugitive if it wasn't known? Sort of a metaphysical question, if you ask me."

Rhandull stood and blinked.

"The point is, my friend here isn't a fugitive," Maarsq said. "And this is his *Rev 2*. And he has places to go. So if you would kindly remove the boot he can be on his way."

"I'm guarding it," Rhandull said. "It's not supposed to leave."

"Obviously, I'm not a fugitive," Hutch said. "Apparently you're guarding the wrong *Rev 2*. Do you even know what *your* fugitive looks like?"

Rhandull pulled a piece of paper from his shirt pocket and unfolded it. His eyes darted back and forth between the image on the paper and Hutch several times before finally declaring "You're not the known fugitive."

"Yes, yes, I believe we've established that," Maarsq said. "But this *Rev 2* that you've booted belongs to my friend Hutch here. I don't know what you've done with the fugitive's *Rev 2*, but clearly there's been a horrible mix-up."

"Here," Hutch said. "Come look at this." He led Rhandull to the rear of the spacecraft. "See that bumper sticker? It clearly says 'My Son is an Honor Student at Northern Huull 4 High.' Would your Blutaarkian fugitive have a sticker like that?"

"I don't know," Rhandull said. He paused. "I didn't like high school."

"No kidding?" Maarsq said. "I would have thought the opposite. I just imagined you resplendent in your letterman jacket, unburdened by any pressure to make passing marks, and getting voted 'Most Likely to Guard Something He's Not Supposed To.' "

"No I wasn't kidding," Rhandull said. He thought perhaps he should be offended, but he wasn't entirely sure. "I think maybe I should talk to my supervisor." He reached for his communicator.

"Oh my," Hutch said. "I am so, so very sorry. Looks like *I'm* the one who's in the wrong. I just noticed the interior of this *Rev 2* is burgundy and charcoal. My *Rev 2* is cinnamon and ash. Honest mistake."

"Sincerest apologies, officer," Maarsq said. He was relieved to see Rhandull putting his communicator away, but annoyed that their only plan was now kaput.

"Well, I guess we'd better start searching for the right *Rev 2*. Sorry to have been a bother."

Charpaqs are stupid thought Rhandull as Maarsq and Hutch left with the footlocker, a footlocker that – to anyone with even a rudimentary understanding of three-dimensional space – was clearly too large to fit inside any *Rev 2*.

After Rhandull was well out of sight, Hutch and Maarsq heard thumping from inside the footlocker. They pushed the trolley between two large vehicles and undid the latch. Peter opened the lid a crack. They heard several cycles of enthusiastic breathing before Peter spoke in a whisper.

"You boys having a good time?" Peter said. "Enjoying aerobic respiration and not having your knees sharing a studio apartment with your trachea?"

"Sorry," Maarsq said. "Plan A fell through, so we're on to Plan B."

"And what does Plan B entail?" Peter said.

"Walking around this parking lot until we think of Plan C."

"Splendid," Peter said. "But I think I have your Plan C. As not-luck would have it, I went to high school with Rhandull. So here's what we'll do..."

After Peter outlined the plan, Hutch went back inside the spaceport to find a customer service phone. Maarsq re-latched the footlocker and pushed the trolley to a location where he could see Rhandull without being seen. This wasn't difficult; Rhandull seemed preoccupied with practicing his "quick draw" technique. Maarsq found this sad and uncomfortable to watch, since Rhandull didn't have an actual firearm. Mercifully, Rhandull stopped when the outdoor PA system crackled overhead.

"Officer Rhandull of Blutaark – please pick up the nearest courtesy phone. Your mother Durlinda has been in an accident."

Rhandull blew invisible smoke from his fingertip, holstered his imaginary gun, and took off running to the terminal. Maarsq wheeled the trolley up to the *Rev 2*. Peter popped out, stretched, and then set to work on the boot with the utility tool from his backpack.

"That should buy us about six minutes," Maarsq said. "Maybe ten if Rhandull sees that 'Cinnamon Buns R Us' in the food court. That going to be enough time?"

"Plenty of time," Peter said. "Just like back at the gym." He looked over his shoulder and grinned at Maarsq.

"You ever remove a boot before?"

"Oodles of times."

"And exactly how many is 'oodles?' "

"Not exactly sure," Peter said. The boot dropped off of the side of the *Rev 2* and the hatch sprung open. "If you count the parking tickets in the glove box it'll give you a rough idea." He threw his backpack into the cockpit, and then vaulted into his seat.

"You'd best be getting out of here," Maarsq said.

"*You'd* best be getting out of here," Peter said. "I'll be forty trillion kilometers away before you get out of the parking lot. Thanks again for everything. I'm looking forward to coming back. I have unfinished business."

"Thank *you*, Peter," Maarsq said. "We'll be waiting."

Peter closed the hatch and threw his helmet on. Maarsq headed back to the terminal. Before he was out of the parking lot, the PA crackled and he heard Rhandull's lugubrious plea overhead.

"Help me somebody! My mamma's been hurt and I can't find her anywhere."

SIX

It was late afternoon when Peter awoke. He rubbed his eyes and blinked. Looking over he saw Brooks driving and remembered where he was. Peter didn't speak at first; he took in the sights and tried to assimilate as much as one could from the passenger seat of a pickup traveling on I-20 between Birmingham and Atlanta.

He had escaped Gyllenhaal 6 without a plan. By the time Earth had presented itself as a convenient place to land, he had only enough time to acquire a cursory knowledge of the planet and to learn one native language. He chose English because he had decided to land in North America. He chose North America because it was a fairly large target. The continent also got points for its temperate climate, reputation for groundbreaking postmodern theater, and free public transportation system known for comfort and efficiency. The Blutaarkian Planetary Database wasn't always accurate.

Peter saw a sign that said "Georgia State Line" soon followed by another that read "Atlanta 40 miles." *Ohhh, ATlanta.* Brooks must have noticed that he was awake.

"Get enough shut-eye?"

"Yes, thanks," Peter said.

"So what's your story?" asked Brooks.

"Not really much of a story," Peter said. He had

learned enough about Earth to know that it was isolated, insular, and avoided by intelligent aliens – except for those rare occasions when their recreational space vehicles were "full," compelling them to land in the middle of the desert for an emergency waste dump. (Although many aliens would argue that owning a recreational space vehicle is reason enough for removal from any "intelligent" list.) With these facts in mind, Peter had cobbled the semblance of a backstory. He just hoped he wasn't pressed too hard for details. "Grew up in Idaho. Spent the last few years working as a naturalist. Mostly documenting, photographing, and cataloging different plants and animals. How about you?"

"Retired now," Brooks said. "Spent more'n thirty years working the steel mills in Birmingham. Moved to 'lanta to be closer to my daughter. I go back to Alabama once or twice a month to check on some property."

"How many children?" Peter asked.

"Just the two. Daughter in 'lanta. And a son who lives near Seattle. You married? Any kids?"

"No to both," Peter said. "I've been traveling too much. Makes it difficult to settle down." They were getting closer to Atlanta. Peter noticed fewer "buckle up" signs and more large signs advertising restaurants, churches, and clubs for "gentlemen."

"Weell, you're still young," Brooks said. He was driving with his right hand draped over the top of the steering wheel; with his left hand he massaged his right shoulder.

"Shoulder giving you trouble?" Peter said.

"Bursitis actin' up," Brooks said. "Among other things. Glad we're almost there. So whatcha gonna do in 'lanta?"

"I was hoping to find a job," Peter said. "Find a

place to stay. Explore the city. I've never been to Atlanta before. What's there to see?"

"Weell, if you like sports, there's the Braves and the Falcons," Brooks said. "Course the Braves don't play again until April. There's the headquarters for Coca-Cola. I hear they give tours, but I've never been on one. Not exactly on my bucket list."

"Bucket list? Peter said.

"List of crap you wanna do before you die," Brooks said. "You know, 'kick the bucket?' "

"Ah. Makes perfect sense." Peter made a mental note to be cautious around buckets while here on Earth.

"There's a pretty good zoo and an aquarium, if you're into that nature stuff," Brooks said. "Lots of traffic, too. It's a real ass-biter. I try to avoid it as much as possible. Shouldn't be a problem for you – not having a car and all. No offense."

"None taken."

"Then there's the CDC," Brooks said.

"CDC?"

"Centers for Disease Control."

"Seems like it would be better to just get rid of disease entirely, rather than just trying to control it," Peter said.

"I hear that," Brooks said. "But they didn't ask my opinion. Anyways, I need to stop and take a leak." He took the next exit and pulled into the parking lot of a fast food restaurant. "This place always has clean restrooms."

Brooks went inside while Peter got out and paced along the sidewalk. After a few minutes, Brooks came out and Peter met him at the truck. Brooks was rubbing his shoulder again.

"Don't happen to have any pain pills on ya do ya?" Brooks said.

"No, sorry," Peter said. "Wait here. I've got something better." Peter grabbed his backpack from the passenger side floor, walked to where Brooks was standing, and unzipped the bag.

"If you make me look at even one of those snack bars I'm gonna puke," Brooks said.

"No worries," Peter said, grinning as he pulled the BAT from the recesses of his backpack. He took a furtive glance at their surroundings before he turned the unit on.

"This some kinda alternative medicine thing?" Brooks said.

"Yes, that's it," Peter said. "You could well consider this an alternative to medicine." He held it in front of Brooks and pushed the first button. "Try not to move. Probably won't hurt."

The light sprayed from the BAT and cast Brooks in a supernatural blue. For a few seconds the BAT, Brooks's bald pate, and his flannel shirt combined to paint an image of Dr. Manhattan as lumberjack in the parking lot of a suburban McDonalds. Then the light went out.

"Purty light," Brooks said. "But my shoulder still hurts. Maybe even worse." He smiled a pirate smile. He wasn't complaining - just being honest.

"Hold on," Peter said. "One final step." He looked at the LCD readout. His heart sank. It wasn't just bursitis. He looked up at Brooks's toothy grin and couldn't help smiling back. "This is going to work wonders," Peter said as he pushed the second button.

Benjamin was sleeping on the floor of the *Rev 9* when he was awakened by someone screeching "The BAT signal!" He hoped this had all been a wretched dream, and that when he opened his eyes they would be greeted by a sixties television program starring Adam West.

"He's outside of Atlanta," Cyril said. "Just over two-hundred kilometers from here. We can be there in a couple of hours if we take your car."

"Number one," Ben said, annoyed that it wasn't a dream, "my car is trashed and in a completely different state. Number two, *no*." He rolled over and closed his eyes.

"Get up," Cyril said. "We'll just find something here. This place is a virtual cornucopia of cars."

"It's a junk yard," Ben said. "None of them run."

"Oh, that's the spirit," Cyril said. "What a downer. You must be a real gas at parties."

"First of all," Ben said, "most parties I've been to I didn't get spat upon, paralyzed, and abducted. Second, no one on this planet has used 'gas' in that context since the last time I was invited to a party."

Cyril picked Ben up by his ear and dragged him down the stairs and back outside. *I hate this,* thought Ben. To give the appearance of being helpful Benjamin suggested a step-wise approach; they would look for a car with four wheels, then look for four non-flat tires, the pop the hood to see if it had an engine. Much to Ben's disappointment, Cyril found a car that fit all of his criteria. It even had half a tank of gas. Unfortunately, the car was a 1990 Jeep Cherokee parked in front of the junkyard office.

"You can't take that," Ben said. "It belongs to somebody who works here."

"There's no one in," Cyril said. "I checked. Besides, I'm in a hurry, and whenever they get back they'll have all those other cars to choose from."

"You don't think that will be a little suspicious?" Benjamin said. "One missing car and a giant suitcase sitting in their junkyard? That's going to raise some questions."

"What suit...*spacecraft?*" Cyril said, glaring a hole through Ben's eye sockets.

"The one you pushed me out of not five minutes ago," Ben said, turning away from Cyril and pointing at the *Rev 9*. Ben did a double take when he discovered he was pointing at not-a-spacecraft. Instead he was pointing at the sky just above the treetops. "What the hell?"

"Hover mode," Cyril said. "Optional equipment on the *Rev 9*, but well worth it. Right now it's sitting 25,000 meters above us, waiting for me until I require its services."

Cyril threw a black backpack into the Cherokee and slammed the door. He opened the driver's door and motioned Ben to get in on the other side.

"Hurry up," Cyril said, climbing behind the wheel. He pulled something from his belt, stuck it into the ignition and started the car.

Ben considered escape. Cyril was inside of the Jeep, out of spitting distance. *I could take off for the trees, maybe make it halfway before he could get out and use that immobilizer thing,* Ben thought. *He missed that other guy, so he's not the best shot in -*"

"And don't even think about running," Cyril said, "or I'll run you over with the car."

Ben got in the car.

"I'll be damned," Brooks said. "My shoulder don't hurt at all. It actually feels good. Hasn't felt this good since back when I worked as a hot bed hooker."

"I'm having difficulty picturing you doing that kind of work," Peter said, giving Brooks an uneasy smile. "I think I'll stop trying before I succeed."

Brooks laughed. "Naw. That's a mill job. Pulling cooled steel rods off a conveyer."

"Ah." Peter saw that traffic had picked up, but other than cars and trucks and trees and signs, there wasn't much to see. A sign told him they were taking 285 north instead of heading directly into Atlanta.

"So you said you're gonna find a place to stay," Brooks said. "That means you're pretty much homeless right now."

"Technically," Peter said. "But it's not a problem. You could just drop me off anywhere. I can sleep in the park. I'll be fine."

Brooks shook his head. "This isn't your own private Idaho. You might sleep in the park here, but the waking up part could be a problem. You might not wake up at all, or worse, you might wake up in the Grady Memorial emergency room."

Peter sat quietly and pondered the implications of what Brooks was saying. He had crashed on sofas of obliging intelligent species in the past – some humanoid, some not – but because of his good nature and resourcefulness it never presented any major problems. He reflected on some of the better experiences: attending theater with Maarsq on Huull 4, ice-climbing the glacial fields of Ordsail with Snaulbitters, and waking up in the emergency room with Bicks on Delden Gamma. Good times. Hanging out with Brooks didn't hold the promise of Hemingway-esque adventure, but if he offered him a place to stay, Peter would accept without reservation. Brooks seemed nice enough, and Peter could use a place to stay while he mapped out a plan for his stay on Earth.

Peter did not see Cyril as a threat. It was a large continent, and Peter was confident that Cyril was still traipsing about the forests of Alabama, shaking his fist and shouting Peter's name. Peter knew that the Blutaarkian Police had stopped searching for him. Tracking a fugitive across a span of millions of light years consumed limited police resources – resources better used to generate income by issuing costly citations for speeding, jaywalking, and for not having received a citation in the previous six months. Besides, six of the seven BATs had been recovered. The police were content to leave the search for Peter to the bounty hunters. Peter had been on the run for seven months and the original field of two dozen bounty hunters had been winnowed to one: Cyril. What Peter didn't know was that the BAT engineers had installed a transmitter in every unit, and that whenever it was activated it sent out a short-range identification signal.

"I'd let you stay with me," Brooks said. "I've got the room, but my doctors say I'm supposed to limit my contact with others. Especially during flu season. But I think I know of a place."

Brooks stayed on 285 – he called it "The Perimeter" – and took the Parkway north when they got to Sandy Springs. A few more turns and they entered the driveway of an apartment complex. It was clean and landscaped, and the parking lot was void of any beer drinking and car maintenance activities so popular at apartments that weren't clean and landscaped. Brooks parked the pickup in front of one of the units and opened his door.

"Wait here," Brooks said. "Shouldn't take long."

Peter rolled his window down and watched as Brooks rapped on the apartment door. A petite young woman answered. She stood in the doorway and a short conversation ensued. Peter could only make out bits and pieces, but the young woman's tone was one of weary frustration. "Really, Dad?" and "not a good time," and "mass-murderer" were the few words that caught Peter's ear. She turned and went inside, but left the door standing open. Brooks practically sprinted back to the truck.

"Get your things," Brooks said. "This is my daughter's place. You can stay here for a while."

Peter grabbed his backpack and followed Brooks inside. Brooks's daughter stood in the living room, arms crossed. She wore jeans and a peach colored t-shirt, and had dark bangs and blue eyes that hadn't blinked yet.

"I'm April. April Robinson," she said.

"I'm Peter."

"It's been a long day," Brooks said. "I need to be getting back to the house. But you let me know if you need anything, 'kay?"

"You mean like a SWAT team, or a medical examiner?" April said. "Sure, Dad, you're on speed dial."

"Super," Brooks said. "I'll talk to ya tomorrow." He turned and left and closed the door behind him.

"My dad's done some crazy stuff before," April said, shaking her head. "And I'm sure it's never ever gonna stop. He said he picked you up hitchhiking in Alabama?"

"Yes," Peter said. "Just outside of Birmingham."

"You're not a serial killer, are you?" April said. She eyed his backpack with concern.

"No, promise," Peter said.

"Pshaww. That's just what I'd expect a serial killer to say," April said.

"You're probably right, I imagine," Peter said.

"Are you a pervert?" April said.

"Again, no," Peter said. "But that's probably just what a pervert would say."

"Got me there," April said. "So what's in the bag? Not that it really matters. I mean, you could kill me in my sleep with a lamp cord if you wanted to."

"I'd really rather not," Peter said.

"Why don't you want me to know what's in the bag?"

"I meant I'd rather not kill you in your sleep."

"So you like your victims wide awake. It's the terror thing, right?"

"No, no, no," Peter said. "I have no interest in snuffing out your life. Asleep or awake. I just came here for a bit of quiet and relaxation. Sort of the exact opposite of murdering someone. Sort of the opposite of this conversation, too."

"I'm sorry," April said. "I'm not the best hostess. I had to attend alternative charm school."

"No kidding?"

"So," April said, "what's in the bag?"

"Some clothes, snack bars, a utility tool – sort of like your Swiss Army knife," Peter said. He hoped she didn't press the issue. He hated lying.

"Okay, well I just got home from work," April said. "If you're hungry there's stuff in the frig. But after tonight you'll need to buy your own food. The bathroom's on the right. I'm going to go take a nap. We'll go over more ground rules later – assuming I wake up. Too bad you're not into killing people in their sleep – perfect opportunity." April went into her bedroom, then closed and locked her door.

Peter wasn't hungry, so he sat in an upholstered chair in the sparsely-furnished living room. He noticed two overbooked bookcases and got up to read the titles. He picked one and sat down, and within a few minutes he was snoring with the book open on his chest. When he awoke April was sitting cross-legged on the sofa across from him, drinking tomato soup form a mug. There was an almost-empty glass of red wine on the coffee table between them. April was wearing the same shirt but snowflake-print pajamas replaced the jeans.

"That's one of my favorites," April said.

"Oh," Peter said, glancing down at the book on his chest. "I didn't get too far into it, but I'm enjoying it so far."

"So far?" April said. "You mean you've never read *To Kill a Mockingbird*? Did you sleep through eighth grade or something?"

"No," Peter said. "I missed a fair amount of school one year. See, there was this accident with a combine..."

"Yeah," April said. "Dad sort of told me. I'm sorry. I didn't mean to be insensitive."

"It's not a problem."

"Well," April said, "It's a really good book. I don't want to spoil it for you, but the underlying motif of...hey, wait a sec. This isn't some kind of creepy foreshadowing, is it?" She sat up and put her feet on the floor.

"I beg your pardon?"

"One of the major themes," April said, "is that it's a sin to kill a mockingbird because they just sing beautiful songs and don't hurt anyone. You could be a well-read serial killer, and you might think I'm attractive, and nothing would be more ironic than to leave that book on my body after you've offed me.

"I do love irony," Peter said. "But again, not so much into the murdering. I think a better analogy is that you're like Scout and I'm your Boo Radley."

April mulled that over. "Guess you're further into the story than I thought." She got up and went into the kitchen and poured another mug of soup. She came back and handed it to Peter. "Thought you might be hungry."

"Thanks," Peter said. "Was feeling a bit peckish."

"So, the ground rules," April said as she sat back

on the sofa. "You might want to write this down."

"I have a superb memory," Peter said. "Proceed."

"You can sleep on the sofa," April said. "I'll get you a blanket. Under no circumstances do you go into my room. And try not to make a mess in the bathroom. No smoking, no drugs, no parties when I'm out. I expect you to look for a job. I can leave my laptop here during the day, and you can use it to look for a job. There's a spare key in a drawer in the kitchen. There's also a smart card for the bus – you'll need it to ride. I think it still has a few dollars left on it. Oh, and my Dad's been sick lately, so don't do anything to stress him out or piss him off."

"Got it," Peter said. "All sounds very reasonable." Peter did consider this to be one of the more agreeable roommate arrangements since he had left Huull 4. He wasn't asked to give a DNA sample, he didn't have to provide an egregious rental deposit, and there was virtually no chance that he would accidentally run into Maarsq wearing nothing but a towel on his head.

"Any questions?"

"Nope," Peter said.

"Good," April said. "Oh, I've got one. I just realized I have no idea what your last name is."

Peter realized that "of Blutaark" would probably raise more questions. He glanced down at the book, then looked back up at April. "Finch. Peter Finch."

"Seriously?" April said. She gave Peter a pirate smile he'd seen somewhere before. "Okay. Well, see you in the morning. Peter Finch."

With that April went into her room and read herself to sleep. Peter finished *To Kill a Mockingbird*, polished off a few dozen other books, and then used the laptop before hitting the sofa.

SEVEN

"Mind if I listen to the radio?" asked Benjamin.

"Yes," Cyril said.

Cyril had been quiet since they hit the interstate. When they left the junkyard he had attached a palm-sized GPS monitor to the dashboard. The monitor displayed a stationary flashing red light that Ben assumed was their destination. Cyril pushed the Cherokee toward the red dot, ignoring the speed limit in much the same way that the two Alabama state troopers ignored him as he sped past their patrol cars. *You never really get pulled over by a state trooper when you want to,* Ben thought. Not long after they crossed the Georgia state line, Cyril took an exit and pulled into the parking lot of a fast-food restaurant. The red light stopped flashing. It now gave a constant glow.

"That sure is an elaborate piece of technology, just to locate a McDonalds," Ben said. "I usually just look for the billboards when I'm in the mood to feel all bloaty."

"Idiot," Cyril said. "This is where Peter last used the BAT."

"Okay. So now what?" Ben said.

"We wait until he uses it again," Cyril said.

Ben was tired, bored, and hungry. "We could go inside, maybe look for any signs of Peter. We could get something to eat, too. I haven't had anything since breakfast."

"I suppose that wouldn't hurt," Cyril said. "Just don't try anything."

Benjamin went to the counter while Cyril waited nearby. Ben – knowing it was a long shot – ordered a Happy Meal, just to see if it helped. It didn't. While Cyril was watching him eat, Ben realized he'd just paid with a debit card. He had been missing less than twenty-four hours, so no one would be looking for him yet. But eventually someone back home (exactly who was uncomfortably vague in his mind) would be concerned with his unexplained absence. His debit card left an electronic trail, just like the trail Cyril was following.

Ben felt a little better after eating, but he certainly would not qualify the feeling as "happiness." He was frustrated with his predicament and irritated with Cyril's presence. *I really don't like this guy,* Ben thought. *Maybe Stockholm syndrome will kick in soon.*

"So, if I understand correctly," Ben said, "whenever Peter uses the BAT you can pick up the signal. But if he doesn't stay in the same place, you'll always be one step behind."

"That's possible," Cyril said. His brow furrowed, as if he'd never thought of that. "Peter will stop eventually. They always do."

When Ben finished eating, they went back to the Jeep. It was starting to get dark, and the prospect of watching Cyril stare at a GPS monitor for an indeterminate length of time overwhelmed Benjamin. He curled up in the back seat and went to sleep.

When April went into the kitchen for her morning coffee, she realized that Peter was gone. *Little early for a job interview* she thought, which was soon followed by *I hope he didn't rob me blind.* Sipping her coffee, April investigated and found that everything in the apartment was the way it was before, except for her copy of *To Kill a Mockingbird* which had been stuffed back into its place on the bookshelf. After coffee and a Danish she got ready for work, locked up, and headed south on the Parkway. *Hope Peter's okay,* she thought when she passed a homeless person at a bus stop near the office. She drove to One Atlanta Plaza, the office tower where she worked as an administrative assistant to the CEO of Dionysus Pharmaceutical.

Dionysus Pharmaceutical was a small biotech company founded by Dirk Reger, who was now its president and CEO. His fledgling company was only seven years old, but he had already established a reputation for his proficiency in converting venture capital funding into disappointment. Dirk charmed investors with a laundry list of promising new drugs in the Dionysus pipeline, but company insiders knew that the "pipeline" consisted of quixotic ideas scribbled on Dirk's yellow legal pad while he gazed at the Atlanta skyline from his 27th floor office. April once caught a glimpse of Dirk's notes during a quarterly meeting, and was able to discern "drug to cure AIDS," "cure for Alzheimer's," "baldness," "halitosis," and "in no particular order" before the lights went down and her Power Point nap started. Despite Dirk's insufferable use of words like "value-added," "proactive," and "synergy," and the never-ending battle with budgetary constraints, researchers at Dionysus had managed to develop a drug for refractory chronic leukemia that had made it to Phase 3 clinical trials.

April had a personal interest in the outcome of this study – her father had chronic lymphocytic leukemia. She convinced him to enroll in the study, and when the time came to fill out paperwork she instructed him to deny any relation to any employee at Dionysus. Any institutional review board would have balked at this ethical violation – but April loved her father.

April spent most of the morning on the phone at her desk placating an irate landscaper at Dirk's 7,000-square-foot home in Buckhead. She checked her cell phone at lunch; there was one message. It was from her father, and he said he had some good news and would stop by her apartment after work.

Peter had slept for a couple of hours. He woke up before sunrise, drank a glass of water, put on a clean shirt, and locked the door quietly so as not to disturb April. He headed south on foot, his backpack slung over one shoulder. Peter, like most Blutaarkians, didn't see walking as a nuisance. After spending days, sometimes weeks, in the cramped *Rev 2*, it was nice to be able to ambulate. Within a couple of hours, he found a doughnut shop with a "Help Wanted" sign in the window. Giving Peter the once-over, the assistant manager seemed reluctant to give him an application, but nodded and acquiesced when Peter simply said "combine accident."

After writing his name, the day's date, and his address (April's apartment), Peter hit the job-application wall. His stellar GPA at Northern Blutaark University and his employee-of-the-month award from the Life Sciences Administration would probably send the wrong message – that message being "Notify the authorities." Peter thought it likely that such candor would result in incarceration and uncomfortable restraints. With great pains Peter wrote "home schooled" under education and "none" under prior job experience. Mercifully, the application did not ask for an exact age. It only asked if the applicant was "over 16." *By about one-hundred-and-seventy years,* Peter thought as he checked the appropriate box. Under references he wrote "Brooks Robinson."

"Brooks Robinson?" said Jess, the assistant manager. "He was one of the greats."

Great, thought Peter. *If this guy knows Brooks, I'm a shoo-in.*

"So," said Jess. "You're applying for your first job?"

"Yes," Peter said. "Well, my first urban job. Worked on the family farm in Idaho for a few years."

"That would explain the combine accident," Jess said. "Do you have reliable transportation?"

"Absolutely," Peter said. He just assumed that the efficient, comfortable, and free public transportation in North America was also reliable.

"No phone?" asked Jess.

"No," Peter said. "But my roommate has one. I'm sure she will let me use it."

"Mmmkay," Jess said. "Well, I'll certainly keep you in mind. But I have other applicants to consider. I'll give you a call."

"But you don't have my phone number."

"If you get the job," Jess said, "I'll send you a letter. I've got your address. Thanks for stopping by." Jess went back to glazing something. Peter turned to go, but looking back he thought he saw Jess wiping his hands with his application.

Disheartened, Peter sat on the curb in front of the shop. None of the jobs he found online seemed intellectually challenging, but he had hoped that obtaining a low-skill position would at least be easy to do. His heart just wasn't into looking for a job. But he needed a place to stay until he sorted things out, and he had made promises to April. He got up and started walking. Before long he found a shopping center with several stores, one of which had a "Now Hiring" sign in the window. The interview at the pizza restaurant seemed to be going well until the manager indicated an oversight on Peter's application.

"What's your social?" said the manager.

"My social what?"

"Your social security number," said the manager. "You left it off of your application."

"Forty-two," Peter said.

"It's a nine-digit number," the manager said. "If you have one you need to find out what it is. If you don't have one I can't hire you. I can't be working any aliens."

For a second Peter thought that his cover had been blown. Then he remembered "an unnaturalized foreign resident of a country" was one definition of "alien" in the dictionary that he read after April went to bed. Peter thanked the manager and resumed his search.

Peter found walking in Atlanta in October a pure joy. The cool mornings, network of sidewalks, and bountiful trees made it difficult to focus on job hunting. An inviting suburban park with walking trails and a playground made job hunting seem categorically irrelevant. Peter sat on a bench, placed his backpack between his legs, and proceeded to people-watch. After a few minutes, he took the BAT out of his bag. He fiddled with it some, and discovered that there was more to it than just the power switch and two scanning buttons. Near the base was an adjustment that altered the size and shape of the beam to accommodate for larger or smaller creatures, or even groups. *Would have come in handy at the gym on Huull 4,* thought Peter. *Should probably have listened to the entire tutorial.*

A middle-aged woman sat on the bench next to Peter. The young boy who had been holding her hand took off for the playground.

Peter turned and smiled at the woman. "How old is he?"

"He's five," she said, a smile of pride breaking across her face.

"I'm Peter," he said, extending his hand.

"I'm Loretta."

"You must be very proud," Peter said.

"Oh, he's not mine," Loretta said. "I just take care of him. Been his nanny since he was born."

"He really seems to enjoy that inclined plane," Peter said.

"The what?" Loretta said. "Oh, the slide. And the swings, too. But I told him my back hurt too much today for that. He'll just have to make do."

"What happened to his parents?" Peter asked.

"They just busy," Loretta said. "His father runs a big company."

"What does his mother do?"

"Shopping mostly," Loretta said. "Spends a fair amount of time at Saks, Tiffany, Jimmy Choo."

"Are those friends of hers?" Peter said.

"Might as well be," Loretta said. "But those are your high-end shopping destinations. I tell little Tyler that if anything happens to me, that's where he can find his momma. Either there or the pharmacy – she spends a fair amount of time there, too. Must be awful stressful bein' that rich."

"I wouldn't know," Peter said. "Right now all I've got is this bag and a vehicle that doesn't run."

"Whatcha got there?" Loretta asked.

"This?" Peter said, looking down at the BAT still in his hands. "It's a camera. I used to do a lot of nature photography. But I photograph people, too."

"Don't look like any camera I ever seen," Loretta said.

"It's pretty special," Peter said. "Very high tech. Do you mind if I take your picture?"

"Son," Loretta said, "you must be out of your mind if you want to take my picture."

"It would be a privilege," Peter said. "You have character."

"Son, where'd you learn to sweet talk a lady like that?" Loretta said. "How could I say 'no' now? Besides, I guess it wouldn't hurt any."

Quite the opposite, thought Peter as he held up the BAT. "Let's see that delightful smile."

Loretta blinked when the blue light washed over her. "That it?"

"Not quite," Peter said. "One more." He glanced at the readout on the BAT before he hit the second button.

Arthritis, vertebral
Hypercholesterolemia (treated)
Diabetes mellitus (treated)
Hiatal hernia
Glaucoma, open angle (treated)

Loretta blinked again when the white light flashed and flickered out.

"There," Peter said. "All done. Thank you, Loretta."

"You're welcome."

"This may sound crazy," Peter said, "but this camera sometimes tells me more about a person than just what they look like."

"That so?"

"It is so," Peter said. "And what it told me is that you've had some health problems that are probably better now. You may not even need your medications anymore. But you may want to check with your doctor to be sure."

"You're right," Loretta said, still smiling. "That do sound crazy."

Loretta and Peter made small talk for a few minutes. Tyler came up to Loretta and begged her to join him on the playground. She did. Peter, still sitting on the bench, surreptitiously used the BAT scan on two other people. One was a young woman with her child and something called "lupus." The other was an older gentleman walking his collie. When Peter looked back at the playground he saw Loretta pushing Tyler on the swings.

EIGHT

Benjamin woke up, sat up in the seat, wiped off his glasses, and put them back on. *Crap. Still not a dream.* The sun was up. Cyril sat in the front seat of the Jeep, eyes transfixed on the monitor. Benjamin mused that Cyril either had an extraordinary ability to concentrate, or he was just dreadfully dull. Ben was leaning toward the latter.

"I need to get something to eat," Ben said.

"I'll have to go with you," Cyril said.

"You know," Ben said, "there's really no reason for Peter to come back here. It's just a fast-food restaurant. On the off-chance that he actually ate here and liked the food, he wouldn't necessarily have to come back to this one. There are literally thousands of them, just like this one."

"What's your point?" Cyril said.

"We don't have to be tied to this parking spot. I was thinking that after we finish breakfast we could get out and walk around a bit."

"All right," Cyril said.

After they finished eating, Cyril drove to the adjacent parking lot and they both got out of the Jeep. Cyril wore his backpack but kept the GPS monitor in hand. Benjamin found a used book store and Cyril followed him in, shadowing Ben as he went to the counter to speak to the young man with unruly blond locks and Buddy Holly glasses. Ben considered asking the clerk if they had *Being Held Hostage for Dummies*, but figured that Cyril would catch on before the clerk did.

"I'm looking for *The Girl with the Dragon Tattoo,*" Ben said.

"Hold on," said the clerk. Soon a young woman with glasses and jet-black pigtails stepped behind the counter.

"Can I help you?" said the young woman.

"Yes," Ben said. "I mentioned I was looking for *The Girl with the Dragon Tattoo.*"

"Okay," the woman said. "What can I do for you?"

"Well," Ben said, "could you tell me if you have it in stock?"

"What in stock?"

"*The Girl with the Dragon Tattoo,*" Ben said.

"Oh," said the young woman. "Seth thought you wanted me." She pushed her sleeve up to her shoulder to reveal an intricate dragon tattoo draped across her deltoid.

"Nice," Ben said.

"Yes," Cyril agreed. "Very nice detail work. Superb shading. It's quite evocative of the pig-eating dragons of Nimdaar 9."

"Uh, thanks," she said, giving Cyril a sideways glance and rolling her sleeve down. "I don't think we have that title right now. But feel free to look around."

Cyril followed Ben as he walked between the stacks. Ben finally found a title to his liking, pulled it off of the rack, and walked back to the counter.

"I've read this before," Ben said. "But there's nothing like a good road story to cheer you up." He sat *The Grapes of Wrath* on the counter and let Aurora – the girl with the dragon tattoo – ring it up.

"Here ya go," Aurora said. "I put a complementary bookmark in the bag for you."

Cyril and Ben went back to the Jeep. Ben got in the back seat, stretched his legs out, and opened his book. Tom had just reached the Joad homestead when Cyril shouted "Yesss!" The monitor light was flashing.

"Atlanta," Cyril said. "He's in Atlanta. That's only fifty-three kilometers."

By the time Benjamin had buckled up, they were speeding east on the interstate. Ben dreaded confrontation, but he hoped that this entire kidnapping-hostage-fugitive hunt fiasco was drawing closer to a resolution.

Fifty kilometers later, Cyril was speeding through Atlanta. Roads lined by houses and sidewalks and trees turned into suburban streets bordered by shopping centers, churches, and gas stations. Ben could see the monitor on the dashboard from the back seat. The flashing red light had not budged since they left the bookstore parking lot. Ben considered the post-capture logistics. *Will we have to drive back to Birmingham to get the Rev 9? Wonder if this Peter guy is a big talker – I hate that on long drives. Maybe I'll get to ride shotgun.*

At a light Cyril took a hard left down a narrow winding street, followed by another left turn into the parking lot of a public park. The red light stopped flashing as Cyril hit the brakes and skidded into a parking spot.

"They teach that in bounty hunter school?" Ben said. "Make lots of commotion when you arrive?"

"Shut up and get out," Cyril said. He grabbed his bag, opened the door, and jumped out of the Jeep.

Cyril was halfway down the sidewalk before Ben was out of the car. Ben trotted to catch up, and when he did Cyril set his bag down and removed the plasma immobilizer from his belt. "There he is," Cyril whispered. He pointed to a man sitting on a bench with his back to them. He was wearing an olive green t-shirt. A black backpack was perched next to him on the bench.

Cyril took aim with the immobilizer. "Dang it!" he said. "Setting always gets pushed up to level 3 for some reason." He flipped it back to the level 2 setting.

"What's level three?" Ben asked.

"Kill shot," Cyril said. "Two is to immobilize."

"What's level one?" Ben said.

"Sort of a Blutaarkian party game," Cyril said as he aimed again. A small glowing sphere shot from Cyril's hand and struck the man. He slumped to one side, then forward until he tumbled onto the ground in front of the bench. Cyril and Ben ran to him.

"Get his bag," Cyril said. He leaned over the man, grasped his shoulder and turned him over. "Uh...put the bag down." Cyril stood up straight and casually turned his head left and right to look for witnesses. "See, uh...I'm going to need you to walk slowly back to the car."

"You're going to lift him by yourself?" Ben said.

"I could if I wanted to," snapped Cyril, "but that's not the point. The point is that we need to go now."

"Did you kill him?"

"No," Cyril said. "I mean, I don't think so. Level 2 almost never kills anyone. Still not the point. The point is that we're here and we need to be not here, and the only thing keeping us from being not here is your incessant yammering." Cyril casually took a piece of gum out of his pocket.

"All right," Ben said. He turned and jogged back to the Jeep and climbed into the back seat. Cyril got behind the wheel and started the car. "So you go to all of this trouble and you're just going to leave him there? I clearly don't understand the bounty hunter business model."

"That wasn't Peter," Cyril said.

"So you shot an innocent stranger," Ben said. "That's just great. Is that guy going to be okay?"

"Sure," Cyril said. "His ears will ring for a few days. And he'll have some challenging laundry issues to deal with. But other than that, no big deal."

"I hope I'm not out of line here," Benjamin said, "but have you really done this bounty hunter thing before? Because from where I'm sitting, I see a definite dearth of professionalism."

"Just shut up," snapped Cyril. He slapped the GPS monitor back onto the dashboard and tore out of the parking lot like drivers with blue handicap tags don't. At that moment, Peter was waiting at a bus stop roughly one-and-a-half miles away from the park. Cyril was headed in the opposite direction.

Peter stood under the bus stop shelter, his backpack over one shoulder, and surveyed the posted bus routes and schedules. A middle-aged woman pulled her car up to the bus stop and motioned Peter to the passenger side window. "Thank you for your service," she said, handing Peter six one-dollar bills and driving off before he could object. The next bus was due in about ten minutes, so he stuffed the money in his pocket and sat on the bench. The bus stop was at the edge of a university campus, and watching the migrating herds of young, bright, idealistic students reminded him of his stint at Northern Blutaark University. Before the bus arrived, a disheveled young man reeking of alcohol and wearing a white shirt and khaki shorts sat next to Peter.

"Got a light, bro?" said the young man. An unlit cigarette dangled from his lower lip.

"No," Peter said, even though he wasn't entirely sure what the young man was asking. He reminded Peter enough of Cyril during their college days that Peter found it difficult to be not nauseated. "Don't you have some plagiarism to commit? Or perhaps a girlfriend to humiliate in a bar somewhere?"

"Hey!" said the young man, "I do. Thanks for reminding me." The young man got up and walked off into an assuredly undistinguished future.

When the bus arrived, Peter used the card April had given him and took a seat near the back. As he settled in he watched his fellow bus riders; a crush of humans of varying sizes, shapes, tints, genders, and degrees of acceptance about having to use public transportation. The naturalist in Peter relished this environment.

Hating to miss a promising data-collecting opportunity, he carefully removed the BAT from his bag. He had learned how to adjust the blue diagnostic beam, and he felt he could scan some of the passengers without being noticed. He scanned a dark-haired young woman who was sitting in front and to the right of his seat. He scanned a middle aged man who was standing in the aisle a few rows up, then a young boy who was sitting with his mother, and finally an older woman sitting to his right. With each scan Peter became more troubled. All species are susceptible to disease, but humans demonstrated an astonishing range and depth of biological dysfunction. *Sure, the Charpaqs of Huull 4 had health issues, as did the Glingecurds of*

Gyllenhaal 6, thought Peter. *But a single human being appears capable of harboring a greater number of maladies than do entire alien species.*

Peter was taken aback by this tragic revelation. On most planets bearing life, organisms are created and evolve over the span of millions of years. Most of the time, evolution is a distasteful but efficient process, using natural selection to weed out the less fit creatures (or more precisely, their genetic data) in favor of those organisms that are better suited for their particular environment. In the best-case scenario, self-aware intelligent beings come about. In the worst-case scenario, overly self-aware intelligent beings come about. Either way, the process of evolution dictates that the "fittest" really are fit, so most species are predisposed to few (if any) health problems. Most creatures already have enough difficulty avoiding being gobbled up by faster living things, or finding enough tasty slower living things to gobble up – or a combination of both.

Evolution doesn't need to waste its time making any particular creature its own worst enemy by giving it lung cancer, clinical depression, or lazy-eye. And on planets not named "Earth," evolution creates a balance where infections are more akin to benign parasitic relationships; the infected organism isn't bothered by the infectious organism, and the infectious organism survives without compromising its host. It's a win-win situation for both, without the need for painful needles and bad-tasting antibiotics.

It was as if evolution on Earth was broken. The natural laws that governed life everywhere else somehow didn't apply here. The upshot was a planet dominated by an intelligent species prone to literally thousands of different diseases - a species with individuals who possessed self-awareness and the ability to communicate, so that they had no qualms about telling everyone else exactly how bad they felt at any given moment. *If anyone deserved to be BATed*, thought Peter, *it was humans.*

Peter at once felt excited about the opportunity to do so much good, but depressed and overwhelmed by the sheer numbers. There were over seven-billion people on the planet, and – based on his cursory survey of the Metropolitan Atlanta Rapid Transit Authority passengers – they each seemed to have at least four or five different health issues.

I'd better get started, Peter thought.

The bus had made several stops when he decided to treat some of his fellow passengers. The brilliant white light from the BAT would not go unnoticed, so he decided to employ the "camera" ruse that he used in the park. He also thought to incorporate their proximity to the university into the subterfuge. He attempted it first on the elderly woman still sitting to his right.

"Excuse me," Peter said. "I'm an art student, and I was wondering if I could photograph you?"

"Nope," said the woman.

"I'll give you three dollars."

"Okay."

Peter dug six one-dollar bills out of his pocket and handed her three. "Smile," he said, knowing full well she wouldn't. After he BAT-scanned her, he convinced others to be "photographed" without remuneration: the middle-aged man still standing in the aisle, a middle-aged woman sitting with her elderly mother, a young boy holding his ear after a doctor's visit, and a young woman in waitress attire. The bus was now almost to the rail station. He decided not to use the BAT scan again until he was on the train. In the back of his mind he knew that whenever he used it, Cyril eventually showed up to ruin the party.

"So close," Cyril said. "Uncanny, really, how much that guy looked like Peter from behind."

"I wouldn't really know," Benjamin said. He kept turning his head, looking out of the rear window of the Cherokee. *You never get pulled over by the Atlanta Police Department when you really want to.*

"Sort of wish I hadn't shot him," Cyril said.

"Yeah," Ben said. "I bet he will wish he hadn't been shot, too. You know, whenever he regains consciousness." Cyril ignored the comment. He drove aimlessly through suburban neighborhoods, looking at drivers and passengers in passing cars and scrutinizing pedestrians on the sidewalk. Ben was about to crack open *The Grapes of Wrath* when the red light flashed on the monitor and Cyril did a U-turn that threw Ben to the opposite side of the car. He cushioned the impact by flinging his face against the window.

"It's moving this time," Cyril said, pointing at the red light. "Not very fast, but definitely moving in a linear fashion. He can't walk that fast. It doesn't make sense."

"Maybe he stole a car too," Ben said.

"Shut up," Cyril said. "We're just borrowing this. I'll return it when we're done, and I'll compensate the owner for mileage, fuel, and wear-and-tear. And I can deduct that from my taxes, so it's a win-win for everyone involved."

"Everyone?" Ben said, rubbing his bruised cheek and trying to catch Cyril's eye in the rear-view mirror.

"It's still moving, following the street," Cyril said. "We're catching up though. Why would he BAT scan people from a car?"

"Maybe he's on the bus," Ben said.

"The bus?"

"You know those large, oblong, white vehicles that you've almost sideswiped a couple of times?" said Benjamin. "They're filled with people and they're called 'buses.'"

The flashing red light kept moving. Cyril drove aggressively, ignoring speed limits, traffic signals, and Ben's whimpering. He blew through a controlled intersection and spied a bus ahead, parked with its tail lights flashing. "There it is!" shouted Cyril. He passed the bus and pulled in front of it, blocking its path.

"I'll wait here," Ben said after Cyril had already opened the door and run to the bus. Ben was reluctant to approach one man in a public park, but storming a bus with a driver and passengers on board seemed like something that would get them featured on the opening segment of the six o'clock news.

Cyril bounded through the front door of the bus holding a badge in one hand and brandishing the immobilizer in the other. (Most witnesses would later report that he appeared to be holding an electric razor in one hand and a sixties-era hippie medallion in the other.)

"Hey," said the bus driver, "I don't mean to be rude, but you can't -"

"Silence!" barked Cyril. "Licensed bounty hunter here – looking for a dangerous fugitive."

Cyril pushed his way down the aisle searching for Peter. Women clutched their purses, a baby started to cry, and a couple of young hipsters rolled their eyes at each other and resumed sending ironic text messages to their friends. Cyril reached the back of the bus and realized Peter wasn't on board.

"Have any of you seen a man on the bus who looks like me?" Cyril said, pushing his way back to the front of the bus. "But less charming? Anybody see him exit the bus? He *must* have been here. My tracking device confirmed that he was on this street just a couple of minutes ago."

"Well," said Theodore, the bus driver, "I certainly don't recall anybody by that description. But this is the Route 30 bus. Maybe he's on the Route 6. It follows the same route we do for a few blocks."

"Great!" Cyril said. "Where is it now?"

"It's headed west, toward the rail station," Theodore said. "It may almost be there by now."

"Thank you very much," Cyril said. "You've been more than helpful."

"You're quite welcome."

"And I'm truly sorry to have inconvenienced you," Cyril said. "I mean, parking my car in front of your bus and everything. That was out of line."

"Don't worry about it," Theodore said. "When you're looking for a dangerous fugitive, you gotta do what you gotta do."

"So true," Cyril replied. "I've been trying to convey that idea to my assistant, but the timid fellow is waiting in the car as we speak. He's not much help there, is he? In fact, you've been infinitely more helpful than he has."

"Just glad I could help."

"You're truly a gentleman," Cyril said. "And this after I've probably delayed you by a good three or four minutes. I hope this doesn't get you into trouble."

"No," Theodore said. "I'm union. Look, that Route 6 is probably close to the station by now. You're welcome to stay as long as you like, but if your man is on that bus he's not gettin' any closer."

"Yes, yes," Cyril said. "Well, sorry everybody!" he shouted to the passengers. "Enjoy the rest of your ride. Bye!" he said, waving to them.

A subdued "Bye" came from a handful of passengers, a couple of them waved back, and one of the hipsters sent a text message: "lame." Cyril exited from the front of the bus and got back into the Cherokee.

"Forget something?" Benjamin asked.

"Forget something?" Cyril replied in a sing-songy voice. "The first thing I'm going to do when I get that BAT is to use it on myself, because you make me sick." He started the car and headed west. "He's not far. He's on the bus headed to the rail station. We'll be there in a couple of minutes, and I expect you to go with me this time."

After violating several Georgia Motor Vehicle and Traffic codes and scattering wide-eyed pedestrians from crosswalks, Cyril pulled up to the rail station in time to see the last passengers disembarking from the Route 6 bus. With no time to spare, he pulled the Cherokee up onto the sidewalk, jumped out, and pulled Ben from the back seat.

"It's good that you parked on the sidewalk instead of in that handicap parking spot," Ben said. "Otherwise people would think you're an asshole."

"Shut up!" Cyril said as he dragged Ben toward the bus. "We'll check the bus first."

"I sort of gathered," Ben said.

Finding no one but the driver on the bus, Cyril broke for the rail station with Ben in tow. They scampered down concrete steps to find rail cars filling with passengers. Cyril instructed Ben to watch for Peter on the platform. Cyril approached the train and crept along the edge of the platform, peering into the large windows of the rail cars looking for Peter. He was almost to the back of the train when he happened by an empty window seat. The seat next to it was occupied by a heavy-set bearded man holding a black backpack on his lap. *Just doesn't look right,* thought Cyril. He stood on tip-toe and leaned against the train to look down toward the floor of the rail car.

Peter had packed up the BAT and hopped off of the Route 6 bus two stops before the rail station. He told himself he needed to stretch his legs, but a sense of foreboding compelled him more than the need to get some exercise. He kept a brisk pace on the sidewalk, and looked over his shoulder whenever a car approached. He made it to the rail station without incident, boarded a car near the back of the train, and took a window seat. From there he watched the steps leading down to the platform like a hawk – if hawks had backpacks, could sit upright in rail car seats, and had arms instead of wings.

The train was almost full when Cyril entered the station, bounding down the steps. Behind him was the man Peter recognized from the salvage yard. Cyril hit the platform and ran toward the front of the train. Peter considered making a break for it out the rear door, but Cyril's partner stood watch on the platform. *This thing should be leaving any second now,* Peter thought. He swallowed hard, dropped down to the floor in front of his seat, and held his backpack out to the bear of a man sitting next to him.

"Could you hold this for me please?" Peter asked. "Just until the train leaves the station?"

"They told us not to accept bags from strangers," the man said.

"Who said that?"

"At the airport," the man said.

"Well, this isn't the airport," Peter said. "Besides, you shouldn't believe everything you hear on an airport PA system."

"You could be a terrorist," the man said, "and that could be a bomb."

"If it were a bomb," Peter said, "it would blow me to smithereens."

"You could be a suicide bomber," said the man, using logic.

Peter could sense Cyril getting closer. "Listen...I'm sorry, what's your name?"

"Wayne."

"Listen, Wayne. Why would I need you to hold it for me if I'm a suicide bomber?" Peter said, using better logic.

Wayne wrinkled his brow. He was thinking. "I don't know," he said. "Maybe you need your arms free for those seventy-two virgins." Cyril was now three windows away.

"Look," Peter said. "Just take it. I've got an angry ex-husband after me and I'd really rather not get my ass kicked."

"Why didn't you say so?" said Wayne. A knowing grin appeared between his beard and mustache.

Peter threw the backpack onto Wayne's lap and scrunched down on the floor in an attempt to make himself into a ball. Cyril approached his window.

"Hey!" shouted a transit worker from the platform. "Step away from the train. It's getting ready to depart."

Cyril backed off of the train, and as he did he caught the glare of the bearded passenger in the aisle seat. He was pounding his right fist into the palm of his left hand. Cyril turned and located Benjamin on the platform and motioned him to the train. But the rail car doors were closing, and by the time Cyril reached the doors they were closed tight and the wheels were rolling.

Cyril pushed his way through the crowd on the platform and approached the transit worker. "Excuse me – I need to know where that train is going."

"North," said the worker. "Ends up at the North Springs station. But it makes four stops between here and there."

"Thank you," Cyril said. He and Ben ran back to the Cherokee.

NINE

"Thanks," Peter said, taking his backpack back from his burly accomplice. "That was close. A little too close."

"I got your back," Wayne said.

"I'm Peter, by the way. I owe you one."

Wayne shrugged. "Naw."

Peter had not forgotten that he was a wanted fugitive, but he puzzled over how Cyril managed to track him from Alabama to Atlanta. His spacecraft was parked in a junkyard outside of Birmingham, so that eliminated the possibility of a tracking device planted on the *Rev 2*. And there were no intergalactic spies on the planet – most would rather retire early than accept an Earth assignment. Perhaps Cyril had somehow found Brooks – but then why would Cyril not look for him at April's apartment, rather than on Atlanta's public transportation system?

Peter looked down at the bag on his lap. *The BAT*. He opened his bag and took the BAT out of its case. He grabbed the utility tool and pried off a panel from the shell. Tucked away at the bottom of the unit, just above where the power module attached, was a transmitter. It resembled the transmitters the

LSA used years ago to track migrating animals, so Peter suspected this was factory equipment installed on all of the prototype BAT units. If it were an LSA transmitter it had a relatively short range, but it had a life expectancy measured in years.

Peter used his utility tool's micro-wire cutter to extract the transmitter from the BAT. He pulled the spare power module from his bag and popped it open. He teased a couple of wires out of the module, and then spliced one of them to one of the wires from the transmitter. He then stripped the plastic coating from the end of the remaining wire from the power module. When touched to the remaining unspliced wire from the transmitter, it would activate it.

"Whatcha got there?" asked Wayne.

"This?" Peter said. "Just a bomb. Kidding!" He nudged Wayne's ribs with his elbow and got an uneasy smile. "Actually it's a camera. But let's just say it had some hardware I didn't really need." Peter set the transmitter aside and reassembled the BAT. "Say, Wayne. Mind if I take your picture?" Peter scanned Wayne. And over the next four stops he also "photographed" a dozen other passengers as they got on and off of the train. Gone was that premonitory feeling that surfaced whenever he'd used the BAT before. After the fourth stop, Peter attached the two remaining wires and stuffed the activated transmitter between two seats. They were less than three minutes from the North Springs station, where Peter planned to exit the train.

Cyril and Benjamin headed north on the parkway. The train had a head start, but the commuter rail tracks ran adjacent and roughly parallel to the northern stretch of the parkway. Cyril thought he could intercept the train at the next stop, but by the time he exited the parkway and drove to the station, the train had emptied and was heading back down the track. Peter was nowhere to be seen.

"What's the plan?" Ben asked after Cyril had wrapped up his tantrum.

"I'm thinking," Cyril said.

"Did you even see Peter on the train?" Ben said.

"No," Cyril said. "But I know he was on it."

"There are four more stops," Ben said, looking at a brochure he had grabbed off of a rack. "If Peter saw you at the very first station, my guess is he would have taken the first opportunity to get off of the train."

"Maybe that's what he wants us to think," Cyril said. "And if he didn't see me, maybe he'll use the BAT again. We'll keep going north." Back on the expressway, Cyril sped in and out of traffic, keeping one eye on the GPS monitor and one eye on the train. Because Cyril had only two eyes, that left no eyes on the other cars. After a few minutes they passed the next-to-last station, and from the parkway they could see the train departing. Cyril sped up, determined to beat the train to the last station. The red light flashed on the monitor. "Ha!" shouted Cyril. "He's still on the train. But the fool will be on his way back to Blutaark before he knows what happened."

Cyril pulled the Cherokee up to the North Springs station. A line of buses idled out front. There was no convenient sidewalk to park on, so Cyril pulled into a handicap parking space. He yanked the tracking monitor off of the dash, the red light still flashing.

"Come on," Cyril said. He sprinted across the lot and then up the steps to the station. Benjamin had trouble keeping up. They made it to the platform just as the train pulled in. "Like a spider in my web. I can practically taste that reward money now."

"Don't you mean 'like a fly in my web?' " Ben said, putting his hands on his knees to catch his breath.

Cyril ignored him, instead focusing on the monitor to locate Peter's rail car. When the train finally slowed to a stop, Cyril was waiting in front of the exit door of the last car. When the doors parted, Cyril found himself face-to-sternum with Wayne's doorway-filling body. He glared at Cyril, but Cyril shouldered his way past and pushed upstream against the mass of weary commuters. According to the monitor, Peter was a few meters away. With the aisle clearing out, Cyril found himself standing in front of an empty seat. Ben came up behind him.

"He should be *right here*," Cyril said.

"He's not," Ben said.

"I can see that!" shrieked Cyril. He inspected the GPS in his hand. "The monitor – it's in perfectly good working order." He crouched and looked under the seat. He got up, then leaned over the seats, stuck his hand between them, and pulled out the kludge Peter had left behind. He examined it, turning it over in his hand, then lifted his eyes toward the ceiling and bellowed. "Arrrghhh! Peter of Blutaark, how you bedevil me!"

"I take it that's not the BAT thingy," Ben said. Cyril took the time to throw the transmitter to the ground and then crushed it under his foot. He ran out of the car and Ben followed. The few stragglers on the platform stood and stared at them. "He was overindulged as a child," Ben said, shrugging his shoulders.

They raced to the middle of the platform and surveyed the thinning crowd. No Peter. Cyril was crestfallen and silent.

"You were right," Benjamin said. "He's like a spider in your web."

Peter had followed Wayne off of the train like a running back trailing his lineman, and escaped unseen by Cyril or Ben. He commingled with the mass of commuters heading out of the station, and once outside he broke from the crowd. Peter was less than half-a-mile from April's apartment, but he eschewed the streets or sidewalks and instead cut through a patch of urban forest to avoid detection. Five minutes after getting off of the train, he was at April's doorstep. He let himself in and locked the door behind him.

Cyril collapsed onto a bench at the station. Ben had the temerity to sit next to him. Nothing was said for a long time. Cyril fumed at having come so close to capturing Peter, but now that the transmitter had been extirpated from the BAT his goal seemed as distant as it had ever been. He wondered how he could possibly locate Peter – a humanoid on a planet of over seven billion humans. *At least I disabled the Rev 2*, thought Cyril. But Peter could end up anywhere on Earth, a planet with a land area of over five hundred million square kilometers. Ben wondered if Cyril was considering calling off the manhunt for Peter and letting Ben go. But Ben didn't get to wonder that very long.

"I guess we'll just get a hotel somewhere around here," Cyril said. "Someplace to rest and regroup."

Now it was Ben's turn to be disheartened. A subdued "I guess so" was all he could muster. *A bed does sound nice though*, he thought. Sleeping in the Jeep was getting a little Joad-like.

They made their way back to the Jeep and found

a nice hotel a couple of miles south on the parkway. Ben used his credit card to check in, and again he wondered if anyone – exactly who was still vague – was looking for him yet.

"One room please, with two beds," Ben said.

"Here on business?" asked the clerk.

"I suppose so," Ben said. "No way this counts as pleasure."

"Are you in that sixties cover band that's playing in the lounge tonight?" she said, noticing Cyril's green paisley shirt.

"No," Ben said. "We're actually here for a fashion intervention."

"I see," said the clerk. "Will you be needing a conference room then? We can move in some sofas and provide coffee."

"No thanks," Ben said. "Just the room."

"Enjoy your stay in Atlanta!"

Once in the room, Ben kicked off his shoes, lay down on the bed, and picked up where he'd left off reading *The Grapes of Wrath*. Cyril sat in a chair next to the bed on the other side of the room. Much to Ben's chagrin, Cyril figured out the TV remote control and started channel surfing. After watching snippets of a reality TV show, a wrestling match, local news, and an infomercial, and lingering on the "adult" channel, he settled on the weather channel.

"You know," Cyril said, "I wasn't exactly a scholar back in college -"

"No!" interrupted Ben, his eyes still glued to his book.

"Anyway, I wasn't exactly a scholar, but this is the worst university I've ever seen."

"This is a hotel," Ben said.

"No," Cyril said. "I mean the educational programming screen. You know the other day when

I called your planet a 'train wreck?' I didn't actually know that at the time. I was using hyperbole to be rude and condescending – just me being me. But it really is a train wreck. No wonder this place has never been colonized. That weather program is the most sensible thing I could find, although you could fairly well garner that same information by stepping outdoors. Now that program on human husbandry was sort of interesting. Until it wasn't. Then it was ghastly."

"That's television," Ben said. "It's not a university. It's entertainment."

"Well that's even worse then, isn't it?" Cyril said.

"Yes," Ben said. "Yes it is. But no one's making you stay."

Cyril got quiet. Ben's remark reminded him that he was still in a hotel room on this horrid little planet and not racing back to Blutaark with the BAT scan in hand and Peter uncomfortably bound in the storage locker of the *Rev 9*.

When April came home from work, Peter was sitting on the sofa reading *The Hobbit*. There were two other books on the coffee table.

"You were up early," April said. "How'd the job hunt go?"

"Not bad," Peter said. "No offers yet, but a solid lead at a doughnut shop."

"Good to hear," April said. "That's another one of my favorites."

"Yes," Peter said. "Especially good with coffee. But all those carbohydrates! Wreaks havoc with the pancreas. Ugh."

"I meant *The Hobbit*."

"Yes, of course," Peter said. "A great read so far. Sort of alarming that a character like Gollum was in possession of a ring that held so much power."

"Uh huh," April said. She was shedding detritus from the work day onto the kitchen table.

"Quite serendipitous that it came into the hands of that Baggins character," Peter said. "He seems like a wise and decent fellow."

"Yeah," April said, coming back into the living room. "Listen, my dad is coming over later, so I'm going to get dinner ready. You're welcome to join us if you want."

"I'd be honored," Peter said.

"And I don't mind you reading my books, but just put them back when you're through."

"Consider it done," Peter said. As April walked back to the kitchen, she turned to see Peter taking the two books from the coffee table and placing them back in the bookcase. When Brooks knocked on the door, dinner was almost ready. He hovered over April in the tight kitchen while she cooked.

"Smells great," Brooks said.

"It's just spaghetti," April said. "Nothing fancy. So what's this great news you have for me?"

"It can wait," Brooks said. "I'm famished." Brooks and Peter set the table after April cleared off her work material. She set three plates of spaghetti on the table, two glasses of red wine, and one beer. Brooks sat across from April, and Peter sat at the end of the table between them. Peter and April made small talk between bites while Brooks cleaned his plate.

"Is there a prize for finishing first?" Peter said, giving Brooks a wry smile.

"Yeah," April said. "It's called 'reflux.' "

"Don't be sassy," Brooks said. "And yes, I'd like seconds."

"Geez Louise," April said. "I'm glad you've got an

appetite, but I'm going to need a raise to afford the food and books." She returned to the table and filled Brooks's plate. When they finished, Brooks leaned back, cradling his head with laced fingers. April, her elbows on the table, sipped at a second glass of wine to rinse away the remaining frustrations from her work day.

"So where do you work?" asked Peter.

"Dionysus Pharmaceutical," April said. "I'm an administrative assistant."

"Dionysus," Peter said. "Wasn't he the Greek god of the harvest, specifically of wine-making and ritual celebrations involving wine?"

"Yep," April said, finishing off her glass.

"Is that what your company makes, wine?" Peter asked.

"Puh-huh," laughed April. "Not exactly. And there are no ritual celebrations, either. Unless you count the five minutes after we get our checks on payday."

"Well," Peter said, "I suppose that since wine contains alcohol, and alcohol is a drug, then the company chose that name as a sort of symbol – or metaphor. The company is like a god that makes people feel better."

"That's a stretch," April said. "But yeah, that's what a lot of people think. Truth is that Dirk – the guy who started the company – is a really big fan of Dion."

"Dion?" Peter said with a quizzical look.

"Yeah," April said. "He was a singer back in the early sixties. Dirk wanted to call it 'Dion Pharmaceutical' but apparently there was some legal foofaraw, so he just added 'ysys' to pretty it up and avoid litigation."

"Speaking of Dionysus Pharmaceutical," Brooks

said, "I think they may actually be on to something."

"You mean like bankruptcy?" April said. "Or criminal charges?"

"Now, April," Brooks said, "You'll change your tune after you hear what I have to say."

"I doubt it," she said. "But try me."

"That new drug they have me on – DPCL2 – it seems to be working," Brooks said. "Went in for my scheduled tests today and before I left Dr. Francis called me back to his office."

"Who's Dr. Francis?" asked Peter.

"Frank Francis," April said. "He's a clinical investigator working for Dionysus. Dad's in a clinical trial because he's got chronic leukemia." April turned to look directly at Peter. "But they can't know he's my dad, or he can't be in the study."

"*Had* chronic leukemia," Brooks said. "They'll need to do some more tests, but Dr. Francis said my blood work showed no signs of cancer cells. Zero. Zilch. Nada."

"*No shit,*" April said. "That's awesome!" April jumped up from the table. She put her arms around Brooks from behind and kissed the side of his hairless head. "I might just get to keep my dad *and* my crappy job."

"Hear, hear," Peter said, raising his glass. Brooks clinked his beer bottle to Peter's glass.

"He wants me to go back tomorrow," Brooks said. "And he wanted to talk to Peter, too."

"Why do they need to talk to Peter?" asked April, now standing with arms crossed.

"He treated my bursitis with some alternative medicine deal," Brooks said. "Frank said that since that was off-protocol they have to ask him some questions about it."

"So help me," April said. "If you get dad kicked

out of this study..."

"April," Brooks said, "It's not a big deal. Just a formality."

"I dunno," April said. "I just have a bad feeling about this." She was looking at Peter. "Well, I guess you're excused from job hunting tomorrow so you can get this all straightened out."

"Nothing to straighten out," Brooks chided. "Like I said, just a formality. Peter will need to bring that thing he used on me and answer a few questions. That's it."

"I'd be happy to," Peter said, forcing a smile.

The knot in Peter's stomach that had started when he saw Cyril at the train station now tightened. He was sure that he could bluff or charm his way through an interview with a clinical investigator, but the last thing he wanted was anybody who wasn't Peter touching the BAT. When beset with similar conundrums in the past, Peter would simply set his alarm for the wee hours of the morning, get dressed quietly, and make his way to the *Rev 2*. Sometimes he'd leave a note that simply read "I'll call you." He would be a galaxy or two away before anyone was the wiser. But with the *Rev 2* out of commission and more than two hundred kilometers away, that wasn't an option. *Maybe I could just "forget" to go*, thought Peter.

"I'll come by in the morning to pick you up," Brooks said.

So much for that plan, thought Peter. He could not just walk or hitchhike his way out of this; Cyril was close by and looking for him. He would have to think of something else.

Brooks did not stay long after dinner. He hugged April and told Peter he'd be by around ten. For the remainder of the evening Peter sat and read. April ostensibly watched TV, but Peter thought she looked lost in thought. She turned in early with a terse "G'night." When her door closed, Peter took the BAT out of his backpack and considered his options.

TEN

Before dawn there was a pounding on the front door. Before anyone could get up the bolt lock surrendered, the frame splintered, and the door swung open. Five men dressed in black – black pants, black jackets, and black shirts – stormed in, their black shoes stampeding across the hardwood floor. The predators found their prey before its bare feet had touched the floor. The capture was swift and efficient: zip ties binding wrists and ankles, duct tape across the mouth, black bag over the head, a struggling body rolled into a long black bag followed by a long zipping sound. A black SUV idled out front.

Four carried the bag, one opened the doors of the SUV, and the four heaved the bag onto the floor of the cargo bay. It landed with a *thunk*. The bag wriggled like a black caterpillar on a hot sidewalk as all five jumped into the vehicle. The SUV took off leaving black parallel marks as the only evidence. Well, that, and the broken front door. And a faint footprint in the hallway. And a disturbed area rug in the bedroom. And the missing person, which is evidence in a negative sort of way. But other than those things, the tire burn-out marks out front was the only evidence.

The hostage was shoved into a wooden chair, the

black bag and duct tape removed, the zip ties left in place. A single light hung tethered to the ceiling, illuminating the hostage like an actor in a spotlight with the audience invisible in the quiet darkness beyond. Finally the silence was broken.

"What do you want with me?"

"I'll ask the questions, Loretta," said a man's voice. "All you have to do is answer them. Honestly."

"There must be some mis -"

"Oh there's no mistake," said the man. "Unless you count the mistake you're making thinking there's a mistake being made. That would be your first mistake."

"I'm confused," Loretta said.

"Let me take this, Brian," said a different man.

"We said no names!" said Brian.

"Sorry. Listen, Loretta, we've already wasted enough time," said the man who wasn't Brian. "This can go very quick and very easy for you if you just cooperate."

"I'm listening," Loretta said.

"Good," said not Brian. "First, is it true that you went to your doctor yesterday afternoon, wanting to be tested to confirm your existing medical problems?"

"Yes it is," Loretta said. "They didn't want to at first, but I can be very strong-willed about things."

"That's a little unusual, don't you think?" said the man. "I mean, you've got all of these medical problems, and then one day you wake up and decide that you may not have them anymore, but to make sure you go see your doctor three months before your next scheduled appointment?"

"Is there a question in there somewhere?" Loretta said.

"Yeah," said the man. "At the very beginning. I

said 'That's a little unusual, don't you think?' "

"Yes."

"Yes, you're agreeing with me? Or yes you think that's a little unusual?" said the man.

"Both," Loretta said.

"Good. Now we're getting somewhere," said the man. "So what did they find out?"

"I was all better," Loretta said. "I don't need any of my medications."

"Really?" said the man. "Just like that? One day you've got arthritis and diabetes and high cholesterol and glaucoma, and the next day you don't? No more expensive prescription medications with forty-dollar co-pays? No more procedures with huge up-front deductibles? No more visits to your doctor every two-to-three months? How exactly, Loretta, does that happen? Herbal supplements? Healing magnetic bracelets? Did you run into a faith healer somewhere?"

"Something like that," Loretta said.

"Could you be more specific?" said the man.

"Well," Loretta said, "I was at the park yesterday. With Tyler. He's the little boy I watch. Such a sweet little boy. His dad is busy with work all the time, and his momma is busy doin' Lord knows what, so they pay me to watch him. And they live close to the park, in one of those big houses with -"

"Not that specific," said the man.

"Sorry," Loretta said. "Well, I met this man at the park. He was sittin' on the bench with me, and asked to take my picture with some fancy camera. After he took my picture he said I might not need my medicines anymore, and to check with my doctor. So I did."

"Really?" said the man. "Just some guy at the park?"

"Yes sir."

"What did this man look like?"

"Sort of a funny little guy," Loretta said. "Little shorter than average, dark curly hair - but his hairline was really receding. Abnormally so, for a man his age, like he'd been the victim of some sort of tonsorial accident."

"What kind of accident?" asked the man.

"Tonsorial," Loretta said. "That means having to do with barbering. My daddy owned a barber shop."

"Of course," said the man, who still wasn't Brian. "Could you draw us a picture?"

"Of the barber shop?"

"Of the man," snarled the man.

"No," Loretta said.

"And just why not?" said the man. He stepped closer, into the spotlight with Loretta, threatening her with his dark sunglasses inches from her face.

"Cause you got my hands tied behind my back."

"Okay, fair enough," said the man. "Maybe later. So what was this man's name? Where does he live?"

"I don't remember," Loretta said.

In frustration the man in black reached for the light in an attempt to shine it directly into her eyes, but it was just out of his reach. He turned away from Loretta and shouted into the darkness. "Didn't I tell you not to forget the gooseneck lamp?"

"Sorry," said Brian.

"Wait," Loretta said. "His name was Peter."

"That's a start," said the man, turning back to face her. "Now tell me about that camera."

"Not your ordinary camera," Loretta said. "It was shaped like a tube – sort of like a potato chip can. But skinnier. It was silver, and had a couple of buttons on the side."

"And where might I find this Peter fellow and his

not-your-ordinary camera?"

"I don't know," Loretta said. "I don't know where he lives."

"We're going to need that information," growled the man.

Loretta looked up into his Ray Bans. "Jason?"

"I beg your pardon."

"You sound just like Jason," Loretta said. "He's the jerk in customer service at my insurance company. I always end up talkin' to Jason whenever I have to call to figure out what they done screwed up. Which is a lot – and I never forget a voice."

"Oh, crap," said Brian from somewhere in the dark.

"Shhh!" said the man. "Listen, Loretta. I don't know who this Jason fellow is. And I don't know what kind of sophisticated hostage mind-games you think you're playing. But if you think it's going to work you've got another thing coming."

"Yep," Loretta said. "You're Jason all right. I could tell by the way you said 'you've got another thing coming.' He's always sayin' that to me."

"Get her out of here," said the man.

Benjamin fell asleep while reading and when he woke up Cyril was still watching TV. Sunlight was peeking around the hotel room drapes, and he wondered if Cyril had slept at all. Ben crawled out of bed and was granted permission to shower, as long as he didn't "try anything funny." Ben wondered what Cyril thought he could possibly get away with alone in a windowless fourth-floor hotel bathroom. Filling the bathtub and dropping a running hair dryer into it was the only thing he could come up with, so Ben decided that "Don't try anything funny" was just another one of the pat phrases Cyril used when he didn't really know what to say. Sort of like "Shut up." After he showered, Ben talked Cyril into going downstairs for breakfast, and over juice and English muffins Cyril started talking.

"I was thinking about our problem," Cyril said, "and I think I've come up with a solution."

"Go back to Alabama and stake out the *Rev 2* until Peter comes back for it?" Ben said.

"Hmm," Cyril said. "I hadn't thought of that."

"Really," Ben said. "Did you ever stop to think that this Blutaark – it is called 'Blutaark,' right, the planet where you're from?"

"Yes," Cyril said.

"Did you ever stop to think that this Blutaark place gave you a bounty hunter's license just to keep you extremely far away for long periods of time?"

"Shut up," Cyril said. "Anyway, we can longer track him remotely. And there are only two of us looking for him in a city of perhaps a half-million people. So the odds are against us."

"Indeed," Ben said. "Assuming he's still in Atlanta. If he's not, the odds are staggering."

"To that point," Cyril said, "I was watching this show called *America's Most Wanted -*"

"Oh, god," Ben said.

Cyril and Ben spent the next few hours crafting a wanted poster for Peter. Cyril drew a freehand portrait of Peter to be placed at the top of the placard. Since "wanted" might imply that Cyril had some sort of legal authority on Earth and could draw undue attention from those who actually did, Benjamin suggested "missing person" under the drawing of Peter instead. Cyril insisted that a reward be offered, and after taking into consideration that he only had one-hundred and twelve bunjits in his wallet, suggested a reward of a million bunjits. Ben recommended using local currency, since bunjits were worthless on Earth. After taking into consideration that he had no cash in his wallet, Ben suggested a reward of one-hundred and twelve bunjits. A compromise was met, and a reward of twenty-thousand dollars was offered. At the bottom of the poster, a phone number was provided – the number of Ben's cell phone that was still in Cyril's possession. After having several hundred copies made at Ben's expense, they spent the afternoon distributing them at bus stops, rail stations, and storefronts. Some were handed directly to individuals, a task handled mostly by Ben, since Cyril's appearance upset several children and a few pets. They returned to the hotel at dusk.

After dinner they returned to the room, where Cyril resumed watching cable and Benjamin sat down, removed his shoes and socks, and propped his achy feet up on his bed. He reflected on the wanted posters they had distributed. Based on his brief glimpses of Peter, Ben thought Cyril's drawing was a good likeness. But he thought that the drawing could pass as a fair rendering of Cyril, too, and wondered how many of the leads they received would be grounded in sightings of Cyril, and not Peter. Ben had now been held captive by Cyril for over forty-eight hours and he could not help but wonder if anyone back in Texas had noticed his absence. Then he heard the ringtone from his cell phone.

April left for work before Brooks arrived to pick up Peter. Before she left she had little to say to Peter, other than to remind him of the meeting with Frank Francis and not to "blow it." Brooks arrived promptly at ten. Peter was ready, and with his backpack on his back, he locked up and followed

Brooks to the truck. Traffic was light, and after a short drive Brooks dropped Peter off in front of the One Atlanta Plaza building.

"I've got to go to the off-site lab," Brooks said. "They want to repeat my blood work. Just go up to the twenty-seventh floor, and they'll take you to Frank's office."

After exiting the elevator, Peter was led down a long hallway to a small waiting area in front of Dr. Francis's office. The cheery receptionist smiled and asked him to take a seat, saying "Dr. Francis will be with you shortly." There were business magazines spread out on the coffee table and hackneyed motivational posters desecrating the walls. Peter wondered if April's desk was surrounded with similar posters. If so, he thought, it's a miracle that she hadn't been motivated to blow her brains out. The receptionist noticed Peter noticing the posters.

"I picked them out myself!"

"No kidding?" Peter said, hoping a conversation wasn't in the offing. He had already come to the conclusion that people who were inspired by motivational posters shouldn't be employed in the first place.

"The one about 'optimism' is my favorite!" she said. "I always try to be optimisticy!"

Just then Frank's door opened. Out stepped a forty-ish gentleman, short and somewhat kyphotic, with glasses, dark hair, and a full mustache. He wore a business appropriate tie and his sleeves were rolled up past his elbows.

"Mr. Finch," he said, shaking Peter's hand. "I'm Frank Francis. I'm here to rescue you from Hannah."

"Oh, Dr. Francis," said the receptionist. "You're a hoot!"

Peter and Frank both ignored her as they went

into the office and closed the door.

"I see you met Hannah," Frank said.

"Yes," Peter said. "She's quite chipper."

"Yeah," Frank said. "Most days I'd like to put her through a chipper. Please, have a seat." Peter sat. The windowless office had the usual accoutrements of a clinical investigator's office: bookcases filled with medical texts, a desk with stacks of papers and professional journals, an ego wall with various academic certificates. Absent were any motivational posters. "I appreciate your taking the time to come in this morning." Frank took a seat behind his desk. "I understand you're Brooks's friend."

"Well," Peter said. "More of an acquaintance. We haven't known each other very long."

"He's certainly taken a shining to you," Frank said. "And he's also under the impression that you cured his bursitis. How exactly did that come about?"

"We were traveling together," Peter said. "He mentioned something about his shoulder giving him problems, so I took the liberty of administering some alternative medical treatment that I've had luck with in the past. I hope I didn't jeopardize his study participation by doing so."

"Probably not," Frank said. "But we can't have any loose ends, so we needed to look into it. He mentioned that you used some kind of device – I hope you brought it with you."

"Yes," Peter said.

"Might I see it?"

"Please be careful," Peter said. "It's rather delicate." He removed the felt-lined wooden box from his backpack and handed it to Frank.

Frank opened the box and removed a silver cylinder with a black base, two buttons on the side, and a horizontal slit near the top. "Interesting." He turned the device over, examined it, then opened a desk drawer and removed a silver letter opener. He started to pry the bottom of the cylinder off.

"I'd really rather you not -" Peter said. Before he finished his sentence Frank had popped off the end of the cylinder. He extracted a couple of "D" batteries and some red and black wires. Peering into the tube he saw two small light bulbs and a mirror.

"Certainly less impressive than I imagined," Frank said. "No offense."

"None taken," Peter said.

"So how exactly," Frank said, "does one cure bursitis with a flashlight made from a painted potato chip can?"

"Potato chip can?"

"Yes," Frank said. "I can still see salt crystals on the inner lining." He licked his finger, traced it across the inside of the can, and then licked it again. "Mmmm."

"Busted," Peter said. "I suppose one might argue that it's not a legitimate medical device, but one can get remarkable results from the placebo effect. Besides, it's not like I received any remuneration."

"Right," Frank said. "The placebo effect." He sat the tube down on his desk and looked at Peter. "But here's the problem I have with that little hypothesis. Brooks had a host of other medical issues besides bursitis. A little arthritis, some hearing loss, prostatic hypertrophy, and chronic lymphocytic leukemia. And now those problems are gone. Non-existent. Poof! Just like that. Chronic leukemia just doesn't suddenly disappear because of the placebo effect."

"Not to point out the obvious," Peter said. "But Brooks *is* taking an experimental drug. Did it ever occur to you that it just might be working? You should try to be more...optimisticy."

"Ahh, DPCL2," Frank said. "Here's the problem with that." He leaned forward, elbows on his desk and fingers interlaced. "Brooks is the only person out of twenty-four in the study who's had any kind of response to the drug. All the others? Nothing. Nada. Bupkis. But Brooks's disease is *completely eradicated* – according to the testing we've done so far."

"Perhaps," Peter said, "he's just an unusual patient who had an idiosyncratic, yet beneficial, result from the drug."

"Here's the problem with that," Frank said, his voice lowering. "Brooks is in a double-blind study."

"I don't follow."

"The patients and investigators don't know what study subjects are getting," Frank said. "Half get the drug, the other half – the control patients – get a placebo. Brooks was not receiving the experimental drug."

"Let me get this straight," Peter said. "In a double-blind study, no one is supposed to know which study subjects are getting the real thing, and which are getting the placebo?"

"Bingo," said Dr. Francis.

"Then how do you know that Brooks wasn't on DPCL2?"

"I'm a man who takes liberties," Frank said. "I get the feeling you are, too."

"I'm a little envious," Peter said. "Apparently the Dionysus Pharmaceutical placebo is superior to my placebo. Perhaps you should market that."

"Nice try," Frank said. "But I think there's more to it than that. And I'm willing to use my considerable resources to get to the bottom of this."

"Well, good luck!" chirped Peter. "So can I have my BAT back?"

"Your what?"

"That thing there that you're holding in your hand," Peter said, catching himself. "I call it a 'bat' because it's sort of shaped like a baseball bat."

"Not really," Frank said. "It's shaped more like a potato chip can."

"Potato chip can – potahto chip can," Peter said. "May I have it back please?"

"Since you asked nicely," Frank said. "And since my eight-year old could reproduce it in less than an hour, sure. You can have it back." He started to reassemble it.

"Ouch," Peter said. "Guess I had that coming."

"I'll be in touch," Frank said. He finished reassembling the faux BAT and placed it into the felt-lined case. He noticed that the can conformed to the indentation in the case very much like a large tabby cat would; he had to twist and squeeze it in order to close the box. "I'll have Hannah show you out."

"So does Brooks get to stay in the study?" asked Peter.

"Probably, for now," Frank said. "Here's a clue: Brooks, in my office, with the bat."

"I understand," Peter said.

He packed the box into his pack as Dr. Francis called Hannah. She led Peter past the motivational waiting area and back down the hallway. He thought about asking Hannah to take him to April's desk, but decided against it. What would he possibly tell her? That Brooks really didn't need to be in the study in the first place, because he was cured by an alien brandishing a miraculous silver baton from a planet almost twelve-million light years away? Or that

Brooks could "probably" stay in the study, but only if Peter gave up the real BAT? That wasn't going to happen – at least not voluntarily. Peter sensed that he should get back to April's apartment as soon as possible and find a more secure place for the BAT. He took the elevator down and waited for Brooks in front of the building.

ELEVEN

Tor Kinney personified the American business success story. He attended a prestigious East Coast university where he made a name for himself both on the lacrosse field and in the classroom. Though Tor was never a member of the lacrosse team, his antics early one autumn morning involving a scantily-clad high school cheerleader, a wheelbarrow full of mayonnaise, and the men's lacrosse practice field ensured that his name would forever be associated with lacrosse in much the same way the name "Katrina" is associated with the city of New Orleans. His presence in the classroom was no less distinguished. He was best known as the student in the back row who wore a bathrobe, drank coffee, and asked thought-provoking questions, such as "Can I borrow a pencil?" "Is this going to be on the test?" and "Can I go now?" After seven years, university administrators decided that, yes, he could go now. They sent him off with an honorary degree in business administration with the understanding that a) he never, ever come back and b) the check that his father donated for construction of a new business building didn't bounce.

With his honorary degree in hand, Tor Kinney

started his business career inauspiciously as a mailroom clerk at the headquarters of the Persona Insurance Corporation. Initially, he was derided by his mailroom coworkers who taunted him with barbs such as "No, you can't have my pencil," and "Seriously, starting your business career in the mailroom? How cliché."

The badgering came to a screeching halt when, on the morning of his fourth day at work, Tor Kinney fired all of his mailroom coworkers. Although technically, at the time they were no longer his mailroom coworkers because Tor's father – August Kinney, founder and majority shareholder of the Persona Insurance Corporation – died on the evening of Tor's third day of work, making Tor the new majority owner and CEO of Persona.

In the twenty years that followed, Tor Kinney navigated Persona through a competitive marketplace, increasing governmental regulations, and shifting societal expectations like a pirate navigating a crowded bar after seven too many drinks. But like a pirate, Tor could also be cunning and ruthless, and he managed to grow the Persona Insurance Corporation from the twenty-fourth largest to the twenty-third largest health insurance company in the country. From his forty-eighth floor executive suite in downtown Atlanta, he would dispense diktats such as "We're in the health insurance premium collection business," and "Don't worry about denying a claim – some sick people get better eventually anyway."

To his credit, Tor was not one of those executives whose work day was divided evenly between his office, board meetings, and the golf course – because he hated board meetings. But he would on occasion roll up his sleeves, take the elevator down to the insurance claims call center, and work the phones along with his employees. "Nothing quite like working one-on-one with a policy holder," he would say after denying one of them a life-saving bone marrow transplant. "It really keeps me grounded."

But on this particular day in October, Tor was not working with policy holders, actuaries, attorneys, or call center employees. He was meeting with an employee unknown to most of the rank-and-file at Persona headquarters – a fringe worker whose name never appeared on the payroll, who was paid under the table to perform unspeakable acts designed to keep the uneven playing field tilted in favor of Persona. And sometimes, when they were shorthanded, he also worked the phones in the claims center downstairs. His name was Jason.

"How did it go?" Tor asked.

"We found the woman," Jason said.

"Good."

"She was cooperative," Jason said. "But didn't have much to give us. Just a general description of the guy and the device he used. She thought it was some sort of camera. She never put two and two together."

"I see," Tor said. "What about a name?"

"Peter," Jason said. "She didn't know his last name or his whereabouts. We spent most of the morning searching by car and on foot. No luck yet. We'll keep looking, of course. Oh, one more thing..." He slid one of Peter's wanted posters across Tor's desk.

"Gross," Tor said. "Is this a policy holder wanting us to pay for their plastic surgery?"

"No," Jason said. "It's a wanted poster we found at a bus stop. The name and drawing match our guy. Looks like we're not the only ones looking for him."

"Interesting. Have you called the number?"

"Not yet."

"Don't," Tor said. "Not until I come up with a plan. I trust you have other copies?"

"Absolutely."

"Good," Tor said. "I think you're off to a good start with this one."

"Thank you, sir."

"You can show yourself out. Keep me posted."

After Jason left, Tor scrutinized Peter's wanted poster, then opened a drawer and filed it away. He picked up the phone and made a call.

"Hello!" Cyril said. "Oh, I'm terribly sorry. Dr. Cotter isn't available right now." Ben recognized an opportunity that might not come again. He jumped to his feet and shouted.

"Help! I'm being -" He was interrupted by the plasma immobilizer.

"Sorry about that," Cyril said, putting Ben's cell phone back to his ear and the immobilizer back on his belt. "That? Well, if you must know – and I trust you will keep this confidential – Benjamin's in detox. Rehab starts tomorrow. We're all cautiously optimistic."

Ben lay on the carpet, unable to move. It felt like a joy buzzer was being pressed against every square millimeter of his skin, creating an intense tingling sensation that he hated. At first. He could barely make out Cyril's half of the phone conversation over the middle-school horn section playing inside his head.

"Yes," Cyril said. "I'm sure finding his car abandoned like that was upsetting. He wasn't hurt physically, but that was the emotional breaking point – rock bottom, if you will – for Ben. Fortunately he made the decision to enter rehab."

Ben managed to pry his eyelids open and from his bedbug perspective of the room watched Cyril ruin his life.

"Again," stressed Cyril, "strictly in confidence, but it was alcohol. And meth. And something the kids call 'huffing.' Yes, I *know*. Well if he was able to hide it from his friends, it's no surprise that he could hide it from his coworkers."

Ben moaned quietly.

"Ninety days," Cyril said. Ben moaned a little louder. "That is, ninety days if he doesn't relapse. Could be longer if he does. So keep him in your thoughts. No, very strict policy here – no phone or electronic communications. But I'll make sure he writes. I'll give him the message. He'll appreciate your being so understanding. Do take care. Bye."

Ben glared at Cyril through glassy half-opened eyes.

"Wendy says 'get well soon,' " Cyril said. "They were all very worried. Now about that little outbur -" Ben's cell phone rang again and Cyril answered it. "Yes?" Cyril listened for a couple of minutes. The only sound in the room was the intermittent moaning rising up from the floor. "Yes," Cyril said. "I'm interested, thank you." Cyril ended the call and turned his attention to Ben. "I have to go. I won't be gone long, but I can't exactly lug your semi-conscious body around with me."

"Mrrgrrbrahmrgumffrr," Ben said.

"Well, I actually could lug you around," Cyril said. "But it would raise questions that I have neither the time nor the inclination to answer. So you'll just have to wait here." Cyril went to his bag and removed a roll of something that resembled duct tape. He peeled off strips from the roll and proceeded to bind Ben's wrists and ankles. "Good thing this material is impervious to drool," Cyril said, placing a final strip over Ben's mouth. Cyril picked up his bag, and noticing Ben's continued potato-like activity, he checked his plasma immobilizer. "Look at that, will you? It slipped to setting 3 again. Must need new batteries – otherwise you'd be...you'll be fine. Probably. I won't be long." Then Cyril left.

Peter waited impatiently for Brooks outside of the One Atlanta Plaza building. *I should really look into getting a cell phone,* he thought. It was well after lunchtime when Brooks finally showed up. He apologized profusely, explaining that the doctors had to do more than just a simple blood draw on this visit. In addition to the routine blood work, Brooks underwent multiple imaging studies, and finally a bone marrow biopsy.

"That smarts like -"

"Like moonshine on a razor burn?" interrupted Peter.

"No," Brooks said. "I was gonna say that it smarts like having a long, hard steel needle stuck through your skin until it hits bone, then it's ground into the bone, then they dig around for a while, then they pull stuff out so it feels like the essence of your soul is getting sucked outta your body. Then they yank the needle out and slap a Hello Kitty band aid on your ass to make it all better. That's what I was gonna say."

"Brooks," Peter said sheepishly, "You're as honest as a gray wedding dress."

"And just as purty, too," Brooks said. He smiled at Peter, then shifted his weight to his left ass cheek.

Peter sat quietly in the passenger seat of the

pickup. He felt ashamed for being impatient and guilty that Brooks had to endure these painful procedures.

"But the good news," Brooks said, "is that it looks like I'm cured. Of course they can't use that word – 'cured' – but they can't find a lick of leukemia."

"Excellent news," Peter said. Brooks dropped Peter off at April's apartment and then drove home to get some well-earned rest. As Peter approached April's front door, he saw that it wasn't completely closed. He nudged the door until it opened enough for him to peer inside. The place was ransacked.

He stepped inside the doorway where he could see both the kitchen and the living room. The kitchen floor was covered in a hodgepodge of soup cans, flour, pasta, milk, eggs, juice, assorted green vegetables, yogurt, and broken beer bottles. It looked like the pantry and the refrigerator had been competing in a fraternity drinking game – and both lost. Cabinets and drawers were open and empty, having given up their contents to the floor and counter tops.

Peter turned his attention to the living room. The coffee table was flipped onto its side and the bookcases were knocked over – their contents scattered about the living room floor as if by a madman riled by the complexities of the Dewey Decimal System. April's bedroom door was open. He cautiously made his way to the doorway. The contents of her closet had been removed and tossed onto her bed. Her dresser drawers had been opened and emptied onto the floor, creating a carpet of shirts, socks, inexpensive jewelry, pajamas, and bras and panties that Peter looked at probably longer than what was appropriate.

Peter stepped out of the bedroom and surveyed

the apartment in toto; it was like a tornado had hit – if tornadoes only occurred indoors and only disturbed the contents of a building without damaging the building itself. Peter felt guilty about Brooks, and now he felt responsible for the pillaging of April's apartment. He was certain that this was about the BAT. He thought that this might be the handiwork of Cyril, but was more likely the doings of Dr. Frank Francis – the man who took liberties. Either way, he was relieved that he hadn't left the BAT here. Peter went to the front door and closed and locked it and set about cleaning up April's apartment.

He started in the kitchen, and when he finished there he moved on to the living room. Cleaning up the living room was relatively easy. He turned the coffee table upright and picked up the scattered magazines and gewgaws. The bookcases were heaved back into position against the wall and the books were returned to the shelves in their original order – to the best of Peter's memory. *In hindsight, maybe I should have cleaned the bedroom first,* thought Peter as he stood amidst the disorganized majority of April's personal effects when she came through the front door.

"What the hell are you doing?" April shrieked.

"I was just getting ready to clean -"

"Get the hell out of my bedroom!" April screamed. "Ugh, I *knew* something like this was going to happen."

"When you're done shrieking and screaming I can explai -"

"I thought I told you never to go into my bedroom," shrieked April. "That's one of the rules, remember?"

"Geez, I didn't realize you were such a strict

constructionist."

"Get out!"

Peter stepped out of the bedroom and maintained what he judged to be a safe distance from April in the living room. "When I got back from -"

"I said get out!" April said. This time she pointed toward the front door. "Get your things and go." Peter was speechless. He got his backpack and left. April closed the door behind him.

Peter walked for a long time after he left April's apartment, and thought about the events that had transpired since breakfast. Cyril was out there, somewhere, still looking for him. But the failed attempt to locate the BAT at April's wasn't typical of Cyril's handiwork. Sure, he could be arrogant. And inept. And a fashion pariah. And no one who wasn't Cyril ever claimed that his critical reasoning skills were above-average. But Peter knew that Cyril was also fastidious, and leaving a mess like that at April's apartment would have bothered him almost as much as not finding Peter and the BAT.

It was obvious to Peter that another party was responsible. Dr. Frank Francis, or someone working under him, seemed to be the most likely candidate. Things were getting too hot in Atlanta for Peter, and being homeless didn't sweeten the pot. *That job at the doughnut shop probably won't pan out, either,* he thought. Peter made the decision to get out of town, but before he hit the road he stopped at a fast-food restaurant. Going through his pockets, he found April's transit card and enough change to purchase a small burger. *I'll mail the card back to her.*

TWELVE

After Peter left the restaurant, it was a short walk to the highway. He faced oncoming traffic, extended his right arm, and trudged backwards. It wasn't long before someone stopped. A large black SUV with chrome wheels pulled over on the shoulder ahead of him and the passenger-side door popped open. Peter jogged to the open door, threw his backpack onto the floor, and hopped into the seat.

"Thanks for the lift. I'm Peter."

"You're welcome." She was a striking woman with jet-black hair pulled into a ponytail. Her pale features were offset by her dark eyes and panic-button red lips. She wore a tight black dress. "I'm Martina."

Peter turned and was taken aback to see three women sitting in the seat behind him, each a mirror image of the driver: thin, pale features, dark hair, red lips, and black dresses that varied only by the length of their hemlines. "I'm Peter," he said again, as if to prompt their introduction. They neither spoke, nor smiled, nor made eye contact. "You girls look familiar," he said. "Have I seen you somewhere before?"

"Might as well face it," Martina said. "You haven't." Peter waited for the customary "Where are you headed?" question posed to hitchhikers who have been picked up, but it never came. He decided to turn the tables.

"So where are we headed?" he asked.

"We're taking I-85 north," Martina said.

"How far?" asked Peter.

"It goes north through South Carolina," Martina said. "Then to Charlotte, then Raleigh-Durham, then up through Virginia where it runs into I-95 near Richmond. But who really knows how far we'll go?" She turned and gave a vacant smile to her friends in the back seat.

Peter thought it was best not to look back. He had lived a long time and been in similar situations in the past. They almost always ended with him being introduced to an icky yet well-financed cult leader. He decided not to jump out of the vehicle, at least for now.

"Okayyy," Peter said. True to her word, Martina took the exit for I-85.

"If you don't mind," Martina said, "we have to stop at a storage facility to pick up a few things. It shouldn't take long."

"No problem," Peter said. *But if it involves loading drugs, firearms, or E-meters into the back of this vehicle, then yes, problem,* he thought.

After exiting the interstate, Martina drove a short distance to the storage facility. She rolled down her window to reach the keypad after stopping at the security gate, then dug into her purse and pulled out a taser. In a coordinated effort, one of the women in the back threw a black bag over Peter's head at the same time Martina zapped him, turning him into a paralyzed, blind, yet not-at-all surprised alien. *Stupid cults*, he thought.

When the bag came off of his head Peter found

himself sitting in a ten by fifteen room with a concrete floor, three corrugated metal walls, and – right in front of him – a large metal door. His hands were cuffed behind his back and his ankles shackled together. The storage unit was completely empty – except for Peter and his chair. And a folding table next to Peter. And Peter's bag. And Martina. But other than Peter and his chair and the table (which, by the way, had a glass of water on it) and the bag and Martina – the storage unit was empty.

"I don't know what you're paying for this space," Peter said, looking around, "but you're not getting your money's worth." Martina opened his bag and dumped the contents onto the table. "If you wanted a snack bar you could have just said so." She grabbed the felt-lined box and opened it. After she removed the faux BAT she tossed the box back onto the table. Martina looked over the painted potato chip can, crushed it with one hand, and threw it in Peter's face. "You're mad because I ate all of the chips."

"I want the real thing," Martina said.

"Don't we all?" Peter said. "I mean, when you get right down to it, when it's all said and done, we just want that special person, a place of our own, and work that's gratifying and productive. What's more real than that? I mean when it comes right down to it, do you really need that European sports car, the beach vacation home, that big promotion -"

"Silence!" shouted Martina. "Tell. Me. Where. It. Is."

"Okay," Peter said. "I'll play along. It's in a locker at the airport."

"Really?" Martina said, rolling her eyes. "Is that the best you can do? A locker at the airport? It's like you actually tried to come up with the most clichéd hiding place imaginable! That's the worst answer ever. Congratulations! I would have found 'My dog ate it' more palatable. I wasn't planning on torturing you, but now I feel I must, just on principle. Even if it *is* at the airport!"

She walked to the large metal door and rapped on it with her knuckles. The door rolled up and Martina whispered something to one of the pale riders waiting outside. She left and then returned with one of the other unnamed women; one carried a cinder block, the other a sledgehammer. They closed the door and then watched as Martina unlocked the shackles from Peter's ankles and removed the boot from his left foot.

"Sorry about the sock," Peter said. "I'm a heavy sweater." With two fingers she peeled the sock off of his foot and tossed it aside. "Okay, now you're only torturing yourself."

Martina watched through watery eyes as one of the women held Peter's bare ankle atop the cinder block with her surprisingly strong hands. The other woman handed the sledgehammer to Martina and then placed herself behind Peter, holding his shoulders down to secure him to the chair. "Did you ever see the movie *Misery*?" asked Martina.

"No," Peter said. "But I did read *The DaVinci Code*. That's gotta be close, right?"

Martina lifted the sledgehammer over her shoulder. "One...two..."

Peter had accurately assessed his situation. He was immobilized. Even with the bony bits inside, his ankles were nowhere near as hard as sledgehammers and cinder blocks. It was currently three against one, not counting the third pale rider who was probably waiting outside. He knew they were clueless about Blutaarkian salivary neurotoxin, but Peter had a propensity for cotton mouth in stressful situations.

He thought he had enough toxin to use against one of his abductors – maybe two – but he would still be handcuffed and outnumbered.

"Wait!" Peter said. "I just remembered something."

"What?" Martina said.

"I really hate pain."

"THREE!" The sledgehammer made a sweeping arc as Martina swung it like Pete Townshend trashing a guitar at the end of a concert. It crashed into the cinder block, sending shards of gray cement and cinder dust into the air. Peter had pulled his foot off of the block at the last fraction of a second, and his ankle was now oozing blood from a nasty abrasion.

"I like it better when villains count backwards," Peter said. "You know, like 'three...two...one...zero.' But I'm hoping that's immaterial, because I'm prepared to tell you where the BAT is. That's the device you're looking for." Martina dropped the sledgehammer and with a slight jerk of her head gestured for her two accomplices to leave.

"And close the door!" Martina shouted to them as they stepped outside. With the door closed she turned to Peter. "So where is it?"

"In my boot," Peter said.

Martina walked over to him. "Lift up your foot." She grabbed Peter's boot by the heel and yanked it off, sending the BAT bouncing across the concrete floor, pinging like loose coins in a clothes dryer.

"You know," Peter said, "You're making a good argument for extended warranties."

"Sshhhh!" She walked to where the BAT had come to rest and picked it up.

"The owner's manual is about nine-hundred and fifty kilometers from here," Peter said. "I'll need to show you how it works. Otherwise, you might disassemble an attractive young woman into her not-so-attractive molecular constituents." He was bluffing. And sucking up a little bit, too.

Martina walked to the table and set the BAT down. She turned toward Peter. With her eyes fixated on his, she bent slightly, slipped her left hand just under the hem of her dress and pushed it up past mid-thigh. With her right hand she removed a Sig Sauer semiautomatic from a thigh holster. After releasing the handcuffs, Martina tossed the BAT to Peter and steadied the gun on him.

"So show me how it works."

"Fairly straightforward," Peter said. "You make sure the power module is in place – which it is. Then you power it up with this small button near the base." Peter turned the unit on. "Then the blue button activates the diagnostic beam. Shall I?"

"Please do."

"The light comes out here," Peter indicated, "opposite the LCD screen." He pushed the blue button. The storage unit fluoresced as the blue light traced across his body. "Now you just look at the LCD readout for the diagnoses." He turned the BAT so she could read the screen. She leaned in just enough.

"Abrasions, moderate, left ankle and foot," she read out loud. "Ventricular tachycardia. What does that mean?"

"Your heart beats, in double time," Peter said. "And now, for the *coup de grâce!*"

"Don't even think about it!" shouted Martina, backing up and thrusting the pistol toward Peter's face.

"Oh, sorry!" Peter said. "I meant *pièce de résistance*. Still having trouble with those French phrases. My bad." He turned the BAT on himself. "The white button is for the treatment mode." The room filled with an astronomical white light which flickered and went out. Martina stepped a little closer and peered at his exposed foot.

"Astonishing," Martina said. "It looks perfect."

"I don't consider it my best feature," Peter said. "But thanks anyway."

"Give it back to me," she demanded, holding out her left hand. Peter stuck out his tongue and dragged it across the entire length of the BAT. "You child. That won't keep me from taking it from you."

"You like to think you're immune to the stuff," Peter said, handing her the BAT. Three seconds later Martina hit the floor. "Oh yeah."

He worked quickly, prying the BAT from Martina's hand and packing it into its black box. The box and his other possessions – save the snack bars – were shoveled off of the table and stuffed into his pack. "You girls might get hungry later," Peter said, estimating that the four remaining snack bars and one glass of water could sustain the four women for a fortnight. Or two. With his pack slung over one shoulder, Peter bent over Martina's body to retrieve the semiautomatic.

"I'm torn," he said. "I could really use a holster, but if I take yours I'll feel guilty for not at least buying you dinner first." He left the holster. Peter stood up and rapped on the metal door. It opened immediately, and he pointed the gun at the two women standing outside.

"Get inside," he barked, and they complied. He made his way over to the SUV and stood next to the driver's side window, where he watched the third unnamed woman using her smart phone to look at photo after photo of adorable cats. She jumped when

Peter tapped the gun against the window, then surrendered the keys and her phone and joined her compatriots in the storage unit. Peter closed the door to the storage unit and locked it, then drove off in the SUV.

THIRTEEN

Cyril was met by security and ushered to the forty-eighth floor where he took a seat in the reception area. The receptionist looked at him and made a face very much like the face a vegan might make on an abattoir tour.

"Mr.?"

"Cyril," he said.

"Mr. Cyril, Mr. Kinney will be with you shortly," she said.

"No mister," he said. "Just Cyril."

"I see," she said. "May I get you anything? Water? Something to read? Another shirt?"

"I'm fine, thank you," Cyril said. "But I was hoping we could move this along. I've got someone tied up back in my hotel room, and I think I forgot to put out the 'Do not disturb' sign."

"You're very funny," she said without changing her facial expression or the pitch of her voice. "You can go in now."

Cyril opened the door and strode across the large Persian rug toward Tor Kinney's monolithic desk. Tor looked up from some documents, tried not to look startled, then stood to shake Cyril's hand.

"I'm sorry," Tor said. "Who are you?"

"I'm Cyril. We spoke on the phone."

"Of course," Tor said. "My apologies again – Margaret usually buzzes me when I have an appointment. Have a seat." He sat down and leaned back in his chair. "I'm Tor Kinney, CEO of Persona Insurance Corporation."

"It's a pleasure," Cyril said. He noticed Tor's generous forehead and wondered if perhaps he had had a Blutaarkian ancestor. Tor's forehead was framed by oily black hair above and by two oily black eyes below – eyes that were set a little too close together. He was either smiling a little, or a mouth breather – Cyril wasn't sure which. "Let's not waste each other's time. You said you had some information that would be beneficial to me?"

"I did," Tor said. "One of my associates saw the wanted poster that you've been circulating." He held up the poster and turned it toward Cyril. "It seems that we're looking for the same person. His name is Peter."

"Duh," Cyril said. "I already knew that – hence, the name 'Peter' appears under the drawing of Peter on the wanted poster of Peter that I made and you're holding."

"Of course," Tor said. "What else can you tell me about him?"

"Whoa, whoa, whoa!" Cyril said. "I'm a bounty hunter, and Peter is *my* fugitive. I was under the impression that you had some information for me regarding his whereabouts."

"He's in the greater Atlanta metro area," Tor said. *Definitely a mouth breather,* thought Cyril, shaking his head.

"What a coincidence," Cyril said. "So am I! Apparently you know less about his whereabouts than I do. Good day." Cyril stood to leave.

"Wait," Tor said. "He has something we both

want. I have enormous resources at my disposal, and if I find him first you walk away with nothing. But if you find him first, I'm prepared to make you a generous offer."

"It's not 'if' I find him first but 'when' I find him first."

"Don't underestimate me," Tor said.

"Too late."

"How does five-thousand dollars sound?" Tor said.

"Like you're making me an offer for Peter's socks," Cyril said. "Actually, he's got this serious foot sweat problem, so bad example. But you get the idea."

"Let me put it this way," Tor said. "If you find him and you don't bring him to me, I will use my vast resources to make your life...well, let's just say that you shouldn't take for granted that your knees only bend in one direction."

"They don't," Cyril said. "Thanks to a mechanical looglack." Cyril turned to walk out.

"Wait!" shouted Tor, getting up from his chair. "Here, take one of my cards."

"Thanks," Cyril said. "Hey, this is really nice."

"Yeah," Tor said. "It's a Vera Wang design. Buck-thirty a card."

"Worth every penny," Cyril said. "You've got to make a good first impression in today's business environment."

"Exactly," Tor said. "Well, I've got your number. Keep in touch."

"You too," Cyril said. He walked out, but before the door closed completely he stuck his head back in. "I'll call you. Maybe we could get coffee sometime."

"I'd like that," Tor said. Cyril smiled a little and left. Tor picked up the phone. "It went exactly as planned. He just stepped out. I'll have security make sure he leaves through the main entrance. You and Brian can follow him from there."

Peter drove back to I-85 and headed north, but without a definite destination in mind. While he was getting the hang of using the brake and the accelerator not simultaneously, he analyzed his current situation. He still had the BAT, and in addition he now had a handgun and an SUV with a full tank of gas. On the downside, the *Rev 2* was still six-hundred miles away and broken, he was broke, he had no job, and he had no place to stay. The handgun and SUV would be reported as stolen as soon as Martina and her accomplices were rescued from the storage unit. He could make a run for it – he had heard nice things about North Carolina – but Martina knew of his plans to leave Atlanta. He thought perhaps he could use that to his advantage – for a little while, anyway. He took an exit, turned around, and headed back toward April's.

Peter ditched the SUV about six miles from April's apartment. Fortunately, he was wearing his seat belt at the time. The ditch was not very deep, but the rear passenger-side wheel was wedged into the muddy bottom of the culvert making it impossible to move the vehicle without a tow truck. He knew he could not leave the SUV at April's complex anyway, so this seemed as good of a place as any. He grabbed his backpack, searched the SUV for anything that might be useful (there was nothing), and started walking. It was dark by the time he got back to April's.

"Uh oh," April said after opening her door. "Looks like someone doesn't quite get the concept of 'getting kicked out.' "

"April," Peter said. "We need to talk."

"I guess having a stalker isn't half as bad as getting hacked to bits by a serial killer," April said. "Come on in." Peter walked in, dropped his bag, and sat in the upholstered chair. April sat on the sofa.

"April, I'm terribly sorry about what happened," Peter said. "But when I got back from my meeting with Frank Francis, your entire apartment had been trashed. I had cleaned up everything except your room. I was about to start on it when you came in."

"I figured something like that happened," April said. "After I finished putting everything back there really didn't seem to be anything missing – except for my copy of *To Kill a Mockingbird*. I finally found it under the sofa."

"Good," Peter said.

"No," April said. "Not good. My life is complicated enough as it is without getting my apartment turned upside-down on a regular basis."

"It probably won't be a regular thing."

"Oh, great," April said. "Because I can totally deal with getting my apartment trashed on an irregular basis. That's *so* much better."

"No," Peter said. "What I meant is that whoever did this was probably looking for something very specific. I doubt they'll be back."

"Something very specific?" April said. "Could *you* be more specific?"

"I'd rather not," Peter said. "It's already caused me enough trouble. I'd rather not get you involved."

"Excuse me?" April said. "I came home from work today to find my apartment had been ransacked. I'm already involved."

"Look," Peter said. "It could get uglier than a ransacked apartment if you knew."

"Fair enough. I could use a beer. How about

you?"

"Sure."

"You're in luck," April said. "They overlooked a couple of bottles in the back of the frig." April went to the kitchen and took two bottles out of the refrigerator. She opened them and brought one to Peter. "Here ya go." As Peter took the beer she reached down, grabbed his backpack, and ducked behind the sofa. "I'm just gonna ransack your backpack. Then we'll be even-Steven," April said, unzipping the main compartment.

"April, please," Peter said, standing.

"Stop!" shouted April. Peter stopped. "Do not move. I can scream loud enough to have that bitch upstairs on the phone to call the cops in a heartbeat." Peter froze, and April started pulling things out of the bag and tossing them onto the sofa. "T-shirts...pants...what's this? Looks like a Swiss Army knife on steroids."

"That's pretty much the case," Peter said. "It's a utility tool. Very handy, but not really something that the forces of evil would conspire to steal."

"Puh-huh," April laughed. "You said 'forces of evil.' Been reading too many comic books much?" Next she unfolded the travel brochure for Gyllenhaal 6. She could not translate the text, but there were plenty of pictures. "What the hell is this? One of those European adult theme parks?"

"Something like that, sure," Peter said.

"Well that's just a little sick," April said, tossing the brochure onto the sofa. She pulled the black box out of the bag. She gently placed it on the back of the sofa and let the empty bag drop to the floor. She looked up at Peter, and then unlatched the box.

"Have you ever heard of Pandora?" asked Peter.

"Yeah," April said. "But I prefer Spotify." April

lifted the lid to the box and with both hands removed the BAT. "What *is* this?"

"Its official name is the 'Bio Analysis and Treatment device,' " Peter said. "Or 'BAT' for short."

"It looks like that memory eraser thing from *Men in Black* and a lint roller had a baby," April said. She glanced back up at Peter and reassured herself that he was not wearing a black suit jacket and pants. He wasn't. "You're not going to erase my memory spotless, are you?"

"What?" Peter said. "You don't remember?"

"Very funny," April said. "So what does it do?"

"It cures disease," Peter said. "Pretty much any disease in any species."

"Right."

"I'm serious," Peter said. "That's what I used on your father. That's why he's cured."

"Bullshit," April said. "He's taking an experi -"

"He's one of the control patients," Peter said. "He never got the drug – that is, if Frank Francis was telling the truth."

"Where did you get this?"

"You'd better sit down for that," Peter said. He sat back down. April climbed over the back of the sofa and sat next to the contents of Peter's now-empty pack. Peter spoke slowly and chose his words carefully. "This technology was developed by a race of beings on a planet millions of light years from Earth."

"Get out," April said.

"Already?" Peter said. "I thought we were good."

"Sorry," April said. "'Get out' is short for 'get out of here' – an idiom used to express utter disbelief."

"Okay," Peter said. "But do hear me out." He paused and took a deep breath. "I used to work as sort of an interstellar naturalist, traveling to different planets to study and document living things. I was given the BAT – the device you're holding – by mistake. A simple bureaucratic snafu."

"So you're an alien?" April said. "What are you doing in suburban Atlanta? I thought you guys were supposed to show up in the rural Deep South, or crash land in the desert."

"Wow," Peter said. "This *is* a little embarrassing. I sort of crash – 'crash' is really too strong of a word – let's just say I inadvertently landed in Alabama, outside of Birmingham."

"Of course you did," April said. "I'm gonna have that beer now." She retrieved her beer from the kitchen and sat back on the sofa. "So, if this BAT thing was given to you by mistake, I take it that somebody wants it back."

"Not so much anymore. Space is a pretty big place, and it's exponentially easier for them just to make another BAT than to expend resources looking for me. Although there is one bounty hunter who is still tracking me."

"So if I smile and nod and go along with this story," April said, "then it's not much of a leap for me to assume that an alien bounty hunter trashed my place."

"You'd be wrong about that," Peter said. "He's actually sort of a neat-freak."

April sighed audibly. "Soooo...who did?"

"Based solely on circumstantial evidence," Peter said, "I'm guessing Frank Francis is responsible."

"Really? What evidence?"

"In our meeting today," Peter said, "he made it clear that he was determined to find out how Brooks was cured. I showed him a fake BAT I patched together. By the way, you're out of potato chips. Anyway, I was hoping to throw him off of my trail. I tried to convince him I was a harmless alternative-medicine guru, but apparently it didn't work. So he came here – or more likely sent somebody here – to look for the device that cured Brooks."

"Allegedly cured him," April said. "Maybe Dad had a spontaneous remission – that happens."

"Spontaneous remission of *all* of his medical problems?" Peter said. "At the exact same time? No, he was cured by the BAT. And Frank Francis knows it."

"Prove it," countered April.

"Let's go," Peter said. "Put the BAT in the bag and bring it with you. You should probably drive." April put the BAT and the remainder of Peter's belongings back into the bag and grabbed her car keys off of the kitchen table, and they headed out the door.

"So where are we going?" April said as they pulled out of the apartment complex. "Not to a large, isolated field somewhere, I hope. My arms are tired from picking up the apartment – I really don't think I could dig a very deep hole right now."

"No," Peter said. "To the hospital. I saw a nice looking one the other day when I was job hunting. It was close to a university."

"Emory," April said. "Oh, that reminds me." She pulled a folded envelope from her pocket. "This came today."

"Thanks for opening it for me," Peter said as he unfolded the letter.

"Hey," April said. "I'd thrown you out, remember? I didn't know where you were and didn't think I'd see you again. But kudos on nailing the doughnut shop job."

"This is great news!" Peter said not sarcastically. April drove and tried to fathom how someone who could travel light-years and who possessed a device that – allegedly – cured illness could be thrilled about getting a minimum-wage job at a doughnut shop in Georgia.

"So," April said. "You know you just can't go into a hospital and walk into some random patient's room. Assuming that's your plan. They have security guards – with guns. And visiting hours – with surly nurses to enforce them."

"We'll try the emergency room," Peter said.

"Same thing. Security guard, lots of doctors and nurses. You just can't waltz back there and pretend to heal people."

"Pish-posh," Peter said. "Doctors do that all the time. No, I get what you're trying to tell me, but if this emergency room is like all of the other emergency rooms I've patronized between here and the M81 group, there will be a waiting area chock-full of ghastly patients without a doctor in sight. Should be easy pickin's."

"We'll see," April said. "But if this goes south, I've never seen you before in my life."

"That's the spirit," Peter said. "Now just play along and everything will go tickety-boo."

April parked in the hospital parking deck, and from there it was a short walk to the emergency room. Upon entering the emergency department, Peter attempted to take a seat in an inconspicuous corner of the waiting room, but was stopped by the triage nurse.

"Sir," said the nurse. "Excuse me, sir. You'll need to stop here, please."

"Odd how she pegged me as the sick one," Peter whispered to April. He walked across the waiting area and took a seat in front of the triage nurse's desk. Her name tag said "Olivia."

"What is your name, sir?" said Olivia. She

glanced at Peter's odd hairline without blinking or changing her expression, a skill honed by years of experience dealing with people whose body parts weren't always exactly where they should be.

"Peter. Peter Finch."

"I'm mad as hell, and I'm not going to take it anymore," said Olivia, looking up from her clipboard and grinning at Peter.

"I beg your pardon?"

"I said 'I'm mad as hell, and I'm not going to take it anymore.' "

"Perhaps some occupational counseling is in order then," Peter said. "Or is it problems at home?"

"It's problems at – no, wait, it's a line from a movie called *Network*," said Olivia. "I'm sure you get that a lot."

"Actually, no," Peter said. "But if it's important, I could go watch it and come back."

"Never mind," said Olivia. "I'll need to ask you some questions and check your vitals. So what brings you to the emergency room this evening, Mr. Finch?"

"I've got this buzzing sound in my head," Peter replied.

"When did you first notice it?" Olivia said.

"I'm not sure, really," Peter said. "Maybe a week ago."

"Why did you wait to come in?"

"It wasn't really bothering me much. But then my girlfriend started to hear it, too, so she thought we should come in. That's her back over there." Peter turned and smiled at April. She crossed her arms and looked up at the ceiling. "She's a keeper!"

Olivia shook her head. "Do you mean to say that she hears a buzzing sound in her head, too? Or do you mean that she can actually hear the buzzing in your head?"

"Yes," Peter said. "The second one. She says the buzzing frequency is about 1024 Hertz. She should know – she collects tuning forks."

"I see," Olivia said. She leaned forward and turned an ear towards Peter. Hearing nothing but snoring and groaning coming from the waiting room, she resumed taking Peter's medical history. "Have you had any other symptoms? Fever? Headache? Earaches?"

"No, no, no, and no," Peter said.

"Do you have any medical problems? Are you taking any medications?"

"No, and no."

"Have you ever had any major injuries or any surgery?"

"Combine injury," Peter said, pointing toward his forehead.

"I see," Olivia said. "Any allergies?"

"Glitter."

"Mr. Finch," Olivia said, trying to put the puzzle pieces together. "Do you take drugs?"

"Just the occasional fermented beverage, if that's what you mean," Peter said. "I had a beer earlier."

"I'll need to check your vitals now," said Olivia as she finished scribbling her notes. She inflated the blood pressure cuff around his arm and pressed the frigid end of the stethoscope against his skin. "Ninety over forty-five," she said after deflating the cuff.

"Wow," Peter said. "That's a little high! Must be because I'm anxious."

"Actually," Olivia said, "that's pretty low."

"Wow," Peter said. "'That's pretty low' is what I meant to say."

"Uh huh," Olivia said. "This goes in your ear."

She placed the thermometer probe in his ear. The electronic thermometer beeped and she removed it. "One-hundred point eight."

"Wow," Peter said. "That's a little low."

"Actually, that's a little...here, just take this clipboard, take a seat, and fill out this form. We'll call you back. In a while."

"Thanks," Peter said. "Take your time." Olivia wasn't sure which she found most disturbing: Peter's appearance, his vital signs, or the fact that he said "take your time" in an emergency room. Peter carried the clipboard back to where April was sitting and sat next to her. "If anyone asks, you collect tuning forks."

"Great."

"Here," Peter said. "Fill this out for me. I'm going to scope out the room."

"Fine," April said. She took the clipboard and wrote Peter's name in the appropriate box. Under "address" she put the address of her apartment, but scribbled "but not for long" in parentheses after it. She checked off the box that said "male" and, in a moment of weakness, put her cell phone as the emergency contact number. "Date of birth?"

Peter thought back to his job application at the doughnut shop. "Just put 'over sixteen.'"

"Whatever," April said. "Do you have a primary care physician?"

"Yes," Peter said. "But his name won't fit in that little space. Just put 'none.'"

April wrote "none" and continued. "There's a long list of diseases with boxes next to them. Do you have any?"

"No," Peter said. "Just the surgery to repair the injury to my scalp and fingers."

April documented the combine injury. "There's

something called 'review of systems' with a lot of different symptoms listed."

"Oh!" Peter said. "Just check all of them. That'll guarantee that they'll put off calling me back for as long as possible." April checked all of the boxes – even the one that said "irregular menstruation."

"Insurance?"

"Boy, they really try to upsell you here," Peter said. "I really don't need any. Just put 'No thank you.'"

"Okay," April said. "But that's what's going to guarantee that they put off calling you for as long as possible." April handed the clipboard to Peter. He returned it to Olivia's desk.

"I hope you're not still mad as hell," he said, smiling. He handed the clipboard to Olivia. She sighed and Peter returned to his seat. "A lot of sick people in here, but no one really *in extremis*. Unless you count the triage nurse."

"Yeah," April said. "That's because the patients who are *in extremis* are usually brought in by those boxy vehicles with flashing lights and sirens. They get first dibs on the stretchers in the treatment rooms."

"Maybe that guy over there," Peter said. With his head Peter gestured toward a tall, heavy-set man wearing a stocking cap and an overcoat. The man was slumped over in his seat, asleep, with most of his chins resting on his mustard-colored knit shirt.

"The guy who's snoring?" April said.

"Yes," Peter said. "I could scan him without drawing his attention."

"How do you know he's not just waiting on someone who's been taken back to a room already?"

"Let's see," Peter said. He opened up his pack, removed the box, and opened it. He looked around;

no one was watching. He powered up the BAT and aimed it at the sleeping giant. He pushed the blue button, and it ran the diagnostic scan without a hitch.

"Pretty light," April said. "But I've never heard of anyone being cured by a rave glow stick."

"Sshh." Peter's eyes swept the waiting room. No one had noticed the light show, or else they were too sick or too tired to care. Peter looked at the LCD readout.

"Wow," Peter said. "If he's not here to be seen, he should be."

"What's that?" queried April.

"It's the diagnostic readout. We still have to perform the therapeutic scan."

"What does it say?"

"That I wouldn't want to be his life insurance agent," Peter said.

"No, really," April said. Peter turned the BAT so she could see the readout. She whispered the laundry list of diagnoses. "Obesity. Narcolepsy. Hypercholesterolemia. Hypertension. Diabetes, adult onset. Sleep apnea. Gout. Gingivitis. Coronary artery disease. Peripheral vascular disease. Herpes zoster, latent. Diverticulitis. Anorect – ewww."

"Yeah," Peter said. "That's probably what brought him in to the ER. I'm surprised that he's able to sit. Also a little surprised that he could sleep through it, but that may be the narcolepsy talking."

Just then the sleeping man snorted, jerked his head up, and looked straight ahead.

"Mr. Finch." Olivia's voice projected across the waiting room.

"Probably more paperwork," Peter said. He handed the BAT to April and approached the triage desk. "Yes?"

"You can go back now," said Olivia.

"Back to my seat? What sort of cat-and-mouse game are you playing with me, Nurse Olivia?"

"No," Olivia said. "Back to see the doctor."

"Already? But I just got here."

"Well if you're right in the middle of reading Highlights," said Olivia, "I'm sure the magazine will still be there when you're through seeing the doctor."

"But all of these other people were here before I was," Peter said. "Like that pregnant woman over there. Or that little boy who's got his snot faucet turned on 'high.' He looks horrible, don't you think?"

"Yes he does," Olivia said. "And that's very Gallant of you. But he's not even here to be seen. He's with his mother – the pregnant woman – who's waiting for the obstetrician. But you're in luck. Our buzzing-noise-in-the-head specialist is freed up and can see you now."

"Oh," Peter said. "Well, see that's the thing. It's gone."

"What's gone?"

"The buzzing sound," Peter said. "April can't hear it anymore, either. But now I've got this pain here." Peter pointed to the middle of his abdomen. "It's really bad. But not so bad that I can't wait, if I need to. So, if you'll just scratch out 'buzzing in head' and write 'tummy pain' on my form, everything will be copacetic."

Olivia sighed. "Just go sit back down. Let's try again later."

Peter went back and sat next to April, who was watching the multi-chinned man in the overcoat. He had fallen back asleep. Peter took the BAT from April, aimed it at the man, and pushed a button. April blinked as the white light filled the room, then flickered and went out. He was still asleep.

"Mr. Finch!" shouted Olivia. "What was that?"

"What was what?" Peter shouted back. Now the man was not asleep.

"That bright light. I saw a bright light flash."

"I didn't see anything," Peter said. "Maybe you're getting a migraine." Olivia got up from her desk and walked through the doors to the treatment area. "Boy, she really couldn't take it anymore."

April nodded in sympathy and guessed that Olivia was now looking for help in the form of pharmaceutical samples. Their attention turned back to the man in the overcoat as he rubbed his stubbleface, removed his sock cap, stood up, grinned for a second, glanced around the waiting area, then walked out of the emergency department.

"See?" smirked Peter.

"That doesn't prove anything," April said. "Besides, one of his diagnoses was 'obesity.' He was still pretty fat when he left."

"The device will reset his metabolism," Peter said. "He'll lose three to four pounds a week until he's at his ideal weight. If you were to suddenly remove all of his excess fat at once, it could actually kill him."

"Hmph. Let's do another one."

"We can't," Peter said. He jabbed the BAT into his bag, grabbed April's arm, and took off dragging her across the waiting area. They passed Olivia's desk just as she was returning through the double doors. "It was just gas!" Peter said as he and April bolted through the same double doors into the treatment area.

"What are you doing?" shrieked April as they ran past patients parked on gurneys behind partially-pulled white curtains.

"Not now," Peter said, as they took a right turn at

the nurse's station and bolted past a handful of men and women wearing various permutations of blue scrubs, green scrubs, and white coats. They all looked up, and then returned to their coffee and chart work like this sort of thing happened all the time. Because it did.

Just past some stainless steel cabinets, Peter and April pushed through another set of double doors and entered a tiled hallway lined with empty gurneys and portable x-ray machines. At the left end was a door with an emergency exit sign above it. "This way," Peter said. He sprinted down the hall, still dragging April by her arm. They hit the door, and once outside April leaned with her back against the wall to catch her breath as the door closed behind them.

"What. The hell. Was that. All about?" April huffed.

"I'd say about twenty-five meters in about ten-and-a-half seconds," replied Peter. "But I can't explain now. If you're finished doing your William Shatner impersonation, we should really head back to the car."

They were almost halfway back to April's apartment before she spoke.

"So what just happened back there?" April said.

"I saw Frank Francis," Peter said. "When that large gentleman was leaving, I looked out of the window behind him to see Frank walking down the sidewalk. He was headed toward the ER entrance."

"Oh my god," April said. "Was he okay?"

"I didn't scan him, if that's what you're getting at," Peter said. "He's probably fine. But the young woman he was with was not fine. Don't get me wrong – she had really nice legs, and if she would have just run a brush through her hair and touched up her makeup...but what I was getting at is that she looked ill."

"What was wrong with her?"

"She had been poisoned," replied Peter.

"How could you possibly know that?" April said. "Don't tell me you scanned her, because I was sitting right there and never saw it happen."

"Because I'm the one who poisoned her," Peter said. "After you kicked me out I started hitchhiking. She, along with three other women, picked me up. They drove me to a storage building where she took the BAT and held me hostage. I escaped by poisoning her."

"Is she going to be okay?"

"I'm fine, but thanks for your concern," Peter said. "Being handcuffed and shackled and robbed and threatened with torture and held at gunpoint – like water off a duck's back. But she'll be fine, too. She wasn't envenomated with a deadly poison, just one that causes intense pain followed by temporary loss of consciousness. She looked a tad underfed, so the effects are probably lasting longer than usual."

"What did she look like?" asked April.

"Sort of tall, dark eyes, long dark hair, pale features," Peter said. "Her name is Martina."

"That's no woman," exclaimed April.

"I saw her gun holster," Peter said. "So I'd beg to differ."

"No," April said. "Martina is Frank Francis's daughter. She's a pout model."

"A what?"

"A pout model," April said. "She works for an agency that specializes in models who pout for print advertising. Pouting is big business. It's her and three or four other women, and they tend to run around together."

"Well, then," Peter said. "I'd like to think that perhaps I've advanced her pouting career by taking the BAT back, envenomating her, escaping, and wrecking her car. I guess sometimes all things do work together for good."

"What are you talking about?"

"April, the universe is trying to tell you that the BAT really works," Peter said. "When Frank Francis couldn't get it from me, he sent his daughter to your place to look for it. And when they came up empty handed, they trailed me. My hitchhiking gave them the perfect opportunity to kidnap me and force me to give up the BAT – under duress, I might add. Do you think they'd go to all that trouble for a movie prop?"

"I suppose not," April said. "You don't think they saw us at the hospital, do you?"

"I don't think so."

"Do you think it's safe to go back to my place?"

"We'll see," Peter said.

FOURTEEN

Cyril returned to the hotel room to find Benjamin mostly conscious. He had rolled onto his back, and when Cyril stepped into the room he was greeted by an angry glare.

"Well that was a total waste of time," Cyril said. "You didn't miss anything. Just some suit interested in finding Peter." He peeled the adhesive strips from Ben's wrists and ankles. "You might want to think about something other than how much this will hurt." Cyril ripped the tape from Ben's mouth.

"Ahhhrrrgggg!" cried Ben while he writhed on the floor.

"Didn't I tell you to think of something other than the pain?" Cyril said.

"I did," Ben said. "I was thinking about how you screwed over my career."

"Nonsense. Wendy sounded very supportive. And from what I understand from the cable TV, rehab is perfectly socially acceptable here." Ben dragged himself off of the floor and into a chair, and then breathed a few deep breaths before attempting to speak.

"You nearly killed me."

"Stop whining," Cyril said. "Lucky for you I'm not

packing the most powerful model PI. This is the Mini-plasma immobilizer. If I'd used the Magnum plasma immobilizer then you'd be mostly liquid and I'd be looking at a huge hotel housekeeping charge."

"So there's a Magnum PI?"

"Of course," Cyril said. "But with the Mini PI, if the batteries are low then setting 3 is almost equivalent to setting 2 fully charged. So I expect you'll be back to your whiny, neurotic self in no time."

"I feel like crap," Ben said. "And I hate that I'm not working and I hate that you're dragging me across the country on some kind of inane escapade that has no apparent end in sight."

"See?" Cyril said. "You're as good as new!"

"So now what?" Ben wheezed.

"Same as before," Cyril said. "Wait here until somebody calls."

"That's worked out great so far," Ben said. "You know, for a bounty hunter you don't seem very – what's the word I'm looking for – proactive."

"What are you talking about?" snapped Cyril. "I thought up the wanted poster, designed it myself, and distributed at least half of them. Seems proactive to me."

"Don't get me wrong," Ben said. "I think it's pretty awesome that you've been able to track Peter across the universe in your *Rev 9* and narrow the search down to one planet out of billions. You should be proud of that. But now it seems like you're having difficulty closing the deal. You're sitting around a hotel room watching cable TV in hopes that someone else recognizes Peter and then makes the effort to call you."

"Maybe it's burnout. I've been this close to catching Peter," Cyril said, holding two nail-less fingers a centimeter apart, "And he always slips away. Anyway, you'll never know the many ways I've tried."

"I'm sure," Ben said. "And I don't want to seem unsympathetic. I just think you could be doing more."

"Well, I'm open for suggestions."

"Really?" Ben said. "Because I totally didn't get that vibe from you. Ever."

"Try me."

"Okay," Ben said. "Do you have any photos of Peter? Or a digital image?"

"Not on me," Cyril said. "But, sure. On the *Rev 9*."

"Good," Ben said. "Now, here on Earth we've got satellites that can take photos of car license plates from outer space. Does the *Rev 9* have anything like that?"

"Why would you want to do that?" Cyril said. "You could just put a camera on a car and drive around, taking photos of cars, buildings, people – everything! Then just make it accessible to everyone on a vast computer network. Much more cost-effective, and less creepy, too."

"Not really," Ben said. "But they're spy satellites. They're put into orbit to monitor strategic...things. Does the *Rev 9* have that capability?"

"It's got a camera that can photograph the surface of planets," Cyril said.

"Okay. Now is it possible to program the computer on the *Rev 9* to recognize a particular individual, and then search for that person from space?"

Cyril hesitated. "I suppose so." He refused to put two-and-two together. Ben wondered if Cyril was really that obtuse, or if he was the only bounty hunter ever paid by the hour.

"Look, when we were in Alabama, you said it was possible to look for Peter from the *Rev 9*. Why don't you do that now?"

"I dunno," Cyril said. "It just seems to take the thrill out of bounty hunting. I mean, any Blutaarkian grade-schooler could climb into the *Rev 9*, put it into low synchronous orbit, flip on the cameras, and find a particular individual in no time at all – provided the target is outdoors. Where's the challenge in that?"

"So the entire time we've been here," Ben said, "you could have just used the *Rev 9* to locate Peter?"

"We haven't been here that long. Besides, room service here is nice."

"Yes, room service is nice," Ben said. "But the game has changed. Didn't you say someone else is looking for Peter? What if they find him first? Did you think about that? No thrill in that – and certainly no reward, either."

"I know," Cyril said. Ben was taken aback; he could not recall Cyril ever agreeing with him. Cyril looked down at the floor and twisted the toe of his boot into the carpet. "Oh, okay."

"Okay, what?" Ben asked.

"Okay we'll search for Peter using the *Rev 9*."

"That's my Cyril!" Ben said.

"I can't exactly land it in the parking lot here," Cyril said. "We'll take the Jeep, find someplace relatively secluded, and board the *Rev 9* there." Cyril gathered his bag and picked up the car keys and motioned for Ben to get up.

They headed north in the Jeep. When driving from a major metropolitan area, it takes a while to find a secluded spot on which to land a large suitcase without drawing unwanted attention. Perhaps it was because of the drive-induced boredom, or perhaps it was because Ben had not attempted to escape for at least a couple of hours, but Cyril felt comfortable opening up to him. He spared no detail in describing the development of the BAT device and how Peter managed to end up with one. He spared many details about the capabilities of the BAT, mentioning only that it was "useful to treat headaches."

On a tight two-lane highway roughly thirty miles north of Atlanta, Cyril spied a break between the trees lining the road. He pulled the Cherokee off of the road and through the opening, and then drove it a few yards, parking it behind a clump of trees where it was invisible from the road. Cyril got out and surveyed the clearing. It was roughly triangular and surrounded by trees on all sides.

"Perfect," Cyril said. He motioned for Ben to get out.

Neither one had noticed that a black SUV had followed them all the way from Atlanta, and was now parked on the shoulder on the other side of the trees.

Peter and April made it back to her apartment, where there were exactly zero forces of evil waiting for them – unless you counted the bitch upstairs. April made some coffee and sat on the sofa. Peter took *To Kill a Mockingbird* off of the coffee table, sat in the chair, and opened the book.

"So how does it work?" April asked.

"Well, I just read these words from left to right, top row to bottom row," Peter said. "And when I finish a page I turn to the next one."

"No," April said. "I mean the BAT."

"Keep in mind that I'm just the end-user. I'm no engineer. But I did listen to almost the entire tutorial. Well, most of it. I bet."

"I'll keep that in mind," April said.

"I'll start with the diagnostic part of the scan," Peter said. "It seems to be based on the same sort of technology that I used to catalog life forms as an LSA scout – something called the BioScan. It employs a highly advanced imaging system. To give you an idea, it's an exponentially greater technological leap from your MRI scans to the BioScan than the leap from cave paintings to your magnetic resonance imaging. Add that to its immense data-processing capability, and you end up with a hand-held device that's able to analyze a living creature anatomically, physiologically, and genetically."

"How much data-processing capability? April asked. "In terms that a young southern woman with a liberal arts degree could understand."

"Are you familiar with Cowboys Stadium?"

"Sure."

"If you were to fill the entire stadium, turf-to-roof, with Cray supercomputers -"

"Then the Cowboys couldn't play football," April said. "As if they could anyway."

"But imagine that stadium filled with supercomputers," Peter said. "Now imagine every square meter of Texas covered by football stadiums filled with supercomputers."

"That would probably be a good thing," April said, grinning at the mental image of Texas crushed under a sea of computer-filled football stadiums.

"That's how much computing power exists in one BAT unit," Peter said. "It uses that power to determine what is out of kilter, biologically speaking. That's sort of the tricky part, as it has to account for pathology, the natural variability seen within a given species, and any co-existing life forms that could be troublemakers, or benign, or even beneficial."

"Impressive," April said. "But you lost me at the end there."

"Did you know that the human body contains a greater number of bacterial cells within its digestive tract than there are cells comprising the human body?"

"Yuk," April said. "I did not know that. Now I want to un-know it."

"Exactly," Peter said. "But the vast majority of those bacteria are considered good. They suppress growth of harmful bacteria and yeast, they neutralize toxins, and they stimulate the immune system and produce vitamins. If you were to eliminate those bacteria, it would most likely make you less healthy."

"You sound like a yogurt commercial," April said. "But I get it."

"So the BAT has to differentiate," Peter said. "And it does. So if you've got an infection like pneumonia or meningitis – viruses or bacteria or fungi that are wreaking havoc – then the BAT knows the difference."

"Then what?" April said.

"Then the treatment – or therapeutic scan – takes over. The best way to describe it is that it's an intelligent beam of energy. It works at the level of the organism's own genetic database by giving it new instructions to direct its intrinsic healing ability. If you've got an infection, it can focus and direct your immune system to eliminate it and repair the damage. If you've got a fractured tibia, it directs the body's healing response to mend it – along with any associated damage like torn muscles, vascular injury, and the like. And it's almost instantaneous."

"And just how does that happen?"

"Not entirely sure," Peter said. "I started listening to a mix tape at that point during the tutorial. But from what I gathered it's a combination of things. Part of it comes from harnessing the organism's own energy stores to make repairs, but much of the energy required is provided by the beam itself."

"There must be limits to what it can do," April said. "Like, what if someone got run over by a train?"

"They should have noticed the tracks and the loud noise," Peter said. "The BAT can't cure stupid."

"But what if they didn't notice, hypothetically?" April said.

"Well, once you're dead, you're dead," Peter said. "The BAT won't resurrect you. But if a trauma victim doesn't die immediately, then the results of using the BAT are mixed. If the injury is sudden and severe – say, getting run over by a train, to use your example – and the systems required to maintain life are too disorganized, then the BAT won't do much good. If your brain is two hundred meters away from the rest of your body, it makes it challenging for your body to try to repair it.

"On the other hand, if the victim of a bullet wound to the heart is treated quickly – before significant brain injury from anoxia occurs, then the BAT could save them. Even some moderate brain damage may be reversed by the BAT, but there may be unpredictable permanent defects. Where the BAT really shines is in the treatment of non-traumatic disorders, like cancer and heart disease. My guess is that once this is widely used on Blutaark, they will still have seat belts and smoke alarms, but no one will ever read a food label again."

"Guess I'd better not take up 'beat the train' at railroad crossings," April said.

"Oh, that's another thing," Peter said. "The BAT doesn't do much for mental illness. Apparently there's too much overlap with what could be considered normal – especially with artists and show biz types. It can treat the extremes – for example, schizophrenia – but for anxiety or other neuroses you might was well just talk about your relationship with your mother."

"No thanks," April said. She got up to add something stronger to her coffee, and then sat back down on the sofa. "Okay, here's the big question. Can the BAT make you immortal?"

"Well, I suppose if I just used it willy-nilly, made a big to-do about it, and self-promoted a lot, then my reputation might last for several thousands of years," Peter said. "But that's not really who I am."

"No," April said. "You know what I mean. If it cures all disease, then it seems to follow that it would impart immortality."

"Your assumption is correct," said Peter. "By curing all illness and degenerative disorders the BAT, in theory, could bestow immortality. But the Blutaarkian powers that be, in a stroke of uncharacteristically sound judgment, decided that the citizens of Blutaark deserved healthy, disease-free lives. But they also recognized that making everyone immortal would be courting disaster."

"How so?" April asked. She took another long sip of strong coffee.

"For starters," Peter said, "there was historical precedent. The Laxbrackles of Cromer 4 were rather clever – clever enough to discover a way to make themselves immortal. But immortality and unbridled reproduction proved to be a bad combination – especially since not one single Laxbrackle realized that discovering space travel *before* discovering immortality would have been the really clever way to go."

"So they overpopulated Cromer 4," April said.

"Precisely," Peter said. "Immortals may be immune to disease and degeneration, but they still need energy. Because of their irrational aversion to birth control and inability to relocate to other planets, Laxbrackles outgrew their food supply. Correction – they outgrew their preferred food supply. Their society collapsed, and to survive they resorted to cannibalism. And it's hard to be immortal when you're being eaten.

"Ironically, most intelligent species in the universe find cannibalism more repugnant than birth control, so Cromer 4 was avoided by those very beings who were in a position to help them the most – aliens who had mastered interstellar travel. Not long after that their star went supernova and put the Laxbrackles out of their misery. Rumor has it that a handful were rescued by a scout team from Pleminkka – but that has never been confirmed."

"But," April said, "Blutaark has mastered space travel. So why not go ahead and embrace immortality?"

"Still a bad idea. And again, there's precedent. The Brimlees of Uffculme 7 were space-savvy long before they took a stab at immortality. And after a few decades they nailed the immortality problem. They were considerably less fertile than the Laxbrackles, and what with being able to travel to other planets, food was never an issue. In fact, early on a few of the Brimlees actually became well-regarded intergalactic food critics."

"Still don't see the problem," April said.

"After a few hundred thousand years," Peter said, "you would think that the Brimlees would be a fount of knowledge and wisdom, sought after for their insight and perspective on topics as compelling as history, philosophy, technology, politics, and the arts. But they weren't. They weren't engaging at all, and they mostly moped around and complained a lot. Number one on the list of complaints was how much better things were 'in the good old days' – which for the Brimlees consisted of an annoyingly vast expanse of time. Everyone found this very off-putting, and a universe-wide restraining order confined them to their own planet."

"Are they still there?" asked April.

"Yes," Peter said. "But their suicide rate exceeds their birth rate, so the population is dwindling. They still communicate with other planets – mostly rambling missives about how no one ever writes or calls or visits. Quite tragic, really."

"I guess," April said. "It still doesn't explain why the BAT doesn't make one immortal."

"It's a design feature," Peter said. "If you've been treated with the BAT you're pretty much guaranteed to live out your normal life span – which on Blutaark is 510 Earth years. But once you've hit that mark, you only have up to another 10 percent of that life span remaining. It's randomized by the BAT device, and no one knows exactly how much time they have left after they turn 510. It keeps you on your toes – until you fall asleep and don't wake up."

"Seems like someone could hack it," April said. "You know, reprogram the BAT so that the mortality code doesn't end up embedded in your genes."

"When I left Blutaark, they only had six other prototypes," Peter said. "So it hasn't happened yet. I'm sure someone will try, but according to the tutorial there are severe consequences for even attempting to do that."

"Like what kind of severe consequences?" asked April.

"They banish you to live on Uffculme 7 with the

Brimlees," Peter said.

"Well, whether or not it makes you immortal," April said, "this BAT thing is phenomenal. No wonder Frank wants it so badly." April paused. "Would that be such a bad thing?"

"What?" Peter said. "If Dionysus had access to the BAT?"

"Sure."

"Well, at first blush it seems reasonable," Peter said. "Dionysus is a company that ostensibly wants to develop drugs to cure disease – the BAT cures all diseases – so it seems like a match made in heaven. But they don't do what they do out of the goodness of their hearts. They're motivated by profit, and that's where things get dicey."

"But they have to make a profit to stay in business, duh," April said.

"I thought you were a liberal arts major."

"I might have taken a business class or two," April said.

"There is nothing inherently wrong or immoral about making money," Peter said. "But if you're motivated by profit only, you're more likely to decide that having two really nice houses, eight cars, and an augmented mistress is more important than a stranger's health and well-being."

"Seems like Dionysus could accomplish both," April said. "Theoretically, they could use the BAT on every man, woman, and child on Earth, only charge a dollar a pop, and come out with about seven billion dollars. Seems like a win-win situation. Heck, the U.S. government could spring for the seven billion dollars – that's less than the cost of two aircraft carriers – and we'd look like the most benevolent country on Earth."

"Ignoring the logistical problems for a moment,"

Peter said, "other countries – or corporations – might think that the BAT is worth more than seven billion dollars. So then a bidding war would start. Or worse, a non-bidding war, with bullets and bombs and lots of dead people. That's sort of the complete opposite of healthy."

"You've used the BAT on other planets, right?" April said. "You didn't incite global warfare, did you?"

"Not yet," Peter said. "But I was working with smaller populations. Humans really need to put the kibosh on this exponential growth fixation. You don't need Laxbracklian immortality to create a problematic food shortage. And, unfortunately, I don't see a merciful supernova in your immediate future."

"I'm doing my part," April said. "But even small populations can start wars."

"True," Peter said. "But I visited planets where the species weren't particularly advanced – they had not yet developed the technology to kill each other in atrocious and efficient ways. Or I would choose planets where species were highly advanced and their civilizations had evolved to the degree where warfare was a distant, embarrassing memory. Earth sits in that treacherous spot on the Venn diagram. Humans have developed the technology to be astonishingly lethal, but they haven't developed the wisdom and good judgment to avoid war in the first place. Nothing personal, April, but when your planet engages in war over a soccer match, a woman, or something that doesn't even exist – other planets talk. And advanced civilizations will avoid you until you're better behaved."

"Yeah," April said. "I have some cousins who used to live in a trailer park. So I get it. So what's your plan now?"

"Thought I'd lay low for a while," Peter said. "Probably ditch the BAT for a while – I'm proficient at hiding things."

"Puh-huh," laughed April. "That thing's a pretty hot commodity. You don't think Frank Francis will be back here looking for it?"

"I doubt it," Peter said. "I gave Martina the impression I was high-tailing it out of the state. That should buy me some time. Maybe I could stay here until things blow over."

"'Blow over,' 'lay low,' and 'high-tailing,' " April said. "Have you been watching a lot of 30's gangster noir films?"

"Is that a yes?" Peter said.

"I didn't hear a question," April said. "But, yeah, you can stay here. Just make sure you lay low, see. It's getting late, but there's one more thing. I was wondering – how did you poison Martina?"

"Blutaarkians have a very potent neurotoxin," Peter said. "We can release it into our saliva. It won't kill you – it just makes you wish you were dead. But it's temporary – fifteen minutes later and you're back to normal. More or less."

"Okay, new rule," April said. "From now on you do your own dishes."

"I'm okay with that," Peter said.

"Say...if it only lasts a few minutes, why did Martina end up at the hospital?"

"I must have given her an extra shot of venom," Peter said. "Or two. Maybe more. I was nervous, things were confusing, she'd just swung a sledgehammer at my foot, she had these legs...so do you like your dishes towel-dried or drip-dried?"

"Drip."

April took her coffee cup to the kitchen and put it

in the sink. She told Peter "good night" and closed her bedroom door. Peter stayed up for a little while; he re-read *To Kill a Mockingbird*, then he took the BAT out of the bag, wrapped it in one of his spare t-shirts, and hid it.

Cyril walked about thirty meters into the clearing and Ben followed. Cyril looked up into the cool, clear autumn sky.

"Are you planning on flagging it down?" said Ben. "Like a taxi?"

"Shut up!" Cyril said. He removed one of the many objects from his overwhelmed belt. The object he removed resembled a small, black cosmetic case – just like all of the other objects on his belt. He flipped it open and deftly pushed a blurred sequence of buttons. Then he closed it and placed it back on his belt and looked back up at the sky. And waited.

"I think a taxi might have been quicker," Ben said.

"Shut it!" snapped Cyril. "It should just take a few more seconds." He looked back up. And waited.

"My neck is starting to hurt," Ben said, looking up at nothing. "How long do we have to do this?"

Cyril glared at Ben, then yanked the black case from his belt. He flipped it open again and pushed some buttons again and looked up at the sky again. Nothing. "Something's wrong."

"Well this is a new and unexpected twist," Ben said.

"No, seriously," Cyril said. "The *Rev 9* is programmed not to land if it's not secure – unless, of course, it's an emergency."

"Of course," Ben said. "It doesn't consider *me* a threat, does it?"

"Ha!" Cyril said. "Good one! Wait here, and try

not to get landed on." He turned and walked back toward the road. As he passed the line of trees he heard a car door slam, and a black SUV took off with its tires squealing. Cyril watched it tear down the highway and disappear. He walked back to where Ben was trying not to get landed upon. "We had some company. It should work now."

A small beige dot appeared against the clear sky. It became a large beige dot in the sky, then just as quickly it became a large beige suitcase sitting on the ground two feet in front of them. The *Rev 9* landed quietly except for the high-pitched yelp made by Ben. The hatch in the side of the suitcase appeared, and after Cyril and Ben boarded, the hatch vanished. They made their way up the steps and took their customary positions – Cyril at the helm and Ben in the back. Ben steadied himself as Cyril's fingers danced over the console. The *Rev 9* made a rapid vertical ascent. Ben made another high-pitched yelp and Cyril sighed loudly – both sounds unheard by Ben due to the loud popping noises in his ears.

The *Rev 9* stopped its vertical ascent at 10,000 meters and Cyril nudged it toward Atlanta. Through one of the porthole windows Ben could see the sun approaching the horizon.

"Does this thing show up on radar?" asked Ben.

"Nope," replied Cyril. "And I know what you're thinking, but the odds that an airplane will crash into us are pretty small."

"I hadn't actually thought of that," Ben said. "So thanks for bringing it up."

"No problem," Cyril said. He opened the floor hatch. "There's food down below, if you like. And if you get tired you can just lie down on the floor."

"So can this thing find Peter at night?" Ben said.

"Not really. But we'll get some great views of the

city. Plus, we'll get an early start looking for Peter first thing in the morning."

Ben went below and found a bin filled with silver foil containers. He opened one, pinched off a piece of what looked like cotton candy, and popped it into his mouth. Ben decided that dryer lint was a food staple on Blutaark, and started looking for some water. He found a bottle of water and a blanket and went back upstairs. It was dark outside now, and Ben curled up on the floor with the blanket and went to sleep.

FIFTEEN

At 10:05 Saturday morning Taryn Yuanuin stormed into the forty-eighth floor boardroom of Persona Insurance Corporation with a latte in one hand and a box of doughnuts in the other. She slid the box of doughnuts across the long mahogany table where sat Tor Kinney and four board members. Tor took notes on a yellow legal pad. The four board members took prescription medications – mostly for anxiety, depression, and unexplained hives.

"Glad you could make it," Tor said.

"This had better be a real emergency," Taryn said. "This little meeting forced me to cut my Krav Maga class short, and I'll probably be late for my Mandarin lessons."

"It is a real emergency," Tor said. "Hence the words 'real emergency meeting' in the header of the email I sent you. And when did you start taking Krav Maga?"

"I'm not taking the class," Taryn said. "I'm teaching it. And before you say something else stupid, Mandarin isn't a musical instrument – it's a language. So can we cut the nano-talk and get down to business?"

Taryn Yuanuin grew up in Atlanta, where early on she demonstrated an aptitude for business and a preternatural disdain for the feelings of others. When Taryn was a child, her father read a story about a seven-year-old boy whose mother drove him out to the middle of a field and left him there alone. As the story goes, she did this to instill a sense of independence and self-reliance in her son, who went on to become a billionaire industrialist – presumably after finding his way back home from the field.

Taryn's father embraced this story, and when she was seven years old he dropped her off in the middle of a forest and drove away. He chose a forest rather than a field because it is easier to find a forest near Atlanta than it is to find a large, empty field. Also, forests are more frightening to seven-year-old girls than fields are. Especially at night. During a thunderstorm.

Taryn never found her way back home. The morning after she was dropped off she squished her way out of the woods and into a suburban enclave, where she happened upon a lemonade stand run by another seven-year-old girl. Taryn used her last quarter to purchase a cup of lemonade. After drinking the lemonade she used the empty cup – and some say the threat of physical harm – to obtain the other girl's lemonade stand in a leveraged buyout. Taryn franchised the one lemonade stand into a chain and poured the profits into complex financial derivatives. Within a few months she had purchased her own home in Buckhead, and allowed her parents to move in with her – after they had completed extensive counseling at the behest of child protective services.

Taryn earned her undergraduate degrees in biology and business at Emory and followed that up with an MBA from Duke University. By her ten-year college reunion she had grown three different biotech companies from inception through initial public offering. When she got the call from Persona, she had her hands full balancing three other board positions, a hedge fund, and her own venture capital firm. She wanted the chair position at Persona to pad her already impressive résumé, but she also saw potential in this stagnant company, and thought it deserved to be saved from "that idiot" Tor Kinney.

Despite calling Tor Kinney an idiot during her interview – with Tor Kinney – she was offered the position of chair.

"There have been some incidents," Tor said. "You know we are able to monitor claims from patients, doctor's offices, and hospitals in real time."

"Yes," Taryn said. "And don't worry about getting to the point anytime soon. I'm sure there are enough doughnuts here to sustain me for a couple of weeks."

"As I said," replied Tor, "there have been incidents. Several individuals with chronic, multiple, and complex medical problems have become the picture of health overnight. Patients who have had diabetes, glaucoma, lupus, what have you – their doctors are filing claims with none of those previously documented diagnoses. Just routine, normal exams. And patients who had been filing claims for prescription drug coverage suddenly stop doing so."

"Could be just a data entry error at the provider level," Taryn said. "And some patients discontinue taking their medications for any number of reasons."

"Thought of that," Tor said. "So we've had operatives obtain the original medical records, and the documentation confirms that these patients have been cured, for lack of a better word."

"So what's the problem?" Taryn asked. "Fewer

claims paid out means a better bottom line for Persona and more value for its shareholders. Tor, I realize that your business classes sometimes interfered with your sleeping, so let me refresh your memory: profits good, losses bad."

"Our concern, Taryn," started Tor, glancing at the other board members, "is that based on evidence we have so far, there seems to be something – or someone – out there that is able to cure incurable disease."

"Jesus Christ," Taryn said.

"He was considered as a possibility early on," Tor said. "But we've consulted distinguished experts in both religion and history, and their consensus is that it really doesn't look like his work."

"You've got to be kidding me," Taryn said. "You drag me here on a Saturday morning to tell me this?"

"Here's the report," Tor said, sliding a sheaf of printouts across the table to Taryn. "It appears to be occurring in geographic clusters. Three of the subjects share the same daily bus route, but they don't seem to know each other. We ran this past the actuaries. They said that the odds of spontaneous disease remission occurring in this pattern are less than one-in-forty-seven trillion."

"Were any of these individuals Persona policy holders?" asked Taryn. Her eyes narrowed as she thumbed through the pages.

"Just one," Tor said. "Her name is Loretta. We've already interrog – we've already interviewed her. You'll find that information on pages five through seven."

Nobody spoke as Taryn devoured the report. "So Loretta wins the health lottery after meeting a total stranger in a public park," she said, looking up from the papers. "Cured after he took her photo with something that didn't look like a conventional camera. Then she went to her own doctor the next day, who confirmed that she was disease-free. Is that correct so far?"

"Yes," Tor said.

"I'm impressed," Taryn said. "Impressed that she could get a same-day appointment with her doctor. But she provided the stranger's name – Peter. And it turns out that someone else is also looking for Peter. A Cyril – is that right?"

"It is," Tor said.

"And you met with this Cyril?"

"I did," Tor said. He wanted to ask if he could step down from the witness stand.

"And what transpired during your meeting with Cyril?" Taryn asked. "Please tell me, Tor Kinney, that this report isn't complete. Please tell me, and the other four board members present whose names I haven't bothered to commit to memory, that this Cyril fellow provided you with information that will enable us to find Peter, take possession of his 'camera,' and save the American health insurance industry."

"No," Tor said. "He wasn't very forthcoming. Apparently he's a bounty hunter, so he stands to lose financially if we find Peter first."

"So is that everything?" asked Taryn. "Some miracle cures, a magic camera, a bounty hunter, and a ghost named Peter?"

"That's not everything," Tor said. "What I'm going to tell you next is classified. I didn't want this information in writing, so it's not in your file. The information doesn't leave this room."

"Tor," Taryn said. "Everybody knows about the lacrosse field incident."

"Not that," Tor said. "Brian and Jason trailed

Cyril. They followed him to a hotel near Sandy Springs. From there Cyril left with an associate, and they drove to a clearing just off of a two-lane highway in northern Cherokee county. Jason got out of the SUV and took a tactical position in the woods to observe them. Brian thought their cover was about to get blown, and he took off without Jason."

"And?"

"According to Jason, while Cyril and his associate stood in the clearing, a UFO dropped out of the sky and landed in front of them. A hatch opened, Cyril and his friend went inside, and the hatch closed. As quickly as it had landed, it took off and disappeared into the sky."

"No wonder you don't want this in writing," Taryn said. "It would be grounds for involuntary commitment – or worse, dismissal. Did Jason happen to get any video of this UFO, perchance?"

"No," Tor said.

"Naturally," sniped Taryn.

"He was in shock," replied Tor.

"I'm not," Taryn said.

"Taryn, these individuals – Cyril and Peter, be they human or alien – have access to extraordinary technology. The ramifications are mind-boggling. We are dealing with a vastly superior intellect."

"Tor," Taryn said. "I get the feeling that you're dealing with a vastly superior intellect every time you walk your dog." She sat back and sipped her latte. "Your evidence isn't exactly unimpeachable, but if what you've told me is true, then I'm compelled to concur that the consequences could be cataclysmic."

One of the no-name board members sitting next to Taryn closed the lid on the box of doughnuts, then removed his glasses and wiped them off.

"People thriving free of disease, leading pain-free productive lives, never paying health insurance premiums," Taryn said. "How horrible would that be?" Her shoulders shuddered. Tor nodded and the four other board members echoed Taryn with one-word responses.

"Tragic."

"Heinous."

"Abominable."

"Sucky."

"So where do we stand now?" asked Taryn. "To bottom-line it for you gentlemen, it looks like all we've got is one healthy customer who will probably cancel her policy, and a couple of names – Peter and Cyril."

"Cyril and his associate never checked out of the hotel," Tor said. "Brian and Jason have it staked out."

"Good. But what about Peter? How can we find him?"

"We don't have much," Tor said. "But we do have a physical description. Here..." He took Peter's wanted poster from under his legal pad, unfolded it, and handed it to Taryn. She stared at it for a few seconds, shook her head, sat her latte down, and stalked out of the boardroom.

"Do I have to do *everything* myself?" came from the hallway before the door closed completely.

"She's hot," said one of the board members. They all nodded.

April slept until her cell phone ringtone caromed around the inside of her skull. A brief conversation with Dirk Reger ensued in which he informed April that her presence at the office was required for a mandatory Saturday morning meeting – in fifteen minutes. She jumped in and out of the shower, pulled her hair back in a ponytail, threw on some jeans and a short-sleeved shirt that were conveniently located on her bedroom floor, and prayed that the meeting was not with HR regarding poor employee compliance with the official corporate dress code. She bolted out of the bedroom and past the kitchen; she would have to jump-start her brain with coffee from the office. As she unlocked the front door she looked back at the living room, where Peter wasn't.

Where the hell is he? she thought, but decided that she needed caffeine before attempting to sort it out. She stepped off of the elevator twenty-five minutes after Dirk's call and sprinted to conference room 101. She hoped for an empty seat near the door so that her tardiness might go unnoticed, but when she opened the door the lights were up and only two others were present. Dirk faced April and was seated at the far end of the conference table. Frank Francis – his back to April – sat closest to the door. One empty chair loomed between them. April sat down and started hyperventilating.

"Sorry. I. Just ran. Down. The hall."

"It's okay, April," Dirk said. "Can I get you anything?"

Xanax. A barf bag. A less stressful job in air-traffic control, thought April. "No thanks, I'm fine."

"Okay," Dirk said. "Then we'll go ahead and get started. April, it goes without saying that you're a valued employee here at Dionysus. But Frank has brought some issues to my attention that we need to address."

"We understand you're acquainted with an individual named Peter. Peter Finch." Frank said.

"Yes," April said. "I just met him a few days ago.

But he's not *the* Peter Finch. That Peter Finch died several years ago."

"I wasn't aware of that," Dirk said.

"Yeah," April said. "Very tragic."

"Anyway," interjected Frank. "I think this Finch fellow is bad news for Dionysus and bad news for everyone in this room. April, I understand your apartment was recently broken in to?"

"It was. But fortunately nothing was taken." Her voice quavered. She hadn't even told Brooks about the break-in. Frank was trying to intimidate her – above and beyond the usual amount of intimidation that April experienced from day-to-day life in general.

"Still," Frank said. "That had to be a little disconcerting. We have reason to believe that the person or persons who committed that crime did so because of Peter. We think Peter Finch came from the West Coast, and that he's up to his hairline in organized crime – specifically, biotech industry organized crime."

"Really?" April said, trying to sound convincing.

"From what Frank has told me," Dirk chimed in, "Peter infiltrates biotech and pharmaceutical companies to steal their intellectual property. April – we know that Peter was staying with you."

"Are you done, Dirk?" Frank interrupted.

"Why do you always get to be 'bad cop?' " Dirk said.

"Not here," snapped Frank. "We'll discuss it on the ride home." He paused. "April, we think that Peter double-crossed someone. And because of that, someone turned your place upside down looking for what he stole and what they feel entitled to. Is Peter still staying at your place?"

"I promise you, when I left my apartment this

morning there was no one else there."

"Good," Frank said. "Security has not been breached at Dionysus, but Peter was most likely attempting to gain access to data about DPCL2 – our investigational drug for leukemia. So it would be best if you didn't associate with him further – it could jeopardize your career here at Dionysus."

April wanted to laugh at the idea that her administrative assistant position might be considered a career, but also at the suggestion that there was any intellectual property at Dionysus worth stealing.

"Easy enough. So, is there anything else?"

"No, that'll be all," Frank said. April stood up.

"Say." Frank's dark eyes met April's. "How is your father doing? You don't mention him often."

"He's good," April said. She paused. "How's your daughter? You don't mention her often."

Frank blinked. "She's uh...she's well, thank you."

"Good to hear." April walked to the door. "Later, Mr. Reger."

"First thing Monday," Dirk said. "Synergy."

SIXTEEN

Benjamin slept fitfully on the cockpit floor of the *Rev 9*. When the first rays of sunlight filled the cabin, he pushed the blanket aside and stood up to stretch. Cyril was still at the helm, watching the monitors as the ship's cameras probed the Atlanta metro area below for any signs of Peter. Ben wondered if Cyril had slept at all. Ben peered out of a porthole window. It was another cloudless day, and it was difficult to gauge whether the *Rev 9* was stationary or creeping along at a snail's pace. That is, a snail's pace if a snail was oozing along a horizontal sidewalk on the Earth's surface – not a snail's pace if a snail were to somehow suddenly find itself 45,000 feet above the Earth's surface where it would plummet vertically at a clip of roughly 32 feet per second squared.

Ben asked if he could go below to get something to eat, and without saying a word Cyril opened the hatch. Ben crept down the stairs to the lower deck and started looking for food that looked like food. No luck. He had just grabbed another foil pouch when he heard shouting from the cockpit; not angry shouting, but jubilant shouting – the way someone might shout if they had successfully completed the running of the bulls wearing a fire engine red jumpsuit. Ben wondered if someone else was in the cabin with Cyril, and climbed the stairs to investigate.

He found only Cyril, who was bouncing up and down in his seat like self-aware adults shouldn't. Ben tore open the foil packet and focused on the images streaming from the monitors. One image was stationary, a bird's-eye view of a several square-block grid of the city below. The other image was moving, tracking an individual walking along a suburban sidewalk.

"That's him!" exclaimed Cyril, pointing his bony nail-less finger at the screen. "That's Peter. We've got a positive ID."

"Sweet," Ben said. He pinched some blue fibers out of the foil pouch and forced it into his mouth. "So you can just sort of swoop down and pick him up, right?"

"Nonsense," Cyril said. "We would lose the element of surprise. He would see the *Rev 9* before it hit the ground, and he'd be off. Remember the salvage yard?" Cyril turned away from the monitor to look at Ben.

"I do," Ben said. "You. Me. Lots of wrecked cars. Grand larceny. Good times. So what's your plan?"

"The first thing I'm going to do," Cyril said. "Is ask you to stop eating my spare air filters." Ben spit the dryer lint back into the pouch. "Then I will monitor Peter until I find out where he's staying. We'll go back and get the Jeep and apprehend him while he sleeps."

"Can't you just use the *Rev 9*?" Ben said. "I mean, if he's asleep and everything."

"Brilliant idea," Cyril said. "I'll just park a ten-meter high alien spacecraft in someone's driveway smack-dab in the middle of the ninth most populous metropolitan area in the United States. What, with all of you humans toting camera phones and firearms, what could possibly go wrong?"

Ben didn't argue. He plopped down on one of the hard plastic chairs in the back of the cabin and consoled himself with the fact that at least Cyril had found Peter. Baby steps. But Ben was more than ready to have this scofflaw apprehended and shipped back to Blutaark, and to get back to his life in Texas. After several minutes Cyril spoke. "Come look at this." Ben got up and dragged himself to the front of the cabin.

"What?" Ben said. He hoped his indifference did not go unnoticed.

"Peter just walked into this small building," Cyril said. He zoomed on the image. "What is that?"

"According to the sign in the parking lot, it's a doughnut shop. He's probably getting breakfast. Like humans frequently do at this hour. When we're hungry. Because we haven't had anything substantial to eat in hours. Making us edgy. And uncooperative. And terse."

"Okay, thanks."

Peter had left the apartment early Saturday morning as April slept. The morning chill quickened his pace, and he arrived at the doughnut shop before he was scheduled to clock in. Peter saw this job as a timely opportunity. He could stay in Atlanta, make some quick money, and then get a place of his own. When the brouhaha surrounding the BAT died down, he could retrieve it and use it in a more discrete manner. April could get on with her life, and not have to worry about Frank Francis or Cyril stopping by to trash her apartment or abduct her roommate.

Jess, the assistant manager at the doughnut shop, told Peter that he could be paid in cash on a daily basis. In return, Peter agreed to leave his apron and quickly exit via the back door should anyone ask any questions not about doughnuts. Jess thought Peter to be a quick study; by the time most new employees had learned which way their aprons go on, Peter had memorized the menu, mastered boxing the doughnuts, and failed to be baffled by the concept of "correct change." Within a few minutes, Jess had Peter making sales and running the register.

Peter was about to take a break late in the morning when a thirtyish blond woman in a dark business jacket, matching skirt, and sensible shoes stormed into the shop. Peter recognized her from earlier in the morning when she stormed in to purchase a box of half-dozen glazed and half-dozen chocolate frosted. This entrance was stormier, and Peter braced himself for his first customer service complaint. She halted her advance at the counter and stood there, hyperventilating. She unfolded a piece of paper, glanced down at it, then glared at Peter with rattlesnake eyes.

"Peter?" Peter remembered what Jess had said about non-doughnut queries, but thought this question seemed harmless enough.

"Yes," he answered.

She turned and strode out of the store. Peter and Jess both watched – Jess with a little more interest – as she walked across the parking lot and got back into her car. Peter turned to Jess and shrugged his shoulders. He was sure he was about to be reprimanded for some rookie doughnut shop mistake.

Jess just smiled. "She's hot."

"Interesting," Cyril said.

Benjamin had been sitting in a hard plastic chair for the last three hours, regretting that he'd left *The Grapes of Wrath* back at the hotel just as much as the Joads regretted not investing in the dust market. Ben longed for the hotel – with its room service, high-definition TV, and furniture that didn't feel like punishment. Hearing the word "interesting" coming from Cyril here in the *Rev 9* was like watching a colorized bad black-and-white movie. But it broke the tedium, so Peter got up and walked to the front of the cabin.

"What's so interesting?"

"Peter has been in there for hours now," Cyril said, his eyes glued to the monitor. "What's up with that?"

"Perhaps he escaped. Again," Ben said. He made a mental note that in the future he should disregard the word "interesting" whenever Cyril used it.

"Impossible," Cyril said. "Unless he tunneled out. Our cameras would have recorded him."

"Then apparently," Ben said, "this intergalactic badass who has transported stolen goods across millions of light-years and eluded capture by Blutaarkian police and an unknown number of intrepid bounty hunters is placing the capstone on his criminal career by working the early shift at a doughnut shop. Makes perfect sense."

"A few minutes ago a young woman ran into the store," Cyril said, ignoring Ben. "Then just as quickly, she ran out. Without any doughnuts. And she's been sitting in her car ever since."

Ben bent slightly and peered at the monitor. "I would have guessed city health inspector. But she's driving a Mercedes. So probably not."

As Cyril and Ben both stared at nothing happening in the doughnut shop parking lot, something happened. A large black SUV pulled into the spot next to the Mercedes, and five men in sunglasses and black suits spilled out of the vehicle. When they reached the sidewalk in front of the shop, the Mercedes backed up and sped off.

Peter could see the SUV from where he stood behind the counter. He watched the five men as they approached the shop. They burst through the front door; two of the men pulled handguns from their jackets and pointed them at Peter. Jess, having lived in Atlanta his entire life, reflexively thrust his hands into the air.

"Geez," Peter said. "You forget to wash your hands one time after going to the restroom -"

"Quiet," shouted the tallest man. "This side of the counter."

"What about it?" asked Peter.

"Get *over* here!" said the man through clenched teeth. One of the armed men traced circles with the barrel of his gun.

"Don't get angry," Peter said, climbing over the counter top. "You can't expect people to get your meaning if you speak in sentence fragments." He stood in front of the men, his hands on his waist.

"Turn around," said the man. With a quick nod he gestured to the other two unarmed men to search Peter. They patted him down and found a cloud of doughnut-flour dust, but no weapons. And no BAT. They cinched zip ties around his wrists and ankles, then picked him up and carried him out like a roll of carpeting. They hauled Peter down the sidewalk and across the parking lot, and then threw him into the back of the SUV. The five suits climbed back into the

SUV. The two armed men sat in the back seat and faced the back of the vehicle with their firearms trained on Peter. At that instant Peter had a strange sense of déjà vu – a sense that he, or someone he knew, had been in this exact same situation before. The SUV tore out of the parking lot, tires squealing and rubber burning.

"How mature," Peter said.

When the SUV finally stopped, all five men got out. Two of them opened the rear doors and dragged Peter from the cargo bed. They were parked in an otherwise empty clay dirt parking lot surrounded by a tall barbed-wire fence. By craning his neck, Peter could see that they were headed toward a neglected building made mostly of oxidizing metal and broken windows. They approached the large sliding doors at one end of the building. One of the men in front unlocked a padlock and pulled the chain from the handles and slid the doors apart.

"So this is food handler's prison," stated Peter. "It's not as bad as I expected." The men kept silent.

The interior was cavernous. It was empty save for a single light fixture hanging from a rafter in the dead center of the structure and a folding chair underneath it. Peter's two porters shoved him – wrists and ankles still bound – into the folding chair.

"I must say," Peter said. "Kudos on your hostage-holding venue selection. Much more spacious than the last place. I'm not claustrophobic, but I definitely consider this an upgrade."

The five men stood in a semicircle roughly ten feet in front of Peter; the two on the end held their guns on him. For the first time, Peter noticed another man – well dressed, but dressed unlike the others – as he walked from the far end of the building. He stopped directly in front of Peter.

"Glad you like the place," said the man. "I'm Tor. Tor Kinney. CEO of Persona Health Insurance."

"I'm Peter Finch," Peter said. "Please to meet you, Tortor Kinney."

"There's just one Tor."

"I wasn't planning to escape. Yet." Peter said. "But I already took note that there's just one door."

"No," Tor said. "My name. It's 'Tor Kinney,' not 'Tortor Kinney.' "

"Ah," Peter said. "Got it. I must say, Mr. Kinney, that your insurance company's sales tactics are a little unconventional, to say the least. To be frank, I think many consumers would find it off-putting."

"Unfortunately," Tor said, "I think you'd be a poor risk to insure at this time. Our underwriters would say that there's a strong possibility you'll incur some catastrophic injuries in the very near future. No, you weren't brought here for a sales pitch. You were brought here because your recent activity threatens our very existence."

"Hey," Peter said. "I just sell the doughnuts. I don't even own the store. If you have issues with addictive carbohydrates in the panoply of poor American dietary choices, you might want to start further up the corporate ladder. Or better still, you might want to better educate the consumers."

"It's not about the doughnuts," Tor said. "I want the device that you've been using to cure people."

"Why?" Peter said, with abrupt defiance.

"Because we can't have healthy people running around," Tor said.

"I would think you'd want healthy policyholders," Peter said. "No claims to pay out."

"It wouldn't work that way," Tor said. "If your device cured everyone, then there would be no demand for health insurance. The industry would collapse. Unhealthy people buy health insurance and pay their monthly premiums. We can always delay or deny claims to boost the bottom line, but we can't force healthy people to purchase something they don't need. That's why I'm willing to take drastic measures to stop this. Here and now. So, hand it over."

"Hand what over?" Peter said.

"The device – what you've been using to treat sick people," Tor said. "We know it exists. Quit stalling."

"Oh, that," Peter said. "It's called a 'BAT.' And if you would have talked to your henchmen here, they would have told you that they patted me down at the doughnut shop and didn't find it. Also – if you haven't noticed – they bound my wrists and ankles. So if I did have the BAT in my possession, handing it over to you would involve some degree of contortion that I really wouldn't be comfortable doing in front of strangers." A couple of the henchmen nodded.

"Where is it?" asked Tor.

"I hid it," replied Peter.

Tor sighed. "Where did you hide it?"

"If I told you that," Peter said, "then it would defeat the purpose of hiding it in the first place. You would go and find it, and it wouldn't be hidden anymore."

"You're being awfully glib, Mr. Finch," Tor said. "But we'll get you to talk. Brian -"

"We said no names!" protested Brian.

"Sorry," Tor said. "Brian, go get the briefcase."

Brian ran out of the building, and a few seconds later he returned with an aluminum attaché. He held the case flat and opened it for Tor. Tor withdrew a file, thumbed through some papers until he found the ones he was looking for, and then started reading. "Here's one. A billing specialist for a physician's group submitted an envelope containing five different claims. Persona Health's unwritten (and secret) policy is to accept one claim per envelope – so one was processed and the other four were fed into the shredder. Every quarter we sell the shredded paperwork to a company that uses it to manufacture insulation. Win-win."

Peter blinked and said nothing.

"Another one," Tor said. "A female policyholder of two-years duration became pregnant. Unbeknownst to her, when she added a dental policy a few months earlier, it reset the starting date of her waiting period. After she chose her Ob/Gyn, Persona Health denied maternity coverage because she was still in her 365-day waiting period."

Peter squirmed a little in the folding chair.

"Still another," continued Tor. "An elderly gentleman was diagnosed with advanced macular degeneration that threatened his vision. He filed a claim for potentially vision-saving treatment – but this therapy has only been around for about a decade. So as per Persona Health's guidelines it was deemed 'experimental' and coverage was denied. He lost most of his vision, but continued to drive – and three months later he ran over a nine-year-old boy and his collie. Don't worry. The dog is fine."

"You bastard," Peter seethed.

"There's more. A middle aged woman with hemochromatosis developed hepatocellular carcinoma – liver cancer. She was a candidate for liver transplantation, which would have given her about a sixty-percent chance of survival. But Persona Health denied the surgery, saying it was 'investigational' or 'experimental,' depending on what day of the week it was. We finally approved coverage for her treatment, but she died on the waiting list, six days after we okayed her surgery. One of our actuaries won an all-expense paid trip to Bali for that little piece of analytical prowess."

"You're a monster!" shouted Peter. He lurched in an attempt to stand and collapsed onto the dirt floor with a thud. Two of the men rushed to him, grabbed him under the arms, and threw him back onto the folding chair. The two with handguns took a step closer.

"You'll especially like this one," Tor said. "A four-year-old boy with -"

"Stop it!" shouted Peter. He sat panting, and attempted to wipe his welling eyes on his shoulder. "Enough already. I'll tell you what you want to know."

"No you won't," boomed a voice from the end of the building. Peter turned his head to see Cyril silhouetted against the open doorway. He walked deliberately toward Peter, Tor, and the five men in suits. The two armed men turned their guns from Peter to Cyril.

"Cyril," sneered Tor. "Looks like you're a little late to the party. Sorry for your loss, but I'm sure you've got a long list of other fugitives not to capture."

"Ouch," Peter said.

Cyril growled under his breath and kept walking.

"I'm going to ask that you stop where you are," Tor said. "Or I'll have my men shoot you." Cyril stopped.

"Tor, I have been tracking Peter for months. He means more to me than he does to you."

"Why, Cyril," interjected Peter. "I'm genuinely touched. I mean, I know we've had our differences – we do have a history. Maybe we can forget all of that and start fresh. I know where there's this perfect little Italian place, and afterwards we could catch a movie-"

"Seriously," Cyril interrupted. "You go to the trouble to abduct him and tie him up and bring him to an abandoned factory on the outskirts of town but you don't bother to gag him?"

"We had questions for him," Tor said. "Torturing someone for information, and yet gagging them so they're not able to answer intelligibly – well, that just seems cruel."

"Right," Cyril said. "As I was saying, why don't you just let me take him? Without the BAT he represents no threat to you. He'll rot in a Blutaarkian maximum security prison until your grandchildren's grandchildren have grandchildren."

"But what if he gets away from you?" Tor said. "Or later, escapes from prison? Or what if someone else here on Earth finds the BAT and figures out how to use it? No, I cannot accept that risk. Besides, he was just about to tell us where he ditched the BAT when you crashed the party. So if you'll just have a seat next to the guest of honor, let him tell us what he knows, and we'll go get the BAT and crush it to smithereens and see what happens next."

"No thanks," Cyril said. "That doesn't work for me."

Tor pointed at Cyril. "Tie him up!" he shouted. One of the gunmen and two of the unarmed thugs descended on Cyril.

"Hands in the air!" ordered one of them. Cyril resisted.

"It's not a statement of fact, like 'oh your hands exist surrounded by a gaseous mixture of nitrogen, oxygen, and carbon dioxide,' " Peter said. "They want you to hold your hands above your head."

Two of the men grabbed Cyril's arms, forced

them behind his back and dropped him to his knees. They zip tied his wrists and shoved him face first onto the floor. A gun was held to the back of his head while his ankles were bound. He was lifted and dragged by his arms and dumped next to Peter's folding chair.

"Heh," laughed Tor. "Now seating losers, party of two. You know, for aliens, you guys are real pushovers. Now, where were we before we were so rudely interrupted? Oh, yeah – Peter – where is the BAT?"

Peter opened his mouth, but the next words heard were Cyril's.

"Now, Ben!" From a broken window behind Peter a glowing blue ball shot through the air like a comet – if comets were the size of softballs and were earthbound and had linear rather than parabolic trajectories. It walloped one of the armed men, knocking him off of his feet. Before he hit the ground another glowing ball hit the second armed man, and a sequential *thud thud* echoed through the building.

Tor reached into his jacket and pulled out a gun. As the other men watched, he ran to Peter and put an arm around his neck and the gun to his head.

"Ben!" shouted Tor. "I know you can hear me. I'm holding Peter and Cyril at gunpoint. You have five seconds to show yourself before one of them eats a bullet."

Ben stepped into the doorway, holding the plasma immobilizer in his right hand. From the ground Cyril turned to look at him, and even from several yards away he could see a fire in Ben's eyes that he'd never seen before. He could also see a flashing yellow light on the PI. It was recharging. *Don't try to fire it now*, thought Cyril.

"Drop the weapon," commanded Tor. "Or I'll

drop Peter."

"Bad pun?" Peter said. "That's my cue. Tor, you're licked!" He flexed his neck and dragged his tongue across Tor's forearm.

"Gross!" Tor said. Then his body stiffened and he fell to the floor motionless. Ben aimed the plasma immobilizer in the general direction of the three still-standing thugs and made his way to Cyril and Peter.

"Me first," demanded Cyril. "You've got to work fast." Ben found a shard of glass in the dirt from one of the broken window panes. He pulled a handkerchief from his pants pocket, wrapped it around the glass, and then kneeled next to Cyril. He made quick work of the zip ties, and when Cyril stood Ben handed off the PI.

"I'm probably going to regret that," Ben said.

"Probably," Cyril said. "Now go release Peter – just his ankles."

When Peter's ankles were freed he stood, and Cyril motioned him and Ben toward the open door. Cyril walked backward, eyes and immobilizer fixed on the goons, then turned and ran toward the *Rev 9* after he cleared the doorway. He made a quick detour to the SUV, pulled something from his belt that looked like everything else on his belt, and tossed it under the vehicle. He caught up to Ben and Peter at the *Rev 9*.

"We've got twenty seconds," Cyril said. He ordered Ben upstairs, then shoved Peter into the lower-deck holding cell and locked it.

"There's been a mistake," Peter said. "I specifically stated my bed preference as 'king-size' and not 'metal floor.' "

Cyril ignored him and scampered up the steps to the cockpit. Ben was already in his seat, buckling up.

As Cyril flew past him on his way to the helm, Ben thought that he saw — for the first time — a smile on Cyril's face.

"Prepare for rapid vertical ascent," Cyril said. He hummed as his fingers danced across the control panel.

"I hate this," Ben said under his breath. He had yet to figure out how to prepare for the sensation that all of his internal organs were trying to become external organs. But then he smiled a little too, realizing this was his last takeoff in the *Rev 9* before Cyril repatriated him back to Texas and transported Peter back to Blutaark.

The *Rev 9* shot silently into the air. On the ground below an SUV decided to turn most of its mass into energy. A bright light penetrated the interior of the abandoned building where Tor started to stir, his consciousness hoping that it was safe to return to his body after most of the horrible pain had departed.

At a few thousand meters the *Rev 9* pitched slightly, allowing Ben to see a puff of black smoke billowing from the dirt parking lot below where the SUV used to be. Looking through the porthole window and above the horizon, Ben marveled at the purity of the blue fall sky. They passed through a few wispy clouds, emerging to an even more striking sea of cobalt-blue. Ben gazed, awestruck, as the blue grew even darker. The sky grew darker still, unsupported by any ground below.

Definitely a shade of black, thought Ben, *except for those tiny scattered bright points of light.* He started to get very annoyed.

"Excuse me," Ben said. "Where the hell are you going?"

SEVENTEEN

"Blutaark," Cyril said.

"Aren't you forgetting something?" Ben asked.

"The BAT?" Cyril said. "I didn't forget. I just thought I'd drop Peter off first, collect my reward, and go back to look for it later. It'll give me something to do."

"No," Ben said. The fire was back in his eyes. "I meant taking me back to Texas! I am *not* going to Blutaark."

"You'll love it. You speak a language that no one will want to bother to learn. Your life span is roughly one-seventh of ours. It'll be just like being a dog on Earth – and dogs seem pretty cool with that arrangement."

"You jerk!" shouted Ben. "I spend three days putting up with your surliness and incompetence and your criminal behavior, and *this* is how I'm rewarded?"

"Criminal behavior?" Cyril said. "I don't recall any criminal behavior."

"The Jeep?"

"Oh, yeah," Cyril said. "I'll return it when I go back. We discussed that already."

"When will that be?" Ben said, angling for a quick ride back.

"Let's see," Cyril said. "Blutaark is about twelve-million light-years away. Accounting for the round-trip and some time on the ground for a little R and R -" Just then the ship shuddered and jerked. "Oh, and a few days for maintenance on the *Rev 9* – we're talking about one year."

"You bastard!" shrieked Ben.

"Oh, sorry," Cyril said. "I neglected to convert to your Earth years. So, more like three years and two months." Ben unbuckled his seat belt and flew at Cyril. He cocked his arm and threw a fist in Cyril's general direction; it had been exactly never since Ben had attempted to hit someone, and it showed. The *Rev 9* shook and shuddered as Cyril turned, grabbed Ben's wrist and threw him to the floor. "Don't make me..." Cyril said, now standing over Ben. The ship settled down. "Why don't you go below deck and chat with Peter. Maybe he'll tell you where he hid the BAT, and we can go back." He released Ben's wrist. Ben stood, twitching with rage, then turned and sank below deck without saying a word.

Benjamin dragged a metal crate across the floor and took a seat in front of Peter's cell. Peter was seated on the floor, his wrists still bound behind his back. He looked at Ben, but Ben avoided eye contact.

"I heard what went on up there," Peter said. "You know, Cyril is actually much more appalling, once you get to know him."

"How long have you known him?" asked Ben.

"Since college," Peter said. "He was loathsome then, too. Lazy, brutish, inconsiderate, narcissistic, duplicitous. I only roomed with him for a part of one semester. I would be asleep, and he would sneak a girl into the dorm room after curfew. Then she would regain consciousness and cause a fuss. Or he would go out drinking and get arrested – but the police would spring him within a matter of minutes and bring him back to the dorm when the others in the drunk tank complained about his behavior. I got out of the housing contract by feigning my own death and re-matriculating as my identical twin brother."

"What happened?" asked Ben, now looking at Peter.

"Well, it set me back a semester," Peter said. "And once your girlfriend has attended your funeral, it really puts a damper on a relationship."

"No. I mean after college."

"Cyril was rejected by the Department of Defense. They diagnosed him with pre-traumatic stress disorder and escorted him out of the recruiting office. Four times. That afternoon. The consensus was that Cyril was a greater risk to Blutaark than he was to any army he might engage in battle. He took it hard at first, but then discovered that his lack of both shame and interpersonal skills made him a good candidate for a career as a bounty hunter.

"I was hired by the Life Sciences Administration, and worked as a field biologist for a few years," Peter said. "It was a great gig. I got to travel, see different planets, and discover unique life forms. I befriended species advanced enough to have developed language. That was rewarding, except for a handful of instances where I was befriended solely on the basis of my potential for deliciousness. The universe is chock-full of carnivores, and not all of them have heard of Blutaarkian neurotoxin."

"I'm familiar," Ben said. He felt a strong shudder, but realized it was the *Rev 9*.

"He really needs to get those stabilizers looked at," Peter said. "So my assignment was to document the gamut of species on any particular planet using an instrument called the 'BioScan.' One day I took my BioScan in for an upgrade, and by virtue of a bureaucratic blunder of interplanetary proportions, I found myself in possession of a device that represented a quantum leap in biological therapeutics."

"The BAT," Benjamin said.

"Precisely. The Bio Analysis and Treatment device. 'BAT' for short. What do you know about it?"

"Not much. You have – you had – one. Cyril wants it. Apparently it cures headaches. If many Blutaarkians are like Cyril, I could see how that would be invaluable."

"Not just headaches," Peter said. A grin spread across his face and he looked Ben in the eye. "It cures everything. Any disease, any species. There are limits, but that's the gist of it. I was halfway to Hillegom 2 when I realized what I had. I thought it was something more than serendipity that it fell into my hands. It felt more like fate. So I spent the next few months on the lam – healing tens of thousands of sick creatures on dozens of different planets."

"Get out!" whispered Ben.

"That's my short-term plan," Peter said.

"That's breathtaking," Ben said. "My breath is taken. This is amazing. So, this entire time, I've been an unwilling accomplice to some royal jerk who has been trying to apprehend - not a brazen, megalomaniacal criminal mastermind - but just a guy practicing medicine without a license?"

"I'd be surprised if Cyril had any aristocratic forebears," Peter said. "But he's definitely a jerk. And in all fairness, the BAT isn't my property. But you get the idea."

"I don't suppose you'd want to give up the BAT

now?" asked Ben. "I don't want to seem petty and selfish, but I sort of like living on Earth." The *Rev 9* shuddered and shook, almost knocking Ben off of the crate.

"We could be on our way back to Earth immediately," Peter said. "If that's what you really want."

Ben nodded and smiled. He trusted Peter in the same way he didn't trust Cyril. Peter leaned with his back against the wall, thrust his left foot between the bars of his holding cell, and told Ben to remove his boot. Ben grasped the boot with both hands and pulled with some trepidation – partly due to fear of the unknown, and partly because of something Cyril mentioned once about Peter's foot sweat condition. The boot didn't budge.

"Pull harder," whispered Peter.

Ben pushed the crate away to make more room, then placed his feet against the cell bars for leverage. He grabbed the boot and yanked. Ben fell backwards into a metal equipment rack, igniting a clangor like marbles in a blender – if marbles were ball bearings and blenders were cement mixers.

"Silence!" bellowed Cyril from above when the noise abated. The *Rev 9* vibrated, then bounced, then shook.

Ben looked into his hands and saw Peter's boot. And on the floor in front of the holding cell he saw a handgun.

"I don't think you'll have any trouble getting him to turn this thing around," Peter said. "Cyril's a pretty big fan of body integrity. Just keep your distance."

"Is it loaded?" asked Ben.

"No idea," Peter said. "I'd have to ask Martina, and she's not here."

Ben picked up the gun with two fingers like it was a dead fish and he wasn't a sea lion. "If it were a revolver I could tell if it was loaded. But it's not, and I don't know how to check."

"Probably doesn't matter," Peter said. "Cyril's a coward. Just point it at him. The threat of getting shot should be enough to get him to change course – well, change the course of the *Rev 9*, anyway. Besides, your options are limited."

Benjamin nodded. He secured the gun in his right hand, took a deep breath, and then broke for the stairs. Cyril was sitting at the helm, staring into space. Ben positioned himself against the back wall of the cabin and aimed the gun at Cyril.

"Any luck?" sneered Cyril.

"Turn around bright eyes."

Cyril swiveled his chair to face Ben. "Oh, seriously?" he said, nonplussed. "Where the hell did you get that? Oh, wait, wait, don't tell me! His name rhymes with 'meter.'"

"Take me back to Earth. Now," Ben said.

"I know this scenario probably worked out for you when you ran it through your adorable frontal lobes," Cyril said. "But the *Rev 9* is on a course for Blutaark. If you shoot me, who is going to pilot it back to Earth? Peter is locked up in a cell below deck, and you don't have the combination."

Ben stood unwavering. "Turn. It. Around."

"No, no," Cyril said. "This is the part where you say 'curses,' and slump into your chair, crestfallen."

The *Rev 9* started to vibrate. Then it shuddered, then bounced vertically before lurching sideways violently, throwing Ben against a bulkhead. The gun discharged. Ben flinched at the *bang*, and before his ears stopped ringing he noticed Cyril slumped in his seat, hemorrhaging from a right chest wound.

"It's loaded," shot Peter's voice from below deck.

EIGHTEEN

"I think April is lying," Frank said. He took a sip of coffee and sat the mug back on the conference table. "If Peter isn't staying at her place, she at least knows where he is."

"I thought your resources said he was leaving the state," Dirk said.

"I think he's still around. April looked a little tense, even panicky – I think she's covering for Peter."

"April always looks tense and panicky," Dirk said. "Everyone in the office has decided to find it charming."

"She was more anxious than usual, Dirk. She looked like she was going to get sick on the conference table."

"Driving the porcelain bus," Dirk said.

"What?" Frank said.

"Calling Europe."

"Uh, right."

"The amusement park yodel."

"That's enough," Frank said.

"Making party gravy."

"Seriously, stop it."

"Back in college we used to have contests to see who could come up with the most euphemisms for the liquid burp," Dirk said. "I usually won. The prize was more beer."

"You've come a long way," Frank said. Dirk stopped talking to puzzle over this comment, which is what Frank was counting on. "But if we could get back to the one item on the agenda -"

"Finding Peter?" Dirk said.

"Yes, Dirk," Frank said. "Finding Peter. While April was here I had a listening device planted in her apartment. And we planted one at her father's house, too. Plus, I've got someone watching her place 24/7."

"They're going to get sleepy," Dirk said.

"Not the same individual all the time," Frank said. "Different people, taking shifts."

"Right," Dirk said. He picked at his wingtips with his fingernail. Then he got a great idea, and scribbled "cure insomnia" on his yellow legal pad. "So how do you think that thing works that he has?"

"I have no idea," said Dr. Francis. "One of my operatives witnessed Peter using it on himself, and she couldn't believe her eyes."

Frank discussed the BAT in detail; how it appeared to be self-contained, was black and silver, hand-held, and that it emitted two sequential beams of light – one blue and one white. He related how the device instantly healed Peter's wounds, presumably the same way it cured Brooks of his leukemia. Technologically, it was not only eons beyond anything he had ever seen, but also beyond anything he had ever dared to imagine. As Frank spoke to Dirk about the BAT, his voice became quieter, almost reverential. He knew that this instrument had the potential to revolutionize medicine.

He also understood that it could revolutionize humanity and life on Earth as he knew it. Frank was also aware that, to the best of his encyclopedic knowledge, no country or university or corporation had this sort of technology, and though he dared to consider the possibility that it was not from this planet, he did not have the audacity to say it. Then Frank looked up at Dirk. He was doodling.

"Dirk," Frank said. "This device that Peter has – it could fundamentally change everything."

"I know!" Dirk kept doodling as he spoke. "We could completely eliminate all of this research and development nonsense. I'm counting on your team to produce functional copies of the device. But even with just one, we should be able to charge out the wazoo for each treatment. Our profits will skyrocket, and our overhead will be basically nil. I just ran the numbers – there's what, four billion people on Earth?"

"Over seven," sighed Frank.

"Even better," Dirk said. "Multiply seven billion times fifty-thousand dollars – that's a reasonable price point to cure someone, right?"

"I suppose."

"So that's what?" asked Dirk. "Thirty-five billion dollars?"

"Three-hundred and fifty trillion.

"Even better," Dirk said. "We'll both be trillionaires! I can hire Bill Gates to do nothing but help me figure out Windows 10."

"I'm glad you get the Big Picture," Frank said. "Dirk..."

"Yeah?" Dirk was now spinning complete circles in his swivel chair.

"Never mind," Frank said, and he got up and walked out of the conference room.

"Synergy!" Dirk said, and the door closed behind Frank.

Ben ran to Cyril. The front of his paisley shirt was soaked with blood. He was conscious, but pale, quiet, and motionless except for short quick breaths and the occasional blink. Ben placed the gun on the control panel and pulled Cyril from the chair, placing him flat on his back on the metal floor of the cabin. He found a pulse. It was rapid and erratic. He then took Cyril's pulse – it was weak and thready. Ben was a trained physician and knew exactly what to do in such situations – provided that he happened to be in an emergency room with things like drugs, IV fluids, and other doctors who didn't mind a little blood here and there. But not being in an emergency room, he panicked. He ran down the steps and up to Peter's cell.

"I accidentally shot Cyril," Ben said.

"Is he spewing a non-stop stream of profanities and swearing vengeance against you and your family by unspeakable means using kitchen utensils and small rodents?" Peter asked.

"No," Ben said.

"Then it's serious. We'll need to get back to Earth where we can treat him with the BAT. Find out what the keypad code is, so I can get out of here and pilot this heap."

"How do I find the code?" asked Ben.

"I'd suggest asking Cyril," Peter said. "Preferably before he loses consciousness. You're more likely to get an answer that way."

Ben ran back up the stairs. His relief at finding Cyril still conscious was short-lived upon realizing that Cyril wasn't flat on the floor where he had conveniently left him. Cyril was now standing, slumped against the helm, holding the gun at his side.

"About that hole in your chest," started Ben. "I

am sooo sorry -"

"Silence!" gurgled Cyril.

"We can make it back to Earth," Ben said. "We'll use the BAT. You'll be okay."

"No," Cyril said. Ben could barely make out what he was saying. "I can make it to Skegness. They can patch me up there until I can get proper care on Blutaark. But..." He paused to catch his breath. "We're not backtracking." He motioned with the gun and Ben sat down.

At that exact moment, another *Rev 9* was skimming through space going in the exact opposite direction. Unfortunately, it was doing so on a collision course with Cyril's *Rev 9*. The pilot of the oncoming *Rev 9* was a well-known elderly Klaghakkit from Rumcorn 4 who sometimes neglected to plot a course before engaging his inflationary drive, and often embarrassed his grandchildren by traveling thousands of light years with the turn signal on. His poor vision made it difficult for him to see the digital display on the ship's navigation controls, so he would input erroneous coordinates or none at all. He compensated for being an intergalactic transportation nuisance by being unpleasant-smelling and surly.

His *Rev 9* was still several light years away, but since both ships were using inflationary drive propulsion they were closing in on each other fast. Space is pretty big, and the odds that these two spacecraft would collide head-on were almost zero – but a direct collision was not necessary to create grisly headlines. If the inflationary drive field that extends beyond one ship overlaps the inflationary drive field from another ship, that particular part of the universe thinks that it's time to quit being very,

very large and instead decides to become very, very, very small. Both ships (and just as importantly, their contents) would be instantly crushed into the volume of a grain of sand. Cyril was well aware of these facts when the amber-colored collision avoidance warning beacon lit up the control panel.

"Well crap," he wheezed. Cyril leaned and with his outstretched hand he slapped a large black button adjacent to the flashing amber light. One of the bulkheads immediately hurled itself against Cyril and Ben, held them like flies on flypaper and then dropped them to the floor like flypaper wouldn't. Ben stood slowly, fighting vertigo and the feeling that his head was now a thumb that had been slammed in the door of a 1969 Pontiac Catalina. He stumbled to where Cyril lay unconscious. Ben kicked the gun from Cyril's hand. This took several attempts – partly due to Ben's vertigo, but mostly because of his innate lack of athleticism. He made a mental note (assuming Cyril survived) to apologize to Cyril for the extra bruises on his arm and ribs when he noticed Cyril's eyes were open.

"Sorry about that, too," Ben said. "What just happened?"

"Collision avoidance system," whispered Cyril.

"It's broken," Ben said. "It didn't keep me from colliding with the wall." Cyril rolled his eyes. At least Ben hoped he was rolling his eyes. *Of all the times I've wanted Cyril to die, this would be the most inconvenient*, thought Ben. He bent over and shook his shoulder and Cyril's eyes rolled back into position. "Tell me the code. I don't think you'll make it to Skegness."

A look of resignation washed over Cyril's already pale face. "All right. It's 867." He paused to catch his breath.

"Eight-six-seven? Got it!' and Ben turned to run below deck.

"Wait!" gasped Cyril, and he reached out for Ben. Ben stopped. "There's more. It's 867...53...09."

"Okay," Ben said. "So it's 8678675309."

"No!" Cyril rolled his eyes again.

"Don't leave me now Cyril!" Ben shook him again.

"No!" snapped Cyril. "You idiot. Just one 867." He panted with the effort.

"So, it's 867...5309?"

"Yes!"

"I got it, I got it," Ben said. "It's catchy." He ran below deck to free Peter.

Ben found a blanket and some bandages, and did his best to stabilize Cyril. Peter put his boot back on, and after standing noticed the orange-colored starter from a *Rev 2* on one of the equipment racks that had not been emptied onto the floor. He made his way upstairs and sat in front of the control panel. He attempted to switch on the interactive on-board computer and was annoyed to discover that this particular *Rev 9* was absent that feature. (Cyril had road-tested various versions, but even the most aloof computer personality found Cyril too disagreeable, and – like every version before it – uninstalled itself.) But the *Rev 9*'s operating system differed little from that of the *Rev 2*, and soon Peter had the ship on a course back to Earth.

"Did you guys leave a car at that abandoned factory?" asked Peter. "I'll need to land this thing in a secluded area, and then drive to where I've hidden the BAT."

"No," Ben said. "But Cyril was driving a stolen Jeep. It's probably still parked where we left it – just off of a highway north of the city."

"That will have to do," Peter said. He searched the ship's flight data and found the coordinates for the clearing in Cherokee county. He calculated that it would take 52 minutes to get to the landing site and then drive to where he had hidden the BAT. He estimated that Cyril had 60 minutes to live.

Taryn was upbeat, driving with the car top down and the speedometer needle up and looking forward to the phone call from Tor. She fully expected the BAT to be in their possession soon, and had already decided on the perfect pair of heels under which she would crush it to bits; that was going to be her reward for finding Peter. Taryn relished the thought that it was her moxie that led to his capture. She was confident that even if Tor and his henchmen had failed to find the BAT, they should at least be able to convince Peter to give it up. She was just as confident that they could deal with Peter once the BAT was secured. Though she was a ruthless businesswoman, she never sullied her conscience with the details of business adversaries who suffered untimely accidental deaths, or who mysteriously vanished while on vacation. She left that to Tor and his associates. All of this made the news even more difficult to accept.

"What?" shrieked Taryn as she sped through the business district, cell phone in one hand and steering wheel in the other. "Please tell me that you did not just tell me that Peter escaped!"

"Well, he didn't really escape," Tor said.

"Thank god," sighed Taryn. "That's your worst practical joke yet, Tor Kinney. For a minute there I thought hara-kiri was going to be the next item on your 'to-do' list."

"No, he didn't escape – he was rescued. By that

Cyril fellow," Tor said. He anticipated Taryn's response and held his cell phone at arm's length.

Taryn shrieked. Not words, but more of a guttural screech, like a rabid howler monkey teaching its daughter to drive. When she stopped, Tor put the phone back to his ear. He heard only panting. Finally Taryn spoke. "Incompetents!"

"It was real bad, Taryn." Tor was almost in tears. "There were laser guns and bombs and a spaceship and I got zapped and I could have been killed and I still can't move my legs right." Tor's whining turned into whimpering, and Taryn found it difficult to squeeze in insults between his bubbly sobs.

"What's your plan now?" Taryn asked.

"I need to go change my pants," Tor said.

"I meant about Peter."

"Oh, I...don't...know," Tor said.

"Well, since I wasn't too busy feeling sorry for myself, I just now took the liberty of coming up with a plan," Taryn said. "Hope you don't mind."

"No," Tor said, his voice still wavering. Taryn could practically see the snot bubbles.

"Good," Taryn said. "Grab the reins, Tor. I'm going to go get doughnuts."

Taryn Yuanuin drove back to the doughnut stop, got out of her car, pushed her way past the crime scene tape and through the front door. There were no inconvenient customers to get in her way. Crime scene tape tends to put a damper on any business by suggesting an establishment with chalk body outlines on the floor at best, and unappetizing bloodsplatter on the walls at worst. Jess was still behind the counter. He recognized Taryn from earlier, but in the fog of Peter's abduction and the subsequent police questioning, he could not remember if she was one of the bad guys or not – so in a sort of compromise he held his hands up just below shoulder height.

Taryn convinced Jess to go into the back office and fetch Peter's employment records. Some say it was because of her stunning good looks coupled with her above-average fashion sense. And some say it was because of her experience as a no-holds-barred business negotiator. And others say it was because Jess had had enough confrontation for one day, and getting Peter's employment records only required that he walk a few feet to the back office, pull the papers from a file, walk a few feet back, and hand them to Taryn. But whatever the reason, Taryn soon found herself in possession of Peter's job application and the home address that he had provided – April's apartment. She whipped out her cell phone. Jess flinched. She called Tor, turned, and walked out of the shop.

"Have you pulled yourself together yet?" Taryn asked.

"This is Jason. Tor's curled up on the floor in a fetal position."

"Good," Taryn said. "That means he's almost back to normal. Listen carefully. I'm going to give you Peter's last known address. You know what to do."

NINETEEN

Cyril was still alive when Peter landed the *Rev 9* in the clearing. Peter removed Cyril's belt and handed it to Ben, and because he was physically stronger than Ben, he used a fireman's carry to get Cyril out of the ship. The Jeep was only a few yards from the *Rev 9*, but before they made their way to the car, Peter pointed to the remote control module on Cyril's belt and instructed Ben to remove it.

"We're going to put her in hover mode," Peter said, and they both turned to face the ship. "Just flip open the top, and push the white button." Ben did as he was told, and they watched as the *Rev 9* shot vertically and disappeared. "We closed the hatch after we left, right?"

"Sure," Ben said unconvincingly as he picked up his pace on his way to the car. Peter lay Cyril down in the back seat, and told Ben to get in with him.

"You're the doctor. You should be with him. I'll drive."

Ben did not have the heart to tell Peter that, as an ophthalmologist, he was fully qualified to ask "better one, or two?" and prescribe Cyril a proper pair of spectacles – but those efforts probably would not have much effect on his impending death spiral. But Ben acquiesced and climbed in next to Cyril. Peter found the keys in the front seat, started the car, and drove out of the clearing and onto the highway.

Peter's driving had improved exactly not at all since he had wrecked Martina's SUV. On several occasions, Ben had to remind Peter to keep to the right side of the solid white line, and not to drive directly on top of it. Peter discovered that driving to the left side of the solid white line made Ben scream, so he stopped doing that for the most part. As Peter sped across the winding rural highway, Ben tended to Cyril, which meant watching him breathe short shallow breaths and roll his eyes back intermittently. His color wasn't good, but that was nothing new. Had Cyril been human, and if anyone had asked, Ben would have opined that this car ride would end with at least one death. But he would also concede that he was clueless regarding the resiliency of Blutaarkian physiology and the powers of the BAT.

Peter managed to get the Jeep on the highway going south to Atlanta, a more linear road that encouraged him to drive faster, but not better.

"My estimate – we should be there in twenty-seven minutes." Peter shouted this, even though the car was quiet and Ben was right behind him.

Ben laughed to himself thinking how they were all out of their element; he would have been more comfortable performing eye surgery, and Peter would have been more comfortable piloting a spaceship through an asteroid belt. And Cyril would have been more comfortable being not shot.

Twenty minutes later, they were in Sandy Springs. Peter exited the parkway and sped down a two-lane road with apartment complexes on one side and a suburban forest on the other. Without any warning, Peter's foot hit the brake pedal like he was crushing an empty beer can. The tires squealed and

Ben's body slammed into the back of Peter's seat like a crash test dummy – if crash test dummies wore glasses and screamed like little girls. Ben was horrified when he realized that he had not bothered to fasten his seat belt on the Ride from Hell. He was distracted from his horror when Peter bolted from the car and ran across a sidewalk and into the woods.

Peter estimated that he had four minutes to find the BAT, get back to the car, and treat Cyril before he died. It had been pitch dark out when Peter had walked into these woods from April's apartment, wrapped his t-shirt around the BAT, and hid it in a tree hollow. Now – surrounded by hundreds of trees that all looked alike – he regretted not drawing a map. He stumbled through the trees in a random fashion that more closely resembled Brownian motion than an organized search. *How many of these trees could possibly have holes large enough to accommodate the BAT?* He had found three so far; one contained an ill-tempered squirrel, but none contained the BAT. Near panic, he wondered if his worst fear had materialized. Had one of Frank Francis's pout models seen him hide it? What if April was coerced into spying on him, watched as he hid it, and then turned it over to Dionysus? Peter tried to keep cool, but he was on the front lines of a panic attack without reinforcements. He guessed he had well under two minutes remaining – or, more precisely – that Cyril had less than two minutes remaining. Peter sprinted from tree trunk to tree trunk. He ramped the anxiety level up to "11" by obsessing over the possibility that he could very well be searching the same trees over and over. He started to hyperventilate. He froze, put his hands on his knees, and took a few deep breaths while trying to quash the mental image of Nathan Radley pouring cement into a tree hole. He stood slowly so as not to faint, and straight ahead – roughly thirty feet away – was an old oak with an elongated opening.

Like an octogenarian approaching a yield sign, Cyril's respiratory rate slowed until it finally came to a complete stop. Ben positioned himself over Cyril's chest and initiated CPR. Ben flashbacked to his first encounter with Cyril and his traumatic brush with Blutaarkian neurotoxin, and was grateful that mouth-to-mouth awkwardness was no longer de rigeur for CPR. He looked up to see Peter running toward the car.

Peter slung the car door open. "Get back!" he shouted. Ben correctly assumed that Peter was talking to him and pulled away from Cyril. Peter had powered up the BAT on his sprint to the Jeep, and now Ben watched with fascination as he held the silver baton at arm's length. A beam of blue light fanned from the BAT and across Cyril's body. Even in broad daylight, it filled the car interior with an intense color that Ben would later describe as "Blue Man Group" blue. A second beam followed, an intense white light that cloaked Cyril and temporarily blinded Ben. It flickered and then went out.

"Where's Cyril's belt?" Peter said. "Get it, now." Ben reached over the back seat and retrieved the clumsy-looking fashion accessory from the cargo bay. "Now remove the plasma immobilizer." Ben eyed the belt and shrugged. "That one!" Peter said impatiently, and he pointed to one of the many small rectangular black devices on the belt. "You're going to need it, like now!"

Ben removed the immobilizer, placed his thumb over what he thought was the trigger, and tossed the belt into the back of the Jeep. He turned back to see that Cyril was now stirring, and his color was a less whiter shade of pale.

Peter slammed the back door, circled the back of the Jeep, jumped behind the wheel, tossed the BAT into the passenger seat, and started the car. Benjamin kept the plasma immobilizer trained on Cyril, who had just opened his eyes. Peter punched the accelerator and turned the wheel, spinning the tires and making a U-turn to head back north. For a fraction of a second, he could see the front of April's apartment across the street and two black SUVs parked side-by-side in the parking lot. He could not tell if anyone was in either SUV. It all had happened too fast.

"He's trying to sit up," Ben said.

"Let him," Peter said. "Just keep the PI pointed at him. Once he's more alert he'll be odious and disgusting...because the BAT doesn't alter personality. Say, there's something I need to ask you."

"Shoot," Ben said.

"Back there, in the Jeep...what were you doing to Cyril?"

"Cardiopulmonary resuscitation," Ben said... "He'd stopped breathing."

"And how does pressing on his spleen help?"

"Would you like me to drive?" asked Ben, changing the subject.

"I've got this," Peter said. "I don't want to pull over – in case we're being followed." He was quiet until they were back on the parkway. Then he told Benjamin about April; how he had hitched a ride with her father in Alabama and cured his leukemia with the BAT, how he crashed at her apartment, and how it got ransacked – probably by someone from

Dionysus looking for the BAT. April knew about the BAT, but not that Peter had hidden it in the woods across the street from her apartment. Peter explained that when he was abducted – once by Martina under the auspices of Dionysus and once by Tor's thugs from Persona Health – a black SUV was used each time. And there were two black SUVs parked in April's parking lot when they retrieved the BAT and saved Cyril's life.

"I don't think they saw us," Peter said. "They were parked facing away from the street. But I'm not taking any chances."

From what Ben could gather, "not taking any chances" meant looking backward using the rearview mirror while driving forward exceedingly fast in heavy traffic. Ben could not see the speedometer, but he felt certain that the phrase "high rate of speed" would be found in his obituary. Cyril sat up and looked around with a dazed expression. He licked his lips repeatedly, but said nothing.

"Uh, oh," Peter said. "We've got company." He was looking in the rear view mirror. "It's one of those black SUVs."

Ben felt the Jeep accelerate, but kept his eyes on Cyril. Their bodies swayed left-to-right and back as Peter swerved in and out of traffic, trying to elude the pursuer.

"They're gaining," Peter said. "How's Cyril?"

Ben reflected on how remarkable it was that Peter had shouldered a significant personal risk and went to extraordinary lengths to save the life of someone who was trying to capture him. *He could have just as easily let Cyril die. Why didn't he?* "He's awake," shouted Ben over the roar of the engine. "He appears stable, but he's very out of it." Ben assumed the BAT had done its job, though he had not yet dared to check Cyril's vital signs.

"Good," Peter said. "Because I'm going to ask you to take your eyes off of him for just a few seconds. I want you to set the PI to setting 1. Then I want you to aim it out of the rear window. See if you can hit the SUV driver behind us."

Ben swallowed hard, turned the PI to setting 1, and turned to look out of the back window. "Uh, Peter?"

"Yeah?"

"Did you notice the flashing red-and-blue lights on top of the black SUV?" Benjamin said.

"Yes. Is that supposed to intimidate me?"

"It is," replied Ben. "But that's not the point. That's not someone from Dionysus, or Persona. That's a Georgia State Trooper."

"What do you suppose he wants?" Peter asked.

"He wants you to pull over. I'm fairly certain he wants to give you a ticket for speeding," Ben said. Then it hit him. They were in a stolen vehicle. "Oh crap."

"What?" Peter had already started to slow the Jeep and had moved into the far right lane.

"This car is stolen. We're going to get arrested." He stuffed the plasma immobilizer into his pants pocket.

"Well, you're not the one driving it," Peter said. "And I'll simply explain that it was Cyril who stole it, not I."

"Look," Ben said. "That's not how it works. They are going to arrest *all* of us." At some level, Ben realized this was the opportunity he had been waiting for since the moment he was abducted by Cyril. Sure, he might be detained for a few hours, maybe even incarcerated for a couple of days. But once they sorted everything out and discovered that he had been abducted and that it was Cyril who stole the Cherokee, then he would be on the next plane back to Dallas. But Ben also realized that he could have escaped the moment Peter left the car to search for the BAT – and yet he didn't. So on another level, Benjamin Cotter understood that he was now part of something much bigger, something more fascinating, and something profoundly more significant than prescribing contact lenses. And he had to admit to himself that he was a little disappointed that Peter wasn't making a run for it.

"Ben, you may be a perfectly competent ophthalmologist," Peter said as he stopped the Jeep on the shoulder. "But I had almost an entire half-semester of Theory of Interplanetary Jurisprudence. Before this is over, they will be apologizing to me for the inconvenience and we'll be back on the road to the *Rev 9*.

Peter rolled down the window, shut off the Jeep, and looked up to see a Georgia State Trooper standing at his window.

"Sir," said officer Rogers. "Do you know why I pulled you over?"

"These are not the droids you're looking for," Peter said.

"I beg your pardon?" said Officer Rogers, dropping his chin to look at Peter over his sunglasses.

"Never mind," Peter said. "So why *did* you pull me over?"

"You were driving *very* irresponsibly," said Officer Rogers. "Speeding, unsafe lane changes, reckless driving. I'm going to need to see your license and registration."

"My apologies. I don't have them on me," replied Peter. "See, this car belongs to my friend Cyril who's sitting in the back there. He was suddenly struck ill after eating some bad walnuts, and I took it upon myself to drive him home, fully aware that my paperwork may not be in order. The things we do for friends – am I right?"

"Wait in the car," said Officer Rogers. He walked back to the SUV and got on the radio.

Ben was dazzled by Peter's confidence. He wondered what miracle Peter would pull off this time to keep them from getting arrested and thrown into jail. Was his first comment to the trooper a clue? Did Peter have some sort of telepathic power that would enable him to coerce the trooper into letting them go with just a warning? Or had he switched the license plates without Ben's knowledge? Or perhaps he used the *Rev 9*'s computer to hack into the DMV mainframe, making it appear that the Jeep was registered in his (or Cyril's) name. He would have considered other possibilities, but his concentration was broken by someone shouting something.

"Get out of the car!"

TWENTY

On Saturday evening, April noticed the two black SUVs parked in her parking lot. The two oversized luxury vehicles with dark tinted windows stood out in that parking lot like two middle-aged men with sunglasses at a high school prom – only more creepy. But it was getting dark, and with the tinted windows she could not tell if there was anyone inside of either vehicle.

When April went outside Sunday morning to get her neighbor's newspaper, she could see two people in the front seat of each SUV. And she was fairly certain that one of them was Martina – Frank Francis's daughter. April went back inside, and within a few minutes she came back out, this time carrying a tray. She walked across the parking lot to one of the vehicles and tapped on the driver's side window. The power window opened with a hum. April forced a smile and spoke to Martina.

"I brought you some food," April said. "Some juice, bagels, cream cheese...Sundays are my stay-at-home and clean house and get-caught-up-on-reading days, so you'll probably be here a while. Can I get you anything else?"

"That's wayyyy too much food," Martina said. She

looked at April with empty eyes and pouted.

"You're welcome," April said. "But I anticipated as much. Here..." She dug a small plastic container out of her pocket and handed it to Martina. "It's a one-hundred calorie strawberry yogurt. You two can split it," she said, referring to Martina's pouting pout-model partner in the passenger seat. "I'll be back to check on you later." April heard the hum of Martina's window closing as she walked to the other SUV and tapped on its window. It opened – but only halfway – revealing a dark-haired young man wearing sunglasses. A red-haired young man, also in shades, sat in the passenger seat. "Like I told Martina, I'm not planning on going anywhere today. So you might be stuck here for a while. I brought some bagels and juice." She held the tray up to the window. "Just leave the tray on the hood when you're done," she chirped.

"Thanks," Jason said. He took the tray, handed it to Brian and shrugged, then rolled up the window. April walked back to her apartment and went inside.

April had made a Herculean effort to maintain the appearance of being upbeat. She hated having to do that; acting cheerful usually made her feel more anxious and depressed than just acting anxious and depressed did. But now she was concerned – not for herself, but for Peter. He was gone when she got up Saturday morning to meet with Frank and Dirk. He left no note, and she had not heard from him since. She sat on the sofa, threw the newspaper onto the coffee table next to *To Kill a Mockingbird,* and replayed their Friday night conversation in her head. Peter did say that he planned to stay with her for a while, to "lay low" until things blew over. He didn't think that the Dionysus thugs would come back to April's to look for him. And yet there they were, right outside, right now. *Maybe Peter came back, saw them waiting for him, and took off,* thought April. *That's the only scenario that makes sense.*

She thought it unlikely that he had been captured again; if they had Peter and the BAT, why would they bother with watching her? *The BAT. He said he was going to hide it. Well, crap. Maybe they have Peter, and they're still looking for the BAT. That would explain the surveillance. Damn. I wish he'd call.* April got up and started cleaning her apartment.

Ben, Peter, and Cyril sat handcuffed in a small room illuminated with harsh fluorescent tubes. They sat at a rectangular table in a rectangular room with a single rectangular door and a large rectangular mirror that Ben assumed was of the two-way variety. They had been arrested, Mirandized, searched, mugshot, and fingerprinted, and their possessions had been confiscated. On the way to the police station, Peter had volunteered to Ben that he had received a grade of "incomplete" in Theory of Interplanetary Jurisprudence. Ben volunteered that he thought Peter should have taken driver's ed instead. Cyril remained uncharacteristically quiet.

"They're going to a lot of trouble to apologize to us," Ben said.

"They are taking their time about it," Peter said. "I'm guessing it's a formal written apology. They want to get the wording just right." Peter turned and looked at Cyril. "How are you doing, buddy?" Cyril turned and gave Peter a wan smile, but still said nothing. "He's been through a lot today – you know, with getting shot and dying and coming back to life and all. Let's say after we blow this joint we take him out for beer and pizza."

Just then a police investigator entered the room.

He was lanky, with brown hair in a pompadour style. He wore blue jeans and a brown sport jacket with the sleeves pushed up past his elbows. He dropped an intimidating seven-inch thick file that rattled the table and Ben's nerves.

"Well, well, well," he said, surveying the suspects. "This has been a long time coming."

"I concur," Peter said. Benjamin winced and slowly shook his head. Cyril stared straight ahead, still smiling. "We've been here almost two hours waiting for this little mix-up to be resolved. Now if you'll just uncuff us and apologize we'll be on our way. We'll need our possessions back. Naturally, you can keep the Jeep."

"Let me introduce myself," said the investigator. "I'm Detective Brady of the Georgia State Patrol, but around these parts they call me 'Tex.' And I'm not about to release the kingpins of the largest crystal meth operation in the southeastern United States."

"Don't change the subject," Peter said. "Just let us go and then you can do whatever you want with those other guys."

"You *are* them, pardner," Brady said. He took a toothpick out of his pocket and twirled one end between his teeth. "We ran the plates to that Jeep you boys were driving." Brady made finger quotes and scowled when he said "driving." "Turns out it's registered to one Hobart Kingpin." Brady glared at Peter. "I'm guessing the mouthy one here is Hobart." He turned and pointed to Cyril. "And that must make you the little brother, Butch Kingpin. And Poindexter over here," he turned to Benjamin, "must be the chemist – Stuart." Brady turned back to Cyril, who was smiling and staring at himself in the mirror. "Is he on drugs?"

"No!" Ben said. "Look, there's been a gross

misunderstanding. Sure, Cyril stole the Jeep. But we aren't drug dealers. Aren't there photographs of the guys you're looking for in that huge file?"

"Honestly, that's not the Kingpin file," Brady said. "It's just a prop we use to intimidate suspects. We have gone dig-it-al. We've got a couple of hard drives chock-full of evidence on the Kingpin cartel, but the fellas in IT tell me it's bad for the hard drives to drop them on the table. Point is – we've got digital images of Hobart *and* Butch."

"So look at these two!" Ben said. "Do they look like any of your photos?"

"Not really," said Brady. "But obviously they have had surgery to alter their appearance and elude capture." He turned to look at Peter and Cyril, and grimaced. "I guess making yourself less attractive is one approach."

Ben sighed. "You have my ID. Run an internet search. You'll see I'm just a doctor from Texas."

"Son," Brady said. "We already Googled you – your website looked very convincing. Just the kind of thing a brainy chemistry-kind-of-guy would do; create a web presence for his alternative identity." Detective Brady pulled out a chair, sat down, and started thumbing through the faux file. "So now comes the fun part. Me and one of my partners will proceed to interrogate you gentlemen until we get a confession outta ya. Although it's not absolutely necessary. Even without a confession, we've got enough evidence for a jury to put you away for forty years. Each. In a row. Without parole. So if you could just go ahead and confess it would save us a lot of time and paperwork. But don't everyone talk at once – let's start with you, Poindexter." He took a digital recorder out of his pocket and placed it in the middle of the table.

Ben and Peter stared at the recorder, refusing to speak. Cyril stared straight ahead.

"Fair enough," Brady said. "Not my first rodeo. If you haven't figured it out already, I'm the 'good cop.' We usually employ the 'good-cop bad-cop' interrogation technique, but our 'bad cop' – detective Howard – is busy moving his mother into a nursing home. Detective Logan will be filling in for him, but he's been passed over for promotion eight years in a row, and will probably take a disability retirement soon. So it'll be more like 'good-cop jaded-cop.' "

"Shouldn't we have attorneys?" Benjamin said.

"Well danggit," Brady said. "That's sort of the exact opposite of a confession. That's not what we're shooting for. Try to be a team player, Stuart."

"I'm sorry," interjected Peter. "Detective Brady, I think we can both agree that we don't need to get lawyers involved. My friend Stu-, my friend Benjamin here is simply attempting to protect me and Cyril. And *not* because we're the Kingpin brothers."

"And what exactly is Stuart protecting you from?"

"It's Ben. My name is Ben."

"He's trying to hide the fact that Cyril and I are aliens."

"Hobart Kingpin," Brady grinned. "According to our sources you're from Oklahoma. I'll admit it's sort of backward, but it don't really count as a foreign country."

"Not that kind of alien," Ben said. "He means like the outer space aliens."

"Well if that don't beat all," Brady said, leaning back in his chair. "This'll be one of those interrogation tapes we play back at the Labor Day Barbeque."

"He's not kidding," Peter said. "My name is Peter of Blutaark. Sitting next to me is Cyril of Blutaark. We've only been on Earth a few days, and have never engaged in the manufacture, sale, or distribution of illegal drugs. We're not the Kingpins, and I can prove it."

"I'm all ears," Brady said.

"Detective Brady – Tex, if I may," Peter said. "Have you ever heard of Blutaarkian salivary neurotoxin?"

"Can't say that I have," Brady said.

"Let me introduce you," Peter said. Ben ducked. Peter leaned forward and spat across the table, covering Brady's face in a mist of spittle. He gasped, threw both palms to his face, and was unconscious before he hit the floor. The door flung open and detective Logan grabbed Brady by the shoulders and dragged him across the floor and out of the room. The door slammed shut. A loud *click* meant they were probably not going to be able to just get up and walk out.

"That went well," Ben said.

Things were quiet for a couple of hours. Cyril had started to blink more, and rather than staring at a fixed point, he looked around the spartan room. He was no longer smiling.

"This is the worst restaurant ever," Cyril said. "Where the hell's out waiter?"

"Good to have you back," Peter said. "But this isn't a restaurant. We've been arrested."

Cyril looked down at his blood-soaked shirt. "Did I kill somebody?"

"No," Peter said.

"Pity," Cyril said. "So what happened?"

"Long story short," interjected Ben. "You were headed back to Blutaark with me and Peter. You accidentally got shot. We came back to Earth and saved your life with the BAT. And on the way back to the *Rev 9* we got pulled over and arrested. Did I mention Peter was the one driving?"

"Did I mention Ben was the one who shot you?" Peter said.

"So we were brought here for questioning," Ben said. "And then Peter spat on the investigator."

"I vaguely remember that," Cyril said. "That's why I thought we were at a restaurant."

"Well I, for one, am glad you're back." Peter said. "For the last couple of hours you've had that post-mechanical looglack ride look in your eyes."

Cyril smiled a little at the memory. "Good times."

Their heads turned toward the door when they heard it unlock. In walked a squat 40ish man wearing a garish orange Hawaiian shirt, khaki shorts, and flip-flops. He had unkempt black hair to his shoulders, and under his arm was a cardboard box which – in fitting with the theme of the room – was rectangular. He sat the box on the table and shut off the digital recorder.

"Good afternoon," he said. "I'm Federal Agent Hays." He sat at the table, opposite Ben, Peter, and Cyril. He spoke softly and moved deliberately and didn't seem to be at all bothered by the fact that the last person who interrogated them was dragged from the room unconscious.

"You don't look like a federal agent," Ben said.

"That's sort of the idea," responded Hays.

"Are you with Homeland Security?" asked Ben.

"Yeah," Hays said. "Something like that."

"If I may ask," Peter said. "Is that Hays, H-A-Y-S or H-A-Z-E?"

"It's Hays, H-A-Y-S."

"Thanks for the clarification," Peter said. Agent

Hays pulled a pair of sunglasses from his pocket and put them on.

"If you gentlemen are through asking questions, I'd like to get started." He paused before speaking again. "I understand you gentlemen are aliens. The outer-space kind."

"Well, Cyril and I are," Peter said. "Ben is just along for the ride."

"I see," Hays said. "Are these your belongings?" He pushed the cardboard box toward them. It contained Ben's personal effects – including his cell phone – Cyril's belt with all of its attachments, and the BAT.

"It appears that everything is there," Peter said. He looked at the others and they nodded in agreement.

"Good," Hays said. "All charges have been dropped. But you're now in my custody. If you fail to cooperate then the charges will be reinstated – with an additional charge of assaulting an officer tacked on for good measure. Am I clear?"

"Yes," Peter said. "Very unhazy."

Agent Hays got up and picked up the box. "We'll go now. Follow me. Single file, please."

"Where are we going?" asked Benjamin.

"West," Hays said.

Agent Hays strolled out of the room, and Peter, Cyril, and Ben followed. Outside of the interrogation room, they were accompanied by armed troopers wearing riot face shields. They were escorted out of the building and to the parking lot where a 1975 Vega station wagon awaited. Under the watchful eye of the troopers, Hays placed the cardboard box in the cargo bay, then uncuffed the three and re-cuffed them with their hands in front of them. He then opened the back door.

"Get in."

"Golly," Peter said. "We really had our hearts set on a black SUV."

"It's a tight fit, but it's a short drive," Hays said. "Don't try anything stupid – there will be unmarked cars following us." Peter, Cyril, and Ben crammed into the back seat. The troopers left. Hays got in and started the car. After several attempts it started, and they left for the airport.

"Bold transportation choice," Ben said.

"Typical government bureaucracy," Hays said. "They wanted something inconspicuous, so they got us these Vega station wagons, not realizing that a running 1975 Vega station wagon would be the most conspicuous vehicle on the road. But at least it's better than when they issued us minivans. It's hard to take someone seriously when they're driving a taupe minivan. It looked like a friggin' suitcase." Cyril started to say something, but thought better of it.

Agent Hays took a little-used road to a remote edge of the airport and pulled up to a locked gate. Two men with sunglasses, black vests, and side arms opened the gate and waved them through. He idled across the tarmac to a small private jet.

"There will be food for you on the plane." Five minutes later they were taxiing down the runway.

TWENTY-ONE

Ben, Cyril, and Peter were seated near the front of the cabin. Agent Hays sat several rows behind them, looking very much like a Miami tourist with his Hawaiian shirt, flip-flops, and shoulder holster. Other than the flight crew of two, they were the only ones on the plane. After takeoff Hays walked down the aisle to speak to them. Despite the engine noise, he spoke softly, apologizing for the four-hour flight. He handed out sandwiches and water bottles, and went back to his seat.

The steady vibration and jet engine hum put Ben to sleep. Cyril and Peter were seated across the aisle from each other. After a while Cyril leaned over and whispered to Peter.

"This thing is soooo slow."

"I *know*," Peter replied. It was several minutes before Cyril spoke again.

"Where's the *Rev 9*?"

Peter looked back down the aisle. Agent Hays appeared to be asleep. "Hover mode."

"Good," Cyril said. He remembered that at some point he would need the remote control unit to retrieve the *Rev 9*, and wondered out loud where his belt was. "I feel sort of naked without it."

"I just ate," Peter said. "So thanks for that image." Peter wondered too. He had not seen Agent Hays or anyone else bring the cardboard box on the plane – the box with Ben's belongings, Cyril's belt...and the BAT.

"Sorry," Cyril said. He was quiet for a while, which was a difficult thing for Cyril unless he was just getting over being dead and then suddenly made not dead again. But he was pretty much over all of that, and he fell back into his old habit of saying things that had not been adequately thought out inside of his head first. "I think we can take them," was just one example.

"What?" Peter said.

"I think we can take them," Cyril said. Because preposterous ideas always sound better when repeated. "There are three of us, and probably just two in the cockpit. That makes three-on-three."

"Maybe that would work if what you're proposing is a three-on-three basketball game. Even that's iffy – we'd be stuck with Ben. Otherwise, that's a ludicrous idea. Assuming you get through the cockpit door before Agent Hays shoots you, attacking someone who's flying the plane you happen to be a passenger on seems like an egregious lapse of judgment."

"You could block the aisle," Cyril said. "I could get into the cockpit and have them unconscious within seconds."

"So I take a bullet," Peter said. "Then you attempt to fly a vehicle that is dependent on the principle of lift and is at the mercy of meteorological whimsy? Do I have that right?"

"I'm sure there's some sort of instruction manual in there," Cyril said. "Besides, if you get shot we can use the BAT, just like you did for me. Even-Steven."

"Do you even know where it is?" Peter said. "I haven't seen the BAT since we got in the car." Before Cyril could answer, Peter looked up to see Agent Hays standing behind them.

"Pardon me," Hays said. "My Blutaarkese is a little rusty. I'm going to have to insist that if you communicate with each other, you do so in English. Once – back in '87, before my time, of course – a couple of aliens from Mowbray 4 attempted to commandeer one of our Learjets in mid-flight. Before they could land the plane, it was taken out by an air-to-air missile. Gentlemen...this isn't our first alien abduction." Peter and Cyril were quiet for the remainder of the flight.

Benjamin woke up and looked out of the window. They were flying west, chasing the sun. Below he saw no roads, no trees, no buildings – only desert stretching to the horizon. The plane banked and initiated its descent, and as it approached the desert floor Ben broke into a cold sweat. The absence of any visible runway or airport triggered a panic attack and a search of the seat pocket for an air sickness bag. When the plane touched down, Ben's relief was short-lived upon realizing the runway was approximately the width of a queen size bed.

The plane slowed, and then taxied a short distance until it stopped next to a military-style Quonset barrack. Agent Hays stood and instructed them to unbuckle and make their way, single file, to the front of the cabin. One of the flight crew stepped out of the cockpit and opened the hatch. Ben, Peter, and Cyril exited to the airstairs and made their way down to the tarmac, where two men with black baseball caps, sunglasses, black vests, and M16s stood next to a gravel pathway leading to the barrack.

"Stop when you get to the door," Hays shouted. When he got to the door he pulled some keys from his shorts and unlocked a simple padlock that secured the door.

"What *is* this place?" Benjamin said.

"Officially," Hays said, "this place doesn't exist. Unofficially it's called Area 52. But the few dozen individuals who know about it and work here call it 'The Rabbit Hole.' "

"That's disgusting," Cyril said.

"Rabbits are mammalian life forms that live in burrows, and hence dig holes," Peter said. "So it wasn't an anatomical reference. Although I suspect that it's more of a literary allusion to *Alice's Adventures in Wonderland,* a story about a young girl who falls into a rabbit hole and is confronted with a multitude of magical and surreal experiences." Ben nodded in agreement. Cyril rolled his eyes. Peter thought of April and her books, and wondered how she was doing.

Area 52, like Area 51, was protected by the United States Air Force. But unlike the activities at Area 51, the Air Force was not privy to the goings-on at Area 52. There didn't appear to be much to it: a single steel barrack, a large steel shed – roughly the size of a small hangar, and one narrow 12,000 foot-long asphalt runway. It sat in the middle of the Nevada desert, unfenced, and miles from any paved roads. The building, the shed, and the runway were painted the color of the desert, making them virtually invisible from the air. The few select planes that landed at Area 52 were equipped with specialized receivers that tracked transmitters placed along the sides and at both ends of the runway, so that every landing – even on a clear day – was an instrument landing. The exterior of the building was unassuming and the interior was unremarkable, save for the out-of-place elevator doors at the far end.

Behind the doors was an elevator with a vertical shaft that plunged almost 9,000 feet underground. It could claim the record for the deepest elevator shaft in the Western Hemisphere, had they been keen to publicize that fact. They weren't.

Below ground, Area 52 was a labyrinth of corridors lined by rooms where a few dozen people lived and worked: astronomers, physicists, mathematicians, biologists, zoologists, aeronautical engineers, electrical engineers, materials engineers, hardware and software engineers, security specialists, weapons experts, psychologists, maintenance and support crew, an accountant and one close-up magician. These workers were under the purview of the Alien Phenomena Agency, an agency spun-off from the CIA in 1957. (It was originally named the Alien Phenomenon Agency, until a second alien phenomenon occurred, prompting the name change.) From the beginning, everyone involved thought that secrecy would be a really good idea, since most Americans wanted nothing to do with aliens unless it was watching them get vaporized on screens in movie theaters. As a result of this super-secrecy, only three people in the CIA were aware of the APA, and two of them thought it was the Amateur Poolplayers Association. Workers at Area 52 were instructed to tell friends and family members that they were employed as insurance salesmen so as to discourage further inquiry.

Agent Hays opened the barrack door. Peter entered first, followed by Cyril and Ben. Hays followed them in, flipped a light switch, and closed the door behind them. The structure was sparsely furnished: against the right wall were a pair of unmade bunk beds, to the left was a large desk perched in front of some dust-clad metal shelving, and at the far end – the aluminum elevator doors.

Hays approached the elevator, inserted a key and turned it, then pushed a white button next to the doors. The elevator hummed. They waited. For a while.

"Is this ship supposed to be going anywhere?" asked Cyril. "And another thing – people say the *Rev 9* is an unattractive spacecraft?"

"It's a building," Peter said. "And despite that fact, it still has more aesthetic appeal than the *Rev 9* by orders of magnitude."

Just then the elevator doors opened and Hays motioned them in. Overhead the Muzak version of "Telstar" played. "Brace yourselves." The elevator doors closed, Hays pushed a button on a panel next to the doors, and the car plunged like it was in free-fall.

"It feels like we're in free-fall," Ben said, suppressing the urge to scream like a nine-year-old girl.

"Pretty much," Hays said. Ben suddenly regretted leaving the air sickness bag on the Learjet. After about a minute the elevator car decelerated sharply, and then stopped. Then the doors opened, and they walked out into a gray corridor with steel doors on each side. Hays led them, and he took a right turn at the first intersecting hallway.

"Well, the privacy factor is off the meter," Peter said. "But I'm not crazy about the color scheme and lack of natural lighting."

Hays stopped at the second door on the right.

"Benjamin, you'll be in here. After your debriefing you'll be sent back to Texas."

"Hey, hey, hey!" Cyril said. "I sort of had my heart set on taking him back with me."

"You're in the Milky Way Galaxy now," Hays said. "I will refer you to the Galactic Code of 1974, article 17, section 4, paragraph 11. In short, just because you have the ability to remove a sentient life form from a sovereign planet doesn't make it legal."

Cyril frowned. "Define sentient."

Hays shook his head, unlocked the door, and showed Benjamin in. There was a wooden table with two chairs (one on each side), a single light hanging from the ceiling, a mirror on one wall, and to the right a smaller door that Ben guessed led to a lavatory. He took a seat at the table, and Hays locked the door behind him.

Hays walked Peter and Cyril down another gray hallway, then another, then yet another. He unlocked a door, and motioned them in. This was a larger room, also with a single light, a mirror on one wall, a door to the right, and a larger table with two chairs on each side.

"Take a seat." Peter and Cyril sat next to one another at the table. "Someone will be with you eventually." And with that Hays closed the door and locked it.

After what seemed like a couple of hours, the door unlocked. A thin man with thinning hair, thin lips, thin-framed glasses, and a sweater vest entered and sat across the table from Ben.

"I'm Dr. Etter," he said. He put his briefcase on the table and extended a hand to Ben.

"I'm Ben Cotter. Aren't you going to lock the door?"

"No need, really," said Dr. Etter. "First, you don't

have a key to the elevator. That's the only way out. And second, you open one wrong door down here and before you know it you're watching your own small intestines being consumed by a ravenous Brawnroggler from Morpeth 7." Ben flinched a little. "Just kidding. They usually keep that door locked." Dr. Etter opened the briefcase and removed an envelope, and from the envelope he removed Ben's keys, wallet, and cell phone and placed them on the table.

"Thank you!" Ben said, reaching for them.

"Ah, not yet," said Dr. Etter. "We have specific protocols here. Just confirm that these are yours, and you'll get them back once you're back up top."

"Yes, those are mine," Ben said. Dr. Etter checked off some boxes on a form, then put the form back in the briefcase.

"Now, I understand you're the victim of an alien abduction," said Dr. Etter. He leaned back, eyeing Ben.

"Yes," Ben said. "Since late Wednesday morning."

"That must have been very traumatic for you. Want to talk about it?" He removed a legal pad from his briefcase.

"Sure," Ben said. "I had just wrecked my car, and I was walking to get help. I ran into Cyril, and then he attacked me and took me on board his spaceship. Then he took me to Alabama – that's across state lines, if that makes a difference." Telling his story made Ben feel a little better.

"Umm hmm," Etter said. He balanced the legal pad on one knee and scribbled some notes.

"Then, when we were in Atlanta, he shot me with something called a 'plasma immobilizer.' That *really* hurt."

"What else did he do?" Etter asked.

"He's just been so *rude*," Ben said. "And condescending. Which doesn't make sense, because he's obviously not as bright or sophisticated as Peter. He's the other Blutaarkian."

"Blutaarkians you say?" Etter leaned forward, resting his forearms on the edge of the table. "Interesting. How did you know they're from Blutaark?"

"Cyril told me."

"Uh huh," Etter said. "Dr. Cotter, is there any history of mental illness in your family?"

"Not yet," Ben said. "That I know of. Why do you ask?"

"Do you take drugs, Ben?" Etter asked. "You know, illegal drugs? Specifically, drugs that make you hallucinate. LSD? Peyote? Mushrooms?"

"Of course not!" Ben said. "You think I'm making all of this up!"

"Not at all," said Dr. Etter. "We just have to cover all the bases. You understand."

"I suppose."

"You said Cyril – the Blutaarkian – attacked you?"

"Yes," Ben said.

Etter reached into his briefcase and pulled out a doll that looked disturbingly like Ben Cotter, and placed it on the table in front of him. "Can you show me on the doll where he touched you?"

"No!" Ben said. "I mean, that's not what happened!" The door burst open and a bespectacled woman with long red hair stormed into the room. Etter threw the doll back into his briefcase. Ben grabbed his wallet and stuck it in his pocket.

"Maynard!" said the woman. "We've been over this again and again. Please step out of the room." Etter picked up Ben's phone and keys, closed his briefcase, avoided eye contact, then skulked out of the room and closed the door. "Sorry about that. I'm Constance, from HR."

"What just happened? Ben said.

"That was Maynard Etter," Constance said. "He's our accountant. He has...issues."

"I suspected as much," Ben said. "He really had me going with that Brawnroggler crap."

"Don't you worry your pretty little head," Constance from HR said. "We haven't had a Brawnroggler incident here in months. And our psychologists are working with Maynard." She sighed. "It's just so darned hard to let someone go after they get on with the agency. You just can't fire them, because they'll just go blabbing about this place to *everyone*." She seemed exasperated, despite her perky floral dress. "But if Etter doesn't turn it around, then I'll have to kill him myself. And *that* sucks. Ugh. You can't imagine the paperwork."

"No doubt," Ben said.

"Again, I apologize," Constance said. "We're a little short staffed – it's the annual canoe trip. But Agent Hays will be back to talk with you shortly. Bye!" She left and locked the door.

Agent Hays unlocked the door, entered the room, and juggled the cardboard box as he relocked the door. He sat the box on the table in front of Peter and Cyril. "It looks like I'm going to have to debrief you guys myself. It's a little unorthodox, but almost everyone is out for the annual canoe trip. So, if you don't have any objections..."

"Not at all," Peter said. "I hope they have a safe canoe trip." He had read *Deliverance* at April's. Cyril said nothing and stared at the ceiling tiles.

"Great," Hays said. "Then we'll get started. First,

a little bit about Area 52. What we do here is analyze alien threats. If we think you're a threat to our planet, then you will be held here and studied."

"When you say 'a threat to our planet,' " Peter said, "do you mean like massive deforestation, uncontrolled population growth, and irreversible climate change?"

"If you're not a threat," Hays said, ignoring the question, "then you will be held here and studied. Eventually you'll be released. And the more cooperative you are in sharing your technology with us, the more favorable your release date."

"Just out of curiosity – how many aliens are you holding here?" asked Peter.

"Eleven different species," Hays said. "Fourteen different individuals – unless you count the two-headed Corpuulon as two. Then fifteen. Well, seventeen with you and Cyril here. Or sixteen if you count the Corpuulon as one."

"Where *we* come from," Peter said "we don't count Corpuulons at all. Their table manners are boorish, and what they try to pass off as professional theater is hackneyed and amateurish."

"Speaking of where you come from," Hays said. "You two are from Blutaark, correct?"

"We are," Peter said. Cyril still refused to speak.

"We know a little bit about your planet," Hays said. "Advanced civilization, developers of a revolutionary spacecraft propulsion system, wicked painful neurotoxin..."

"You've done your homework."

"The Corpuulons have provided us with some background information," Hays said. "And we used to have an intergalactic trader from Bubjai. He was a fount of information – but mostly about what kind of throw rugs and occasional furniture Blutaarkians favor. We take what we can get. But you two are the first Blutaarkians we've actually had the pleasure to meet."

"Well," Peter said, "I apologize that half of them had to be Cyril." Cyril said nothing but shot Peter a look, then crossed his arms and resumed examining ceiling tiles. "But since you know about Blutaark, then you must know that we pose no threat to the people of Earth."

"I've seen video of you driving in Atlanta," Hays said. "But assuming that you don't get behind the wheel of a car, then, yeah, I'm guessing you're probably not much of a threat to Earthlings. So that brings me to the big question...why are you here?"

Peter had anticipated this question. He didn't think that divulging his status as a fugitive would help matters, but as long as Cyril kept quiet he could keep that under wraps. Peter was loath to surrender the crown jewels of Blutaarkian technology: the BAT and the inflationary propulsion system installed on both the *Rev 2* and Cyril's *Rev 9*. But telling Hays that he and Cyril were just "dropped off" on Earth to find jobs, settle down, and raise families would be met with justifiable skepticism, if not outright torture (above and beyond exposure to Hays's Hawaiian shirts.) If Peter was going to be coerced to give up one of the spaceships, if would have to be the *Rev 2*, which – the last time he checked – was broken. Cyril's *Rev 9* was their ticket off of the planet, so its existence could not be acknowledged. Peter hoped that Cyril played along, or at least kept his mouth shut.

"Why are we here?" Peter said. "Bad luck, mostly. Cyril and I were returning from a survey mission on Gyllenhaal 6. We're naturalists for the Life Sciences Administration on Blutaark, and our work entails seeking out and documenting the flora and fauna of whatever planet we're assigned."

"After your mission on Gyllenhaal 6, were you assigned to study life on Earth?" asked Hays.

"No," Peter said. He looked at Cyril, who seemed to be playing along. For now. "There was a technical problem with the inflationary drive on our spacecraft. Earth was the closest planet that was compatible with Blutaarkian life. To make matters worse, we were running low on conventional rocket fuel, so we came within a muon's width of crash landing."

"Where did you land?"

"In Alabama," Peter said.

"That's entirely consistent with an emergency landing," Hays said. "No one lands in Alabama on purpose. But could you be more specific about where you landed?"

"In an auto junkyard," Peter said. "Near Birmingham." Agent Hays changed his tack. He reached into the cardboard box and pulled out the BAT.

"What, exactly, is *this*?"

"Careful," bluffed Peter. "That's a death ray."

"It's a pretty crappy death ray," Hays said. "Our boys in the tech department have been shining it at each other for the last couple of hours without any of them getting so much as a sore throat. The blue and white lights are rather striking, but they tell me this thing has way more computational power than one could possibly need for a flashlight. Or a death ray."

"Mind if I take a gander?" Peter said. Agent Hays obliged, and handed it to him. Peter looked at the BAT. It appeared to be intact, but as he turned it over he noticed that the LCD screen had been smashed, making any readout unintelligible. The

Alien Phenomena Agency had no idea what they had. At least for now. He couldn't resist pointing out the broken screen to Hays. "See? This is why Earthlings can't have nice things." He handed it back to Hays.

"So what is it?"

"It's called a BioScan," Peter said. "It's what we use as LSA scouts to scan and document alien life. It can analyze the anatomy, physiology, and genetic composition of any given life form, then archives the data.

"Then what do you do with that information?"

"Take it back to Blutaark," Peter said. "We're just the scouts. I can't say for certain what the LSA does with the data, but it doesn't seem to be for any nefarious reasons. Historically, Blutaarkians have been big on knowledge for the sake of knowledge. Sure, we're practical too, and we'll use our pansophy to make our lives a little easier. But you won't find us imploding entire planets just because our leader's psychological development got stuck on 'adolescent.' In fact, Blutaark shares its knowledge and technological advances with other planets, provided they are not outright hostile to us. Just about anyone with enough bunjits can purchase a quality spacecraft equipped with our patented inflationary drive system."

"So if it's just a BioScan, why would you lie to me about it?" Hays said.

"It's proprietary technology," Peter said. "The LSA put a lot of time and effort and funding into R&D for the BioScan, and they hate it when one gets lost or stolen. They'll probably dock me two weeks' pay just for that cracked LCD screen."

Agent Hays put the BAT back into the box, and removed Cyril's belt. "Cyril, can you tell me what all of these devices are?" Hays held up the belt with one hand, and swept the other past the belt like a model presenting a matching washer-dryer on a TV game show. Cyril sat, arms folded, and scowled. "I see. Well, we've removed one item that appeared to be some kind of stun gun. But frankly, we're sort of clueless as to what some of these things are. Peter, perhaps you can tell me?

"The 'stun gun' is what we call a plasma immobilizer," Peter said. Hays knew what it was, so Peter saw no reason to lie about it. "It has three settings, if you haven't figured that out yet. Setting 3 will kill most anything smaller than a giant Reptoglyph of Oosterhaut 3. Setting 2 will immobilize anything with a nervous system for at least five minutes. It will also make anything with a digestive system a pariah for the better part of an hour. Setting 1 is handy for warming up tea or coffee. As for those other items on Cyril's belt, I'm not sure I'd be much help. Cyril is very protective of it, so I just never really paid it much attention. Just between you and me, Agent Hays, I think Cyril wears it mostly to impress the ladies. You know...to compensate for other arenas in which he might be lacking."

Cyril snorted, turned to Peter and tried to scowl harder.

"What about this?" Hays pulled the *Rev 9*'s hover control device from the belt, flipped it open, and started pushing buttons at random. Peter suppressed a gasp as he pictured the *Rev 9* plunging 25,000 meters and smashing into a field in northern Georgia. Then he remembered they were currently beneath 3,000 meters of rock, where the transmitter was useless.

"I think it's a garage door opener or something," Peter said. He glanced at Cyril and caught him grinning.

"What about this?" Hays said. He removed a small black container, opened it, and poured dozens of pearl white button-sized tablets onto the table.

"Again," Peter said, "and this is just a guess, but it probably has something to do with the ladies. Either breath mints or a vasodilator." Cyril stopped grinning.

"Okay," Hays said. "I can see we're not going to get very far tonight, so let's just call it a day." With his hand he swept the tiny white tablets off of the table and back into the container, and then he gathered the BAT and Cyril's belt, put them back into the cardboard box, and stood up. "I'll take you both to a room where you can rest for the night. You'll want to get a good night's sleep. We'll be leaving first thing in the morning – for a field trip. I'm assuming your spacecraft is still in that junkyard near Birmingham?"

"I suppose," Peter said. "Unless it's been parted out."

Hays led Cyril and Peter to a small dormitory-style room. It had one desk with a chair, a small refrigerator, indoor-outdoor carpeting, a bathroom, and bunk beds.

"Dibs on top!" Peter said as he leaped into the upper bunk. Cyril sat on the lower bunk.

"I will be back in the morning," Hays said. "We'll leave early." And with that he closed and locked the door. He walked back to Benjamin's room and stuck his head in the door. "It's been a long day for all of us, and I really don't feel like debriefing you tonight. I'm taking Peter and Cyril to Alabama in the morning. You'll go with us and I will debrief you on the plane." Ben hated to drag this out longer than necessary, but he really had no say in the matter.

And it had been a long day. He nodded. "Good,"
Hays said. "I'll take you to a more comfortable room
for the night." He took Ben to a room identical to
Peter and Cyril's room, told him 'goodnight' and
closed the door.

TWENTY-TWO

Ben washed up, turned out the lights, and then crawled into the lower bunk under a blanket. His thoughts meandered, and just as he got cozily warm he decided that he was thirsty. He climbed out of bed and found a bottle of water in the fridge. His eyes adjusted to the dark while he drank, and he noticed a dim light streaming under his door from the corridor. He finished his water, walked to the door, and found it unlocked. His curiosity piqued, Ben walked barefoot into the corridor, turned left and kept walking.

It was quiet except for the faint whir of the ventilation system. The doors lining the corridor were unmarked and windowless, and when his corridor intersected another, Ben took a right turn. An elevator loomed several feet ahead. He pushed a white button on the wall, and when the doors opened he stepped into the elevator. The doors closed, and Ben pushed the one illuminated button and braced for a rocket ride to the surface. Instead, the car seemed to sink. When it stopped, Ben exited into another corridor. Down this hallway there was one door on the left with a small window and a sign that read "quarantine." Ben edged up to the window and peered in. Lying on a cot was a frail young woman with white hair and pale features. Seeing Ben, she struggled to sit up, then looked at him with sunken eyes. The door was locked by a simple latch on the outside. Ben slid the latch and opened the door.

"Are you okay?"

"No," she said in a faint voice. "So tired. So cold." Ben helped her to her feet. He saw that she was humanoid, but not human. Her pale green eyes were set too far apart, her teeth too white, and instead of four fingers and a thumb she had four elongated digits on each hand.

"What is your name?" Ben asked.

"Barbaxaquottlmangaporellianfori," she said, catching her breath.

"Can I call you Barb?" Ben asked.

"No."

"I'm Ben. Let's go." Without knowing why he was doing this or where he was going, he led her out of the room and into the corridor.

"Thank you," she said in a faint voice. "We need to go this way, to the hangar." They crept down the corridor. She took Ben's hand for support. After a few minutes and little progress she stopped to rest, leaning against a wall. "I am languishing here. I need to get home soon. Or I will die."

"How long have you been here?" Ben asked.

"Months. They are not trying to kill me, but they cannot get my nutrition right. It is just a matter of time. Let us keep walking. Just go slowly." They started back down the hallway.

"Are you a threat?" asked Ben. He told himself that perhaps a better time to ask that question was before he had let her out.

"I am," said Barbaxaquottlmangaporellianfori. "But only if I tell them what they want to know. That is why they have not allowed me to return to my home planet of Nog. I will not talk." They reached another hallway, and she led him to the right.

"What do they want to know?" Ben said.

"The secret of longevity," she said. "My race developed a way to extend life span. It is really not so difficult. It just involves some tweaking of the genetic code, a low-carb diet, and reading poetry at least twelve minutes a day."

"Twelve minutes a day?" Ben said. "Ouch. Almost defeats the purpose. But if that's all they wanted, why don't you tell them?"

"It would destroy this planet," she said. "Earth is not ready. The population explosion would result in famine, water shortages, wars, really really bad parking. And do you really want to see a Rolling Stones 100th Anniversary Tour?"

"Not to mention all of that poetry," remarked Ben. They were interrupted by the sound of footsteps in the distance, followed by an alarm. A pulsating red light filled the corridor.

"They are coming," she said. "We are almost there." They took a left turn, and then another right. She stopped next to a utility door. "Open it." Benjamin opened the door. "There, get the mop and bucket." Benjamin grabbed the bucket and the mop, the bucket still half-full with dirty mop water. *Yeah, I can totally see how this is going to help.* For good measure he picked up a yellow "wet floor" sign. "Now what?"

"Follow me this way." The deafening alarms muted the sound of the approaching footsteps, but their rhythmic pounding shook the floor. Barbaxaquottlmangaporellianfori came to a long window that looked into a hangar housing a half-dozen alien craft. She touched a pad next to the window and an opening appeared in the wall. "Start mopping, moving slowly this way. I just need you to slow them down, I need a minute to get my ship onto the lift, and then I am home free." She took some deep breaths. "Please do not tell them anything."

"Good luck," Ben said as he made wide, sloppy sweeps across the floor with the wet mop.

"You too." She moved from the door to where Ben was standing, stood on her toes, and kissed him full on the lips. "Thank you. You saved my life. And perhaps your planet." She turned and went into the hangar, and the door *whooshed* shut behind her.

Ben mopped, backing slowly toward the hangar window, his gaze fixed toward the far end of the corridor. Out of the corner of his eye, he could see one of the smaller spacecraft rolling across the hangar floor toward a metal platform.

The guards appeared, rendered in stop motion by the blinding red lights that strobed through the corridor. There were maybe eight or nine of them, wearing helmets with visors, dressed in fatigues, and carrying weapons that just happened to be pointing toward Ben. He mopped faster.

"Where is she?" shouted one of the guards. They all moved closer.

Ben looked in their direction, but in his peripheral vision he saw the spacecraft in the hangar creeping onto the lift. "Who?" he yelled over the cacophony.

"Barbaxaquottlmangaporellianfori," he said. They were now just a few feet away.

"Sorry," shouted Ben. "I'm not good with names over five syllables. What does she look like?" He swung the mop in an arc across the floor in front of him, then turned his head toward the window and saw her spacecraft sitting dead still on the lift.

"Drop the mop or we'll shoot!" A ruby red laser beam traced from one of the weapons to Ben's forehead. Ben dropped the mop.

"Careful, wet floor." Two of the guards were on him in an instant and forced Ben against the wall. A third man hit the pad and dashed into the hangar. Two more men ran up to the open hangar door, and despite the conspicuously placed warning sign, one slipped on the freshly-mopped floor. His rifle discharged as he hit the ground.

Ben felt his chest explode and watched his blood splatter onto the helmets of the men holding him against the wall. The gray corridor that had been illuminated by the red flashing lights went black; not black like night, but black like the underground darkness he had once experienced on a family vacation tour of a cave when the tour guide shut the lights off.

Ben now had that same sense of panic – but with less shrill screaming this time. Back in the cave of his childhood, the lights had come back on almost immediately. This time the blackness lingered, until eventually he saw a dim light in the distance. His eyes adjusted, and the light seemed to intensify and grow closer. His head throbbed hard.

Ben realized that he wasn't dead, that the beam of light was from light in the corridor spilling into his room under the door, and that his head throbbed because he had sat bolt upright during a bad dream after falling asleep in the lower bunk of a not-quite-adult-sized bunk bed. He got out of bed and turned on the light and went into the bathroom. He was already developing a nasty bruise on his forehead. He tried to piece together the dream, but his recollection was spotty.

It wasn't all bad. There was the kiss. *Please, do not tell them anything*, she said.

TWENTY-THREE

The next morning Agent Hays roused Peter and Cyril, and then stopped by Ben's room. He was still in bed.

"Be ready to go in fifteen minutes."

"I'm really not up to this," Ben said, pulling the blanket over his shoulders. "Do I have to go?"

"Sorry," Hays said. "I have my orders. You're going."

Twenty minutes later, Agent Hays, Peter, Cyril, and Ben were in the main elevator. Mostly due to gravity, it was taking significantly longer for the elevator to get from the bottom of Area 52 to the surface than it did to get from the surface to the bottom of Area 52. Cyril chose this moment to break his silence.

"This thing is sooo slow." Cyril turned and looked at Ben for the first time that morning. "What the hell happened to your head?"

"I hit it on the bed," Ben said. "It's rather small."

"It's a little bigger now with that lump," Cyril said, demonstrating why sentient life forms throughout the universe were known to sit and debate in pubs for hours on end as to whether Cyril of Blutaark was more insulting when he was trying to be insulting, or whether he was more insulting when he was just trying to make ordinary conversation.

"I meant the bed."

"Right," Cyril said. Then he resumed being silent and irritated.

The elevator doors opened and they stepped into the barrack with its bunk bed, desk, and metal shelves. There were five men waiting for them; four of them carried automatic weapons and wore camo and helmets with visors. Ben's chest started to hurt a little bit. Hays introduced the fifth man.

"This is Dr. Mitchell," Hays said. "He will be joining us for technical assistance. Dr. Mitchell is an aeronautical and an electrical engineer. He's also well-versed in computer technology and Lithuanian folk medicine." Dr. Mitchell stood with one hand on his hip. He was fit and muscular, wore a short-sleeved knit shirt and khaki trousers, and he smiled more than most people associated with super-secret government agencies smiled. In one hand he held an athletic bag, prompting Peter to look at Agent Hays to see if he was holding a not-athletic bag. Mitchell gave a quick nod, and they all nodded back.

"Peter," said Mitchell. "We analyzed satellite photos from all of the salvage yards in and around Birmingham. I saw nothing that looked like an alien spacecraft."

"It's not very big," Peter said. "And we disguised it with body parts."

"Body parts?" said Mitchell, now not smiling. "What kind of monsters are you?"

"He means car body parts," Cyril said. He rolled his eyes. "Duh."

"Do you recall the location of the salvage yard where you and Cyril landed the spacecraft?" Hays said.

Where you and Cyril landed the spacecraft, thought Ben. *He thinks they arrived on Earth together in Peter's ship. Great.*

"Not exactly," Peter said. "I recall lots of trees. Green ones. And dirt roads. They were sort of reddish-brown. Like the desert plains of Elspeet 2. Does that help?"

Hays sighed. "After we land we'll drive to each salvage yard until we find one that looks familiar to you. Let's go, shall we?" Hays and Mitchell led the way out of the building, followed by Peter, Cyril, and Ben. The four armed men brought up the rear. Once on the plane, Peter and Cyril were instructed to sit at the front of the cabin, and Ben sat with Agent Hays in the back. Mitchell sat alone in the middle, and the four guards were scattered throughout the cabin. After takeoff, Hays took a small recording device out of his shirt pocket, switched it on, and put it back into his pocket. "Let's get started."

"You know," Ben said. "I'm not so sure this is a good idea. My thinking is all fuzzy. I took a pretty good blow to the head. Maybe I need a CAT scan..."

"I'm sure you'll do fine," Hays said. "Just answer the questions truthfully and to the best of your knowledge. So where did you first meet Peter and Cyril?"

"Oh, gosh," Ben said. "That was right after I wrecked my car. I was driving from Dallas to Hilldale. Hilldale is a small town in North Texas. Well, everything's relative, right? I mean it's much smaller than Dallas, but it's actually a little larger than say – Elgin. I have a satellite office there – in Hilldale, not Elgin. And by satellite, I don't mean like it's orbiting the planet. I just mean that it's a remote office, smaller than my main one, which I travel to once a week. I'm an ophthalmologist. Did I mention that?" Ben wondered if he could keep this up for the duration of the flight. "My parents were so proud when I got accepted into medical school. Proud, but also a little surprised because of that little dorm incident during my sophomore year -"

"Dr. Cotter," said Agent Hays. "Do you remember the question I asked you?"

"Why, yes," Ben said. "I'm pretty sure I do."

"Answer it. Now."

"Sorry, little trouble focusing," Ben said. "I took a pretty good blow to the head. Did you guys get those bunk beds from an orphanage or something?"

"Answer the question!" Hays barked.

Well that worked for all of three minutes, thought Ben. *Time for Plan B – playing stupid.* "Yes, the question you're referring to is where did I meet Peter and Cyril?"

"Yes."

"Well, that's easy," Ben said. "Actually, I only recall meeting Cyril. I was walking across this field after I had wrecked my car. I saw this spaceship sitting in a clearing, and when I went to check it out Cyril appeared from behind the spacecraft."

"Continue," Hays said.

"Well, we exchanged pleasantries," Ben said. "I thought his behavior – and appearance, too – seemed a bit odd. I got the same feeling in the pit of my stomach that I get whenever I'm in a room with a conspiracy theorist. He seemed a bit irritated, annoyed that I had stumbled upon him and his spaceship. I distinctly recall that he didn't want to let me leave. I explained that I had patients waiting who needed my attention, and I started to walk away."

"What did the spacecraft look like?" interjected Hays. This question threw Ben off of his narrative. He wondered if Hays was trying to trip him up, and he told himself to not think about the *Rev 9.* "It wasn't very large, and it certainly didn't look like a suitcase." *Crap!* "It was somewhat larger than an SUV. And it was sort of a battleship gray, or primer gray. And it had sort of a partial domed window over the cockpit...are you familiar with 'The Jetsons?' "

"Sure," Hays said. "Ruh-roh!" came out before he caught himself. He reminded himself to redact that portion of the transcript.

"Well, it looked sort of like The Jetsons space car, but with less canopy and more fuselage."

"I see," Hays said. "Why did you say that it didn't look like a suitcase?"

"I don't believe I did," Benjamin said.

"You most certainly did," said Agent Hays. "I am recording this. I can play it back for you if you like. You said 'it certainly didn't look like a suitcase.' "

"That's odd," Ben said. "I guess maybe I said that because some spaceships do look like suitcases. You know, like the one on *Star Trek*. What's it called?"

"The Enterprise?"

"Yeah," Ben said. "That's the one."

"The U.S.S. Enterprise looks nothing like a suitcase. And I've seen more than my share of suitcases. And spaceships."

"Sure it does," Ben said. "You have to be looking at it from just the right angle."

"What kind of suitcase?" Hays asked.

"What do you mean?"

"What kind of suitcase resembles the U.S.S Enterprise?" Hays persisted.

"There's that Samsonite model," Ben said. "It's rather modern looking, and it very much looks like a spacecraft. And very much unlike Cyril's ship." Ben knew that his argument was unraveling, but he felt powerless to stop the onslaught of questions.

"Nonsense," Hays said. "That model looks nothing like the Enterprise. If anything, it vaguely resembles The Millennium Falcon. But not at all like the Enterprise."

"I think that's what I meant," Ben said. "I meant The Millennium Falcon. I get *Star Trek* and *Star Wars* confused."

"I don't believe you," Hays said.

"What?"

"No one confuses *Star Trek* and *Star Wars*," Hays said. "Sure, they're both dramatic works of contemporary science fiction that feature alien life forms and a variety of spaceships, but they're entirely different. It would be like confusing The Beatles and The Rolling Stones."

"I did that once, too," Ben said.

"You confused The Beatles and The Rolling Stones?"

"I thought the song 'I Wanna Be Your Man' was by The Rolling Stones," Ben said. "But it's actually The Beatles."

"You're still confused," Hays said. "Lennon and McCartney wrote it, The Beatles recorded it, but so did The Rolling Stones."

"Which version do you think I was listening to?" Ben said. He was relieved that he had managed to divert the conversation away from the topic of spaceships and suitcases.

"I have no idea," Hays said in exasperation. "It doesn't matter. I was simply trying to get at why you would say that a spaceship did not look like a suitcase."

"Because it didn't," Ben said.

"Yes, yes, I get that," said Agent Hays. "But there are probably millions of objects that don't look like spaceships. I'm simply dumbfounded as to why you chose suitcase instead of say, a yardstick, or a Box Elder, or a suspension bridge."

"Well it didn't look like any of those either," Ben said.

"I know!" Hays said. He rubbed his temples.

"Ah!" Ben said. "I've got it."

"You've got what?" Hays asked.

"I know why I said 'suitcase,' " Ben said. "When I was a child I had this sort of verbal dyslexia, where I would unconsciously substitute one compound word for another compound word that started with the same letters. For example, instead of 'foothills' I might say 'firehouse,' or instead of 'backspin' I might say 'bullshit.' So instead of 'spacecraft' I said 'suitcase.' That blow to the head probably triggered it."

Hays rubbed his temples harder. "Okay. Let's just go back to your meeting with Cyril. What happened next?"

"I tried to walk away," Ben said. "But he must have shot me with something, because the next thing I knew I was flat on the ground in the middle of that house fire, suffering through the most intense pain I'd ever experienced. And then I passed out."

"House fire?"

"Oh, sorry," Ben said. "I meant hayfield. There I go again."

"But house fire isn't a compound word," said Agent Hays. "It's two separate...never mind. What happened after that?"

"Well, I regained consciousness," Ben said. "And I was sitting in the back of a Jeep Cherokee with Cyril. I think he was napping. And Peter was driving. And I'm using the word 'driving' very loosely here. He was speeding and swerving in and out of traffic. It's no wonder he got pulled over."

"So," Hays said. "You don't recall anything between that field in Texas and getting arrested in

Atlanta?"

"Afraid not," Ben said. "Maybe it was that blow to the head." Hays reached into his pocket and turned off the recorder.

"Neurotoxin."

"I'm sorry?" Ben said.

"Blutaarkians have a neurotoxin that they use to incapacitate other living things." Hays said. "It causes extreme pain, and usually loss of consciousness. I guess we can add amnesia to the list. At least in your case." Ben picked up a hint of skepticism in his voice.

Agent Hays swallowed some aspirin and closed his eyes. He didn't open them again until the pilot announced that they were on approach to Birmingham. The plane was met on the tarmac by a large, black, windowless van. They all piled in. Mitchell drove, and they took off for the first junkyard. At the third junkyard, Mitchell pulled the van into an empty red-dirt parking lot next to a double-wide mobile home that doubled as an office.

"This looks like the one," Peter said. Mitchell maneuvered the van closer to the junkyard's fence and parked.

For once in his life, Peter was without a solid game plan. He had anticipated staying on Earth indefinitely; he would maintain a low profile, use the BAT discreetly, catch some live theater, and maybe master the doughnut trade. Once Cyril gave up searching for him, it would have been easy enough to call for a towship and get the *Rev 2* back into commission on Gyllenhaal 6. Then the universe would be his again. But now the Alien Phenomena Agency had the BAT. And it looked like they were about to get the *Rev 2* as well.

TWENTY-FOUR

It was an unseasonably warm October afternoon in Atlanta. April mixed a pitcher of lemonade, gathered a handful of red plastic cups, and went outside. She walked across the parking lot to Martina's SUV, and before she could tap on the window it buzzed open.

"It's kinda warm out," April said. "I brought you some lemonade. Sorry, it's not fresh-squeezed." She handed Martina two cups and poured.

"Thanks," Martina said. She handed a cup to her twin in the passenger seat. They both stared down into their cups without drinking.

"I know what you're thinking," April said. "It's okay. I used low-cal sweetener." They looked at her, smiled and nodded, and took sips from their cups. "Oh, it's not drugged or poisoned or anything, if you were wondering." They weren't. They ignored April and sipped their lemonade. April poured a cup for herself, gulped it, and walked to the other SUV. This time she had to tap on the window. "I imagine it's pretty warm in there. I brought you guys some lemonade." She handed two cups to Jason and poured.

"Thank you," Jason said. He handed a cup to Brian.

"I'm sorry it's not fresh-squeezed," April said.

"But I made up for it by adding lots of real sugar. I mean a *ton* of sugar. I like my lemonade really sweet." She poured herself another cup and drank, but Jason and Brian were already drinking.

"It's good," Jason said.

"Thanks," April said. "And as I told Martina, it's not poisoned or drugged or anything." She topped off her cup and drank some more, as if to make her point. "So how much is Dionysus paying you to watch my front door?"

"That's none of your – wait, who's Dionysus?" Jason said.

"Dionysus Pharmaceutical. Look, I know. Marina over there is the daughter of one of the guys in corporate. It's no big secret."

"She's a corporate investigator too?" Jason said. He made a face like he had just said something he shouldn't have. "We thought they were...party girls."

"Party girls?" April said. "I suppose that's a euphemism for something. No, she's here for the same reason you are. Peter. Or more precisely – Peter and that BAT. I'd like to know where they are, too. But I don't. But feel free to hang out in my parking lot. Just watch out for my neighbor who lives above me. If she asks what you're doing, just tell her you're stalking me, or that you're a drug dealer, because if she thinks you're a Mormon missionary she'll call the cops."

"Thanks for the heads up," Jason said.

"So if you're not with Dionysus, who do you work for?" April said. Jason closed the car window. "Never mind," she shouted. "Enjoy the lemonade." April took the tray off of the hood and started back to her apartment. She stopped, went back to the SUV, and tapped on the window. Jason opened it a crack. "There's been a change in plans. I just remembered that I need to get a few things from the store this afternoon. I really don't think both of you need to follow me, so maybe you could get together with Martina and coordinate who will go and who will stay here. It would save Dionysus some gas money."

"I work for Persona," blurted Jason. He made that face again.

April smiled and walked back to her apartment, and when she reached her door she turned to see Jason standing next to the other SUV, talking to Martina.

"Everybody out," said Agent Hays. The four armed guards were instructed to wait in the parking lot to guard the gate. Ben, Peter, and Cyril followed Hays and Mitchell. The gate was padlocked, but Hays removed something from his pocket, picked the lock, and led them in. "So which way to your spacecraft?"

"I think it's over there, in that direction," Peter said, pointing toward a long row of junked vehicles to his right. Hays nodded and Peter led the way.

Peter found the *Rev 2* without difficulty. The canopy had been exposed when Cyril had removed some auto body parts to gain access to the cockpit, but it had since remained untouched. Agent Hays and Dr. Mitchell stood on one side of the vehicle, and Ben, Cyril, and Peter stood on the other.

"No wonder we couldn't find it in the satellite photos," said Mitchell. For the first time since they were at Area 52, Peter noticed Mitchell holding the athletic bag.

"You guys start pulling the rest of that crap off of the ship," Hays said.

Ben and Peter started removing the shell of junked auto body panels from the *Rev 2* as Cyril stood and watched with his arms folded. It did not take long to unveil the *Rev 2* – a marvel of technology, even by intergalactic standards.

"Impressive," said Dr. Mitchell when the spacecraft was almost completely uncovered. He knelt on one knee, opened his athletic bag, and removed the BAT. When Mitchell stood, Peter was both delighted and disheartened to see the BAT.

"Planning on analyzing some biological samples out here, are we Dr. Mitchell?" Peter said.

"Your BioScan story was so close to believable," said Hays. "But we're thinking that the BAT is somehow critical to the operation of the *Rev 2* – either for propulsion or navigation. Either way, it should prove to be quite valuable to us."

"Well this is turning out to be the worst field trip ever," Peter said. "Don't you guys have a natural history museum, or planetarium that we could visit instead?"

"We're in Alabama," interjected Ben.

"How about you just pop the hood on this thing, and we'll see where this BAT goes," Hays said.

"You're going to be more disappointed than Cyril's parents," Peter said. Cyril growled.

"Do it," insisted Hays.

"Don't say I didn't warn you," Peter said. He entered a code and popped open the canopy of the *Rev 2*.

"Welcome back," chirped Soledad. "If I had known you were bringing company, I would have freshened up a bit."

"No worries," Peter said. "It's just that these gentlemen rarely have the opportunity to see an inflationary-drive equipped spacecraft that hasn't been smashed to bits on the ground, so I thought I'd let them check you out."

"That's fi – wait a minute," Soledad said, her tone changing from perky to apprehensive. "You are not planning on getting rid of me, are you? After everything we have been through together?"

"Soledad, no," Peter said. "That's not it at all. There aren't enough bunjits on this entire planet to convince me to sell you."

"It's about that landing, isn't it? I should have deployed the chutes automatically. But I *did* apologize. Doesn't that count for something?"

"Calm down," Peter said. "I promise, once we're done here I will take you back to Gyllenhaal 6 for a nice tune-up and some premium fuel. Doesn't that sound nice?"

"I guess," Soledad said. "Promise?"

"Promise," Peter said. "Okay, we just want to take a little look-see under the hood." Hays put his hand over his holstered gun as Peter reached into the cockpit. He pulled a lever and the hood popped open.

"Really?" Ben said. "Intergalactic spaceships have hoods? I suppose it has a trunk, too." Everyone ignored him. Mitchell leaned against the spacecraft and peered into the propulsion unit bay. He held the BAT in various locations and configurations, but nothing seemed quite right.

"What about there?" Hays said, pointing to the spot where the orange-colored starter used to be. Peter looked at Cyril and frowned.

"No," said Mitchell. "It sure looks like a component is missing, but the BAT has an entirely different size and shape." He moved on to the cockpit and leaned in, and like a prince with a size-14 crystal slipper in a kingdom of dainty-footed lasses, resumed his search for the spot where he thought the BAT belonged. Still no luck. He stood, looked at Hays and shrugged.

"No matter," Hays say. "We'll get one of the trucks to haul this back to the hangar in Nevada, and go over it with a fine-toothed comb." He paused. "Hold on. What about the trunk?"

"Oh. My. God," Ben said. "Seriously? It's got a trunk?"

"You know the drill," Hays said to Peter. "Open the trunk." Peter reached into the *Rev 2*, slid a latch and the trunk lid swung open. Mitchell moved to the rear of the vehicle. Peter joined him.

"It's just a trunk," Mitchell said after taking a look-see. "Strictly for storage, apparently. No functional components that I can tell." He reached in and picked up a pair of worn sneakers, and just as quickly dropped them back into the trunk. "Good Lord." His eyes pooled with tears and he retched. "Remind me to warn the lab that they'll need a biohazard bag for those." Mitchell quickly moved back to the side of the *Rev 2* and stood next to the cockpit. Peter put his hand on the trunk to close it. Looking in, he spied a red-and-gray box, roughly the size of a pack of cigarettes, stuck on the inner surface of the trunk lid. He grabbed it, pocketed it, and slammed the lid shut. He looked at Agent Hays, who was now next to Mitchell, gazing into the cockpit. Peter walked away from the rear of the vehicle and stood with Ben and Cyril. Hays looked up from the cockpit, and his eyes locked onto Peter's. Hays was wearing his Very Serious Face – the expression that humans wear when they have to deliver bad news, or attend the opera. And Peter knew why.

"There is only room for one person in this space vehicle," Hays said.

That's when the shooting started.

After talking with Martina, Jason returned to his SUV. He had a phone call to make. Jason hesitated to call Tor Kinney; it was very likely that Tor had not recuperated from yesterday's brush with humiliation and Blutaarkian neurotoxin, but Taryn's intensity scared the bejesus out of him. He decided that he would rather have a woman verbally berate him than to hear a grown man sob uncontrollably, so Jason called Taryn.

She was in the middle of archery practice. She grew visibly irked when her private cell phone ringtone sounded. Taryn told her mother to remove the apple from the top of her head and "take five" while she fielded the call. Her annoyance with the interruption was superseded by an even greater annoyance with an upstart startup pharmaceutical company after Jason informed her that Dionysus was also in the hunt for Peter and the BAT. She lauded Jason for being proactive, and for his diligence and good judgment in informing her of the situation. Taryn murmured something about "shoo-in for employee of the month" and a "nine-dollar Shoeland gift card" and ended the call.

Taryn Yuanuin wanted to know why another corporation was looking for Peter, how they knew about the BAT, and how much they knew about it. She had been dragged into that emergency meeting by Tor on Saturday, and she relished the thought of inconveniencing others by demanding an emergency meeting on a Sunday. It only seemed fair. Besides, it *was* an emergency. And unlike Jason, she had no qualms about calling Tor. His tears always seemed to cheer her up, for some reason. (Then again, so did everyone's.) But before she called Tor, she needed to get in touch with someone at Dionysus.

Calling the corporate headquarters for Dionysus

Pharmaceutical on a Sunday afternoon will only give the caller a brief recorded message that politely asks the caller to leave a message, or – if it's a dire emergency – to call during regular business hours. "That won't do," Taryn said out loud to herself, and she then proceeded to scour the internet for contact information for anyone connected to Dionysus. She managed to find the cell phone number for an administrative assistant by the name of April Robinson.

"Hello?" April said.

"Is this April Robinson?" Taryn asked.

"Yes it is."

"I need Dirk Reger's cell phone number please," Taryn said. "It's an emergency."

"May I ask who's calling?"

"Look," Taryn said. "I said 'please' *and* I used the word 'emergency.' That should be enough to tear you away from your Velveeta-inspired snack-making for your jersey-clad beer-swilling marginally-employed boyfriend while he watches the Falcons get their asses handed to them. I don't really have time to fax you my full nine-page resume, so suffice it to say that I am Taryn Yuanuin, Chairperson of Persona Health Insurance Corporation. And I need to speak to Dirk. Now."

"Okay," April said. She took a deep breath. April wanted to tell Taryn that she was wrong, that she did not actually have a boyfriend, and if she did he probably wouldn't be a Falcons fan. But she thought that that sounded sadder than having a boyfriend who swilled beer, was marginally employed, and made her prepare Velveeta-based hors d'oeuvres. "Give me a second to look it up."

"Tick-tock, tick-tock," Taryn said.

April found Dirk's private number on her

smartphone and read it to Taryn. "He's probably on the golf -" April said before Taryn abruptly ended the call. Amber grabbed her purse and headed out for the grocery store. She left her phone at home on purpose.

"Hello?" Dirk said.

"Dirk, my name is Taryn Yuanuin. I'll be brief. I'm the Chairperson of Persona Health Insurance. You and I share a common interest in locating a presumed alien named Peter and the device known as the BAT. I would like to arrange a meeting to discuss consolidating our efforts as soon as possible, and by 'as soon as possible' I mean before you take another swing with that golf club."

"Health insurance, you say?" Dirk said. "I'm happy with my current provider. But if you can stand a little constructive criticism, you really need to dial back the high-pressure sales pitch."

"Dirk, listen carefully and just for a minute pretend you don't have ADHD. I am not a salesperson. I chair the board of a major health insurance company in my spare time, but I also manage a hedge fund that could take out Dionysus Pharmaceutical in a hostile takeover, and you would be oblivious to that event until your administrative assistant read the story to you from a two-week old copy of the *Wall Street Journal* while you argued with your landscaper about where the Italian-marble garden fountain should go. I have a significant financial interest in finding Peter. And the BAT. And apparently so does someone at Dionysus, or they would not have gone to the trouble to send investigators to look for him. Perhaps you need to direct me to that individual, because clearly they are a couple of standard deviations smarter than you are."

"Oh, you must mean Frank Francis," Dirk said. "Yeah, he's really smart."

Taryn sighed. "I will be at your corporate office in fifteen minutes. You and Mr. Francis meet me there."

"Do I hafta?" Dirk said. "We're only on the ninth hole."

"No," Taryn said. "You don't hafta. But if you meet me at your office in fifteen minutes, I'll tell you a secret that will knock twelve strokes off of your golf score tomorrow."

"Ohhh, okay," Dirk said. "Just one other thing."

"What?"

"How did you know about the fountain?" Taryn hung up.

Fifteen minutes later, Taryn and Tor Kinney strode into the Dionysus board room on the 27th floor of One Atlanta Plaza. Dr. Frank Francis was seated, his briefcase opened on the table in front of him. Dirk was seated at the head of the table, wearing his tartan golf cap and thumbing through a two-month old issue of *Golf Digest*.

"Hi!" Dirk said. He did not get up.

"Welcome," Frank said, standing as he greeted them. "I'm Dr. Frank Francis. Did you have any trouble getting in?"

"None whatsoever," Taryn said. "But you should probably buy your security guard a cup for Christmas." Taryn sat at the opposite end of the table from Dirk. Tor shook hands with Frank and Dirk and took a seat next to Taryn.

"I am Taryn Yuanuin, and this is the CEO of Persona Health, Tor Kinney."

"So what do we owe the pleasure?" Frank said.

"I'm not one to waste time," Taryn said. "I'm not just going to cut to the chase. I'm going to fast forward past the chase, arrest, conviction, incarceration, and multiple stays of execution and cut to the lethal injection."

"That was really kind of wordy," Dirk said, eyes still glued to his magazine.

"So sorry," Taryn said. She glared at Dirk. "Maybe Dr. Francis can explain everything to you slowly and in monosyllables after the grownups are finished talking. As I was saying, we know about Peter, and we know about the BAT and its capabilities. Its continued presence is a threat, not just to Persona, but to the entire health insurance industry. We are committed to tracking down Peter, destroying the BAT, and making sure that another one is never deployed."

"Whoa, whoa, whoa," Dirk said. He sat his magazine down and leaned forward. "We are committed to tracking down Peter, taking that BAT thing from him, and using it to make boxcar loads of money. Destroying the BAT would make that really hard."

"What I think Dirk is trying to say," Frank said, "is that our goals seem diametrically opposed. So, pooling your resources with ours in order to find Peter – and the BAT – doesn't seem to be in the best interest of either party."

"We have already come very close to apprehending Peter," Taryn said. "You stand to suffer an extraordinary loss if Persona finds him before Dionysus does."

"We've been close to finding Peter as well," Frank said. "And if we find him first, you would also lose – how do the kids say it? 'Bigtime.' "

"The kids don't say that anymore," Dirk said.

"What?" Frank said.

"They don't say 'bigtime' anymore," Dirk said. "I

have kids. And they never say that."

"The point," Frank said, "is that we're at an impasse. I don't see how we can help each other. When the BAT is found, either Persona or Dionysus will lose whether they have been working together to find it or not."

"You are assuming that each party has an equal chance of finding Peter," Tor said. "And I don't think that's the case. I think the odds favor Persona."

"On what do you base that assumption?" Frank said.

"Are you aware that there is a third party who is also searching for Peter and the BAT?" Tor said.

"Were we aware of that?" Dirk said, looking to Frank.

"Just read your magazine," Frank said. "What third party?"

"Obviously we cannot show all of our cards," Tor said. "But suffice it to say that there is an alien bounty hunter with a keen interest in this matter. We know his name, what he looks like...if we find the bounty hunter, he's practically our ticket to Peter."

"So, gentlemen," Taryn said. "That changes the equation in favor of Persona. In fact, our actuaries tell me that there's a sixty-five percent chance that we will find Peter – and the BAT – before you will." Taryn never shied away from making up statistics to bolster a point.

"Then why do you need *us?*" Frank asked.

"Because I don't care to leave anything to chance," Taryn said.

"But if – when – we find the BAT, Dionysus could not stand idly by and watch Persona destroy it," said Dr. Francis. Dirk winced, then drew a deep breath and placed his hand on the table.

"I think it was Robert Frost who said 'A thing of

beauty is a joy forever.' And our revenues and profit margins with the BAT would be gorgeous. Why would you want to destroy that?"

"It wasn't Frost," Taryn said. "It was Keats. And at this point I'd destroy the BAT by crushing it under my designer heels just so I could be the person responsible for the biggest disappointment in your already disappointing life." She turned and spoke directly to Frank. "Persona could not stand idly by and allow Dionysus to destroy the health insurance industry by making health insurance obsolete overnight."

"One other consideration," said Dr. Francis. "If you destroy the BAT – if you eliminate the singular piece of technology that can cure any illness in any human being – it would cause needless pain, suffering...and death...for billions of people."

"Whatever," Taryn and Dirk said in unison.

"Jinx!" Dirk said. "I said 'jinx' first. That means the bad luck's on you."

"No kidding," Taryn said. Dr. Francis removed his glasses, pulled a handkerchief from his pocket, and dabbed his eyes. Then he gestured to Dirk Reger, leaned toward him, and whispered in his ear. They spoke back and forth for several minutes as Tor and Taryn looked on.

"Ms. Yuanuin," Frank said. "Are you concerned about the health insurance industry, or just Persona, per se?"

"I have some minor holdings in other health insurance companies," Taryn said. "But by far, my largest holding in that sector is in Persona."

"I see grounds for compromise," Frank said. "If Dionysus and Persona work together, and Peter and the BAT are found, we could preserve the BAT, use it, and share the profits."

"Ginormous profits," interrupted Dirk.

"Your share — and Tor's as well — would more than compensate you for any losses incurred by the collapse of the health insurance industry," Frank said.

"What sort of share did you have in mind?" Taryn asked.

"Eighty-percent Dionysus, twenty-percent Persona," Frank said. "You and Tor can divide that as you see fit."

"Fifty-fifty," Taryn said. "Anything less is unacceptable."

Frank whispered to Dirk. Dirk nodded, and Frank made a counter offer. "Seventy-five twenty-five."

"Are you deaf?" Taryn said. "I just said anything less than fifty-fifty is unacceptable. In fact, I find Dirk's hat so annoying that my offer is now sixty-forty in favor of Persona."

"Then I guess this meeting is adjourned," Frank said. He started to close his briefcase.

"Not so fast," Taryn said as Tor handed her some papers from his attaché. "It seems that Dirk Reger has his health insurance coverage through the Persona Health Insurance Corporation."

"I don't see how that changes anything," said Dr. Francis.

"You're not threatening to raise my premiums, are you?" asked Dirk. "You're playing hardball now."

"Here's a copy," Taryn said, sliding papers across the table to Frank. "According to our records, Dirk Reger required medical attention for an infection he contracted while he was in Singapore on business last July. Apparently, this pesky infection required a *lot* of penicillin, and probably a fair amount of soul-searching on Dirk's part. Refresh my memory, Dr.

Francis. Does STD stand for 'sore throat disease?' "

"No," Frank said.

"Dirk," Taryn said. "Did you ever mention this infection to your trophy wife?" Taryn had never seen or met Dirk's wife, but she assumed that, like a trophy, any wife of Dirk's would be hard on the outside and empty on the inside.

Dirk and Frank whispered back and forth. Finally Frank turned to Tor and Taryn. "Fifty-fifty."

"Deal," Taryn said. "But only if Dirk agrees never to wear that golf hat in my presence again." Dirk quickly removed the hat. "That concludes our business for now. Good day, gentlemen." Taryn stood and headed toward the door. Tor grabbed his attaché and followed her.

"Excuse me," Dirk said. "Aren't you forgetting something?" Taryn stopped at the door and turned to look at Dirk. "You were supposed to tell me how to drop twelve strokes from my golf score."

"Only play sixteen holes," Taryn said. She walked out with Tor right behind her.

After the door closed Dr. Francis and Dirk sat quietly for a couple of minutes. Finally Dirk spoke. "I don't like her. But she's hot."

"They might actually help us find Peter and the BAT," Frank said. "But still, I think it would be in our best interest to find them first. I just do not trust Taryn or Tor. And, unfortunately, they seem to have a slight advantage over us with that alien bounty hunter. Dionysus needs to leverage its position."

"What did you have in mind?" Dirk said.

"How much trouble would it be for you to hire a new administrative assistant?"

TWENTY-FIVE

Agent Hays, Dr. Mitchell, Peter, Cyril, and Ben were too focused on the *Rev 2* and too far away to hear the front door of the junkyard office swing open, but they heard the shots that followed. Two men stood side-by-side on the porch of the double-wide and flooded the parking lot with semiautomatic rifle fire. The four armed APA guards had been facing the gate, prepared for any attempt by the aliens (and Benjamin) to escape; they were unprepared for an ambush from behind, and never had the opportunity to return fire. As the guards lay dying in the dirt parking lot, the two men turned their attention to the junkyard.

Bullets peppered the rusting hulks of junked cars like hailstones on a roof – if hailstones had a horizontal trajectory, could pierce metal, and could kill you instantly. Hays and Mitchell instinctively dropped to the ground on their side of the *Rev 2*. Peter, Cyril, and Ben hit the ground on the opposite side of the spacecraft, not so much from instinct, but more as an acknowledgement that standing up while being shot at was probably a bad idea.

"You'll never take the Kingpins alive!" shouted one of the men from the porch. He was thin, had short sandy hair, and wore blue jeans and a blue, oil-smudged t-shirt.

"Hold on, Butch," said the other man. He was heavier and stouter, with dark hair pulled into a ponytail. "I don't recollect that we ever discussed any sort of suicide pact. I think under certain circumstances – say if we were faced with overwhelming firepower and no running car with which to attempt an escape, then being taken alive wouldn't be such a bad option." Both men continued to fire sporadically toward the *Rev 2*.

"Sorry, Hobart," said Butch. "I didn't really mean it anyways. I was just trying to be intimidating." Butch stopped shooting, turned toward the junkyard, and shouted. "Correction – under certain circumstances – say if we were faced with overwhelming firepower and no running car with which to attempt an escape, then being taken alive wouldn't be such a bad option."

"Thanks for the clarification," shouted Agent Hays. Butch and Hobart resumed shooting.

Ben sat with his back against the *Rev 2* and his head between his knees. Cyril was on the ground, his arms over his head. Peter stretched out prone on the ground, and when he opened his eyes he could see the BAT lying in the dirt underneath the *Rev 2*.

Peter stretched his arm under the *Rev 2*, but the BAT was just out of reach. He spied a stick on the ground in front of the spacecraft, and belly-crawled toward the front of the vehicle. He hesitated before he left the cover of the *Rev 2*. The junkyard echoed with the staccato popping sound of metal piercing metal. When the shooting paused, Peter leaped for the stick and grabbed it. Bullets hit the ground in front of his nail-less fingers, and he retreated behind the *Rev 2*. Shots ricocheted off of the body of his spacecraft, spraying wayward bullet fragments into nearby cars.

"That smarts," Soledad said. Peter flinched at nearby explosions that made his ears ring, and then he realized that Hays and Mitchell were now returning fire. He looked back under the *Rev 2*. The BAT was still there. Hays and Mitchell had taken cover behind the car next to the *Rev 2*. Their attention had been diverted from Ben, Cyril, Peter, and the BAT to the metal projectiles coming toward them at roughly twice the speed of sound from the porch of the junkyard office. Shooting their own high-speed metal projectiles back at the porch seemed like the thing to do.

Peter reached under the *Rev 2* with the stick and rolled the BAT toward him until it was within his grasp. He shoved the BAT into his boot and turned to Cyril, who still had his arms over his head. "Pssst," Peter said. "I'm betting that home maintenance isn't high on the list of Kingpin priorities."

"What?" Cyril said. "They're shooting at us, and you're concerned that their place needs a paint job?"

"It really does," Peter said. "And I wouldn't go with the drab olive green next time. What were they thinking? But what I was referring to was that hole you cut in the fence."

"What about it?"

"Well, since the APA and the Kingpin brothers are sort of preoccupied with killing each other, I just thought it presented the perfect opportunity for us to escape."

Cyril pondered this idea for a few seconds. "You first."

"My pleasure," Peter said. "Just stay low and follow me. Ben, are you in?" Ben had not heard them; his head was still between his trembling knees. Peter shook him to get his attention. "Ben, we're making a break for it. Are you in?" Benjamin nodded briskly. Or flinched from a particularly close shot. Peter wasn't sure, but either way he assumed Ben would join them.

Peter crawled to the back of the *Rev 2*, and then made his way behind the long row of cars that angled away from the front of the junkyard. Cyril and Ben followed. From the vantage of the junkyard office, it was impossible for Butch and Hobart Kingpin to see them, but the bullets continued to strike uncomfortably close to the two aliens and the ophthalmologist.

"I dare say," Peter said, looking back at Cyril, "that they are worse shots than you are."

For once Cyril didn't argue with Peter. "Lucky for us," he replied.

Peter crawled behind the last car in the row and peered around the bumper. Cyril came up beside him. They could make out the semicircular cut in the fence. A 40 foot gap loomed between them and the opening. Any person (or alien) in that clearing would be visible to anyone standing on the junkyard office porch.

"I think we should make a break for the fence together," Peter said.

"What sense does that make?" Cyril said. "A larger target will be more likely to get their attention and get us shot."

"If we go separately," Peter said, "then who goes first?"

"You're probably the fastest," Cyril said. "You go first."

"But what if I get shot?" asked Peter. "That would be rather demoralizing, don't you think? To have the swiftest member of the team get mowed down in front of you? You'd be paralyzed with fear, and either get shot or re-captured."

"Then we'll have Ben go first," Cyril said. "He's probably the slowest."

"But what if Ben gets shot before he makes it to the fence?" Peter said. "It's going to be a little awkward for us when we have to crawl over his lifeless body to make our escape. Not to mention that it'll slow us down, and make it more likely that we'll be shot, too." Ben cleared his throat. The Kingpin brothers continued to exchange fire with Mitchell and Hays. In the distance, the rhythmic thumping of helicopter blades could be heard between gunshots.

"We don't have time for debate," Cyril said. "It sounds like one side has reinforcements coming." Neither Ben, Cyril, nor Peter was presumptuous enough to guess if the reinforcements were for Agent Hays and Dr. Mitchell, or for Butch and Hobart Kingpin. Drug lords could afford helicopters, and they were a long way from Area 52. "Let's vote on it. I say we go separately."

"Together," Peter said. Peter and Cyril looked at Benjamin.

"I feel like I'm going to throw up," Ben said.

"That wasn't one of the choices," Peter said. He leaned over and whispered into Ben's ear.

"We go together," Ben said.

"It's settled then," Peter said.

"What did you say to him?" Cyril asked.

"There's no time," Peter said. "The vote was two-to-one. Get ready. We're going on the count of three." Peter, Cyril, and Ben got to their feet and crouched behind the trunk of a 1965 Chevy Impala. The helicopters were almost upon them. "One... two... three." After "three" Peter bolted across the clearing with Ben and Cyril at his heels.

Butch Kingpin saw them just as they reached the fence. "Looky, they're runnin' away. We're winning!" he said to Hobart. In his euphoria, Butch could not resist taunting Peter, Ben, and Cyril. "Get outta here you chickenshits, and don't come back," he shouted. A bullet from Agent Hays's gun grazed Butch's scalp, and he dropped into a crouch behind the porch railing and returned fire.

"Butch," Hobart said. "That was uncalled for." He fired off a couple of shots. "Your haughty airs, derogatory tone, and humiliating words have no place on the battlefield. Disrespecting your opponent almost got you killed. As Lao Tzu said in *The Art of War*, 'There is no greater danger than underestimating your opponent.' "

"You're right again, brother," said Butch. "I have much to learn." He stood and again shouted toward the general direction of the junkyard. "I apologize. My haughty airs, derogatory tone, and humiliating words have no place on the battlefield. To quote Lao Tzu, 'There is no greater danger than underestimating your opponent.' "

"No problem," Agent Hays shouted back.

By now Peter had pushed on the severed chain-link fence to fashion an opening. He waved Cyril and Ben through. As Peter followed, he felt a bullet whiz past his ear and heard another ping the fence post. The three scurried across the dirt road, and Ben and Cyril dashed into the woods. Peter paused before joining them. He looked back to see two black helicopters hovering over the junkyard parking lot, throwing vortexes of red dust into the air. He ducked into the forest, and seconds later he heard a barrage of machine-gun fire and deafening explosions behind him. Peter sprinted until he caught up to Ben and Cyril.

"This way. To the road." Peter led them through the woods, and then stopped at the dry creek bed where he had tended to his wounds days earlier. This time he stopped to get his bearings. "Not much farther," Peter said. "If I remember correctly."

"Not much further," gasped Ben, "until I go into cardiac arrest."

"Stop," gasped Cyril, "whining." Gunfire erupted in the distance behind them. There was another explosion, and a thick plume of smoke billowed over the treetops.

"We need to go," Peter said. And before any objections could be raised, he bolted. Peter did not stop running until he reached the road. Ben and Cyril stopped running long before that, but slogged onward until they were standing on the shoulder of the empty road with Peter.

"Brilliant plan," Cyril said. "So do we wait for a bus, or hail a taxi?"

"Quiet!" Peter said. He held up one finger, and turned an ear toward the road. "I call shotgun." From behind a curve a white pickup appeared. Peter extended his arm and stuck out a thumb as the truck approached them. "Gentlemen, do try to make yourselves presentable."

The truck slowed, then stopped right in front of them. Peter stepped up to the open passenger-side window and spoke to the driver, who was wearing a red flannel shirt. "I was wondering if we might bother you for a ride. We're in a bit of a fix."

"After everything you've done for me," Brooks said, "I should just give you the keys to my truck. Climb on in." Ben and Cyril stood and stared, mouths agape. Peter opened the door and climbed in.

"Don't look at me all butt-hurt," Peter said. "I *did* call shotgun." He slammed the door and Ben and Cyril climbed into the back of the truck.

Brooks drove his truck down the winding road like there was a tomorrow, and after a few miles Peter composed himself enough to initiate conversation.

"Extraordinary good timing back there, Brooks."

"I s'pose. What are you boys doing out here?"

"My associates – Cyril and Benjamin – and I were unlawfully abducted by government agents, and were being held hostage," Peter said. "Our abductors were distracted by trying not to get killed by drug dealers, and we took the opportunity to become un-hostages."

"Glad you and your friends made it out okay," Brooks said. "Ben and Cyril, you say?"

"Yes," Peter said.

"Are they aliens, like you?" asked Brooks.

Peter was momentarily taken aback. "Well, Cyril is. Benjamin is just awkward."

"I see," Brooks said. He paused for a moment. "April pretty much told me everything. To an old broke-down retired steel worker it sounded pretty far-fetched at first. But there's no denying that I'm cured of my leukemia – and everything else. I'm healthier now than I was forty years ago. And it wasn't from that crap Dionysus was treating me with. No, you can't argue with empirical evidence. Or April Robinson either, for that matter." Brooks laughed.

"So what are *you* doing out here?" Peter said.

"Had an emergency on one of my properties that I had to take care of," Brooks said. "Tenant had a busted water heater that I had to replace."

"Well, again, your timing was impeccable," said

Peter. "I mean, for you to drive by moments after we had escaped, while we were standing helpless on the side of the road – it smacks of *deus ex machina*."

"*Deus ex machina*?" Brooks said. "You mean the plot device where a seemingly unsolvable problem is resolved by introducing a new character, event, or object in a contrived and unexpected manner?"

"Exactly."

"Well, I beg to differ," Brooks said. "Granted, the timing was coincidental, with you three in the midst of an escape just as I happened to be driving by. But if you'll recall, when we first met I told you that I come back to Birmingham to take care of my investment properties, so it's not unreasonable that I'd be driving along this road again. My reason for being here isn't so much *deus ex machina* as it is *aerugo in aqua calefacientis*."

"Ah. Rust in the water heater," Peter said. "But still, you really saved our asses back there."

"Not so much," Brooks said. "About two miles down this road there's an old gas station with a pay phone. You could have called April and she would have picked y'all up in a couple of hours."

"Still, and I think I speak for Ben and Cyril as well, I'm very grateful you were there to rescue us. Sorry I don't have a snack bar to offer you." He smiled at Brooks.

Brooks smiled and winked. "You've done enough." Ben and Cyril coped with the two-hour ride in the bed of the pickup as best as they could. Cyril complained, annoyed with the wind, with the diesel fumes from passing trucks, and at not having a proper seat to sit on. Benjamin sat without speaking, annoyed with Cyril's complaints about the wind, diesel fumes, and lack of a proper seat to sit on. Peter and Brooks mostly made small talk, but as they neared Atlanta Brooks asked Peter what his plans were, then offered to let the three of them stay at his place. Brooks informed Peter that investigators working for Dionysus (and investigators from some health insurance company now, too – the name escaped him) were watching April's place, so crashing there wasn't an option. He had not seen any suspicious individuals around his place, but he suspected that his home, as well as April's, was bugged. Brooks suggested that an unused Winnebago parked in his back yard would give Peter, Cyril, and Ben a relatively inconspicuous and secure place to stay until they sorted things out. Peter noticed that the word "comfortable" was never mentioned during the discussion about living quarters.

"What's their story?" Brooks asked, alluding to Ben and Cyril. Peter explained how Cyril was an intergalactic bounty hunter who was tracking him because he failed to return the BAT in a timely fashion. Ben was just an unfortunate human from Texas who ended up getting abducted by Cyril, mostly due to Cyril's profound lack of attention to detail and Benjamin's very bad luck. Peter confided in Brooks that he planned to negotiate a deal with Cyril that would get the bounty hunter back into space and off of Peter's back. It would also allow Benjamin – Dr. Cotter – to return to Texas. After Peter got the *Rev 2* repaired, he would be free to explore the universe, and perhaps someday find a nice place to settle down – preferably a planet with warm sandy beaches, respectable live theater, and an absence of pharmaceutical and health insurance company executives.

It was late afternoon when Brooks pulled his pickup truck into the driveway. He lived in a small ranch-style home on a half-acre lot filled with pine trees. It was not far from April's apartment, and the space and trees provided a modicum of privacy. It had been a long day for Peter, Cyril, and Ben; after an early flight that took them halfway across the country, they had dodged bullets from drug lords and escaped from their super-secret government agency captors. It culminated in the "worst part," according to Cyril – having to ride in the open bed of a pickup truck from Birmingham to Atlanta. Since he had to ride with Cyril, Ben was inclined to agree.

Ben and Cyril stretched after they climbed out of the back of the truck. Brooks looked up and down his street after he got out, then held a finger to his lips to keep the three quiet. He motioned them to follow him. They went to the side of the house, through the gate, into the back yard, and up to the Winnebago. Brooks opened the door and let them in.

"It's not much," Brooks said. "But it isn't home. I'll bring you some food and some coffee. There's a coffee maker in the kitchen." Peter looked around and noticed that he was standing in the kitchen. And the dining room. And part of a bedroom. Ben and Cyril each found a bed and were asleep within minutes. Peter sat at the diminutive dining area table, closed his eyes, and waited for Brooks. He awoke about an hour later when Brooks swung the door open and walked in carrying two full grocery bags. "If you need anything else, let me know."

"Thanks again for everything, Brooks," Peter said. After Brooks left, Peter made some coffee and drank a cup. He decided to turn in, and after getting up from the table he found two beds, each one already occupied and each one large enough to accommodate one average-sized human and a medium-sized dog, or one above-average sized human and no dog at all. Cyril was smaller than Ben, so Peter opted to squeeze into bed next to Cyril. The BAT was starting to chafe his ankle, but he left his boots on and ignored it, and slept like a baby.

Peter awoke the next morning to the smell of bacon, eggs, and fresh coffee. Ben was up cooking and Cyril was still sleeping. Peter crawled out of bed, stretched, and found the bathroom. When he got out he joined Ben at the table. Ben had already set a plate for him.

"I trust Blutaarkians can eat bacon and scrambled eggs?" Ben said.

"Absolutely," Peter replied. In his travels Peter had encountered several advanced life forms who eschewed cooked eggs. But to the best of his knowledge, a love of fried bacon was a constant in the universe - the one exception being a civilization of rather bright pigs on Brabant 3. "But brace yourself. Cyril will probably complain about the bacon being too crispy."

Ben took a sip of coffee. "So what happens now?"

Peter looked over his shoulder; Cyril was still asleep. Still, he whispered to Benjamin. "I've devised a plan. I think I can get Cyril out of our hair and me safely off of this planet. Just play along." As an afterthought he added "But I do sort of like this place."

"What about the BAT?" Ben asked.

"That part of the plan," Peter said, "is sort of irritating me right now."

Ben stared at his coffee, and when he heard Cyril stirring he set out another plate. Before long Cyril joined them at the table.

"You overcooked the bacon," Cyril said.

"You snore a lot," Benjamin said. "In fact, I think there's a good chance you have sleep apnea. It could explain why you're perpetually moody."

"I'm moody because you overcooked the bacon."

"You are *always* moody," countered Benjamin. "I just now gave you overcooked bacon. Now unless you're the victim of some heretofore unrecognized time-travel phenomenon, I fail to see how my serving you crispy bacon this morning could make you retroactively grumpy."

"The eggs are okay," Cyril said.

"Thank you," Ben said. "But seriously, you should have your doctor check you out when you get home." Cyril finished his breakfast without further complaint, then got up and stood next to the table.

"Speaking of getting home, we should probably start heading back to Blutaark. We're rested and fed, so it seems as good a time as any." Benjamin anxiously wondered if he was included in Cyril's "we," but reassured himself with the thought that he was included in whatever it was that Peter had planned.

"Just out of curiosity," Peter said. "How do you plan to get there?"

"In the *Rev 9*," Cyril said. He wanted to add "stupid," but wanted to see if he could be not moody for another minute or two.

"It's in hover mode, right?" Peter said.

"Yes."

"Well then, I suppose if you land it next to Brooks's RV, we'll get on board and be on our way."

"Thank you for being cooperative," Cyril said. "You were way overdue." He reached for the hover control module on his belt, only to realize that the belt (and the attached module) was most likely still in a cardboard box at Area 52, approximately 2200 miles from his waist. "Arrrgggghhhhhhhh," shrieked Cyril with a ferocity that shook the RV's walls like a temblor – if earthquakes were localized to the area of a large driveway and had bad breath.

"Oh yeah," Peter said. "That won't draw any attention at all." Cyril started pacing back-and-forth with his hands behind his back, but in the limited confines of the RV it looked more like poorly choreographed square-dancing than fitful pacing. "Cyril, why don't you sit down? Relax, take some deep breaths. Let's talk it out." Cyril stopped pacing and stood next to the table, panting, with his hands on his hips. "That's really more like hyperventilating than deep breathing."

Cyril took a seat and avoided eye contact. Eventually his breathing slowed. "What is there to talk about?"

"Clearly, I've put more thought into our current situation than you have," Peter said. "And I have some ideas."

Over the next few minutes, Peter laid out his plan while Benjamin and Cyril listened. He started with a basic outline of the problem and a solution: the Alien Phenomena Agency was in possession of both the BAT and Cyril's belt (and the *Rev 9* hover control module), so Cyril should go and get them. Peter would relinquish any claim to the BAT and allow Cyril to return it to Blutaark for the full reward. In return, Peter asked that Cyril cease and desist in his attempts to apprehend Peter and remand him to Blutaarkian authorities. Additionally, Peter would assist Cyril in his efforts in getting from Georgia to Nevada. He was confident that Brooks would be willing to help with the transportation issue, either by renting a car or purchasing a bus or plane ticket for Cyril – provided it was a one-way ticket. Peter admitted that those details were sketchy, and would not be finalized until he discussed the matter with

Brooks. Lastly, Cyril would go to Area 52 without Benjamin, and in return Ben would not press unlawful-abduction-of-a-sentient-life-form charges against Cyril in intergalactic court. Peter summed it up by framing his plan as a reasonable compromise for everyone: Benjamin would be able to go home, Peter would avoid incarceration, and Cyril would get his *Rev 9* back and claim the reward for returning the BAT.

Cyril sat quietly for a minute after Peter stopped talking. "What does 'desist' mean?"

"It means that once you stop doing something, you don't go back later and start doing it again," Peter said.

"Hmm," Cyril said. "Do you know what the penalty is for unlawful-abduction-of-a-sentient-life-form?"

"I do not," Peter said.

"Mandatory ten years riding around in the back of an open pickup truck," interjected Ben. "At least in this jurisdiction."

Cyril rubbed his temples. His expression suggested that he was in deep thought, or that perhaps the overcooked bacon disagreed with him. "Benjamin really hasn't been much help -"

"What about the time I recommended that you use the cameras in the *Rev 9* to locate Peter?" interrupted Benjamin, before he stopped himself, realizing he was making the point to remain Cyril's hostage.

"And I could really use the reward money from the BAT," Cyril said. "The *Rev 9* needs some work."

"We noticed," Peter said.

"But I really had my heart set on seeing you get thrown into prison," Cyril said.

"You never know," Peter said. "Perhaps someday

I'll make off with another bit of cutting-edge Blutaarkian technology, and we can do this all over again."

"Yeah..." Cyril's voice trailed off and his expression grew wistful. Then he turned at looked at Peter. "I'll do it."

TWENTY-SIX

April rolled in late to work Monday morning, but she told herself that it really didn't matter. She was Dirk Reger's sole administrative assistant, and he typically did not make it into the office until after 10:30. April's ongoing concern about Peter, the continuous surveillance, and the Saturday morning interrogation session with Dirk and Dr. Francis made the weekend seem like a bust anyway, so she felt justified in getting the extra hour of sleep.

Dirk arrived at 11:00 and with a terse "Morning" he stepped into his office and closed his door. After a few minutes, he rang April and asked her to come in. Usually, when Dirk called April into his office he was specific with his reason for doing so. He might ask her to order some authentic tiki lamps for a weekend pool party, or to pick up his daughter at school because "somebody" forgot to, or to make travel arrangements for his wife's shopping vacations, or to pick his wife up at the airport because she couldn't find her car because there were so many gray Mercedes-Benzes that all looked alike and not because she drank on the plane. And one time Dirk asked April to come into his office to take dictation. But this morning he simply asked her to come into his office. Dirk was sitting behind his desk, looking straight ahead at nothing in particular until he turned and looked at April.

"Take a seat, April." He was wearing his Very Serious Face.

April's stomach knotted. Dirk never looked this serious. In a flash she remembered Sunday's phone call from - what was her name? Terry? Karen? She couldn't remember now and it wasn't helping that her ears were ringing and she felt like she was going to throw up. Hyperventilation was the next stop for this anxiety bus. *Why did I give her Dirk's phone number? And why am I worried about getting fired from a job I hate?*

"April," Dirk continued. "I know you love your job. And I would really hate for anything to jeopardize your employment here at Dionysus."

"Okay," April said in a near-whisper. The ringing in her ears was getting less ringy, but was replaced by an ancient echo of her father's voice admonishing her about the folly of pursuing a liberal arts degree in this economy. "Listen, I'm sorry about that phone call yesterday. That woman was really pushy. And she said she knew you -"

"April," Dirk said. "It's not about that. If I could be frank with you for a minute – I mean honest – not Frank Francis. I mean, that's not to say Frank isn't honest. And there are times when I'd like to be Frank – I mean Frank Francis this time – because he's really smart, and he's a doctor, too, so I could write my own prescriptions. But what I'm trying to say is that I'm going to be very honest with you. I mean, it's not that I'm not always honest with you, but right now I'm going to be more honest than usual. Okay?"

"Got it," April said.

"See, Dionysus isn't doing well," Dirk said. "Our

funding is drying up, and there are no new investors willing to step up to the plate. The only drug we have developed that has made it to Phase 3 – DPCL2 – only worked in one study subject. Well, it seemed to have worked at first, until we realized it wasn't our drug that cured him, but something else entirely. And I think we both know what that was."

"The placebo effect?" April said.

"Peter Finch," Dirk replied. "Or more specifically, his BAT."

"Are you trying to tell me that this Peter Finch guy beat leukemia out of a patient with a baseball bat?" April said. She hoped that her feigned naïveté sounded convincing. "I thought you said he was some kind of intellectual property thief."

"No," Dirk said with a hint of condescension. He bought the feigned naïveté. "The BAT is a device that...April, how much do you know about this Peter Finch?"

"Not a lot. My father met him in Alabama. He said he grew up in Idaho, and worked as a biologist for a while. He was a voracious reader - seemed intelligent, but not really focused. He crashed at my place for a couple of days, but when I got up Saturday morning he was gone. And I haven't seen him since - I told you that at our meeting."

"I remember," Dirk said. "April, Peter possesses something that could save Dionysus Pharmaceutical. Not only save the company, but make it profitable beyond our wildest dreams. Is there any way you could get in touch with him?"

"No," April said. "I don't even think he owns a cell phone."

"Think hard," Dirk said. "Because if you can't lead us to Peter, then we will have to get Peter to come to you."

"Honestly, Mr. Reger," April said. "I don't really know where he came from, and I have no idea where he went."

"That sucks," Dirk said. "I hate what I'm about to do, but I'm left with no choice."

"You're going to fire me?" shrieked April.

"Heavens, no!" Dirk said. "Don't be such a drama queen. That would be a little drastic, don't you think?"

April breathed a short sigh of relief until Dirk reached into a desk drawer, pulled out a handgun, and pointed it at her. April gasped and clutched the arms of her chair to keep from passing out on the floor. Dirk picked up the phone and buzzed Hannah, and within seconds she had sprinted into Dirk's office and closed the door behind her. She stood next to April, and sat her canvas knitting bag with the kitten-chasing-a-bumblebee applique on the floor.

"Hannah," April said. "He's got a gun!"

"Oh, sweetheart, I know. But he's the CEO so I'm sure he has a really good reason." Dirk nodded at Hannah and she reached into her bag and pulled out a length of rope. "Hands behind your back!"

"Hannah!"

"Oh, April," Hannah said. "Try to be optimisticy. I'm sure this is what's best for the company. You know what they say. 'Teamwork is the fuel that allows common people to attain uncommon results.'" Dirk waved the barrel of the gun at April, and she put her hands behind her back. After Hannah had tied April's wrists, she took another piece of rope and secured her ankles. Hannah dug into her bag and pulled out a roll of duct tape. April shook like a chihuahua in detox, and she flinched when Hannah ripped the duct tape into two short segments. "I just love your bangs," said Hannah as she pressed a strip of duct tape squarely over April's mouth, followed by the second strip for good measure. Hannah stepped out of Dirk's office with a "Be right back!" Dirk dropped the handgun into the drawer and closed it.

"God she's annoying. I wanted to shoot her a little bit." April laughed reflexively, but winced in pain when the duct tape tugged at the skin around her mouth. "Sorry 'bout that. Listen, April - it's going to be a long ride. Do you need Hannah to take you to the restroom before you leave?" April's eyes widened and she shook her head back and forth. Dirk's office door swung open, and Hannah entered the room pulling a dolly. It wasn't until Hannah parked the dolly next to her that April could see the oblong wooden crate.

April shook her head again, and her eyes welled with tears. "Uhmmm mmmm, uhhhmmmm mmmm."

"April," Dirk said. "We know where Brooks lives." April acquiesced, took a deep breath, closed her eyes, and stood up with help from Hannah.

"Why, Pumpkin, you're shakin' like a leaf," said Hannah. She guided April into the wooden box that she had thoughtfully lined with blankets.

April felt the back of her head touch a pillow, and in her mind's eye she couldn't help but see herself laid out at her own open-casket funeral. *And to think I took this job for the health insurance.*

April kept her eyes closed as Dirk and Hannah dropped the lid and secured it with a padlock. The crate lurched as Hannah pulled the dolly out of Dirk's office and into the hallway.

"You should probably use the freight elevator," shouted Dirk.

"Okay!" said Hannah. Twenty-eight levels below,

Martina and two of her pout-model associates waited in an idling black Hummer parked at the One Atlanta Plaza loading dock.

A few miles away, Taryn Yuanuin stared out at the Atlanta skyline from her plush executive chair. She slept fitfully the night before and it showed. Taryn had managed to wrangle an agreement with Dionysus to share in the future profits generated from the BAT by convincing Dirk and Dr. Francis that Persona had the advantage in the hunt for Peter. But they were playing poker, and she had bluffed. She realized that Persona may have already botched its only opportunity to obtain the BAT when Cyril rescued Peter. By now they – and the BAT – could be light years away. Taryn had called Tor at 4:30 a.m. for an update. Despite the 24/7 surveillance and bugging of Peter's last known address, there was nothing significant to report - unless you counted April Robinson's penchant for making extraordinarily sweet lemonade. Taryn didn't.

From high above the street in her corner office, Taryn heard the faint wail of a police siren. Her tired eyes widened. She spun her chair around to face her desk, slung open a drawer, and pulled out a thick file. Digging through the morass of documents and spreadsheets, Taryn found what she was looking for - Peter's job application form that she had taken from Jess at the doughnut shop. She traced her finger down the page until it landed on the name Peter gave as a reference: Brooks Robinson.

Peter was eager to ship off Cyril back to Area 52. Since Brooks was an integral part of his plan, Peter thought it would be best if he let him know about it. He rapped on Brooks's back door, and within a few seconds he opened it and let Peter in. Peter apologized for being a bother, especially this early in the morning, but Brooks assured him that he was no trouble, and that he had been up since sunrise anyway. Brooks rarely got to see April during the work week, so having guests was a pleasant diversion. And he enjoyed Peter's company almost as much as April's.

"I was wondering if we could talk," Peter said.

"You want some breakfast?" Brooks asked.

"Thanks," Peter said. "But we already ate."

Brooks pulled out a chair for Peter and they sat at the kitchen table. "So what's on your mind?"

Peter hesitated. He understood that Brooks would probably do any favor Peter asked of him, but he did not want to take advantage of him, or put him in harm's way. Brooks was already putting himself at risk by harboring three fugitives, and Peter was loath to further complicate his life. But he needed Brooks's help. Peter took a quick breath and spat the words out. "I need a favor."

Brooks listened intently as Peter gave a thorough accounting of his current predicament and the pertinent events that led up to it. He explained how he and Cyril were from the same planet, and how Cyril was a bounty hunter who had tracked him across the universe to Alabama, then to Georgia.

"April told me everything," Brooks said, smiling and nodding.

Peter detailed how he, Cyril, and Benjamin were apprehended by the Alien Phenomena Agency and escaped when the agents holding them were ambushed by members of a Southern crystal meth cartel.

"The Kingpins?" Brooks said. "My property in Alabama was in the same neighborhood as theirs.

We were members of the same homeowner's association."

"That must have been horrible," Peter said.

"Yeah," Brooks said. "I never cared too much for homeowner's associations – always run by precious little tin gods who want to tell everyone else what to do. Makes me want to puke. But the Kingpins were always cordial to me. And they always barbecued for the neighborhood Labor Day picnics."

"Well, they were sort of adamant about shooting at us yesterday," Peter said. "And I'm guessing someone else will have to provide the barbecue for the next Labor Day picnic."

"That's too bad," Brooks said. "Their brisket was to die for."

"Apparently," Peter said, "so was their crystal meth." He paused and considered the possibility that the Kingpin brothers made it out of the junkyard alive, and that Hays and Mitchell did not.

"So?" Brooks said.

"So what?" Peter replied.

"I think you mentioned something about a favor."

"Ah, yes," Peter said. "I've made a deal with Cyril. He's agreed to stop trying to apprehend me and return me to Blutaark if I let him take the BAT. But to do that – and also be able to retrieve his spacecraft – he will need to return to Area 52. In Nevada. We were looking for some assistance with his transportation – perhaps a plane ticket. Or even one for a train. Or a bus. We just need to get him there, and the sooner the better."

"Is this place close to Vegas?" Brooks asked.

"Not particularly, no."

"Too bad," Brooks said. "I would drive Cyril there myself – if he didn't mind riding in the back of the pickup. But I've garaged an old Chevy Impala. Still runs, just needs a battery. It used to belong to Mrs. Robinson...before she passed." He got up from the table and went to the pantry. He opened the door and then reached in and plucked the car keys from a glass bowl sitting next to a tray of cupcakes. Brooks walked back to the table and handed them to Peter.

"You sure about this?" Peter said.

"Yeah," Brooks said. "It's not doing me any good. And April won't drive it."

"You understand that if you let Cyril take your car, you may never see it again?"

"That's okay," Brooks said. "It's insured, and I've got my truck."

"God bless you please, Mr. Robinson," Peter said.

"I can run to the auto parts store and have a battery in her in half an hour."

"That would be perfect," Peter said. Brooks grasped Peter's shoulder, smiled, and shook it gently. He went out the front door, and Peter heard the sound of the pickup motor start up, and then fade as Brooks drove off. Peter went back to the RV.

Peter presented the idea to Cyril of using Brooks's car to drive to Nevada. Cyril's halfhearted approval became completely hearted when presented with the other option of being transported back to Area 52 by riding in the back of Brooks's pickup. Benjamin spent several minutes teaching Cyril as much as he could about driving an automobile and the fundamentals of motor vehicle laws. Cyril boasted "If Peter can drive, I can too." Ben found this statement roundly unsettling.

Before Brooks returned, Peter, Ben, and Cyril went into the house and found the door leading into the garage. Ben hit the automatic garage door opener, and as the door lifted daylight spilled over the beast. It was a four-door 1975 Chevy Impala, burnt orange, with bench seats, and an automatic transmission. It had the bulk of a small dinosaur, and with a 400 cubic inch engine it required the by-products of roughly three dead dinosaurs to propel it to the nearest gas station. Ben opened the driver's door and had Cyril sit behind the wheel. Ben reviewed the critical control features: steering wheel, gear shift, accelerator, brake, and parking brake. Cyril asked about the "death ray," and was genuinely miffed to learn that Earth cars lack that feature. Benjamin reflected on his experience with inconsiderate Dallas drivers, and was compelled to agree with Cyril that a death ray would be a nice option. He showed Cyril where to put fuel in the tank, then removed his Chevron gas card from his wallet and handed it to Cyril.

"You can use this to pay for gasoline, but only at Chevron gas stations," Ben said. He pointed to the logo on the card. "Look for a sign that looks like this."

"Or how about I just look for the word 'Chevron,' " Cyril said, discourteously reminding Ben that at least he had the courtesy to learn English before he landed on Earth.

"Right," Ben said. He made a mental note to report the card stolen in a couple of days. "I'm guessing it gets about 18 miles to the gallon on the highway, and it probably has about a twenty-gallon tank, so you'll need to gas up about every 350 miles."

Cyril snickered a little, caught himself, and then leaned over to whisper into Peter's ear. "Fossil fuel! How quaint. Is it getting warm out here, or is it just me?"

Peter shook his head with disapproval. "We're still guests here." Just then Brooks pulled up in his pickup truck and parked in front of the house. He lugged the new battery up the driveway and told Benjamin to pop the hood. Five minutes later, the battery was installed and the Impala was ready to go.

"Start 'er up," Brooks said. Ben turned the key. The engine turned over and the car purred like a kitten – if kittens weighed four thousand pounds and did not mind being locked in the garage for a decade. Benjamin pulled the car out onto the driveway, put it in park, and got out. Brooks handed Cyril an interstate road atlas. He had already highlighted the route to Nevada. "You'll just take 285 south until you hit I-20, then go west. The rest is pretty self-explanatory."

"Thank you," Cyril said. He shook Brooks's hand. Then he turned and shook Ben's hand "And thank you, too. Sorry about the abduction. And the neurotoxin. And the plasma immobilizer. And your job."

"It's okay," Ben said. Cyril's sincerity surprised him. "Getting shot with the plasma immobilizer hurt like hell. But I think I've been less depressed since it happened." Cyril smiled.

Peter stepped in, turned Cyril around by his shoulders, and hugged him. "Safe travels, my friend. You think you'll have any trouble finding Area 52 after you get to Nevada?"

"Not a problem," Cyril said. "It was a clear day when we took off in that infernally slow aircraft. I made it a point to memorize the pattern of the roads in the area. I thought it might come in handy for escaping. Never dreamed that I'd use it to find my way back."

"Yeah," Peter said. "Life is strange. Here, I want you to take this. Just in case." Peter reached into his pocket, pulled out the red-and-gray box that he had removed from under the trunk lid of the *Rev 2,* and handed it to Cyril.

"What's this?" Cyril asked.

"It's Charpaq technology," Peter replied. "It's called a BAMN box. If you find yourself in an impossible situation, you just flip the lid and push the white button. You can only use it once."

"Bam box?" Cyril said. "You're giving me an explosive self-destruct device? Thanks?" Cyril was at once touched and puzzled.

"No, Cyril," Peter said. "It is not a bomb. BAMN stands for 'By Any Means Necessary.' Like I said, if you have no other options, you can use it. You may not see immediate results, but it can be remarkably effective. Best of luck."

"Thanks," Cyril said. "I guess this is goodbye." He shoved the BAMN box into his pocket, climbed into the Impala, and closed the door. He gave a quick wave, and Brooks, Ben, and Peter reciprocated. Cyril threw the transmission into drive and hit the accelerator. The engine roared as the car fishtailed off of the driveway and sped across the front yard. Cyril narrowly missed colliding with Brooks's truck, but he thickly hit his mailbox, catapulting it into the neighbor's yard across the street. They winced at the screech of metal on concrete as the Impala leaped off of the curb and bottomed out on the pavement. Cyril regained control, steered the vehicle into the right side of the street, and then accelerated again before disappearing around the corner. The squeal from his tires reverberated throughout the neighborhood long after he was out of sight.

"Benjamin," Peter said. "Did you at any time discuss the use of seat belts with Cyril?"

"No."

"Pity."

Brooks retrieved his mailbox, then closed his

garage door and went into the house. Peter and Ben walked around the side and through the gate and then back into the RV to wait and see how Peter's plan unfolded.

Taryn pulled her rental car into Brooks Robinson's driveway and stopped with a screech before Cyril had even made it to the interstate in the Impala. She got out of the car, slammed the door, and sprinted down the sidewalk. Ignoring the doorbell, she rapped on the front door frame with her fist until the door opened – and then for a few seconds longer. Before Brooks could utter a word, she had pulled her wallet out of her purse and flipped it open to reveal a badge, and then just as quickly shoved the wallet back into her purse. The badge wasn't real, but it did not matter. It often allowed Taryn to get what she wanted when her money, near-genius intellect, and willingness to be the most ill-mannered person in the room did not.

"Brooks Robinson? FBI. We need to talk." Taryn pushed her way through the door and past Brooks until she was standing well inside the front entry way. She stood in place and turned in a circle, taking in the expansive house. To one side was a large dining room furnished with luxurious cherry wood table and chairs, and a china cabinet displaying an impressive Wedgwood collection. Toward the back she glimpsed a gourmet kitchen with granite counter tops and professional appliances. She wondered how someone like Brooks could get mixed up with a loser like Peter.

Brooks looked more puzzled than concerned as he closed the front door behind them. "FBI you say? What is this all about?"

"We have reason to believe that you may be

harboring a fugitive who poses an immediate and grave danger to our country," Taryn said. "I'll need to do a thorough search." With that she took off. She searched the kitchen, then a living area, then a downstairs bedroom and bath. Brooks followed as she ran up the stairs, where she searched an additional four bedrooms and three bathrooms. Finding nothing, she trotted back down the stairs where she searched a study, then what appeared to be an entertainment room where she stopped to catch her breath. There was a large-screen high-definition TV at one end of the room, and across from that a sofa. The remainder of the room was dedicated to baseball memorabilia: posters, pennants, gloves, jerseys, and a large trophy case filled with...trophies.

"Look, lady," Brooks said as he strolled into the room after Taryn. "You've gone to a lot of trouble just to get an autograph. I'm going to have to ask you to leave or I'm calling the police."

"So you're Brooks Robinson, the baseball player," Taryn said. "And not the Brooks Robinson who the alien menace put as his reference on his doughnut shop job application?" Brooks reached into his pocket and pulled out his cell phone. "Oh, okay. Before I go I guess I'll go ahead and get that autograph."

Brooks watched Taryn walk down the sidewalk and get into her rented Corolla. *Yeah. She's hot.*

As she was driving back to the private jet that awaited her at the Baltimore-Washington International Airport, Taryn rebuked herself for wasting five hours on the round trip to Baltimore instead of first investigating the Brooks Robinson who lived in Smyrna, Georgia. Sometimes her instincts failed her. She was still feeling uncharacteristically unsure of herself when she parked her Mercedes behind the white pickup in front of the modest, ranch-style house. This time she rang the doorbell.

"Brooks Robinson? FBI. We need to talk," Taryn said when Brooks opened his door. She flashed the faux badge and returned it to her purse, but without the sense of urgency and confidence she had in spades in Baltimore.

"Say your piece," Brooks said.

"We have reason to believe that you're harboring a fugitive who poses an imminent and significant security risk to our country," Taryn said.

"Do you have a search warrant?" Brooks asked.

"Yeah," snapped Taryn. "I've got it right here." She reached back into her purse and pulled out a Glock 19. Brooks backed into his house with his hands up, and she followed him inside and closed the door. She smiled a little to herself – she could feel her mojo rising.

"I knew you weren't FBI," Brooks said.

"Ah," Taryn said. "The geezer has an eye for detail. You must have noticed that the eagle was missing from my counterfeit badge. Or that it says 'FBI' instead of 'Federal Bureau of Investigation.' Or that instead of gold, my badge has a silver border."

"No," Brooks said emphatically. "It's because you're driving a car that's worth more than my house."

Holding Brooks at gunpoint, Taryn searched the entire house, but found no evidence of Peter, the BAT, or the enigmatic bounty hunter. Taryn and Brooks ended up standing in the small dining area off of the kitchen. She was tired and frustrated.

"Do you live alone?"

"I do," Brooks said.

"Then who is that?" Taryn pointed to a photo stuck to the refrigerator with a magnet.

"That's my daughter, April," Brooks said. "But she doesn't live with me."

April Robinson, thought Taryn. *No way that's a coincidence.* "Does she work for Dionysus?" Brooks kept his mouth shut. "She does! That's your connection to Peter. That's how your name ended up as a reference on his job application. Listen, not a word about my coming here gets back to Dionysus, *capiche*?" She raised the barrel of the Glock to his jaw.

"I have no idea what you're talking about," Brooks said with a steely stare. "Maybe this Peter guy was a big fan of that hall-of-fame third baseman who played for the Orioles."

"Nope. Already looked into that possibility. A total waste of time – except for the sweet autograph." As the words left her lips, Taryn looked past Brooks and out of the window where she saw the Winnebago. "What the hell is that?"

Taryn bolted out the back door and was halfway across the yard before Brooks yelled at her from the back porch. "Wait! You can't go in there!"

She stopped and turned to look at Brooks. She was determined to search the RV, but she was curious as to what Brooks would say to try to keep her from doing so. "Why not?"

"It's my...meth lab. It's loaded with toxic chemicals." Brooks yelled at her like she was a kid on his freshly-mowed front lawn.

"Oh really? Name two chemicals used in the production of crystal meth."

"Pseudoephedrine and anhydrous ammonia," shouted Brooks at the top of his lungs.

"Lucky guess. Name two more."

"Toluene and hydrochloric acid."

"Oh, for the love of..." Taryn turned and started back toward the RV. The next-door neighbor's mastiff barked ferociously, then let out a yelp and stopped barking just as Taryn slipped between the RV and the fence.

"Acetone and sodium hydroxide," screamed Brooks in one last heroic effort to stop her.

Taryn slung the RV door open and stepped back against the fence. With arms extended she held the Glock with both hands, the barrel trained on the empty doorway, and listened. It was quiet, save for the faint whimpering of the mastiff, unseen on the opposite side of the fence. She crept up the steps of the RV, and once she cleared the doorway she swung the pistol to her left and hit the floor; she had a perfectly clear shot at absolutely nothing. She stood, brushed herself off, and then held the gun in one hand while she readjusted a strap on her heels with the other. A short walk-through revealed dirty dishes in the sink and unmade beds. *Men,* she thought. Then she corrected herself. *Alien men.*

She opened the bathroom door and just as quickly closed it. No aliens, just several inhospitable species of mold. Taryn went through the motion of looking in cabinets and under the beds, but she knew it was pointless. Peter was still one step ahead. She bounded out of the RV and stormed across the yard to where Brooks stood. When he realized that Peter and Benjamin had somehow escaped, he turned cocksure and glib.

"Sorry about the yelling earlier," Brooks grinned. "I forgot that I left the meth lab in my other RV."

"Oh shut up," snapped Taryn. She was incensed that Peter eluded capture, but she took comfort in knowing that the alien – and probably the BAT, too

– was still on Earth, still within her grasp. And she was determined to find him before those incompetents at Dionysus did. "I know Peter was here, Brooks Robinson. My people will be watching you 24/7. Count on it." She turned to leave, then stopped and spoke again. "By the way, I would trench your front yard on my way out, but some punk teenager beat me to it."

TWENTY-SEVEN

April heard a muffled *ding*, then felt two jolts as Hannah pushed the dolly into the elevator. Despite Hannah's earnest attempts to make the crate comfortable, April was already starting to feel cramped and achy. With her ankles tied, hands tied behind her back, mouth duct-taped, and her body contorted inside a wooden shipping crate, April was more shocked than frightened. She had been in relationships that she thought might end like this, but she never suspected anything like this would happen at Dionysus. Dirk was narcissistic and inept, but when April overheard break room criticism of her boss, she would often come to his defense with a "Well, at least he's not pure evil." Now she wasn't so sure.

Hannah pushed the dolly out onto the loading dock. Martina climbed out of the Hummer and opened a back door, and with assistance from Hannah and two pout-model accomplices, she hoisted the crate and slid it across the back seat. "Be brave, little one," Hannah said as she patted the crate. "Remember, courage is resistance to fear, not the absence of fear." April heard the car door slam –

and she wished Hannah's head had been in it. Martina and her girls climbed back into the front seat. Martina pulled the Hummer out of the loading dock and headed toward Interstate 20. They would make the Outer Banks of North Carolina in about ten hours.

April could feel the constant hum of the tires on the highway. She wondered where they were taking her, and how long this crate that looked a-little-too-much-like-a-casket would be her living quarters. She closed her eyes and took slow deep breaths. April distracted herself by imagining Hannah strolling through a warehouse, then getting crushed under a falling crate filled with motivational posters. Then she remembered that Dirk had neglected to make her clock out before she was abducted, and the thought that she was getting paid to be kidnapped made her chortle. The duct tape over her mouth made it sound more like moaning.

"Are you okay?" asked one of the pout models.

What an inane question. The question was so preposterous that April would not have answered it even if she could have. *Am I okay? I'm bound and gagged and stuffed in a box. At least they haven't killed me. Yet. Dirk said they need me to get Peter. But what's going to happen after that?* She started to hyperventilate, and her surroundings seemed to get darker than they already were. April had successfully distracted herself from her physical discomfort by inducing a panic attack. She now distracted herself from her panic attack by slipping out of consciousness.

Brooks watched from the side of the house as Taryn drove off, then he walked back to the Winnebago. He looked under the RV, walked around the back, and then up the side next to the fence until he was standing in front of the door. "Hello?" he shouted inside. He heard scuffling behind him and turned to see Benjamin making his way over the top of the fence. As soon as Ben dropped to his feet next to Brooks, Peter bounded over the fence, landing next to Benjamin.

"Hello!" Peter said. "Did we miss anything?" When Peter heard Brooks shouting to Taryn, he hustled Benjamin out of the RV's side door and boosted him over the privacy fence and into the next-door neighbor's back yard. Peter leaped over the fence before Taryn got to the RV. This simple escape was complicated by Borgnine, the neighbor's territorial mastiff, who charged at Peter and Ben with teeth bared. Blutaarkian neurotoxin uncomplicated things.

"Just some broad who claimed to be with the FBI," Brooks said. "Turns out she wasn't. But she was looking for you, Peter."

"Dionysus again," Peter said.

"Nope," Brooks said. "She made it a point to tell me not to tell anyone at Dionysus about her little visit."

"Then she's with Persona Health," Peter said.

"What about the Alien Phenomena Agency?" asked Ben.

"Unlikely," Peter said. "If she were from the APA, there would have been more than just one of her, they would have been men, and there would have been black vehicles and helicopters and explosions and mayhem and excessive high-fiving."

"One other thing," Brooks said. "She claimed that she was gonna stake out my house, to see if you showed."

Peter had planned to camp out in Brooks's

Winnebago with Benjamin until he was certain Cyril was no longer a threat. But Cyril had just departed for Area 52, and Peter estimated that it would take another two or three days (at best) until his Cyril problem was solved. Having operatives from Dionysus or Persona parked in front of Brooks's house would be inconvenient, but not disastrous. Peter understood that with twenty-four hour surveillance and the strong possibility that Brooks's house was bugged, he and Ben would be compelled to remain inside the RV. Discretion was imperative. There could be no noise, no visitors, and no lights after sundown. It would be like living in a monastery, but without all of the excitement of chanting and calligraphy. Brooks excused himself, went inside the house, returned with a walkie-talkie, and handed it to Peter. In an emergency they could communicate with Brooks, and vice-versa, without the risk of leaving the RV.

"You don't know how invaluable your help has been," Peter said. He hugged Brooks and retired to the Winnebago with Ben. As Brooks went back inside, a black SUV pulled up and parked across the street. Brooks planned a morning fit for a retiree; he would read his newspaper, and then later call his daughter at work.

April awoke. She had no idea what time it was, or how long she had been unconscious. It was still dark, but it seemed quieter than before. The tires hummed at a lower frequency, and April heard fewer passing vehicles. She guessed that they were no longer on the interstate. April was positioned on her side, and she attempted to shift her body to relieve the pressure on her shoulder. She was exhausted, and hungry, and needed to pee. It reminded her of a bus trip she took as a teenager from Birmingham to Albuquerque, but without the pregnant nun, the colicky babies, and the burro. She could hear Martina and one of the pout models talking, but could not make out what they were saying. After a while she gave up trying.

After what seemed like two or three hours, the Hummer slowed even more and the ride became bumpier. *Great*, thought April. *We're off road now.* Twice the vehicle lurched violently, and April's head slammed against the side of the crate. "Mmmrrrmmph." Despite Hannah's best efforts at padding the box, it still hurt.

"Sorry," came from the front seat. The Hummer stopped and the engine shut off. April heard the front doors open, then the rear door closest to her head. She felt someone struggle to slide the crate across the seat. The box seemed to hover briefly before Martina and her friends let gravity do the complete opposite of heavy lifting, and the crate fell to the ground. April expected a jarring crash but was pleasantly surprised when it hit the ground with a jarring thud.

"Sorry," Martina said. She unlocked the crate and lifted the lid.

April attempted to open her eyes, but was temporarily blinded by the light spilling into the briny night air from the oceanfront beach house. She shut her eyes as Martina and one of the other girls grasped her arms and lifted her to her feet. She stretched as much as she could with her wrists and ankles bound. April felt someone untying the rope around her wrists, and as her eyes adjusted she peeked through squinted lids. The beach house was massive and luxurious. It was bone white, built on three levels, with a wide wooden staircase rising to a second-floor deck that extended the length of the house. Light cascading from dozens of windows lit up the sand like stadium lights illuminating a ball park infield. Through the wall of windows, April could make out furnishings and appointments fit for a mansion in the Hamptons. She half expected to see Gatsby raising a glass of champagne on the deck. April felt the rope drop from her wrists, and she stretched by extending her arms in front of her. She turned her head to look around, but all there was to see was sand and beach grass behind her, and in front of her – beyond the house – the ocean. There was no paved road adjacent to the beach house. It could only be accessed by four-wheel drive vehicles. One of the girls knelt to untie April's ankles.

"Wrrrurrrhheehhh?" April said, forgetting the duct tape.

"It's a vacation home on the Outer Banks," Martina said.

"Uhmmeppuhee."

"Don't worry," Martina said. "This place has seven bathrooms." April was more than a little disturbed that Martina seemed proficient at understanding someone who was gagged with duct tape. Once the ropes loosened from her ankles, April stepped out of the box and onto the sand. Martina approached her and grasped the edge of the duct tape. "Brace yourself. And it's okay to scream – no one can hear you out here. Fast like a Band-Aid." And with that Martina ripped the duct tape off of April's face. The pain left April momentarily breathless, but once the moment passed and her breath returned, April let out a scream so shrill that the International Banshee Federation voted unanimously to make her an honorary member. When the pain finally waned, April noticed that she was on her knees in the sand. They helped her back up, and the four of them walked toward the house. April made a note to herself to never, ever make an appointment for a Brazilian wax.

Once inside, Martina led April upstairs to a bedroom on the third floor, and showed her the attached bathroom.

"Sorry we don't have a change of clothes that will fit you," Martina said. April rolled her eyes. "But at least you can clean up. I'll have one of the girls bring you some food. Do not attempt to leave this room. We have orders to tase you if you so much as open the door. Try to get some rest tonight. You are going to have a long day tomorrow."

Martina left and closed the door behind her, and April went into the bathroom to pee. It was taking a while, so she took in the bathroom. It was larger than the bedroom in her apartment, with a glassed-in shower on one end and floor-length windows overlooking the ocean on the other. The Jacuzzi tub looked inviting, especially to someone who had been contorted inside a wooden crate for ten hours. Two white porcelain bowl sinks rested on the granite vanity that complemented the granite tile floor, and two billowy white bathrobes hung from hooks on the wall. The absence of toothpaste splatter on the mirror, makeup stains on the counter, and towels and lingerie on the floor made it seem a bit sterile, but April would work on that later. She got up and flushed and started running hot water into the tub. She soaked her achy muscles in the hot tub for half an hour. The warmth of the water and the buzz of the Jacuzzi were hypnotic, and for thirty minutes she was able to forget that she was a pawn in a complicated game.

April got out of the tub and showered to wash her hair. After drying off she donned one of the fluffy cotton bathrobes. It was too big for her, but it did not matter. The weight and warmth and texture were exquisite, and for a few seconds April thought that this sensation was totally worth being kidnapped and locked in a box.

April walked into the bedroom, where a tray of food was waiting next to the bed: a turkey sandwich, a pickle slice, a bag of chips, two chocolate-chip cookies, and a glass of iced tea. It felt good to be not horizontal, so she stood as she nibbled the sandwich and looked out the windows at the whitecaps. Floodlights illuminated the beach below, reaching almost to the water's edge. To the right a long wooden walkway extended from a second-level deck to a small oceanside gazebo. April eventually sat on the edge of the bed and thought about her father, and she hoped nothing bad happened to her because it would kill him, and he had been hurt enough. Brooks usually spoke with her at least once a day. He would be missing her by now.

She didn't feel sleepy, but – still wearing only the bathrobe – she curled up in bed. She wondered where Peter was, and what Dionysus might do to get him before she nodded off.

Brooks had called April around lunchtime, and her phone went straight to voice mail. He tried again right after her usual dinner time, still with no answer. This was not particularly unusual. April was often busy at work and unable to answer personal calls, and Dirk never hesitated to give her take-home work if the demands of her job could not be shoehorned into an eight-hour day. Or she could have been out shopping. Occasionally, April would unwind after work by stopping by Smith's Bar, a local music venue not far from the office. There were any number of benign reasons why April failed to answer her phone, but Brooks sensed something was amiss. It was that gut feeling, or sixth sense, that most parents have that enable them to know at some not-completely conscious level that they are about to get a phone call from a school counselor, emergency room, or bail bondsman, that told Brooks April was in trouble.

He considered driving to Sandy Springs to check on her, but if she were home she'd just be annoyed if she had work to do and he dropped in unannounced. And if she wasn't home, Brooks wasn't sure what he would do other than worry more. He went into the front room and peeked around the drapes. The black SUV was still parked across the street. Brooks checked in with Peter and Benjamin via walkie-talkie. They were fine. *Maybe I'm over-thinking things.* He attempted to watch the news, but halfway through realized that a worried parent watching the late local news was like giving a hypochondriac a subscription to *The New England Journal of Medicine*. He turned the TV off and turned in, and decided to try to reach April again first thing in the morning.

It was just after two a.m. when April's bedroom door burst open and the lights came on.

"Sorry," Martina said. "But we've got our orders." April squinted to see Martina. She was accompanied by two of her friends, and they all still looked the same: overdone makeup, perfect black hair, and fitness-instructor bodies wrapped in tight black dresses. April wondered if they went to the trouble to change just for her, or if they always just slept like that.

"What do you want?"

"This won't take long," Martina said. "Here, put these on." She handed April a pair of running shorts and a t-shirt. April went to the bathroom to change, and only then did she notice that the t-shirt had "Life is Good" printed on the front. She gasped a little and her eyes welled up with tears. It wasn't from fear, or stress, or sadness. April had an unusual trait that she had never disclosed to anyone – not even her parents. She teared up whenever she was confronted with profound irony. It happened often enough and with such consistency that she coined her own word for it: *cryrony*. She dabbed her eyes with the bathrobe and went back into the bedroom.

"I gotta tell you guys," April said. "This is the worst slumber party ever."

"Sorry," Martina said. "We were going to do this tomorrow, but for some reason Dirk insisted on doing it tonight."

"You mean this morning."

"Whatever," Martina said. "Follow us." They walked down the hallway and into another bedroom. April was instructed to sit in a simple wooden chair perched on the hardwood floor next to a bed. A white bed sheet fastened to the drapes by clothespins provided a uniform and unidentifiable background. A studio light on each side of the chair illuminated the linens. After she sat down, April noticed a video camera on a tripod set up a few feet in front of her.

"We're not going to be making an internet dating site profile on me, are we?" April asked.

"Oh, you poor thing. Do you already have one?"

"No!" replied April.

"Here, take these." Martina handed her a couple of sheets of paper with text. Then she handed her a copy of Monday's edition of the *Raleigh News and Observer*. "You'll need to hold up the front page when we get started, then just read from the prepared text."

One of the girls spent an inordinate amount of time and effort to adjust the lighting and camera to her satisfaction, as if "hostage video" was going to be a new category at this year's Academy Awards. April started reading the newspaper.

"How about that," April said, perusing the entertainment section. "Looks like Tarantino is going to start filming *Kill Bill Volume 3*. He'll probably be done before we are." Even the usually stolid Martina grew impatient.

"Let's just do it. Now."

"Hold up the front page," said the camera girl. "Upright and facing the camera." *Duh*, thought April. She held up the paper. "Camera rolling."

"Cut," Martina said after a few seconds. "Now put down the paper and read from the text when I point at you."

"Camera rolling." Martina pointed at April.

"My name is April Robinson. I have been kidnapped, and I am currently being held hostage. My captors do not want money." April looked up at the camera and shook her head. "Puh-huh. Yeah, right."

"Cut! Just read what's on the paper!" Martina reprimanded. "From the top."

"Camera rolling." Martina pointed. April read.

"My name is April Robinson. I have been kidnapped and I am currently being held hostage. My captors do not want money." She paused and looked directly at the camera, then resumed reading. "They want me to be rescued, but my rescue must be carried out by one particular individual. His name is Peter, and if he's watching this, he knows who he is. If I am not rescued within 36 hours, you will never see April Robinson again. Peter, if you are watching this, call the local TV news station, and they will ask you a security-screening question to confirm that you are who you are. You will then be told how to find me."

Martina gestured to the camera girl to stop recording. "We're off."

"I'll say," April murmured. She immediately got sick to her gut and regretted cooperating for the video. They planned to kill Peter, but they could not do that and let her live, too. *I should have kept my mouth shut. At least Peter would have been spared.* Wooziness overcame her, and she closed her eyes and steadied herself by placing her hands on the seat of her chair. As she focused on taking slow, deep breaths, a little voice in the back of her head consoled her. *He's smarter than they are. Everything is going to be okay.*

"April," Martina said. April opened her eyes and looked up. "We need to come up with a security question. What's a question that only you and Peter would know the answer to?"

April thought for a minute. "What literary character is he like?" As the words left her lips she started to cry again. Maybe it was stress, or fear, or sadness. Or cryrony. She wasn't sure. Or maybe it was "all of the above," her default answer on every multiple-choice test she had ever taken.

"So what's the answer?" uttered Martina in a monotone. Apparently, the vaccination against empathy had taken.

"Boo Radley."

"What book is he in?"

"*Catcher in the Rye*," April said. "Duh."

"Oh yeah, that's right," Martina said. April wanted to jump up and push her out the door and down the stairs. "Oh, and don't worry about that 36-hour deadline. It doesn't actually start until this video gets aired on the six-o'clock local Atlanta news."

"That's *great* news," April said. The sarcasm was lost on Martina. She took April back to her room. April went back to bed and slept past sunrise.

Cyril was making good time. He was heading west on I-20 and had just crossed the Alabama line into Mississippi. He estimated that the drive to Area 52 would take 32 to 33 hours – maybe 34 if he stopped to rest. Blutaarkians – especially if they're occupied – require relatively little sleep, averaging about one hour during a 24-hour period. Cyril seemed to get by on even less, sometimes sleeping only an hour or two during a seven-or-eight day stretch. This unique trait would have given a talented bounty hunter a significant advantage when tracking his prey across the vast, empty expanse of the universe. Cyril was not that bounty hunter, and it was clear to those who knew him that he only filled the extra waking hours with baseless complaining. This spawned intense debate over billions of drinks in millions of pubs across the universe. Was Cyril's ability to go without sleep a gift, some kind of reward, for reasons that no thinking creature could fathom? Or was it some kind of punishment to all other living creatures for reasons that were not yet clear? The general consensus tilted toward the latter.

Four hours later, Cyril stopped in Shreveport for gas, and by the time he stopped again in Amarillo it was two a.m.

TWENTY-EIGHT

Brooks got up at 6 a.m. He showered and shaved and prepared bacon, eggs, and toast, but he ate only the toast and drank some coffee. At eight-o'clock – when he knew April should be up and still at her apartment – he called. She did not answer.

At nine o'clock the 27th floor elevator doors opened and Brooks walked into Dionysus corporate headquarters. He strode though the hallways unnoticed until he was standing in front of April's desk. His heart sank, because not April was sitting there. Instead it was a young man with dark hair, a receding hairline, and squinty eyes – eyes that looked like he was wearing contact lenses that were trying to escape, and he was holding them in by sheer force of his eyelids. He wore a blue shirt and a black tie. He was doing exactly nothing, and seemed okay with that.

"May I help you?" Matt said, ambivalent about finally having something to do.

"I'm Brooks." He searched for the right words. "I'm a little disappointed."

"I'm a temp," Matt said. "I get that a lot."

"I'm looking for April."

"Who's that?" Matt asked.

"She's the person who's usually sitting where you are."

"Oh. I'm a temp," said Matt again, hoping with his entire being that that would be explanation enough for Brooks. It wasn't.

"I don't suppose you know where she is?" Brooks asked.

"No sir," Matt said. "The agency called yesterday afternoon and told me to be here this morning."

"I'd like to see Dirk."

"Who's that?" Matt asked.

"He's the CEO of this operation," Brooks said. "You're sitting in front of his office."

"Oh. He's not in yet. Probably."

"Then I'll just wait for Mr. Reger," Brooks said.

"Who's that?"

"Same guy," Brooks said. "Dirk Reger." Brooks took a seat in the waiting area across from the desk that used to be April's. Watching Matt doing exactly nothing only compounded Brooks's discontent, so he got up and walked to Frank Francis's office. Hannah was also doing nothing but in an excruciatingly perky fashion. She informed Brooks that Dr. Francis was out for the day, so Brooks returned to Dirk Reger's waiting area. Around eleven, just as Brooks had finished reading all of the Forbes magazine articles about leveraging something to get lots more of something else, Dirk showed up. Brooks intercepted him at his office door.

"Dirk, we need to talk," Brooks said.

Dirk turned to him. "And you are?"

"Brooks!" interjected Matt. "His name is Brooks." Matt patted himself on the back for being a productive member of the Dionysus juggernaut despite his temp status, then as both Dirk and Brooks stared at him he came to the stark realization that he did not know Brooks's last name. He looked away and hoped the phone on his desk would ring.

"He's the temp," Brooks said. "And I'm Brooks Robinson. April's father."

"Ah, yes," said Dirk, reaching out to shake his hand. "Brooks Robinson! What can I do for you?" Dirk broke out in a smarmy smile, and Brooks felt certain he was about to be sold a juicer, a home gym, or life insurance.

"April is missing," Brooks said. "Can we talk in your office?"

Dirk's eyes darted up as he searched his memory. "Sure," he said, after he was certain that there was no telltale rope, duct tape, or ammo in plain view. They went into his office and Dirk closed the door.

"So where the hell is she?"

"Whoa, cowboy!" Dirk said. "Slow down. Last time I saw April was when she left for lunch yesterday. She called later and said she wasn't feeling well, and that she was going straight home."

"She's not at home, she doesn't answer her phone, and her car is still parked in the garage."

"Brooks. I know you're concerned, but April has been a little stressed lately. She probably just hit her favorite bar for lunch, had one too many cosmos, found some guy, and spent the night at his place. That would explain everything."

Brooks felt like he had been punched in the gut by Dirk's derogatory accusations about his daughter. Dirk felt like he had been punched in the gut by Brooks's doubled-up fist. Dirk gasped for air and – blinded by the tears in his eyes – felt his way around his desk until he was sitting doubled-over in his oversized executive chair.

"I *know* something has happened to April," Brooks said. "And I know that you – or somebody at

Dionysus — know where she is. And if anything happens to her, I will ruin your life just as sure as you are gonna amusement park yodel all over your carpet." Brooks walked out and slammed the door. Dirk threw up all over his desk, but avoided getting a single drop on the carpeting. He wiped his mouth on his sleeve.

"Showed him."

Brooks stormed toward the elevators, then turned and walked back to April's desk. He pushed Matt aside and slung open the bottom desk drawer. He removed a black leather handbag and popped it open.

"That's mine," Matt said.

"Sorry." Brooks closed it and put it back, then took April's purse from the drawer. He opened it and found her cell phone with all of his unanswered calls. He took the purse and cell phone and headed toward the elevators.

Around noon Cyril stopped at a diner just outside of Kingman, Arizona. He wasn't fatigued; in fact he was enjoying the drive through the desert with its deceptive uniformity and starkness and absence of living things that talked. But he was getting hungry, and he thought it best not to storm Area 52 on an empty stomach. He stopped at a roadside diner that had a dirt parking lot, one of those signs on a trailer, and a location that probably put it just out of reach of any sort of health inspector's jurisdiction.

He sat at the counter and ordered the chili and a glass of water. Cyril was still wearing the same disturbing (and now bloodstained) paisley green shirt he was wearing when he first encountered Benjamin. That, and his shoulder-length hair and laissez-faire approach to hygiene, drew the attention of the waitress and the two young men sitting at the end of the counter. After Cyril finished his meal, he paid and walked out into the sun-drenched parking lot. The two men followed. They each wore jeans and boots and feared nothing except – apparently – sleeves and a tenth-grade education. They caught up with Cyril as he reached the Impala.

"Hey hippy," sneered Avery. Cyril turned and scowled. He had gone well over 24 hours without speaking to a difficult human, and this jerk just snapped his winning streak.

"Well looky-here," Baron said. "Looks like we got somebody here who just went through a time warp from 1975."

"Actually, not," Cyril said. "Time warps are a ridiculously impractical way to navigate spacetime, especially since the advent of inflationary drive technology. Now if you'll excuse me..." Cyril turned away and dug the keys out of his pocket. He was less than five hours away from Area 52, and he wasn't in the mood to attempt a discussion of advanced physics with two humans who looked like they just recently mastered the use of scissors.

"Hold on, freak," Avery said.

"What?" snapped Cyril.

"See, we can tell you ain't from around here," Avery said. "You ain't very hospitable like."

"That's right," Baron said. He nodded enthusiastically and did not stop until his friend glared at him and shook his head.

"So sorry," Cyril said. He shoved his hand into a pocked and withdrew a stick of gum. "Would a stick of gum help?"

"Naw," Avery said.

"Suit yourself." Cyril unwrapped the gum and popped the stick into his mouth.

Baron looked deflated. "I wanted some gum."

"Shut up, Baron," Avery said. "See, it's tradition in these parts – when a stranger comes to town we get to test drive their car. I'm surprised you didn't know that." Baron perked up, and resumed nodding in anticipation of getting to call "Shotgun!" in the very near future.

"Guess I missed the sign," Cyril said. "But it looks like I get off on a technicality. This isn't my car." He turned to unlock the car door. Cyril knew what Avery and Baron were up to. He could have easily neutralized them and been on his way, but Earth made him cranky. He had been burdened with babysitting Benjamin from the get-go, then shot to death, arrested, held captive by a supersecret government agency, shot at by drug lords, forced to ride in the back of a pickup, and – when he thought it could not get any worse – coerced to live in a recreational vehicle. Cyril was accustomed to being the bully (though the general consensus was that he was a mediocre one at best) and it had been far too long since he had attempted to compensate for his slightly unhappy childhood by acting out. He was looking forward to this.

Avery grabbed Cyril's shoulder and spun him around. "How 'bout you hand over those keys?"

"How about you go pick on someone from your own level of stunted psychosocial development?"

A look of befuddlement panned across Avery's face. He wasn't sure he had been insulted, but it was obvious that Cyril was not making any effort to hand over the keys to the Impala. He grabbed Cyril's shoulder with his left hand and drew back his right fist. Blutaarkian neurotoxin splashed across Avery's exposed left arm, and he collapsed to the ground in a writhing heap of denim and regret. Avery would have bet his truck that his arm was on fire. When the pain exploded to the rest of his body, he opened his eyes but saw only blackness. *I'm in Hell*, thought Avery, but then quickly dismissed that idea because he saw neither an evil tormentor with horns and a pitchfork nor his second-cousin Rupert, who preferred the company of men. Loss of consciousness temporarily delivered Avery from his pain and stupidity.

Seeing Avery incapacitated in the dirt, Baron stopped nodding and stared slack-jawed at Cyril until he put two-and-two together and got something approximating four. He turned and broke into a trot toward the black pickup. Cyril pulled the gum from his mouth, and from twenty feet away pegged the back of Baron's arm.

Baron collapsed in much the same way Avery did. Baron was bulkier, and a cloud of dust arose when he hit the parking lot. The convection oven known as the Mojave blew dust particles into Cyril's face, irritating his eyes and annoying him in general. Through tear-filled eyes he spied the mirage-like image of Avery's truck, and he wondered if it contained anything that could potentially compensate him for the pain and suffering of red, watery eyes. Avery and Baron were still occupied with being unconscious, and were in no condition to object when Cyril asked with uncharacteristic politeness if he might have a look.

"It's sort of a Blutaarkian tradition," Cyril added. "When someone makes you cry for no good reason, you get to loot their vehicle." This was not actually a Blutaarkian tradition, and in fact during his college days Cyril received a 30-day sentence for doing this exact same thing to an ex-girlfriend. But this wasn't Blutaark and Cyril harbored no restraining-order defying obsession with Avery or Baron, so he made his was across the parking lot to the lifted black Ford pickup. Cyril tiptoed to reach the door handle, and then climbed inside to look around.

Cyril discovered the glove compartment and dug out a Smith & Wesson snub-nosed revolver, then stuck his arm behind the seat and found a Remington 700 rifle. Cyril had not put much thought into how he would launch an assault on a fortified installation like Area 52, but now that he was just a few hours away from his target, he recognized that having weapons other than sarcasm and neurotoxin would be advantageous. Plus, the guns looked cool, too. He hopped out of the pickup with the rifle and revolver and skipped past his still-unconscious lootees.

"Thanks fellas," chirped an upbeat Cyril. Things were looking up. He tossed the rifle into the back seat of the Impala, stuffed the revolver into his pants, and got behind the wheel. He headed north and forty minutes later he crossed into Nevada.

Brooks drove to April's apartment and let himself in with a key she had given him for emergencies. Nothing in the apartment looked amiss, and he found that both comforting and disturbing. He locked up and drove home. April had now been missing for over 24 hours, so Brooks called the police to file a missing person report. He informed them that he was certain someone at Dionysus was responsible, and in return he got a perfunctory "We'll look into it." He spent a couple of hours going through her cell phone contacts and calling her friends, but none of them had seen or heard from her in the last 24 hours. Finally, he picked up the walkie-talkie and called Peter.

"We should go look for her," Peter said.

"I've already done that," Brooks replied. "I don't know where else to look. Besides, it crossed my mind that they may be using her to draw you out. That black car is still parked out front, by the way."

"So what do we do?"

"We sit tight, for now," Brooks said. "I'll think of something." He paced about through every room of his house, then sat in April's old bedroom for a spell, then paced some more. After a couple of hours on his feet, he decided to sit down in the living room and turn on the TV to drown out the sickening silence.

April woke up around ten to find breakfast sitting on a tray next to her bed. She went to the bathroom, then crawled back into bed and enjoyed her breakfast of Belgian waffles with blueberries, sausage, milk, and juice. When she finished, she sat and ran her fingers across the 1500 count Egyptian cotton sheets, and for the first time took a good look at the bedroom where she was being held captive. She remembered what Martina had said the night before. *You are going to have a long day tomorrow.* That had sounded ominous, but April struggled to generate any comforting, familiar anxiety.

Weird, she thought. She was having a pretty good day, so far. April felt less stress and anxiety than on a typical Tuesday morning working under Dirk Reger at Dionysus. *Dionysus. If they wanted to really torture me, they could just play a loop of Dirk repeating "synergy" and "value added."* She got out of bed, opened the plantation shutters, and explored the room. The windows could not be opened, and other than the bathroom door, there was just the one door that led to the hallway. When Martina opened her door to retrieve the tray, April could see one of the girls standing guard outside of her room. April attempted to engage Martina.

"So what's on the agenda for today?"

"Well...you just keep being a hostage for now," Martina said.

"Any more video productions?" April said. "Perhaps an enhanced interrogation session? Maybe a field trip to the beach? I forgot to pack a swimsuit when I was being shoved into a crate at gunpoint, but a walk on the sand might be nice."

"No. There are icky things in the sand," Martina said. "I have to go. If I keep holding this tray I'm going to develop unsightly arm muscles. You understand."

"Ohhkay." April decided that, given the option, she would choose waterboarding over a walk on the beach with Martina. Martina closed and locked the door, and April looked for something to do. There was a bookcase decorated with shells and starfish and sand dollars. The few books it held looked as if they came from a display bookcase at a second-hand furniture store: *Gregg Shorthand for Beginners, The Illustrated History of Animal Husbandry,* and *The Panama Canal – Pros and Cons*. A flat-screen TV adorned the wall opposite the bed, and April found the remote control in a nightstand drawer. She sat cross-legged at the end of the bed and channel-surfed until she stopped on a movie she had seen a half-dozen times before, but decided to watch anyway because it seemed appropriate: *Girl Interrupted*.

After the movie, April settled on the weather channel. It was going to be a lovely day on the Outer Banks. Her attention was broken by a metallic thump-thump-thumping that echoed rhythmically, like a calypso steel drum was migrating from the second floor to the third via the hardwood staircase. Once it reached the top of the stairs the thumping stopped, replaced by the sound of something being dragged down the hall until it faded into another room. This sequence of sound effects was repeated two more times, interrupted only once by a "Crap, my nail!"

April turned off the TV and started digging in drawers looking for paper and pen. She was bored and the compulsion to write tugged at her psyche like a needy two-year-old tugging at the hem of a mother's skirt. April yearned to dump her emotions onto paper – the vague fear, the free-floating anxiety, the relentless depression, the saudade she felt for the time before she lost her mother, before Brooks got sick, and before she worked for Dionysus. As she searched the room, her thoughts turned more practical. She might not have much time left, so she would document everything that had happened to her over the last few days. She would write about meeting Peter, how he cured Brooks, and how Peter overcame her skepticism by demonstrating the miraculous capabilities of the BAT. She would document the evil, incompetence, and corruption at Dionysus that led to her abduction and her current unresolved status as hostage.

The only blank paper she could find was a few practice pages in *Gregg Shorthand for Beginners*. She could find no pen or pencil. *Duh. Who writes at the beach?* The needy two-year-old wanted to throw a tantrum.

April guessed it was around two or three in the afternoon when Martina returned with lunch. Martina stayed and watched from a chair next to the door while April sat on the edge of the bed and ate from the tray. Martina slumped and looked tired and distraught.

"Hey, who's the hostage here?" April said with a grin.

"You are," Martina said without a grin. "Can I get you anything?" April dismissed the obvious requests: a SWAT team, a "no locked door" policy, an anti-anxiety medication that lived up to its hype.

"How about something to write with?"

"Sorry," Martina said. "Dirk said no phones or laptops."

"I meant like a pen and paper." Martina stepped out of the room, and a few minutes later she returned with a yellow spiral notebook and a black ball-point pen. "So is this Dirk's place?" asked April. "He never mentioned it."

"No," Martina said. "But he chose it because it's large, isolated, only accessible to four-wheel drive vehicles, and the constant sound of the ocean drowns out all of that annoying screaming."

"Screaming?" April shuddered. "Even after everything that's happened so far, I didn't think you'd resort to torture."

"We won't," Martina said. "I was talking about Dirk's spoiled brat she-child. She's a monster if she doesn't get her way – actually, she's a monster even when she gets her way. Dirk thought he might bring his kids out here for the weekend if Peter didn't show."

"Who does this place belong to?"

"According to the mail in the mailbox, David and Ruth Laskin," Martina said. "Dirk found it online, had us scout it out, and since it was listed as vacant we broke in and commandeered it."

"Why didn't he just rent it?"

"Dirk didn't want to lose the security deposit,"

Martina said.

"Great," April said. She made a mental note to not bleed on something expensive if they shot her inside the beach house. Martina took the food tray and left, and April started writing. When she stopped for a break it was almost 6 p.m.

TWENTY-NINE

Cyril pulled off of highway 50 and turned onto an unmarked dirt road that led north. He stopped the Impala and unfolded a map of Nevada, a page torn from the road atlas Brooks had given him. Cyril recognized the roads and landmarks – the images had been seared into his memory during the flight out of Area 52. He estimated that it was now about 18 miles away. He started the Impala and headed north in a cloud of desert dust, and after 12 miles he pulled the car off of the dirt road and stopped.

Cyril climbed out of the car and stretched. The sun had dipped below the peaks to the west, and an October chill was already settling onto the desert. Under the dome light, Cyril spread the road map onto the seat and oriented it with his surroundings. The dirt road was not on the map, but Cyril used the odometer to determine how far he had driven from the highway. One of Cyril's aptitudes (some might argue the only one) was his uncanny ability to know his exact location and maintain his orientation on the surface of any solid planet with only a paucity of external cues, coupled with his ability to walk in a straight line for many, many kilometers at a time without deviating so much as a degree. The general consensus was that Cyril developed these skills as a toddler when his parents abandoned him in the most remote locales planet Blutaark had to offer. He would need these skills again tonight. He stuffed the map into a pocket, retrieved the rifle from the back seat, closed the car door, and headed toward Area 52.

Cyril made the six-mile trek to Area 52 in a brisk ninety minutes. He felt the unpredictable surface of the desert floor give way to the uniformity of the asphalt runway before he made out two structures in the darkness: the steel barrack, and beyond that, the rusting shed. He crossed the runway and jogged to the padlocked door of the barrack. So far, Cyril had encountered no resistance. There had been no fence, no armed agents watching from a sentry tower, no guards patrolling the premises in armored personnel carriers. *Stupid humans.* Cyril convinced himself that reclaiming the BAT and the *Rev 9* would be a cakewalk – only more fun – because he hated cakes, carnival games, and not being allowed to shoot at others enjoying themselves.

Cyril felt the padlock in the dark, then took two steps back, looked around, and pulled the revolver from his waistband. He cocked the gun, aimed in the general direction of the lock, and fired. He decided that he should have taken three or four steps back when hot metal fragments ricocheted off the metal door and onto his forehead. He examined the padlock. It was still intact.

"Arrrgggghhhh!" Cyril thrust his shoulders from side-to-side in frustration. Ignoring the fact that the revolver had a finite number of bullets, Cyril took four steps back and fired four more times.

The sound of gunfire filled the desert valley and echoed off of the peaks to the west and the north.

Cyril turned to scan the desert behind him, and seeing exactly zero armed humans approaching, he returned to the locked barrack door. One of the bullets penetrated the body of the padlock, but when Cyril yanked it the shackle held tight. He circled the barrack and found a small window in the back. He lifted the Remington 700 and with the butt of the rifle he broke out a window pane, then cleared the shards from the frame and reached in to unlock the latch. It was a lot of trouble for a window that was not locked. He opened the window and climbed in and stood in front of the elevator.

The glow from the white button next to the elevator reflected off of the silver doors and provided Cyril with an irresistible target. Cyril raised the handgun and fired. Sparks flew, the light was successfully snuffed out, and the elevator doors parted. He reflected for a moment, recalling that Agent Hays had simply pushed the white button to activate the elevator. *Boring!* Cyril stepped into the elevator. "Telstar" was still playing overhead. He was tempted to shoot, in no particular order, the overhead speaker and the white button on the panel. But he considered the close quarters and his earlier unpleasant experience with shooting the padlock and decided to just push the white button and hum loudly instead.

The elevator doors closed and the car plummeted, and in his abrupt near-weightless state Cyril took a moment to regret ordering the chili at that diner in Kingman. The elevator slowed and Cyril prepared himself for an all-out assault on Area 52. He clutched the rifle in his left hand, drew the revolver with his right, and took cover just inside the door next to the control panel. His heart pounded with anticipation.

The elevator stopped, a bell rang, and the doors parted. Cyril waited, and when the expected fusillade failed to develop, he leaped from the elevator and stormed down the dim corridor, aiming his (now empty) handgun at the courageous lone defender of Area 52: a jumpsuit-clad custodian with a mop.

Cyril stopped, caught his breath, and reassessed the situation. He surmised that the human guardians of Area 52 had decided that it would be a breach of etiquette to wage a bloody battle to the death on a freshly mopped floor. He stuck the handgun into his pants and headed down the corridor in search of unmopped floors and his manners-conscious adversary. His footsteps echoed down the length of the corridor, but the custodian ignored him until Cyril was upon him.

"Watch it!" he said. "Wet floor." The custodian pointed a gnarled finger at a yellow plastic sign emblazoned with the international symbol for "wet floor."

"Sorry," Cyril said. "On Blutaark that's the symbol for skateboarders ahead."

"Go around," snarled the custodian. He resumed mopping the floors of Area 52, a thankless task that he would have to start all over again the minute he completed it, a job he approached with all of the joy of Sisyphus with a mop and marginal benefits.

Cyril turned right. He wandered about a labyrinth of long, poorly lit, and empty corridors, and with each new turn he grew more irritated and distraught at the lack of armed humans to engage in battle. Cyril considered backtracking to find the custodian and shoot him, just to try to cheer himself up a bit, but was too disoriented to know which way to go.

Everything looked the same. Nothing looked

familiar. He tried to open several unmarked windowless doors, but they were locked. Finally, he turned down another gray corridor to find harsh fluorescent light spilling into the hallway from a large rectangular window. Cyril drew the revolver and edged closer to find a middle-aged woman sitting behind a white linoleum counter, poring over a voluminous ledger. Directly behind her was a room filled with metal shelves, government-issue desks and chairs, and a mimeograph machine. Directly in front of her was Cyril.

"May I help you?" she asked without looking up. Cyril sensed a trap. The dowdy matron with her horn-rimmed bifocals and her hair in a bun was an obvious diversion to lull him into a sense of complacency. He was prepared to shoot her, but he needed some answers, and from past experience Cyril understood that the "shoot first and ask questions later" approach generally produced lots of screaming that made it difficult to understand the answers.

"Yes," Cyril said. "I'm looking for the alien spaceship hangar."

"Aren't we all?" said the clerk.

"I beg your pardon?" Cyril said.

"The right man. We're all looking for the right man." She finally looked over the top of her glasses and gave Cyril the once-over. "But in your case, your tragic sense of fashion is going to work against you."

"That's not what I said. I simply asked where the alien spaceship hangar is."

"Suit yourself. To your left to the second corridor. You'll take a right, then another left at the third corridor. That one runs directly to the hangar entrance. You can't miss it." Cyril turned to leave but froze when the clerk shouted at him. "Hey! Is that a

Remington 700?"

Crap, thought Cyril. His back was to the clerk. He could not be less vulnerable. He half expected a bullet to enter the back of his skull at any second, but clearly this clerk had a "ask questions first – shoot later" policy.

"Why, yes it is." He still had the revolver in his right hand, and wondered if he could spin and get a shot off before she did.

"Nice," said the clerk. "I've got a scoped Remington 700 BDL. It was a present from my third husband." Cyril had slowly turned and was now facing her. His thumb stroked the hammer of the Smith & Wesson. "We used to hunt together until he mysteriously disappeared on that elk expedition in Montana." She chuckled and broke into an unnerving grin. Cyril wasn't sure, but he thought maybe the gray-haired clerk winked at him when she said "disappeared." But he was positive that she had made air quotes with her index and middle fingers.

"Sorry for your loss," Cyril said, using finger quotes when he said the word "loss." "But I have to go – they're not expecting me."

"Good luck."

Cyril followed her directions, and within a couple of minutes he was standing in front of the spacecraft hangar. Through a long horizontal window he saw six unfamiliar alien ships, and in the far corner – the *Rev 9*. The corridor was quiet, and he saw no one in the hangar guarding the vehicles. Cyril pushed a pad next to the window and a door appeared. He sauntered into the room, and seeing nothing threatening, he put the revolver back in his pants. To his right was a large platform. From each corner taut metal cables ascended into a black shaft cut into the ceiling. Cyril guessed that this freight elevator ended at the large shed adjacent to the steel barrack on the desert floor 9,000 feet above.

The *Rev 9* was parked on a flat dolly, and its hatch had been left open. He circled the craft, inspecting it as best as he could, then went inside. Nothing was amiss. Everything seemed to be in working order, the keys were still in the ignition, and someone had painstakingly detailed the cabin. He was a little disappointed that the bloodstains from his gunshot wound had been wiped away – that sort of thing would sometimes get you complimentary drinks at intergalactic bounty hunter bars. But overall, Cyril was not unhappy at the care they had shown the *Rev 9*. He climbed out of the craft and onto a bright yellow tow tractor. He backed it up to the *Rev 9*, hitched the dolly to the tractor, and pulled forward toward the platform.

After Cyril centered the *Rev 9*, he unhitched the dolly and drove the tow tractor off of the elevator. A brick-sized metal box with two black buttons dangled from a corrugated metal tube at one end of the platform. Cyril walked to the box and placed his thumb on the "up" button. Despite leaving Earth without Peter, he was looking forward to piloting the *Rev 9* again, to the emptiness of space, and to being unwelcome at any restaurant with a reasonable dress code. A tiny grin broke across his face. *Hold on*, he thought. *Seems like I'm forgetting something.* The grin disappeared. Then Cyril frowned a little. Then a lot.

"Arrrggghhhhhh!" He let go of the box and thrust his shoulders back and forth until the self-induced vertigo tossed him from the elevator platform and onto the hangar floor. "The BAT! And my belt! Stupid, stupid, stupid!" Cyril wallowed in self-pity, and when he was done he picked himself up, brushed himself off, and walked out of the hangar to find his belt and the BAT and – if he got lucky – to shoot somebody. He decided that the clerk would be the best place to start, so he reversed the clerk's directions to the hangar until he was standing at her window again.

"May I help you?" This time she looked up and tossed her unnerving grin into Cyril's face.

"Sorry to bother you again," Cyril started. "Your directions to the hangar were spot-on, so thanks for that. But I was wondering where you store the personal effects of detained aliens."

"That would be the detained alien personal effects storage," said the clerk.

"Yes, yes," Cyril said. "That is very helpful." He used air quotes when he said "helpful." "But where is detained alien personal effects storage located?"

"From where you're standing, go right. Take the first right, then another right two corridors down. It will be the third door on the left."

"Thanks," Cyril said.

"You are very welcome," said the clerk. She used finger quotes at "very welcome."

Cyril took off to his right and made a right turn at the first corridor. He was a few steps away from the second corridor when he heard a door open behind him, followed by the distinct sound of a gun being drawn from its holster.

"Freeze, maggot! Hands in the air!" Even from behind Agent Hays recognized Cyril. A night of binge drinking had failed to erase the image of Cyril's paisley shirt.

Cyril turned slowly with his hands in the air. From the corner of his eye he caught Agent Hays's multicolored Hawaiian shirt, which stood out in the gray corridor like a clown on a battleship. In a split second, Cyril recalled the gunfight at the junkyard in Alabama, and how everyone was shooting and no one was getting shot. Cyril liked his odds. He ducked to his right and bolted down the second corridor. A gunshot rang out and echoed down the hallway, followed by the sound of Hays's labored footsteps. Cyril found a door, and as Hays rounded the corner with his gun drawn, Cyril grabbed the door handle and yanked as hard as he could.

"Arrrrggghhh!" Cyril dropped the rifle, grabbed his wrist, and crumpled to the floor. The door was locked. "I think I broke something."

"On your belly," shouted Hays. "Hands behind your back."

Cyril snorted but did as he was told. Hays kicked the rifle away, and then held his gun against the back of Cyril's head with his right hand and cuffed him with his left. Hays holstered his gun and pulled Cyril to his feet. He patted him down, confiscated the Smith & Wesson, and then led him down the hallway.

"I could have been halfway to Dulder 4 by now if I hadn't come back for the BAT," Cyril grumbled.

"The BAT?" said Agent Hays. "When you find it give me a call. Then we'll both know where it is."

"It's not in detained alien personal effects storage?" Cyril was incredulous.

"I wish." Hays laughed. "I haven't seen the BAT since that salvage yard fiasco."

"But...but..." Cyril doubled over, then stood and arched his back. He unleashed a guttural scream that reverberated throughout the labyrinthine corridors and elevator shafts of Area 52, and made Agent Hays consider both early retirement and an appointment with an ear specialist. "Peter," snarled Cyril. He spat on the floor.

"Hey, hey, hey," Hays said. "It'll be weeks before our janitor mops this sector." Hays grabbed Cyril by the arm and walked him through a convoluted path through the hallways of Area 52. "So where's Peter?"

"He's back in Atlanta. At least that's where he was when I left."

"Great," Hays said. "Technically I'm off the clock, but I'll be back in the morning to interrogate you. We'll go after Peter once our security personnel get back."

"Where's your security?" Cyril asked.

"I take comfort in knowing that I can retire with a decent pension and benefits in six years. And that I've got the respect of my children. Well, three out of four, anyway. Things sort of went bad between me and Ted after that time he was away at church camp and I was cleaning his room -"

"No, no, no," Cyril said. "I meant the people who guard Area 52. Where are they?"

"Oh," Hays said. "It's their week for the canoe trip." They stopped in front of a door marked "quarantine." Hays told Cyril to put his feet together, then he zip-tied his ankles. He unlatched the door and tossed Cyril onto an army surplus cot, and with a terse "See you later" walked out and slammed the door. Cyril turned to see a gaunt, sickly-looking alien on a cot adjacent to his. He wasn't familiar with her race.

"Who are you?"

"Barbaxaquottlmangaporellianfori," replied the woman, without lifting her head or even opening her eyes.

"Can I call you 'Barb?' " Cyril asked.

"No," whispered the alien.

THIRTY

It was the lead story on the local six o'clock news. A young Atlanta woman had been kidnapped, and her abductors had emailed a link to a video to each local news outlet, demanding that it be aired. They weren't asking for money – they simply wanted someone named Peter – and only Peter – to attempt her rescue. If Peter was watching, he was to call the news station to answer questions to confirm his identity. The kidnappers threatened to kill April within 36 hours if their demands were not met.

One news station decided not to air the video – not for ethical reasons – but because they calculated that April's murder would make for more interesting TV than her rescue would, and thus pull higher ratings. But two of the news stations decided to air the video, mostly because they forgot to carry the "1" when they ran their calculations. Luckily, Brooks Robinson happened to be watching one of those stations.

Brooks watched the video and, despite being overwhelmed with emotions, tried to absorb as much information as possible. He scrutinized the image of April's face, looking for clues to her well-being, state of mind, and location. He thought that she looked tired, and maybe a little annoyed – and she could have taken a couple of minutes to brush her hair and touch up her makeup – but she did not appear distressed. The only clue to her location was the Raleigh paper. He was relieved that April was alive, but infuriated that someone – or more likely, some corporation – was using her to get to Peter. At the conclusion of the video, the number for the station scrolled along the bottom of the screen.

Peter. Brooks closed his eyes and took a few seconds to sear the images from the video into his memory, then dashed out the back door. Brooks raced across the back yard and barged into the RV. Benjamin had been nodding off at the table over the July issue of *Georgia Highways*. Peter was lying in bed, hoping that April was okay, and that Cyril wasn't. Brooks startled them; they expected him to communicate via walkie-talkie, and assumed he would do so before coming out to the RV unless it was an emergency.

"What's wrong?" Peter said as Brooks caught his breath.

"April is being held hostage." Peter had never before heard panic in Brooks's voice. "They just played a hostage video on the news. She seems okay, but they are threatening to kill her in 36 hours if their demands aren't met."

"What demands?" Peter asked. "I've seen her apartment, and – nothing personal, Brooks – but the word 'pauper' springs to mind."

"They don't want money. They want you to rescue April. There's a number you're supposed to call." Brooks had scribbled the number down and he handed it to Peter. "They are gonna ask you questions to make sure you're the one."

"Just so there aren't any math questions," Peter

said. Brooks handed him a cell phone. Peter entered the number that Brooks had written. It took several minutes to get through to the news station. More than two dozen men in the greater Atlanta metro area who happened to be named Peter – and a handful who were not – called the number thinking that it was some kind of reality TV contest, and that the prize was a date with April. Or an all-expense paid trip to Raleigh. Understandably, the station intern who was given the job of fielding these calls was short when Peter's call finally went through.

"Are you calling about the hostage video?"

"Yes," Peter said.

"State your name."

"Peter...of Blutaark."

"Fine. We would have also accepted 'Peter Finch.' Now the second and final question. What literary character are you like?"

Peter smiled. "Boo Radley."

The intern gave Peter another phone number that he was to call immediately. Peter did. A man with a gravelly voice answered and immediately delivered detailed instructions that Peter committed to memory. Peter was told to drive directly to Charlotte, North Carolina. He was given explicit directions to a used book store. There he would find a copy of *Ten Minutes from Normal* by Karen Hughes. Peter would find a slip of paper on page 119 with another phone number to call for additional instructions. Obviously, Peter should come alone, and there should be absolutely no police involvement. Otherwise, he would be putting April in grave danger. And they would know, because they will be watching him every step of the way.

"You do have access to a car, right?"

"Sort of," Peter said. "It's called a 'Winnebago.' "

"Not ideal, but acceptable. You will need to leave now. You have less than four hours to get to Charlotte and make the next call. The bookstore closes at ten. Any questions?"

"Yes," Peter said. "What if someone buys that book before I get there?"

The voice on the other end broke into raucous laughter that continued for several seconds until it turned into a raucous hacking cough. Then the phone went dead.

"I have to get to Charlotte," Peter said, handing the phone back to Brooks.

"You mean April," Ben said.

"No, no. The kidnappers instructed me to drive to North Carolina for further instructions. I have to leave immediately."

"Then let's get a move on!" Brooks said.

"Brooks, I know you're concerned, but that's a bad idea. They specifically told me to come alone. Besides, if we leave in the RV, I'm betting that black car that's still parked out front is going to follow us. I doubt that they are connected to the kidnapping – I'm betting you're being watched by Persona, or government agents. But either way, they could detain us, or at least keep us from getting to Charlotte before the deadline."

"When's the deadline?" Brooks asked.

"Ten p.m." Brooks stood, shaking his head and looking at the floor, not saying a word. Peter could see he was conflicted, but the clock was ticking. "Brooks, we need you to create a diversion. Or we'll never make it."

"You always seem to know what's best," Brooks said. Peter outlined the plan. He would drive, and Ben would accompany him, hidden in the back of the RV. Brooks ran back into the house and returned with the keys to the Winnebago. "Godspeed. And you'll probably need this, too." He handed the cell phone and keys to Peter, and hugged him. He went to Ben and hugged him too, then whispered something in his ear. Brooks bounded out of the RV, opened the gate at the side of the house, walked to his pickup, and climbed in.

Brooks started the truck and then ripped down the street, leaving behind a cloud of smoke in the air, a trail of rubber on the pavement, and a neighbor on the phone with the HOA president to lodge a formal complaint. Before Brooks reached the end of the block, the black vehicle had made a U-turn and was in pursuit. As soon as it was out of sight, Peter fired up the Winnebago, drove through the open gate, and floored it. As they headed toward the interstate, Benjamin desperately searched for a seat belt.

"You look dreadful," Cyril said.

"I know," said Barbaxaquottlmangaporellianfori.

"How long have you been here?"

"Several months," she said. "I am dying here. I am malnourished. My captors cannot provide an adequate low-carb diet, but they will not let me leave."

"You should have escaped," Cyril said.

"You should have not been captured."

"They got lucky," Cyril quipped.

"Actually, I had one opportunity," she said. "My race has the ability to insinuate our thoughts, our desires, into the minds of other sentient creatures – but only when they are asleep, dreaming. They were holding a human who was known as 'Ben.' He seemed kind, if not overly bright. I tried to compel him to facilitate my escape. He was supposed to come to this very cell and release me, then expedite my safe passage to the spacecraft hangar where I could have reclaimed my captured vessel and escaped this sick planet. Something went wrong. He must have hit his head or something."

"You know," Cyril said. "You verbalize a lot more than most species do when they are dying." He was in no mood to talk or listen – now, or ever, really – and he was convinced that acknowledging his passing acquaintance with Benjamin Cotter would only lead to more talking and listening.

"You must hail from V'shogg," she said. "The planet with the most rude, insensitive, and socially inept creatures in the known universe. Either that, or you're Cyril of Blutaark."

Cyril decided that this was going not at all like he wanted. He changed the subject. "So what's there to do around here?"

"Wait."

"Okay." Cyril said nothing. He was uncomfortable lying on the cot with his hands behind his back, so he shifted and rolled onto his side so he was facing her. "What are we waiting for?"

"What do you mean?"

"You told me to wait," Cyril said. "I hate waiting. What are we waiting for?"

"You asked me what there is to do around here," she said. "That was my answer. Wait. There is nothing else, really. No future, no hope for escape, no adequately equipped gym with both cardio equipment and free weights. You just wait."

Barbaxaquottlmangaporellianfori faced Cyril's cot, but she had kept her eyes closed ever since Agent Hays had thrown him into her cell. Now she opened her eyes like someone waking from prolonged anesthesia. She gasped, a look of disgust washed over her face, she raised her frail arm, and with one spindly digit she pointed at a rectangular bulge in Cyril's pants. "What...is *that*?"

Cyril looked down at the front pocket of his pants and recognized the outline of the device Peter had given him when he departed for Area 52. "It's called a BAMN."

"That is a horrid nickname."

"No," Cyril said. "It's an acronym – for a device. It stands for 'By Any Means Necessary.' It was given to me by...an acquaintance. He said I could use it if I ever...found myself...in an impossible...situation."

"You mean...like the one you are in now?"

"Sure," Cyril said. He shrugged. "I suppose – from the perspective of a casual observer – it might appear that I'm kind of in an impossible situation."

"Kind of?" she said. "You are on an alien planet, locked in a cell 3,000 meters underground, you have not a plasma immobilizer to your name, you are not particularly bright or charming, and after the canoe trip there will be armed guards stationed outside the door and patrolling every corridor."

"I bet you're a drag at parties," Cyril said.

"I bet you are a drag everywhere." She paused. "So how does it work?" She made a point not to look at it.

"There's a button. You just open it and push the button. But I can't get to it."

Barbaxaquottlmangaporellianfori shuddered. "I suppose I could retrieve it. This had better not be some kind of vile trick."

"I just hope it's not a garage-door opener," Cyril said. "Or a bomb." Cyril was having second thoughts about putting his trust in Peter and making the trek to Nevada. If Agent Hays had been forthright, and the BAT wasn't here, then where was it? Did Peter still have it? If so, then clearly Cyril had been conned into returning to Area 52 just so Peter could be rid of him. *Maybe permanently*, thought Cyril. The sinking feeling in Cyril's gut told him that he would know, one way or the other, the second Barbaxaquottlmangaporellianfori pushed the white button.

She took a slow deep breath and extended her arm. She could just reach Cyril. She worked two fingers into his front pocket and pinched the BAMN. She tugged, but in her weakened condition she could only advance it a centimeter at a time before letting go to rest. When the top half of the gray-and-white box was exposed, she grasped it with all four digits and pulled. It escaped Cyril's pocket, but slipped through her fatigued fingers, bouncing off of the cot and crashing onto the concrete floor.

Cyril flinched, then realizing that they had not been blown to tiny bits, decided that the moment should not be exempt from sarcasm. "Nice job."

"Sorry," she whispered. With one final effort she reached to the floor, lifted the box, and flipped it open. She placed the tip of her finger on the white button.

"Hold on," Cyril said. "Could you maybe hold it over that way a little bit?" She ignored him and pushed the button. Then nothing happened. Lots of nothing. Seeing the huge amount of nothing that was going on, Cyril flung himself into a state of rage. He would have rather been blown to pieces than to be forced to confront this overwhelming tidal wave of nothing. "Arrrgggghhhh." With his hands still cuffed behind him, he thrust his shoulders back and forth with unbridled anger, rocking the cot and nearly ejecting his body onto the floor. He stopped, and – panting and sweating – demanded that Barbaxaquottlmangaporellianfori throw the BAMN box against the wall.

"Why?"

"Because it will give my tantrum closure! Now throw it!"

She lifted her twig-like limb, and with all of the energy she could muster, heaved the BAMN box toward the concrete wall. It fluttered short of its mark, landing with a *coosh* onto a blanket at the end of Cyril's cot.

"Arrrrrrgggggghhhhhhh! You throw like a girl!" She turned away from Cyril and shut her eyes. She sensed something – something other than Cyril's ill-tempered grumbling. It wasn't auditory, but something she understood to be inside of her – a deep, profound, resonant force. She wondered if she was dying. It seemed to fade, and she drifted off to sleep.

"What time is it?" shouted Benjamin from the back of the RV. He sounded panicky.

Peter attempted to reassure Ben by shouting back at him. "It's about nine forty-five. Plenty of time." Ben was reassured. "If the clock on the microwave is right." Then he wasn't.

The Winnebago barreled through the streets of Charlotte. Ben had secured himself to a barrel chair in the back of the RV with a crude cocoon fashioned from pillows and bungee cords. But the chair swiveled, and that fact – combined with Peter's reactive, choreiform driving – made Ben's trip from Atlanta to North Carolina a nauseating, non-stop, three-and-a-half hour amusement park ride. Used bookstore or not, he was ready for the ride to be over.

"How much farther?" Ben asked.

"Judging from the directions they gave me, about

four kilometers." Peter said. "And no sign of the robots yet."

"What?"

"No robots!" shouted Peter. "I didn't want to alarm you, but the orange robot warning light came on about 40 minutes ago."

Benjamin unhooked the web of bungee cords and staggered to the front of the RV. He steadied himself against the back of Peter's seat and peered at the dashboard. "That's a gas pump. We're on empty. You need to find a gas station. Now." Ben felt a subtle lurch that told him the motor had just stopped. "Correction. You need to find a gas station ten minutes ago." He reached in front of Peter and threw the transmission into neutral. He squinted through the windshield, and through his thick glasses he thought he could make out a gas station two blocks ahead.

"We're coasting," Ben said. "But I think that's a gas station on the right. Just pull into that driveway. If we make it there." The road sloped gently in their favor at the moment of total fuel depletion, but now it leveled off, and the RV was creeping toward a standstill. "Just...a few more...feet."

The silent behemoth lurched again as it crossed the threshold of the gas station driveway. Peter strained at the steering wheel, guiding the beast to its final resting place – next to the gas pump. Peter never touched the brakes. Ben looked at the clock; it was nine forty-eight.

Benjamin jumped from the RV and found the gas cap. It was locked, staunchly protecting the dozen or so molecules of fossil fuel that remained in the tank. He shouted to Peter. "Throw me the keys!" Peter pulled the keys from the ignition, leaned out the door, and tossed them to Ben. Ben found the gas cap key, unlocked the cap, and grabbed a pump handle.

"How long will this take?" Peter asked.

Ben shook his head. He thought Peter appeared inappropriately unpanicky. "Ten, twelve minutes, maybe longer," he said with a look of despair.

"Not enough time," Peter said. "I'm going on foot." Ben did the math. They were probably more than two miles from the bookstore with less than twelve minutes until the deadline. Peter would need to run consecutive five-minute miles to get there in time. By the time Ben checked his work, Peter had leaped from the Winnebago and sprinted into the darkness like a greyhound – if greyhounds were bipedal and completely oblivious to traffic. Still holding the pump handle, Ben remembered that he had given his good gas card to Cyril. After a desperate search, he found Brooks's card clipped underneath the driver's side sun visor.

People in Charlotte honk a lot, thought Peter as he turned right on a service road, ran down a grassy slope, and across a busy expressway. He dashed up a slope on the opposite side and then followed the service road for over a mile. He was making good time by sprinting and taking short cuts that he could not take with the Winnebago without eliciting rude gestures from other motorists. (Blutaarkians are known universe-wide for their effective neurotoxin, but no Earthlings and few aliens are aware of their superior foot speed – probably because of the effectiveness of their neurotoxin.) Peter turned down a side street and saw the bookstore two hundred yards ahead. It shared a small building and a smaller parking lot with a tattoo parlor. The lights were on and a red-and-black "open" sign hung inside the window. A sign on the door said "Elaine's Used Books."

Peter pushed himself, running harder than he ever imagined he would really want to run. This was for April. And Brooks. As he approached the building, a clock in the window of the tattoo parlor read 9:57. *I'm going to make it.* Then the bookstore lights went out. He could see the silhouette of a woman in the doorway, backlit by a yellow light from a storage room. She locked the door and flipped the sign to "closed." Peter skidded to a stop, almost crashing into the glass door, but the woman had already turned around and was walking toward the back room.

No! It's not fair. It's not ten o'clock yet! In an act of pure desperation, Peter raised him arms, and with both fists pounded repeatedly on the glass door. The door rattled, the "closed" sign swayed in the window, and next door in the tattoo parlor a unicorn's horn became markedly longer than originally planned. And Peter screamed.

"Elaine! Elaine! Elaine! Elaine! Elaine! Elaine!" The woman in the bookstore flinched when Peter hit the door. She turned and stormed back to the front door, unlocked it, and opened it enough to poke her head out and scowl.

"Waddya want?"

"*Ten Minutes from Normal*," Peter said.

"I think it's going to take you a lot longer than that," Elaine said, giving Peter the once-over. She slammed the door.

"Wait!" shouted Peter. She opened the door again. "It's not even ten yet. Oh, and I'm trying to save someone's life!"

"How so?"

"My friend has been kidnapped. Her abductors hid a phone number inside a book in this store, and if I don't call they're going to kill her."

"I don't believe you," Elaine snapped. "But points for originality." She flipped the lights on and waved Peter into the store. "Come on in. But make it snappy."

"Where would I find it?"

"What?"

"*Ten Minutes from Normal.*"

"Try the nonfiction/ politics section." She pointed to the back corner of the store. "Alphabetized by author." Peter ran to the back of the bookstore and scanned the shelves.

"I don't see it!"

"Hold on," Elaine said. The pause seemed interminable as she searched the racks. "Here it is. In the horror section."

No sooner than she pulled the book from the shelf, Peter yanked it out of her hand. He flipped through the pages with his thumb, and on page 119 he found a yellow slip of paper torn from the bottom of a legal pad. He called the number.

"That was cutting it close," said the voice on the other end. "But if you ran all the way from Atlanta to Charlotte, color me impressed."

"The Winnebago ran out of fuel," Peter said. "I just ran from the gas station." The caller – or one of his accomplices – was watching, but had not seen Benjamin. "I'll need time to go back and fill it up."

"Fair enough. Now listen carefully." Peter was instructed to drive to Raleigh via the interstate, then to the Outer Banks by highway 64. "You have six hours. If I don't get a call from you by 4 a.m., then April's life is in danger, come alone, do not involve the police, blah blah blah."

"Then I call this number?"

"No. After this call ends this phone will no longer work. You'll find a new number at a 24-hour doughnut shop in Nags Head -"

"Ahh, does it have to be a doughnut shop? I've had some unfortunate experiences."

"Work with me here Peter. You will go to the men's restroom, and taped underneath the lid of the toilet tank you'll find a piece of paper with a new phone number."

"Eww," Peter said. "Seriously, the toilet? You couldn't have stuck it under a ceiling tile or something?"

"Did not think of that," said the man. "But I like it. Maybe for the next kidnapping. But the restroom there is very nice, with a sink and some nice scented liquid soap and one of those push-button hand dryers. Good luck Peter." The call ended.

Peter slipped the phone into his pocket and handed the book back to Elaine.

"You're not going to buy it?" she asked as Peter headed toward the door.

"Not a word of it." Once outside, he sprinted back to the gas station. Benjamin had just finished filling the tank and was locking the gas cap in place.

"How'd it go?" Ben asked.

"Tickety-boo," Peter replied. "We're going to the Outer Banks. Get on board." He took the keys from Ben, climbed into the driver's seat, slid the keys into the ignition, and turned the motor over. He took a couple seconds to confirm that the robot warning light was off, and then pulled out of the gas station.

"I'm getting hungry," Ben said.

"Good news. We're going to a doughnut shop."

Taryn Yuanuin stopped playing the harpsichord and sat and stared at her sheet music. She had just finished her Tuesday evening practice session, and now only the tick-tick-ticking of the metronome pierced the empty mansion air. It was too quiet. She had not heard from Dirk Reger or Frank Francis since that confrontational meeting at Dionysus headquarters on Sunday. Taryn's reverie was shattered when the opening bars of "Another one Bites the Dust" – her ringtone – erupted from the adjacent room.

It was Tor Kinney, calling with his daily 10 p.m. briefing. He was a couple of minutes late. Taryn was a stickler for punctuality, but tonight she failed to notice Tor's tardiness. She had demanded these briefings from Tor ever since she became Chair of the Board. These updates typically consisted of a mundane laundry list of Tor's recent activities, such as "Got a haircut, weekly sailing lesson, berated an underling, didn't run company into the ground." But Taryn found today's briefing to be more interesting – and disconcerting.

Tor reported that there had been no sign of Peter, and nothing out of the ordinary, save for a puzzling occurrence just after six that evening. Brooks Robinson had run from his house like it was filled with home-repair contractors, jumped into his pickup truck, and sped off. Jason and Brian tailed him as he took a serpentine route through his neighborhood, where he finally stopped at a convenience store. He purchased a can of soda and some beef jerky, then took a slow, meandering drive back to his house. There, Brian pointed out to Jason that the unsightly monstrosity that had been parked in Brooks's back yard (yet visible from the street) was now missing. Despite the obvious aesthetic improvement, they both thought that that was a bit odd, and they passed that information on to Tor, who passed it on to Taryn. Taryn ended the call and immediately called Dirk Reger.

"Hello?"

"Dirk?" She did not recognize the voice. It sounded like the voice of a fossilized whiskey-soaked blues musician with a two-pack-a-day habit.

"Sorry, hold on," Dirk said. He cleared his throat. "Okay."

"Did you hire Tom Waits to take your calls?"

"I just have an upper respiratory thing going on."

"I'm concerned," Taryn said.

"Thanks, but I sound worse than I feel," Dirk said. "With some zinc and throat lozenges and plenty of fluids I'll be fine in no time."

"I meant about Peter. And the BAT," she snapped. "It's been over two days since our parties came to a good-faith agreement, Dirk, and while there are no new developments on our end, I was curious as to whether Dionysus had anything to report."

"Nope," Dirk replied.

"That's it? No sightings? No rumors? No new leads?" Taryn said. "So help me, Dirk Reger, if you're holding out on us..."

"Taryn, I share your concerns," Dirk said. "But we've been working our darndest here to find that scoundrel. Besides, it was my understanding that Persona had the edge in locating Peter, what with that bounty hunter and all."

Taryn hated the fact that Persona was having no better luck at finding Peter than Dionysus was, but she hated even more that Dirk had just pointed that fact out to her. "I told you there was nothing new on our end. If I knew where Peter was, would I be wasting my time calling you?"

"Well, yeah, I would hope so," Dirk said. "That's sort of the deal. If one of us finds him, we're supposed to let the other know. Taryn, it's mission-critical that we leverage our core-competencies in a synergistic fashion to move the needle on this project."

"You know what I mean," Taryn said, suppressing the urge to vomit. She didn't trust Dirk, and she thought there was a strong possibility that he was lying to her. But she was one-hundred percent certain that he didn't have the BAT. If he did, he would have used it on himself already. His sandpaper-on-a-chalkboard voice told Taryn that that had not happened.

"Look, I have to go," croaked Dirk. "I will let you know if I hear anything."

"Goodbye Dirk."

As soon as the call ended, Dirk called Martina. "He's on the way."

"It's me, Martina. You don't have to disguise your voice."

"I'm not," Dirk said. "I'm sick. He should be in Nags Head by 4 a.m., then the beach house not long after that. I'll call you when he leaves the doughnut shop."

"Perfect."

"How's April?" Dirk asked.

"She's holding up."

"Good," Dirk said. "I'm going to miss her."

"Don't get all sentimental now," Martina said.

"I'm not," Dirk said. "It's just that the new temp is horrible. Listen, I've got to go. I'll call you."

April was holding up okay. Try as she might, she found it difficult to sustain a heightened level of fear and anxiety in a secluded, quiet, oceanfront luxury beach house. *That's probably why they're so expensive*, she thought. But Martina's prediction had been accurate. It had been a long day for April, a sort of marathon of exactly-nothing-to-do punctuated only by three above-average meals, and now she was hitting the boredom wall. She tried watching cable TV, but realized that an activity that you really don't enjoy all that much to begin with is not enhanced in the least by solitary confinement. With a guard at her door, April was denied access to the beach and the rest of the house. For a while, she occupied herself by trying to imagine all of the activities that well-to-do beach house owners were wont to do: billiards, croquet, horseback riding, shuffleboard, tennis, cigar smoking and brandy snifting, air kissing, and prescription drugs. April thought that horseback riding on the beach sounded sublime, but that everything else sounded dreadful, and she told herself she was glad she wasn't wealthy.

She pulled a book off of the shelf – *The Panama Canal: Pros and Cons* – turned to a random page, and read one sentence: "The Panama Canal is an intricate system of locks and dams that allows for the transfer of over 300 million tons of cargo a year between the Atlantic and the Pacific oceans." April dropped the book and steadied herself against a sturdy wardrobe, overwhelmed by sheer boredom. She eased her way back to the bed and curled up under the sheets. She told herself that in the unlikely scenario of getting polled for such a thing, she would have to rank boredom somewhere below waterboarding, but just above "the rack."

When she felt a little better, she got up and took a warm bath, then turned off the lights and climbed back into bed. It was dark outside, and she wondered where Peter was. For his own sake she hoped that he stayed away. But the selfish voice inside her head told her that being rescued would be, by far, the coolest thing that ever happened to her. It would, in fact, be "the only reason I could possibly have to attend my high school class reunion" cool. She looked at the clock and closed her eyes. It was a little after ten.

THIRTY-ONE

Barbaxaquottlmangaporellianfori woke up with a start. A harsh, guttural rhythmic gnarr reverberated off of her eardrums, like the echoes of Satan's gargling emanating up from the bowels of hell. She sat up and reached out to give Cyril a nudge, and he stopped snoring. But now she felt that same odd sensation she experienced before she fell asleep; a constant, low-frequency vibration that resonated throughout her body like a soothing voice, reassuring her that she was at harmony with the universe. She had only experienced something this transcendent one other time in her life – but this time it wasn't a vibrating bed in a seedy hotel on Baskoop Delta.

Something caught her eye. A faint white light pulsed from the bunched-up blanket at the foot of Cyril's cot. She struggled to her feet and pushed the blanket aside to find the source of the light. A tiny diode on the BAMN was flashing, and as she watched the pulses became more frequent and intense. She did not bother to wake Cyril. Other than the flashing diode, and the surreal vibration, there still seemed to be a huge amount of nothing happening. She astutely guessed that waking Cyril to point out that mostly nothing was going on would be rewarded with scorn and more demands for her to throw things. She curled up back on her cot, closing her eyes only to blink, and allowed the periodic flashes bathe her retinas while she waited for something.

There was also a great deal of nothing-much-going-on on the surface of Area 52, but high above the steel barrack and rusted shed there was practically no nothing-much-going-on. A massive Charpaq battle cruiser had settled into Earth's atmosphere. It was licorice black in color with obelisk smooth surfaces, and it was roughly the size and shape of New Hampshire. Stealth technology made it invisible to radar, but if a camper had looked upward from the northern Nevada desert, they would have marveled at a New-Hampshire shaped black hole in the night sky that blotted out the constellations. But on this particular night there were no campers who were also ancient Greeks, so no one seemed to notice the missing constellations.

The battle cruiser halted its descent at 5,000 meters, and a helmsman positioned the massive craft so that a football field sized hatch was centered over the two nondescript buildings on the surface of Area 52. The doors to the hatch slid apart with a whisper and 3 million white leaflets fluttered to the ground, carpeting the desert floor like snow – if snow were a fire hazard and contained environmentally hazardous ink. There were no guards or sentries on the surface of Area 52 that night, what with the canoe trip and all. But if there had been somebody on the ground at that moment, and if they had been nimble enough to escape getting crushed under 15 tons of paper, then they might have picked up one of the flyers and read the following:

To whom it may concern:

This Charpaq battle cruiser has been dispatched in response to an emergency BAMN signal that seems to be transmitting from your underground facility, suggesting that a fellow Charpaq (or someone well-connected to a ranking Charpaq) is in eminent danger, or is being held against their will. If said Charpaq (or well-connected friend of a Charpaq) is not released to our custody immediately, then we will be forced to take action. This would most certainly involve invading your facility. Since we're rather bulky and ungainly, things often get broken and feelings get hurt during this kind of operation. Also, attending to this BAMN emergency took us well out of our way to a skirmish on Weert Beta, so we're a bit moody. You have been duly warned.

Sincerely,
Vice-Admiral Perch
The Royal Charpaq Fleet

After tapping his foot and drumming his fingers and hearing no response whatsoever from Area 52 for well over eight minutes, Vice-Admiral Perch ordered a contingent of 72 battle-tested Charpaqs to land on Earth, storm Area 52, find the BAMN device, and hit the "snooze" button. And if it wasn't too much bother, rescue whoever activated it.

Another hatch whispered open and six landing craft – each laden with a dozen Charpaq troopers – dropped out of the battle cruiser and onto the Area 52 runway. One-hundred and forty-four hooves beat across the desert floor as they charged the barrack.

They blasted the lock off of the door, and a dozen troopers trotted inside while the others waited outside. Resistance came early in the form of an "out of order" sign taped to the elevator doors. The popular Charpaq commander shrugged and turned to head back to the landing craft. When he reached the door, one of the less popular soldiers spoke up.

"What about that other building?"

"Oh, okay," grumbled the commander, and the lot of them sauntered out of the barrack and over to the shed. They entered to find it empty, save for a large metal plate covering the floor and a metal box suspended from the ceiling by a silver corrugated tube. The box had two black buttons, one marked "up" and one "down." After some healthy debate and a quick game of the Charpaq version of "rock, paper, scissors" the commander opted to push the "up" button. The ground beneath their feet vibrated as a high-pitched whine echoed off the corrugated metal walls. Hydraulic pistons pushed open the roof to reveal a New Hampshire shaped empty space hovering in the night sky. After a minute or so, the whine diminished, the metal plates on the floor separated, and a *Rev 9* appeared in front of them.

They rolled the *Rev 9* off of the elevator, out of the shed and onto the runway, and then half of the contingent boarded the platform while the other half stood in the desert to watch over the Blutaarkian spaceship and the six landing craft. The commander pushed the "down" button – there was less debate this time – and the elevator plunged 9,000 feet into the Earth until it stopped inside the Area 52 alien spacecraft hangar. The Charpaq troopers rushed through the hangar and out into the corridor, winding their way through the Area 52 maze toward the source (according to their sensors) of the BAMN transmission.

They stormed through the corridors, the only resistance coming from a window clerk who – with her nose buried deep in a ledger – shouted "Take a number please!" as they stampeded past her window. One of them did, and that seemed to placate her. Down another corridor, they found the source of the signal behind a metal door labeled "quarantine." Never a strong adherent to the germ theory of disease, the commander lifted the latch and flung the door open.

Barbaxaquottlmangaporellianfori had been watching the BAMN device; the flashing light had increased in frequency until it was now a solid white light, and she knew that the nothing-much-happening-at-all was about to come to a screeching halt. When the cell door swung open, she sat up slowly, blinked, and smiled.

Two Charpaqs rushed to help her to her feet, and the commander followed them in. He picked up the BAMN and hit the "snooze" switch.

"You look horrible," blurted the commander. "It's a good thing you had the BAMN."

"It is not mine," she said. "It belongs to Cyril." She pointed to the alien snoring on the cot. One of the Charpaqs rousted Cyril, while another lifted Barbaxaquottlmangaporellianfori into his arms.

"You guys are Charpaqs," Cyril said, rubbing his eyes.

"Yeah," said the commander. "That's generally what happens when you activate the BAMN. You push the button, the alert gets transmitted, we show up, you get rescued. We're sort of stalled here between steps 3 and 4, and if it's not too much trouble I'd like to get you out of here before the humans show up with their lead-and-sulfur-and-potassium nitrate-based weapons and their fossil fuels and infomercials and what have you."

Cyril pointed out that his ankles were zip-tied and his wrists were handcuffed. One of the Charpaqs drew his plasma gun and offered to blast the constraints from Cyril's extremities. When the commander proffered his opinion that such action might result in Cyril having one or two limbs, instead of four, Cyril protested. They decided to use the cot as a stretcher to carry Cyril out of Area 52 and up to the landing craft.

"Wait," said Barbaxaquottlmangaporellianfori. "There are more of us. Thirteen more, imprisoned against our wills. Fourteen, if you count the Corpuulon as two." She paused to catch her breath. "Most of us have our own ships, so it would simply be a matter of setting us free and getting us to the hangar."

"Now, look here, missy," said the commander. "We went well out of our way to respond to this distress signal. But that's not good enough for you, is it? No, now you want us to initiate some sort of mass jailbreak. And the kicker is, it's not even your BAMN device! It belongs to Mr. 'Please Don't Shoot My Limbs Off' over here. So to your request, I politely say no."

"Please?"

"I just said no. Now if you'll just -" Barbaxaquottlmangaporellianfori fainted. "What just happened?" he asked the trooper holding her limp body.

"She fainted. I'm guessing from overwhelming emotional stress."

"Oh, that's just perfect." The commander put his hands on his substantial hips and sighed. "Just perfect. I tell her no – politely, I might add – so she swoons. Now that makes *me* the bad guy if I don't put six dozen Charpaqs in harm's way just to cater to her trifling request. I hate this job." He grudgingly issued orders for thirty-two troopers to search for and rescue all imprisoned aliens, while two Charpaqs carried Cyril on the makeshift stretcher and one carried Barbaxaquottlmangaporellianfori. The "search" part of the mission came to an abrupt conclusion when – approximately three steps down from the quarantine cell – the Charpaqs discovered several locked steel doors to their left and right, each with "alien prisoner inside" stenciled under a small, square window. Two troopers went from door-to-door, blasting each lock with a single blinding burst from their plasma guns. Other troopers followed, entering the cells to assist the liberated aliens. By the time they got to the end of the corridor, all thirteen prisoners were accounted for – fourteen, if you count the Corpuulon as two.

The commander led a phalanx of armed Charpaqs at the front and the rear, sandwiching a diversity parade of thirteen sundry aliens, Cyril and his orderlies, and the chivalrous Charpaq carrying Barbaxaquottlmangaporellianfori. This hodge-podge of alien life walked, trotted, slithered, hopped, and clip-clopped through the halls of Area 52 with all of the grace and subtlety of a broken grocery cart in a revolving door. They moved past a door marked "lounge," took a right turn, and made their way back toward the hangar.

Inside the lounge, Agent Hays was finishing up some paperwork – an incident report to explain why corridor 6H-885 now had a new bullet hole. He had just checked the final box on page 11 when he heard footsteps, hoof steps, and assorted snorts and brays coming from the hallway. Under his breath he cursed the Alien Phenomena Agency's much too lenient pets-at-the-workplace policy. But when he heard "Arrggghhh, my wrists!" it triggered an auditory memory. *Cyril.*

Hays burst out of the lounge with his handgun drawn, hoping that this did not result in more paperwork. He was taken aback when he was confronted with sixteen armed, burly Charpaq troopers who all turned to look behind them to see what the commotion was. He smiled and waved and ducked back into the lounge just as a plasma ball ripped down the hallway, singeing his ponytail. He bolted out through a back door into another corridor, fumbling for his walkie-talkie. He sprinted through Area 52 toward a strategic location that would cut off the interlopers and escapees from the spacecraft hangar.

"Code green!" he shouted into the walkie-talkie. "Code green! Multiple aliens, aided by armed troops. Last seen in corridor 8H-489, heading toward the hangar."

Agent Hays ran down a parallel corridor, but stopped short at an intersecting hallway. He peered around the corner, drawing the attention of one of the Charpaqs, who took the liberty of firing a volley of plasma balls in his direction. Hays pulled back, cringing as a half-dozen softball-sized blue orbs blasted into the adjacent drywall, creating plumes of acrid smoke and six perfectly round holes. Hoof beats thundered toward him from down the hallway. Hays backtracked and ducked into a conference room, then exited through a back door that led to yet another corridor. He drew his gun with his right hand, held the walkie-talkie to his face with the left, and ran faster than large men wearing oversized Hawaiian shirts should be legally allowed to run.

"All available personnel, rendezvous at the intersection of corridors 8H-489 and 3H-227. Alien escape attempt in progress. Repeat, alien escape attempt in progress. They are armed and hostile." Hays was the first to arrive at the rendezvous site. As he stood there alone, panting with his hands on his knees, he chided himself for issuing a "code green." Since Area 52 was currently protected by a substitute team of a few field agents and a dozen-or-so office personnel, he suspected that attendance might have been better had he announced a "code beige" – a mandatory meeting with doughnuts provided. He could hear the escapees and the Charpaq landing party approaching. Their only possible escape route to the hangar passed through the code green rendezvous site, where Agent Hays now stood patting his pockets, searching for his inhaler. This fact, combined with the strategic configuration of the Area 52 corridors in the vicinity of the hangar, meant that even a small force of Area 52 personnel could prevent the escape of a much larger force of armed aliens. But Hays knew that attempting to stop the approaching horde single-handedly would be suicide.

Sweat trickled down his temples as he held his gun against his heaving chest and peeked around the corner. Down the corridor, he could see the aliens' shadows stretching across the recently mopped floor. Within seconds, the crush of three-dozen armed Charpaqs and fourteen not-at-all-pleased-about-being-locked-up-for-no-good-reason aliens would be in plain view.

Something grabbed Hays's shoulder from behind. He spun around, flinging beads of sweat from his forehead and blindly pointing his gun. Agent Shelby stepped back and held both hands up in mock surrender.

"It's me!" said Shelby.

Hays had never shot another agent, and he cringed at the thought of the paperwork should such a thing happen. He sheepishly mouthed "sorry" and turned his attention back to the alien threat. Behind his back, Area 52 personnel seemed to materialize from adjacent hallways, offices, labs, and closets until the corridor to the hangar was defended by a crack force of six field agents, Etter from accounting, a couple of biologists, Constance from human resources, and the surly custodian whose name no one wanted to commit to memory.

"Stop where you are!" shouted Hays. The Charpaq commander wordlessly held up one hand, and everyone behind him came to a stop with the precision and coordination of a derailing freight train. Three more steps and they would all be sitting ducks for the better-positioned forces of Area 52. "You cannot escape. Return the prisoners to their cells, and we will grant you passage back to your ship."

"Well that just figures," said the commander. "No good deed goes unpunished." He had turned to look back at Barbaxaquottlmangaporellianfori when he said this, but she was still busy being unconscious. He stood and thought for a minute, then turned and shouted back to Agent Hays. "Do they have to go back in the exact same cells that we rescued them from? I think we sort of lost track."

"Oh come on!" protested one of the aliens – the smart money was on Cyril – before he was silenced with a plasma gun butt to the ribs. But this triggered a roar of grumbling and objections from the others.

"Okay, okay," beseeched the commander. "I guess we'll do it *your* way." He turned back to address Agent Hays. "You know I could have my battle cruiser drop a couple of Higgs bombs down your elevator shafts with just one call, right?"

"Would not the resultant blast annihilate this facility and create a blast cavity that would be instantly crushed under the weight of trillions of tons of rock that's currently sitting above us?" Hays asked.

"Yeah. So?"

"So...that would kill everyone down here," Hays said.

"He called my bluff," whispered the commander to the trooper next to him. The trooper thought it best not to explain the difference between calling someone's bluff and pointing out a painfully obvious fact. "Okay, well how about this, then? We'll just camp here until you let us pass."

"You're going to eventually get hungry," Hays said. "Not to mention the fact that the restroom facilities in that sector haven't been properly maintained. The custodian bristled. Hays ignored him.

"What about you guys?" answered the Charpaq commander. "Every minute that you spend thwarting our egress is another minute that form A-52-17b doesn't get filled out, or that a Power Point presentation goes unfinished, or that a workplace sexual harassment seminar doesn't get scheduled."

Hays turned to assess the morale of his rag-tag Area 52 fighting force. The Charpaq commander had hit a nerve. Foreheads were beading with sweat, eyelids were twitching, and even the non-accountants were avoiding eye contact. *At least we're adequately armed*, thought Hays. All of the field agents, Constance from HR, and the two biologists had semiautomatic pistols. Etter from accounting had a samurai sword. And the custodian cradled an AK-47.

If Hays and his band had attempted to charge the Charpaq landing force, they most certainly would have been met with plasma gun fire that in all likelihood would have resulted in inconvenient softball-sized holes in their torsos. But Hays and his ad hoc Area 52 militia were entrenched in a superior strategic position, so that if the Charpaqs had advanced down the corridor to the spacecraft hangar, they most assuredly would have ended up with bullet-sized holes in their torsos. Since no one on either side was willing to accept holes of any size in their torsos as a viable outcome, the two opposing forces stood stalemated.

Benjamin slept in the back of the RV during most of the drive from Charlotte to the Outer Banks. Peter woke him just as they were entering the bridge over Croatan Sound. Ben made his way to the front of the lumbering vehicle and looked outside in an attempt to get his bearings. There was no other traffic on either side of the narrow four-lane, and the expanse of water on each side of the bridge was still and dark. There wasn't much to see, until Ben turned his gaze upward. Because of a new moon and the absence of urban light pollution, he could clearly make out the Milky Way. For a few seconds he pretended that he was back in the cabin of the *Rev 9*, but this time it was traveling through the vast emptiness of space instead of through the skies of the southern United States, and *he* was the pilot instead of some boorish, irascible alien with –

"We're almost there," Peter said, interrupting Ben's fantasy. "Maybe fifteen more minutes." Peter had made good time on the highway and was on pace to arrive at the doughnut shop in Nags Head well before 4 a.m. Ben stumbled back to the rear of the RV without saying a word and sat on the edge of the bed. He avoided the barrel chair; for some reason sitting in it nauseated him. Sixteen minutes later, Peter pulled into the doughnut shop parking lot. "Do you want anything?" Ben realized that they had not eaten since lunch on Tuesday. He told himself that deadlines and hostage situations make for an amazing appetite suppressant, then told Peter that he'd like a couple of glazed doughnuts and some milk.

"And please get the food before you handle that toilet lid," Ben said.

"Will do." Peter walked into the doughnut shop with all of the verve of someone who had been on the road all day, shuffled up to the counter, and gave a nod to the clerk who had the verve of someone who had just been awakened by the ringing bell hanging from the front door. Peter ordered a bottle of orange juice, and for Ben, the two doughnuts and a carton of milk. He looked around while the clerk bagged the doughnuts. Peter saw nothing out of the ordinary for a doughnut shop at 3:47 in the morning – just a middle-aged man wearing only a purple thong and matching cape sitting at a booth sipping coffee and flipping through the pages of the latest edition of *Investor's Business Daily*. Peter took the milk, juice, and doughnuts back to the RV, and then returned to the shop.

The clerk's initial alarm at seeing Peter return turned to genuine relief when Peter headed to the men's restroom instead of complaining about the doughnuts or committing armed robbery. Once inside the men's room, Peter locked the door and stepped into the stall.

He lifted the lid to the toilet tank, and taped underneath – right where the gravel-voiced man said it would be – was another torn strip of yellow paper. Peter peeled the paper from the lid and then put the lid back on the tank. He unfolded the paper to find a befuddling "cure impetigo" written on one side and a ten-digit phone number on the other. He pulled Brooks's cell phone from his pocket, and in one horrific instant it slipped and tumbled and landed with a *splash* in the toilet.

Peter instinctively reached toward the waterlogged phone, then stopped himself before his fingers plunged into the water. *Yuk.* But through the rippling water he could read the time on the phone's screen: 3:55. He closed his eyes and thrust his hand into the water and fished the phone out of the bowl. He yanked paper towels from the dispenser and wrapped them around the phone to dry it. Peter keyed the new phone number and hit "send." *Oh please oh please oh please.*

Nothing. Desperate, he pushed the silver button on the hand dryer and let it blast hot air over the phone for two full cycles. He keyed the number again and hit "send" again and again nothing happened. Peter dashed out of the restroom and back up to the clerk at the counter.

"Do you have a cell phone?" Peter hoped his sense of urgency was conveyed to the clerk who was busy counting straws.

"Yeah, but we're not supposed to use them while we're on the clock. Company policy."

"I need to use it," Peter said. "It's an emergency."

"Sorry. I've already been written up twice."

"Certainly you could allow me to borrow it? It's literally a matter of life and death."

"You know most people do that," said the clerk.

"Do what?" Peter said. He glanced at his comatose phone. It was 3:58.

"Say 'literally' when they say something that's really figurative in nature, or a metaphor, or an exaggeration." That community college rhetoric class was finally paying off.

Peter raised his voice. "It's no exaggeration! It is truly a life-or-death situation. Someone will literally die if I don't make this call by 4 a.m.!"

"Excuse me," shouted the man in the booth from across the room. "You can use mine."

Peter darted across the restaurant to the caped man. "Thank you. You're a hero."

"I know." He reached into his thong, removed his phone, and held it out on his palm for Peter.

Peter hesitated. Until five seconds earlier, he would have concurred with anyone who told him that the most disgusting thing he would do all year would be to handle a cell phone that had fallen into a toilet bowl. But he was running out of options, and the clock on the screen read 3:59. He snatched the phone, keyed in the number, and hit "send."

"You certainly have a flair for the dramatic," said the voice. "You only had fourteen seconds to spare. What happened? Did your battery die?"

"No," Peter said. "Dropped the phone into the toilet."

"You know you can fix that by immersing the phone in rice overnight."

"Good to know," Peter said. "But I didn't have rice. *Or* overnight."

"Touché. Well, enough banter. Listen carefully." The kidnapper instructed Peter to drive 15 miles north on Highway 12, then at a specific mile marker he was to pull the Winnebago well off of the road and park it. From there he would be on foot. April could be found at an abandoned oceanfront house approximately a mile-and-a-half north. Because of the dunes, it was only accessible by foot, by horseback, or by four-wheel drive vehicle.

"Sucks that you don't have a Jeep," said the kidnapper. "You will need to get there before six a.m. You have been cooperative so far, so don't blow it. Come alone, no police, et cetera, et cetera."

"Got it," Peter said. The call ended. Peter pinched the cell phone with two fingers and handed it back to the caped stranger. "Thanks. You're a lifesaver." Peter turned his head and looked at the clerk. "Literally." The clerk shook his head and Peter bolted out of the door.

"How'd it go?" Ben asked.

"The good news – we're almost there. The bad news – I really need to wash my hands." Peter started up the RV and headed north. Fifteen minutes later he pulled the Winnebago off of the road and turned the engine off.

"What's wrong?" Benjamin asked.

"They're holding April at a beach house that's only accessible by foot. I'm afraid this is where we part ways, my friend."

"You know it's a set up. It's suicide to go alone," Ben said.

"It's murder if I allow you to go with me. They haven't seen you yet, but clearly they're watching me. When they see you traipsing over the dunes behind me, they will kill April. Wait here and that won't happen. I promise."

Ben was hard pressed to mount a convincing counter argument. "I never really liked the beach anyway," he rationalized. "Icky things in the sand. Here, you'll need this." He stood and reached into a cabinet and removed a red tool box, then handed it to Peter. "This belongs to Brooks. I have no idea what's in it, but he wanted you to have it. He said it might come in handy."

"Thank you, Ben. And tell Brooks 'thanks.' For everything." Peter stood and hugged Ben. Ben recognized the hug. It was the same kind of hug that he got from his now ex-wife the very last time he saw her. She whispered "goodbye" in his ear, then left for a two-day conference in Vegas with a moving van and a motorcycle mechanic. "Goodbye," Peter said.

Peter took the toolbox from Ben and stepped out of the RV into the early morning darkness of the barrier island, and disappeared behind the dunes.

THIRTY-TWO

Martina stood in the dark and watched the ocean from a balcony. The beach house was dark; all of the lights had been turned off, save for one in a third-floor room on the north end. Had a beachcomber been walking on the sand below, the only light he would have seen penetrating the darkness of the Outer Banks would have been the pinpoint stars in the sky, the whitecaps on the waves, and Martina's phantasmal face hovering over the balcony. He probably would have turned around, or at least walked a little faster. Martina was expecting a call, and when it came just after 4 a.m. she stepped back inside to take it.

"He's on his way," Dirk said. "You know what to do."

"Consider it done," Martina said.

"Perfect. How's April doing?"

"She's fine. She's sleeping now – but not for long."

"It's too bad, really," Dirk said. "She should have never stuck her nose in where it didn't belong."

"What the hell do you mean?" Martina said. "She was just minding her own business when you made the decision to kidnap her."

"Well..." Dirk cleared his raspy throat. "She should have never gotten mixed up with Peter in the first place."

"If I understand correctly, she didn't really *want* to have anything to do with him. Her father found him and just dropped him off at her place."

"Well..." Dirk struggled to come up with a justification for getting rid of April that didn't make him sound like a greedy, narcissistic sociopath. "She should have never had such bad luck," was the best he could do.

"Yeah," Martina said. "That's it. Bad luck. Look, I need to go." She ended the call with Dirk, then went into April's pitch black bedroom and eased her awake with a nudge. She took April's hand and guided her out of the room and down the darkened hallway, around a corner, and toward another room where light cascaded through multi-paned French doors, across the hardwood floors of the hallway, and down the grand staircase to the second level below.

"Where are we going?" April asked, rubbing her matted eyes. Her hair was pulled back in a ponytail, and she was wearing a dark blue t-shirt and pajama pants. Martina – as always – was in her skin-tight black dress. There were no other pout models around, that April could see, and the only sound echoing throughout the mansion was the *clip-clopping* of Martina's heels against the hardwoods.

"Sshhh," Martina said. "It's almost over. Peter is on his way."

"The big rescue scene? It's about time. Any chance I could shower, brush my teeth, throw on some makeup, and put on some clothes?" April asked. "If there's going to be media, I don't want it to look like that I just gave up – you know, like how I look when I'm at the office."

"That won't be necessary," Martina said. April was trying her best to put on a brave face, and with those four words Martina had just slapped the heck out of it. A rush of adrenaline boosted her hostage fueled anxiety to a new level: stark fear. As they stepped closer to the illuminated room, April flinched and her nostrils burned from the pungent vapor of gasoline, and the stark fear turned into blind panic.

This could be my only chance. April yanked her hand from Martina's grip and ran past her. *If I can just make it outside.* Before she made it to the top of the staircase, the taller, stronger Martina grabbed her by the shoulder and spun her around.

"I need some help out here!" Martina shouted. The French doors burst open, and two black-clad pout models emerged like bats out of hell – if hell had hardwood floors, a stone fireplace, and nautical -themed furniture. Each one grabbed an arm and forced a struggling April into the large, well-lit room. Martina followed them in and shut the doors.

The standoff in Area 52 was now more than an hour old, and the Charpaq commander was growing impatient. He had been charged with putting a landing force on the ground, finding the BAMN, affecting a rescue, and returning to the battle cruiser with all troops and landing craft accounted for. For a commander of his pay grade, this sort of mission should have taken a little over twenty minutes. The fact that he was now past that mark by well over two standard deviations weighed on him, especially with his quarterly performance review looming. As much as he hated the idea, it looked like he was going to have to fake some leadership.

He thought for a minute, then turned to the trooper to his right and whispered to him. The trooper crouched and scampered to the back of the horde, then disappeared down a back corridor. The Charpaq commander wanted to create a distraction, and decided that engaging Agent Hays in faux-negotiations would buy him the time he needed. "What's your name?" he shouted down the corridor.

"I'm Agent Hays. Hays for short. What's your name?"

"I am Commander Brasher. Hays, it looks like we're at an impasse. I'm prepared to negotiate."

"I'm prepared to listen," Hays said. Etter from accounting shook his head in disgust, sheathed his samurai sword, and sat on the floor.

"How about you let our landing party *and* all liberated aliens go?" Brasher said. "Then we'll put in a good word for Earth for planet of the month with the galactic landscape committee."

"No," Hays said.

"You drive a hard bargain, Hays," Brasher said. "Okay, how about this? You let us all go, and when I get back to the ship I'll send down a couple of crates of t-shirts that say 'My dad just annihilated Flachsmeer Beta, and all I got was this crummy t-shirt.' "

"Uh, no."

"Hoo-boy!" Brasher said. "Your negotiating skills are unparalleled." (You don't make commander in the Charpaq fleet without at least an above-average aptitude for brown-nosing.) "How about you let us all go, but we let you keep one alien?" In the unlikely event that Hays agreed to this deal, Brasher was prepared to leave Barbaxaquottlmangaporellianfori behind. She was still unconscious, and would probably not put up much of a fuss. Besides, if they did rescue her, her ungainly name would be a time-consuming burden when it came to filling out reports back on the ship. Brasher's wrist cramped up just thinking about it.

"Still no," Hays said.

"This is going well," said Brasher without a hint of irony or sarcasm.

"Not really," Hays said. But it *was* going well for Brasher.

While Brasher was negotiating with Hays, the dispatched scout had located the out-of-order elevator, pried open the doors, and climbed into the elevator shaft via the utility door at the top of the car. From there, he relayed a message to a Charpaq lieutenant on the surface, who by now was well aware of the delay, as well as the fact that with every passing minute his chances of getting promoted past Brasher and landing the large corner office increased exponentially.

The scout, acting on Brasher's orders, requested two three-thousand meter carbon nanofiber ropes from the battle cruiser. The lieutenant confirmed the request, finished the crossword puzzle he had just started, then forwarded the request to the ship's supply officer. Ten minutes later the lieutenant relayed a message to the scout from the battle cruiser. "They don't have two three-thousand meter ropes. Will two four-thousand meter ropes be okay?"

"Yes, yes, of course," the scout said. The lieutenant finished an energy bar, flossed thoroughly, and relayed the message back to the supply officer that, of course, two four-thousand meter ropes would be fine. Within ten minutes, two four-thousand meter carbon nanofiber ropes were on the ground at Area 52. One end of each rope was secured to a high-speed winch on one of the landing shuttles, and the other end of each rope was threaded through the steel barrack, between the open elevator doors, and down the 3,000 meter shaft.

At the bottom of the shaft, the scout fed the two ropes through the opening in the top of the elevator car, then hopped down and made his way back to the huddled mass of Charpaq troopers, Cyril, and the alien escapees. Commander Brasher was still addressing Agent Hays, effectively stalling by proffering frivolous, absurd, and unreasonable demands. It reminded Hays of potential home buyers when he was trying to sell his bungalow in a down market. He was tempted to step out and open fire on Brasher just on principle.

"Okay, how about this?" Brasher happened to turn and look behind him to see the scout approaching from the rear, and nodded to acknowledge his safe return. The scout returned the nod, confirming to Brasher that the first stage of the operation was a success. "We skirmish a little – maybe each side fires off a few ill-aimed shots, nobody gets hurt, but then you let us go and we give you exclusive rights to the story of how you repelled an entire alien landing force. A couple of us can even 'play dead' if you want to take pictures."

"When you were in officer training school," asked Agent Hays, "was there any compulsory coursework in negotiation techniques?"

"Yes," Brasher replied. "I got an A in the class, but I was able to talk the instructor into giving me a B-minus."

"An accredited officer training school?"

"Yes. Why do you ask?" Brasher continued to engage Hays in conversation while, one-by-one, a

Charpaq trooper in the rear would tap one of the escapees on the shoulder, motion them to follow, then escort them through the winding corridors of Area 52 until they arrived at the final leg of their evacuation route: the out-of-order elevator. At that point, both the Charpaq and the alien were secured to the ropes by carabiners, then whisked 3,000 meters to the top of the elevator shaft.

It took a good half-dozen Charpaqs and aliens getting dragged over the hard dirt floor of the barrack, across the desert, and halfway to the Area 52 runway before the winch operator learned to decelerate the ascent before they reached the very top of the elevator shaft. The last two aliens to be evacuated from the depths of Area 52 were Cyril and Barbaxaquottlmangaporellianfori. She had regained consciousness, but was still in no shape to hold on to a rope for the three-minute ride to the surface. "Hang on as tight as you can," said the trooper who had been holding her diminutive frame. As he secured himself to the rope, he anticipated the lengthy report he would later be required to submit (made lengthier by her multisyllabic name) regarding his role in her rescue.

"Can I call you 'Barb?' " he asked.

"No."

Cyril was evacuated last – partly because no one wanted to grapple with the problem of how to get a handcuffed ankle-bound alien to the top of a very deep shaft – but mostly because of his nasty attitude. After his two Charpaq attendants had removed him from the standoff, Cyril groused about the ineptness of the entire rescue effort.

At the elevator, one of the Charpaqs suggested, out loud, that the problem of getting Cyril out of the bowels of Area 52 might be solved by looping the rope around his neck several times before giving the winch operator the figurative thumbs up. Cyril protested, pointing out that rather than being a benign mode of transportation, pulling a rope that has been wrapped around someone's neck was actually a gruesome method of execution on several less-evolved planets.

"I was only kidding," said the offending Charpaq.

"Not really," mouthed the other Charpaq, shaking his head while looking Cyril dead in the eye. Cooler heads finally decided to have one of the stronger Charpaqs hold Cyril as they ascended the elevator shaft together, much in the same way that Barbaxaquottlmangaporellianfori was evacuated. Cyril was – to everyone's pleasant surprise – uncharacteristically quiet during the 3,000 meter ascent, probably because the Charpaq's meaty arm compressed Cyril's ribs like a python suffocating a house cat.

One-by-one, the liberated aliens were brought to the surface. They were surrounded by Charpaq troopers and pitch dark, the only light coming from the landing craft on the runway and the stars above – save for that portion of the sky that was blotted out by the battle cruiser. The lieutenant allowed them a few minutes to enjoy their new-found freedom; it had been years since some of them had seen the night sky or inhaled fresh air. Some of the aliens wept. A couple of them coughed.

Each alien was then accompanied by two armed Charpaqs to the shed, down the freight elevator, and into the spacecraft hangar. Charpaq scouts had encountered no humans in the hangar. The vehicle maintenance crew wouldn't clock in for another five hours, and even during non-canoe trip weeks the hangar was not routinely guarded by security personnel. As each alien identified his particular vehicle, it was dollied onto the elevator platform, then lifted to the surface and towed to the runway. The entire operation proceeded without a glitch until a brief scuffle broke out between the Corpuulon – who claimed that a late model *Moebius 8* was his – and a Vudgkull. The situation was defused when four Charpaq troopers (who logged a lot of time at the gym) intervened, and the Vudgkull produced a valid claim ticket.

As the menagerie of alien spacecraft collected on the Area 52 runway, the lieutenant insisted that a thorough background check be performed on every alien in their custody. A digital image of each one was run through the Intergalactic Database of Criminals, Bail-Jumpers, Scofflaws, and Individuals Who Are Just Very Annoying in General. Excepting the Corpuulon, all of the aliens cleared the background check and were given permission to board their spaceships. The Corpuulon was flagged because of his outstanding status of being just very annoying in general. But he, too, was allowed to board his ship. The Charpaqs had a convenient rule (that the lieutenant just made up) that prevented them from transporting the very annoying.

Barbaxaquottlmangaporellianfori was cleared, then was carried into her ship by her steadfast Charpaq trooper, who was by now growing fond of her. They found a couple of protein bars in a pantry, and after consuming them she perked up considerably and insisted that she was well enough to survive the two-day journey to the closest authentic Nog-cuisine restaurant. "It is only two stars," she said. "But it will do." The Charpaq gave her a gentle hug, and she promised to write.

"I'll see you in my dreams," said the trooper.

"Count on it," she replied.

One-by-one, every alien who had been imprisoned at Area 52 powered up his (or her) spaceship, then – without looking back – broke free from the invisible shackles of Earth's gravitational field. A couple of them, in their giddy haste, also neglected to look up and nearly collided with the Charpaq battle cruiser. The embarrassed aliens offered multiple apologies, then resumed the long but much-anticipated journey home. Every Charpaq felt a deep sense of pride for a mission well done with each spacecraft that left the runway and disappeared into the blackness of the early morning Nevada sky. When the Corpuulon's ship took off, what started as a smattering of applause grew into a standing ovation. With the Corpuulon's departure, only three aliens remained – excluding Cyril. These three were now milling about the desert, making small talk, and wishing they had thought to bring sweaters. Save for the Charpaq landing vehicles, just one spacecraft remained on the Area 52 runway: the *Rev 9*.

The Charpaqs dubbed the three remaining aliens "The Orphans," because they no longer had spaceships of their own. (This perturbed one of the aliens, who was an actual orphan – he kept silent so as not to stir the pot.) Two of them had crash-landed, while the third suffered the ignominy of having his ship disassembled by Area 52 scientists. The Orphans cleared their respective background checks, then were crowded into one of the Charpaq landing craft. They were to become guests of the Charpaq fleet's preeminent battle cruiser, able to enjoy modestly discounted food and lodging until there was a more opportune time for them to be repatriated. Each Orphan hoped that when that time came, he would be welcomed by friends and family (perhaps not a realistic expectation for the "real orphan") with open arms, and that there would be no awkward questions about the missing spaceship.

When Cyril and his rescuer reached the top of the elevator shaft, the trooper released his grip on Cyril and tossed him into the barrack, where another trooper awaited with bolt cutters. With a *clink* and a *snap* the Charpaq severed Cyril's handcuffs and the zip-ties. Cyril stumbled forward, then bent over with his hands on his knees, panting until he was less blue. He stood, then strode across the floor of the barrack and out of the door into the chilly desert air. Through his watering eyes, Cyril spotted the *Rev 9*. It was about 100 meters away. The hatch was open, and there did not appear to be anyone standing guard. His first impulse was to break into a sprint, but he stopped himself. *I don't like running*, he thought. *Also, what about my belt? And the BAT? And what if Agent Hays was telling the truth and they really lost the BAT after the salvage yard fiasco? Should I go back and look for it, or at least get my belt back? Naaaahhhh.*

Cyril started walking toward the *Rev 9*. He avoided eye contact and stuck his hands in his pockets to suppress the rattling links of his broken handcuffs. He was only a few steps away when someone grabbed his shoulder from behind.

"You're not going anywhere."

For the better part of fifteen minutes, Agent Hays had delivered a harsh diatribe critical of Commander Brasher's abominable negotiation skills. To soften the criticism, Hays spent another half-hour presenting a tutorial that outlined the fundamentals of successful negotiation tactics. The Charpaq commander resisted getting defensive and instead listened with rapt attention, occasionally interjecting a "Yes, yes, I think I understand," or "I'm not quite clear on that. Could you elaborate?" whenever Hays paused or made a particularly cogent point. This served two purposes. On a practical level, it allowed Brasher to rest his voice. More importantly, it perpetuated the standoff, enabling all of the Charpaq troopers and the aliens in their custody to escape via the main elevator shaft.

Brasher looked over his shoulder, and the empty corridor behind him told him it was time to make his move.

"I hope some of this has sunk in," said Agent Hays. "But I truly think it could reap benefits for you in your future galactic empire-building endeavors if you have a keener understanding of the art of negotiation. Negotiation isn't a matter of just repeatedly presenting terms that are only favorable to your side and wholly unfavorable to the other in the futile hope that your adversary will eventually break down and acquiesce. It's a process whereby two parties engage in a mutual and fair discussion to reach a compromise that both parties can agree to and benefit from."

"Yes, yes, I think I get it now," said Brasher. "Would you mind if I try again?"

"Please do," Hays said.

"Okay. How about...you let my landing party go, we take nine of the aliens with us, and you keep the rest."

"Are you counting the Corpuulon as two?"

"No."

"That's still a bit one-sided," Hays replied. "But it's much better than your previous attempts."

"Thank you," Brasher said. "I'd like to try one

more time." He was lining Hays up in his sights.

"I was hoping you'd say that." Hays felt a surge of pride at his new-found mentoring skills. This did not go unnoticed by his colleagues encamped in the corridor behind him, one of whom spat on the floor and muttered "insufferable..."

"Here goes," Brasher said, moving in for the kill. "How about you let *me* go. Then at the count of one hundred, you can have all of the aliens back."

"What about the rest of your landing party?" Hays said.

"You drive a hard bargain," Brasher said. He paused for effect. "Okay, I'll let you have them, too."

Agent Hays was incredulous. Did Brasher – in an attempt to reach a compromise using his laughable bargaining skills – overshoot and propose a deal that was glaringly one-sided in favor of Hays and the Alien Phenomena Agency? He couldn't risk giving Brasher time to reconsider. "Deal," Hays shouted down the corridor.

Brasher smiled. "Whew! I hope I did okay."

"You did great," Hays replied.

THIRTY-THREE

The third-floor room extended the entire breadth of the north end of the luxury beach house. An ocean breeze fluttered the curtains at each end of the room; one window faced west and overlooked the dunes of the barrier island, the other window faced east and overlooked the beach and the sea. A massive stone fireplace was centered on the north wall. A few feet in front of the fireplace sat two simple wooden chairs, side-by-side, facing the French doors and the hallway and the staircase beyond. Between the chairs and the fireplace sat three 26-gallon red marine gas tanks. Their black fuel caps had been removed.

Despite struggling with her captors, April was able to assimilate this entire image in an instant, and it horrified her. The two pout models threw her into the chair on the left and held her there while Martina attempted to bind April's ankles with a rope. April resisted the only way she knew how – by screaming and kicking and using biting sarcasm.

"Calm down!" Martina said, "Don't make me tase you!"

"Oh *that's* an awesome idea," April said. "Firing off 50,000 volts of electricity in a room filled with gasoline fumes – what could possibly go wrong?"

Martina hadn't actually thought of that and offered April a gracious "Yeah, right...thanks" as she finally managed to secure April's legs and tie the rope around her ankles. Martina moved on to April's wrists, tying them together, then using another rope to secure them to the back of the wooden chair. The gasoline vapors burned April's eyes and stung her throat. Screaming didn't seem to help. She started to hyperventilate instead, but was compelled to calm herself and slow her breathing when the decreased carbon dioxide in her bloodstream and the petrochemical fumes in her head made her dizzy and sick to her stomach.

Martina stood in front of April, but looked down at her own shoes to avoid eye contact. "Don't worry. It will all be over soon."

Hundreds of questions flooded into April's head, but with the hypocapnia and the gasoline vapors and the sleep deprivation and the fear and the anxiety her brain seized up, and by the time she uttered "What the hell does that mean?" Martina and the two pout models had left the room, closed the doors, and disappeared down the staircase.

"What the hell does that mean?" snarled Cyril.

"It means that you're coming with me," said Lieutenant Daan. "You have an appointment for a debriefing back on the C.S.S. Lewis. It's standard operating procedure for anyone who's set off the BAMN device."

Cyril wanted to point out that by going to the Charpaq ship he was going somewhere, and not "not going anywhere," but he had attempted arguments based on technicalities with authority figures in the past, and it never ended well. "What about the *Rev 9?*"

"You mean your luggage?" the lieutenant asked. "I'll have one of the bellhops take it up." Cyril bristled. "Just kidding. I'll have one of the troopers pilot it up to the battle cruiser. We'll hangar it until you're done."

Perhaps this isn't a bad thing, Cyril thought. *Maybe they looted the place and came across my belt, or the BAT.* Lieutenant Daan led Cyril to one of the landing craft, and within minutes they were walking to a debriefing room on the Charpaq Space Ship Lewis. The doors parted with a *woosh* before Cyril could read the sign on the outside. It read "Interrogation."

"Okay," Commander Brasher said. "I'm leaving now. Implicit in our agreement that you allow me to leave via the hangar elevator is that you won't shoot bullets into me while I attempt to do so."

"Of course," Hays said. He turned to look behind him, then frowned and shook his head at the custodian who had just shouldered his AK-47.

"And after I pass, I want you to count out loud."

"Wouldn't have it any other way," Hays said. Brasher headed down the corridor with his hands in the air and his plasma gun slung over his back. As he sauntered across the intersecting corridor where Hays and the ad hoc APA security team were entrenched, he gave a weak smile and waved one hand, like a movie theater-goer walking past the usher with a purse full of home popped popcorn – if movie theater ushers were armed with Glocks. Once he passed out of their view, Brasher broke into a trot for the hangar.

There was a period of indecision while team Area 52 debated whether Hays was simply supposed to count to one-hundred, or whether he was supposed to count in "one one-thousand, two one-thousand" fashion as if he were counting off 100 seconds. A consensus was reached that Hays should just count to one-hundred, since it was unlikely that the Charpaq race shared the Earth system of time measurement based on seconds, minutes, hours, and days.

By the time Hays had counted to seventeen, both Cyril and the *Rev 9* were on board the C.S.S. Lewis, the Area 52 runway was empty save for two remaining Charpaq landing craft, and Brasher had made it back to the surface and ordered two-dozen armed troopers to surround the shed.

By the time he had counted to seventy-two, Hays was immersed in a daydream about the promotion that was sure to be his reward for recapturing the alien escapees, thwarting the Charpaq interlopers, and not shooting holes into any Area 52 walls for well over eight hours. *The only thing that's standing between me, a bigger desk, and an expense account is roughly seventeen hours of paperwork*, thought Hays. At the count of ninety-eight (who would know, really?) Hays charged around the corner, gun drawn, fully prepared to single-handedly apprehend a very empty corridor.

Hays stood perplexed until his sense of bewilderment was blown away by a feeling of overwhelming shame. It was the kind of shame one only experiences when a historic personal failure is played out in front of coworkers – coworkers who will remember every excruciating detail of the embarrassing episode and not hesitate to bring it up at every meeting, performance review, and office Christmas party.

Hays turned to face his colleagues who had gathered behind him. As if attempting to run away from his shame – or those colleagues who were still armed and now very annoyed – Hays feigned an epiphany, shouted "To the hangar!" and then took off down the corridor. The cluster of Area 52 personnel parted, allowing him to pass, then followed him – like villagers with torches and pitchforks – as he ran to the hangar.

Hays burst into the hangar to find it as empty as the corridor he had charged into a minute earlier. As he considered the unpleasant ramifications of both the en masse alien escape and the loss of every spacecraft from Area 52, profound shame welled up inside of him again, and to suppress it he turned and shouted to the Area 52 personnel who had just caught up with him.

"To the elevator!" Hays ran onto the platform, then turned to face his now miffed, defeated, and battle-weary substitute soldiers. They stood unmoved and unmoving and stared at him. "Oh, come on, guys!" Hays pleaded, thinking back to a leadership seminar he had once attended. After some grumbling and several audible sighs, the six agents, two biologists, Constance, Etter, and the custodian all shuffled across the hangar floor and onto the platform. Hays pushed the black "up" button and they shot toward the surface. After a dizzying climb up the elevator shaft, the platform slowed, then settled to a stop level with the dirt floor of the shed. Hays saw exactly no Charpaqs or escaped aliens, and so went with the default strategy that had been such a rousing success so far.

"To the desert!" Hays shouted, and he bounded off of the platform and out the shed door. Like a defensive squad pursuing a scrambling halfback in the open field, the eleven coworkers ran after Hays. Some of them wondered how much longer this could go on. Sprinting to the hangar and then to the elevator took relatively little time and effort, but the enormity of the desert seemed daunting. To make matters worse, most of them did not have appropriate footwear. They immediately stopped wondering when they were forced to skid and slide across the desert floor to avoid colliding with Hays, who had come to a dead stop in front of them. Some tried harder than others. As Agent Hays picked himself up out of the dirt, the others looked around them and found they were surrounded by a dozen armed Charpaq guards.

"Drop your guns," barked the commander. Twelve guns hit the desert floor with a *thud*. "And you – drop whatever it is you're holding there." Etter looked around as if somebody else were clutching a samurai sword. The commander frowned and pointed to him. "Yes, you!" The unsheathed sword hit the ground with a *clink*. With all of the humans disarmed, he addressed Agent Hays. "Are you the leader?"

An image of the Alien Phenomena Agency's organizational chart popped into Hays's head, and he visualized his name in the general area where a great-great-great-grandchild's name would appear in a family tree. "No," he said, without elaborating.

"Where is he?"

"Probably home in bed," responded Hays with palpable envy. "He should roll in around ten."

"We can't wait. We've already wasted enough time here. Are there any others remaining in your bunker?" Hays admitted that there were others – though he wasn't sure how many. "You should probably have them join us. And mention that they might want to bring along any easily-carried personal belongings that they don't want to get crushed under tons of rock."

Agent Hays stared at his walkie-talkie and struggled to remember the code to order an Area 52 evacuation. *What's the mnemonic device? Oh, yeah,* Hays thought. "Code brown! This is a code brown! You must evacuate via the hangar elevator. This is not a drill. Repeat, code brown!" After a few minutes, seventeen additional employees of the APA had crawled out of the underground labyrinth and joined Hays and the others in the desert.

"Is this everyone?" Commander Brasher asked.

"Yes," Hays said with confidence, although there was no way he could be certain. But at this point he didn't really care. If any Area 52 personnel had ignored (or slept through) both a code green *and* a code brown, he figured that they deserved whatever was coming to them.

Brasher put his hands on his hips and cleared his throat, as if he were preparing to deliver some official pronouncement. "It probably goes without saying," he began in a booming baritone. He paused, noticing that several of the under-dressed humans were trembling. "Oh, come on. I haven't even mentioned the really terrifying part yet."

"They're cold," Hays offered.

"I'm *terrified*," volunteered a female voice in the crowd.

"Well, as I was saying, it probably goes without saying that Vice-Admiral Perch isn't happy. Not. One. Bit. He's not keen on governments or organizations that incarcerate aliens and confiscate their personal property for no apparent reason."

"A couple of them crashed their spacecraft into our planet." Most of the imprisoned aliens had *not* crashed their vehicles into Earth. Hays hoped the commander wouldn't point that out, and resorted to the only argument he had at his disposal. "There was property damage..." Hays trailed off, trying to recall the specifics. "A bird feeder, a wheelbarrow, one of those above-ground pools..."

"Were there any charges brought?" Brasher asked. None of the aliens had been charged, but Hays did not know that, so he answered with a shrug. "Just as I thought. I'm no intergalactic attorney, but I'm guessing that there are laws against incarcerating non-threatening alien beings on a random and capricious basis. And Vice-Admiral Perch is no intergalactic attorney, but he guesses that there are probably such laws, too. Long story short – he has decided that your punishment shall be the immediate destruction of your underground facility."

*I sort of wanted to retire anyw*ay, thought Hays. He shuffled his feet. *Maybe get a job in the private sector running leadership seminars. Leadership. Hmmm. No one is saying anything Maybe I should say something leader-like.* "You're willing to destroy Area 52 – an irreversible and disproportionate act – without mediation, or some sort of hearing or tribunal? That seems a little heavy-handed."

"Consider yourself lucky," Brasher said. "Perch wanted to terraform the entire area that you call 'Nevada' into a vast, barren, rocky wasteland void of any moral code or decent live theater.'

"Too late," muttered one of the humans in the crowd.

"I talked him down to just obliterating this place that you call 'Area 52,' " Brasher said. "Besides, while a terraform project looks great on a résumé, we just don't have time for that." At that moment a Charpaq trooper emerged from the shed and nodded to Brasher, who nodded back. "There will be no further discussion. We are leaving now, and once our landing craft have lifted off I will activate a Higgs bomb that is set to detonate in 60 minutes." The armed troopers headed for the landing craft, and Brasher pointed to a hill that stood a quarter-mile away. "You might want to go stand over there."

Hays and the other APA personnel trudged off in the dark and disappeared behind the hill. They watched as the lights of the landing craft shot into the air, then disappeared into the underside of the battle cruiser. As the hatch at the bottom of the C.S.S. Lewis slid shut, a few of the Area 52 workers – mostly men who had been married a long time, or who had teenaged children – broached the subject of going back down into the depths of Area 52 to search for the bomb. "We've got 60 minutes," one argued.

The interrogation room was a small, oblong room filled with a large, oblong table. Lieutenant Daan sat on the side closest to the door, positioned in front of a monitor and a touch pad built into the table. Cyril was directed to sit on the opposite side.

"State your name please for the record," the lieutenant said.

"Cyril of Blutaark." The lieutenant entered the name into the system. In a fraction of a second the database spewed Cyril's vital information onto the screen.

"Cyril the Bounty Hunter," mused the lieutenant. He looked over the monitor and into Cyril's eyes. "Can you confirm that the *Rev 9* in our possession is registered to you?"

"It is." Cyril thought this might be a good time to ask about the BAT and his utility belt, but was cut off before he could speak.

"So how did you come into possession of the

BAMN device?" With this question, the lieutenant's tone went from matter-of-fact to accusatory and brusque, so that Cyril – despite his stunted social skills – sensed that it was probably not a good time to ask questions.

"It was given to me by...an acquaintance."

"Lieutenant Daan opened with an eye roll, then for his closer he sighed heavily. "Does your acquaintance have a name?"

"Yes," Cyril said. He sensed another imminent eye roll, so he elaborated. "His name is Peter. Peter Finch. At least that's what he's been calling himself since he's been here on Earth."

"Pray tell, what does he call himself when he's not on Earth?" Cyril squirmed; he was not accustomed to being on the receiving end of practiced condescension.

"Peter of Blutaark," Cyril said. Lieutenant Daan stared at Cyril, then blinked, then stared some more.

"Did you say...Peter...of...Blutaark?"

"Yeah, I did."

"Do. Not. Move." The lieutenant stopped staring and sprung from his seat and ran from the room. His footsteps disappeared down the corridor before the interrogation room door *whooshed* shut.

The Charpaq trooper who was chosen to plant the Higgs device was lowered down the "out of order" elevator shaft after the aliens, including Cyril, had been rescued. He walked a random route through the underground maze, then entered a random, unlocked door with "storage" stenciled on it. There were several rows of gray metal shelves that filled the room and stretched to the ceiling, and from one of those random rows he chose a random shelf, and from the random shelf he removed a random wire basket that contained a tacky, cumbersome, black utility belt. He considered keeping it for himself, but decided that it would make him look too much like a boorish, amateur bounty hunter. He removed the utility belt, armed the Higgs device, placed it at the bottom of the basket, and then draped the utility belt back on top. Gingerly.

As far as Higgs devices went, this one was not particularly notable. It was the size and shape of a loaf of bread, and had the usual assortment of stickers warning one not to drop it, immerse it in fluids, or speak ill of it within earshot of the device. When detonated, a Higgs device assumes the mass of an object exponentially larger than the Higgs device itself. Then it contracts to its original mass and reverts to an inert state. The cycle of expansion-contraction is explosive, taking only milliseconds to complete. A smaller device, such as the one placed in the storage basket in Area 52, can expand to the size of a domed professional sports stadium. A device the size of a railroad car can expand to the size of a small planet or a large moon. If one were to detonate a Higgs device in deep space, he would likely be reprimanded for wasting a lot of money. Nothing much happens, other than a momentary distortion of the local time-space continuum. But the Charpaqs – who invented the Higgs device – discovered that if you detonated a Higgs device in close proximity to (or inside of) another object, the result is something that they like to call "pretty cool." Charpaqs found the device useful in military endeavors, civil engineering, and at boring parties at somebody else's home.

The Charpaq trooper found his way to the Area

52 hangar and took the elevator back to the surface. Upon exiting the shed, he nodded to his commander to confirm that the Higgs device had been hidden and armed. The trooper and Brasher sat together in the landing craft during the quiet flight back to the C.S.S. Lewis. As the shuttle entered the hangar inside the battle cruiser, the commander turned to the trooper.

"You heard my speech down there, right?"

"Yes sir, most of it, I think," said the trooper. "I thought that you were stern, yet fair, sir.

"Thanks," Brasher said. "Just one question."

"What's that, sir?"

"Did I say sixty seconds, or sixty minutes?"

THIRTY-FOUR

Lieutenant Daan darted back into the interrogation room and stood at silent attention until Vice-admiral Perch entered.

"Vice-admiral Perch, I give you Cyril of Blutaark." Perch's torso was disproportionately large, even for a Charpaq. His bison-like thorax distracted Cyril, and it took him several seconds to grasp that the small head atop the generous torso was speaking. "Answer the Vice-admiral!"

"Could you repeat the question?" Cyril asked.

"What have you done with Peter?" asked Perch in measured tones.

"Well, we went to college together, shared some classes, played on the same intramural farfelball team."

"No!" shouted Perch. "What I mean is...*where is Peter?*" He slammed his fist into the table, demonstrating a mix of anger and solemnity that baffled Cyril. It seemed like an irresponsible waste of resources to deploy a battle cruiser just to apprehend an inconsequential fugitive like Peter, whose recent highlight reel would include working at a doughnut shop and living in a recreational vehicle.

Cyril could not have known that in the weeks

since Peter had escaped Huull 4 with the Blutaark Police on his heels that he had become part folk-hero, part icon, part guy-who-cured-a-lot-of-us-and-told-us-he'd-come-back. Adult Charpaqs held mass vigils, anticipating his return. Parents named their newborns Peter, spawning an entire generation of Charpaq women who hated their names and resented their parents more than usual. Pre-teen Charpaq girls doodled pictures of Peter on their school binders. Teenage Charpaq boys taunted the girls about their pictures, but then wrote angst-y poems in the privacy of their bedrooms. Those poems weren't always about Peter; not everything had changed.

When Maarsq and Hutch were aiding and abetting Peter in his attempt to elude the authorities, Hutch had placed a BAMN device in the trunk of the *Rev 2*. The Charpaqs believed that Peter would return when he could, but they also knew that there was a strong possibility that he might find himself in a situation from which escape would be impossible. Knowing that Peter had the BAMN device gave the Charpaqs hope. When they discovered that Cyril possessed the BAMN device intended for Peter, they were incensed.

"Well," Cyril started. "The last time I saw him he was in Smyrna, Georgia."

"Show us where that is," Perch demanded. Lieutenant Daan swept his fingers across the touch pad and an image of the Milky Way galaxy appeared on the wall.

"You can zoom in. A lot. It's actually located on the planet you're terrorizing now." The image of a rotating Earth appeared. Cyril pointed to the general area of the United States. "Zoom on this. Good. Now here. That's Georgia. Zoom on this urban center – that's Atlanta. Now zoom in here. A little more. Good. Right there." The image displayed was of a neighborhood in Smyrna. Cyril recognized it and pointed to Brooks's house. "That's where I saw Peter last." Cyril noticed that the recreational vehicle was missing, but decided not to mention it.

"We're setting a course for Smyrna," said Perch to the lieutenant. "I will see you on the bridge." He stormed out of the interrogation room.

"You're welcome," Cyril said. Cyril assumed that the debriefing was over and he remained seated, expecting that Lieutenant Daan would offer heartfelt apologies for the inconvenience before taking him to the *Rev 9*. Cyril also had expectations that – before he was sent off as a hero – there would be a fruit basket, a brass band, and some kind of honorary sash – the details of which were sketchy.

Three of the men volunteered to go back and search Area 52 for the Higgs device. They had two things in common: all three were agents, and none of them were Agent Hays. The others said "Good luck," "Godspeed," and "Make sure the coffee pot is off." The three men laughed at the gallows humor of the coffee pot joke, but the office safety officer persisted, saying "Seriously, check the coffee pot."

One of the agents said "It's time," and after hugs and goodbyes they turned away from the group and took somber steps into the dark, heading back up the hill toward Area 52. Their send-off lasted approximately eight times longer than their mission. The three men froze when a seismic rumble reverberated from beneath the desert floor and into the marrow of their bones. The scampered to the crest of the hill in time to see the desert floor bulge, then explode upwards to sculpt a dome of rock that eclipsed the hill where they stood in awe. They fell to the ground as a massive roar – like a freight train, or a tornado (the three would argue this point for years) – washed over them and shattered their eardrums. Deep fissures opened up in the dome in front of them like crevasses on a glacier while tons of dust and a fusillade of rocks filled the air. A portion of the runway shattered like glass, and the shed and steel barrack crumpled and were swallowed by the earth.

They felt the ground shudder beneath them and watched in horror as the umbral massif that had consumed Area 52 imploded. The Higgs device had obliterated the underground installation as well as a sizable portion of the bedrock that enveloped it. Nature strongly disliked the resulting vacuum, and the stunning collapse of 3,000 meters of rock created an ever-expanding hole in the desert floor. As the earth imploded in front of the three agents, the dirt beneath them gave way in a landslide. One scrambled to safety over the crest of the hill, but two tumbled toward the maw of the voracious crater. The lead agent crashed into a creosote bush and held on, then reached out and grabbed the other agent by his arm to arrest his fall. His feet dangled over the edge of the now quiescent crater that had grown to a depth of 60 feet and a span that could engulf the Brooklyn Bridge. In the still dark desert morning, he turned to the agent who had just saved his life. "Did he say sixty seconds? Or sixty minutes?" he shouted over the ringing in his ears.

The other agent shouted back. "What?!"

THIRTY-FIVE

It was well before sunrise when Peter trudged north across the dunes toward the beach house. His usual sprightly pace was slowed by the sand, his inappropriate footwear, and Brooks's weighty toolbox. The BAT wedged in his right boot had blistered his ankle, and the sweat and sand stung him with each step. It got easier after he traversed the dunes. He picked up his pace a little on the more level, compacted beach sand.

Peter approached the house from the south. Even in the dark, from a distance it appeared enormous. Seeing only the silhouette of the unlit house, Peter initially mistook it for a grounded freighter. As he drew closer he realized his error – most freighters didn't have plantation shutters and tennis courts. The kidnapper had told him that April would be here, but provided no other specifics about where she could be found, or how Peter might gain access to the house. He thought that the toolbox might contain something that would help him to break in, and he was grateful to Brooks for his prescience. The toolbox might even provide an alibi if he were caught – although he wondered if trying to pass as a contractor up before dawn might strain credulity.

He thought the place looked vacant; there were no vehicles, and no pets or toys in the yard. More importantly, there were no sinister-looking gunmen with automatic weapons – often a deal breaker on your luxury vacation rentals. Peter made his way to the back of the house, opposite the oceanfront, where his eyes were drawn to a light in a third floor window. The window was open and the curtains danced in and out, but all was quiet save for the muffled roar of the ocean. He walked up the wide staircase to the second level deck, set the toolbox down, shielded his eyes with his hands, and pressed his forehead against a window. The interior was shrouded in darkness, devoid of even the dim glow of digital clocks or electric appliances. After a few seconds, Peter thought he could make out a faint light on the left, deep inside the house. He guessed that it came from the third floor.

Peter stepped to the door, turned the handle, and nudged it open. He was surprised that it wasn't locked, and a little disappointed that he didn't get to break in. He toyed with the idea of looking for a locked door, but let it go. He picked up the toolbox and stepped inside. The sand from his boots scratched against the hardwood floors as he walked through the entryway and crept toward the center of the house. With an outstretched hand, he located a wall switch. He took a slow, deep breath and flipped it. Nothing happened. He found another, and flipped that one. Still nothing – unless you counted all the darkness that was still hanging around. Peter wondered if there might be a flashlight in the toolbox, but realized that rummaging through tools in a metal toolbox might attract unwanted attention. Besides, it was as clear as any college freshman's intro to behavioral psychology operant conditioning lab experiment that he was supposed to stop flipping switches and head toward the light.

Peter walked into the main living area on the second floor, where the stench of gasoline fumes provoked at least two of his senses. *Ugh. Fossil fuels.* To his left, a stairway climbed to the third floor where a soft light fell from a room at the top of the stairs. The light bathed the left side of the living area in a faint golden glow, but it failed to reach the right side of the room that remained as dark as Cyril's adolescent free verse poetry. Peter turned and headed for the staircase, when a Colt revolver clicked in the darkness behind him.

"Don't move."

"Martina," Peter said. He never forgot a voice. "Stunning place you have here – I bet. You might want to check your fuse box."

"Shut up," Martina snapped. "Up the stairs."

"Okay, you're sending mixed messages," Peter said. "But if you give me a minute, perhaps I can think of a way to go up the stairs without moving." She jabbed the barrel of the gun between his shoulder blades. "Up the stairs it is."

"Drop the box while you're at it." Peter set it on the floor, and from the corner of his eye he saw a figure dart from the shadows, grab the toolbox, and vanish to his right. In the darkness he heard an outside door open and the metallic rattle and thud of a heavy metal toolbox crashing into the sand.

As Peter approached the top of the stairs, he could see light coming from a single room, and through the panes of the French doors he saw April sitting in front of the fireplace. Her eyes turned up to meet Peter's, and despite being tied to a chair in a room filled with gasoline and tacky nautical-themed furniture, she smiled. Her sense of utter relief at her imminent rescue was crushed when she saw Martina standing behind Peter with a gun.

"You're doing the hostage rescue thing wrong," April said as Peter entered the room.

"It'll be more fun this way. Trust me," Peter said. She knew he was being flippant, but she trusted him. Two of the pout models had followed them into the room, and they proceeded to tie Peter's wrists and ankles while Martina held him at gunpoint. They pushed him down onto the wooden chair next to April and secured his wrists and ankles to the chair. His eyes watered as he surveyed the room. "You know, usually people put the boathouse closer to the water, rather than on the third floor."

"I'm really going to regret what I have to do next," Martina said. April closed her eyes, certain that they were about to get shot. Martina handed the revolver to one of her accomplices and knelt in front of Peter. She closed her eyes and gagged a little as she thrust her hand into Peter's right boot. She found the BAT and yanked it out. Peter grimaced. She stood and quickly handed it off to the other pout model. "I'm going to go wash my hands now." At this, Peter winced a little more, recalling the caped thongman at the doughnut shop.

"Now what?" Peter said when Martina returned.

"Now we wait." Martina and the pout models went downstairs, but before they left Martina threatened Peter and April. "I *will* shoot you if you try to escape."

"Get up," said Lieutenant Daan. "We're leaving."

Worst apology ever, thought Cyril. He followed the lieutenant out of the interrogation room and down the corridor. "You *are* taking me to the *Rev 9*, aren't you?" asked Cyril when he had caught up.

"No. We're going to the bridge."

"I was under the impression that I could leave after the debriefing," Cyril said.

"Not until we find Peter." Cyril wanted to grumble, or to shoot something, but he still didn't have his utility belt and was short of breath from the brisk pace. "Cyril, you're a Blutaarkian bounty hunter – were you trying to apprehend Peter?"

"At first. But we came to an agreement," Cyril said. "I agreed to let him go, and he agreed to relinquish any claim to the BAT." The doors in front of the lieutenant opened with a *woosh* and they walked onto the bridge. Cyril and Lieutenant Daan positioned themselves at the rear of the compartment. The bridge was smaller than Cyril would have guessed; Vice-admiral Perch commanded from a seat near the center, facing a wide omni-screen that spanned the forward semicircular wall. Several peripheral support stations surrounded Perch, each one manned by a Charpaq officer working diligently to look busy. The lieutenant continued their conversation in a whisper.

"How did you track Peter?"

"The BAT. When it's activated it transmits a signal."

"Ah, the BAT signal," the lieutenant said, like it was something he had always known but had forgotten about. He excused himself to speak to the ship's communications officer, and then returned with more questions. "Where is the BAT now?"

"I was sort of hoping you guys had it," Cyril said.

"Negative."

"Well if you guys don't have it, then it's either with Peter, or it's in Area -"

"Engage the floodlights," barked Vice-admiral Perch. Cyril and the crew stood awestruck as the

Nevada desert below lit up on the omni-screen, revealing a cyclopean crater where Area 52 used to be.

"It's probably with Peter," Cyril said.

Vice-admiral Perch summoned commander Brasher to the bridge, and (forgetting about the BAMN rescue, the standoff, and the alien evacuation) complimented him on an impressive crater. Perch then swiveled his chair 180 degrees and addressed Lieutenant Daan.

"Where are we going again?"

"Smyrna, sir."

"Chart a course for Smyrna," Perch ordered. Then he swiveled back to admire the crater.

It was just after daybreak when Peter and April heard a four-wheel drive vehicle roar over a sand dune and park behind the beach house. Seconds later, they heard footsteps on the downstairs hardwood floor. April and Peter had only engaged in small talk – if any talk at all – during the two hours they had been tied up together. Early on, April had broached the touchy subject of how Peter planned to rescue her, a subject made more touchy by the fact that he was tied to a chair. He had been wondering that, too, but not wanting to trouble her, he murmured something about a plan that was "too complicated to explain" and "would probably work better" if she wasn't privy to the details. April did not press the issue, and after that exchange they each spent the remaining time attempting to get as comfortable as one could while tied to a chair. As footsteps approached, April stretched her legs out, and Peter realized that while her ankles had been tied together, they had not been secured to her chair.

"Peter Finch," Dirk said. "I'm Dirk Reger,

president and CEO of Dionysus Pharmaceutical. You've already met Martina." Dirk was wearing a white button-down shirt, no tie, and matching dark gray slacks and suit jacket. Martina stood behind him with her arms crossed. She wore the skin-tight black dress that April and Peter had never seen her not wear. "How are you, April?"

April was accustomed to fielding absurd questions from her boss. In the beginning it annoyed her, but after a while she just thought of it as sport, and she would try to answer with an equally absurd response. "I'm good. Say, after you let me go, could you give me a ride home?"

"About that," Dirk said. "Not gonna happen."

"The letting go part or the ride home part?"

"Both."

"You just can't leave us here *forever!*" April said.

"Riiight," Dirk said. He paused to let the ramifications of what he was saying sink in. "I have to agree with you there."

It didn't take long. "You *can't* kill us!" April shrieked.

"Look," Peter said. "You've already got the BAT. Why don't you just let us go?"

"That's an easy question. I'll let Martina take that one," Dirk said.

"If we let you go, then you'll go to the police, and then they'll arrest us, and take the BAT, and I'll have to live in jail," Martina said with a bothered sing-songy delivery, like a mother explaining to her five-year-old for the fortieth time why he shouldn't stick a wire coat hanger into an electrical outlet.

"You can't get away with this," Peter said. April turned to Peter and shook her head in disbelief, wondering if Peter's complicated escape plan involved repeating clichés until their captors were bored into submission.

"Oh, Peter," Dirk said. "Your naïveté is adorable." He turned to Martina. "Am I right? Is he not adorable?"

"He's very adorable," deadpanned Martina.

"If you could see the big picture, Peter, you'd understand that this is the best possible outcome," Dirk said. "Dionysus will be able to duplicate the BAT and use it to treat millions – no, *billions* – of people to cure them of *everything*. So what if I become the wealthiest person on the planet? Children won't have brain tumors, adults won't have obesity and coronary artery disease, my mother-in-law won't have that ghastly rash that she's always harping about. And with a healthy, pain-free work force, the economy will skyrocket!"

"Even if you really believed that," Peter said, "that's not what will happen. It will take you decades to replicate a functional BAT. But with even just one, being the wealthiest person on the planet won't be enough for you. You're greedy to the core, and you'll commoditize the BAT, using it to treat only the highest bidders. The result will be more social inequality, more illness, more riots, and ultimately – wars. *You're* the one who doesn't get the big picture. I've seen this go down on other planets – not with the BAT, but with food, water, energy, parking spaces...it never ends well."

"Earth is different," Dirk snapped. He paused, then started pacing back-and-forth. "I've come too far and worked too hard to let this slip through my fingers now, Finch." Amber rolled her eyes. "Even if your scenario plays out, I'll have more money than God. That's the real bottom line. The two of you get sacrificed, I get rich, and sick people get cured – if not everyone, at least the pretty, important ones.

Besides, I'm willing to bet that *you* didn't invent the BAT. And with a bounty hunter on your trail, odds are that it wasn't yours to begin with. I'll actually be doing someone a big favor by offing you -"

"Okay," April interrupted. "Enough with the Villain Speech already."

"What did you say?" Dirk asked. He stopped pacing and squinted at April.

"The Villain Speech – where the bad guy pontificates after he's captured the hero," April replied. "Often resorting to taunting and ridiculing the hero at length instead of killing him outright. Then the villain provides the hero with details of his nefarious plot, including how he plans to kill the hero. It's trite and overused – but it can allow time for another character to rescue the hero." Both Peter and April looked around the room, out the windows, and behind Dirk and Martina as inconspicuously as possible.

"Nice try," Dirk said. "It looks like you're all out of heroes. If no one objects, I'll move on to the next action item on the agenda – killing the two of you."

"Are you going to shoot us?" Peter asked.

"Oh, you'd love that, wouldn't you?" Dirk said. "With all of this gasoline, we'd probably all go up in flames together. Besides, just shooting you leaves too much evidence. I've got an RPG launcher in the back of the Hummer. Martina and I will just step outside, then I'll fire a rocket into this room. No more April, no more Peter, no more beach house." He looked around at the kitschy room decorations. "And if any room deserved getting blown up, this one does."

"Finally," Peter said. "Something we can agree on."

"Death Trap!" shouted April.

Dirk sighed. "Now what?"

"Death Trap. It's a plot device where the bad guy devises an elaborate and sadistic method of death for his victim," April replied. "Rather than something quick and effective – like shooting him – he plans something more complicated that fuels the tension, but also gives the hero an opportunity to escape."

"Not to beat a dead horse," Dirk said, "but I *just* explained why we can't shoot you where you sit. And if you think you can escape in the time that it takes me to walk to the Hummer, pick up the launcher, and pull a trigger, then go for it."

"Puh-huh," laughed April. "Game on."

"So brave, little April," Dirk said. "But life isn't an English lit course – I'm guessing. This is goodbye. If it's any consolation, the new office temp is awful." He turned to Peter. "You've been a worthy adversary. So long." Dirk and Martina walked out of the room and down the stairs.

Benjamin waited until after sunrise to head out. During the pre-dawn hours, he berated himself for not insisting on a contingency plan before Peter took off to find April. Questions haunted him as he sat in the Winnebago and gazed out of the windshield at the empty highway. *How long should I wait for him? What if they come after me? Why didn't we get more doughnuts back there?* By the time the first rays of sunlight cascaded over the barrier island, Ben's uncertainty had turned into a sick uneasiness. He realized that Peter should have had enough time to get to the house and back, with ample time to spare for a bold, climactic rescue of April Robinson. Something was amiss. *Peter would want me to wait*, Ben thought. *But he would do the same thing if he were in my shoes.* Ben stuck the cell phone in his pocket and headed east across the dunes, then north toward the beach house.

"We have precious little time." Peter looked into April's eyes. "Do exactly as I say, no questions, and you'll get out of here alive." April understood and nodded. "Put your feet on the floor and turn so that the back of your chair is against the back of mine." April discovered that she could stand, albeit in a crouched position. With her ankles together she could hop, and though she could not walk she managed to rotate her chair with ease. At the same time, Peter lunged and twisted in his chair with the grace of a raccoon trapped in a garbage can, and managed to position it so he was facing the east window.

Outside, Dirk came to the conclusion that the Hummer was parked uncomfortably close to a beach house that was about to be turned into an exploding fireball. He climbed into the behemoth with Martina, started it up, and drove it to the leeward side of a low dune. From her vantage point facing the west window, April could see Dirk get out of the vehicle. Both April and Peter heard the car door slam.

"Push right up against the back of my chair," Peter said. "I can almost reach your ropes." April lifted and pushed with her legs until her chair collided with Peter's, and in an instant she felt Peter's fingers tugging and pulling at the knot. She found this reassuring, until she saw Dirk open the back door of the Hummer and remove the rocket launcher.

"Listen," Peter said. "When your hands are freed from the chair, your ankles and wrists will still be tied together. But there's no time to untie them. Just get up and hop to the door – it's not locked – then get down the stairs any way you can."

"But what about -"

"I'll be fine. Trust me." April could see Dirk standing with the rocket launcher. Martina stood a few feet behind him, her fingers stuck in her ears. "Almost done!" Peter said.

"That's just what I was thinking," April said in a desperate whisper.

"You're free. *Go!*" Peter shouted. April stood, teetered and watched as Dirk lifted the launcher to his shoulder. With her hands tied behind her back, April hopped toward the French doors, hit them with a shoulder, and bounced into the hall when the doors gave way. Two short hops brought her to the landing, where she turned with her back against the wall, looking for support from the bannister. Her bare feet landed with a *thunk* as she slid them off of the landing and onto the uppermost step. A slight hop and another *thunk* to the next step. Another hop, another *thunk*. Dirk tilted his head to aim. There was a *boom* as white smoke wafted from the launcher and dissipated in the sea breeze. April's feet hit the step near the middle of the stairs coincident with the *boom* from the RPG launcher. She gasped and started to falter, but there was not enough time for fear to register between the *boom* and the hellish explosion that followed.

April would remember a roar that hammered her eardrums, a furnace blast of air that propelled her off of the stairway and onto the second-floor hardwoods, and a wall of black smoke that billowed down the stairs from where the north wing of the third floor used to be. Peter's admonition to *get down the stairs any way you can* rattled in her head and made her laugh a little – on the inside. Outside, Dirk and Martina flinched as the rocket instantaneously converted the upstairs room into an expanding ball of fire and a hurricane of shrapnel generated from exploding wood, nails, drywall, and kitschy furnishings.

"We should probably go," Dirk said, clearly staking his claim for the Atlanta Area Businessmen's Understatement of the Year Award. He threw the launcher into the back of the Hummer, then he and Martina jumped in. They disappeared behind the dunes and headed for the highway.

Benjamin heard the explosion, then saw the smoke rising into the Carolina blue October sky from the gasoline-and-luxury-beach-home fueled fire. *That's not how rescues work*, Ben thought, before breaking into a sprint. Ben soon ground to a stop at the back of the house, coughing and gasping – not from smoke – but because he was overweight, in his late thirties, and was foolish enough to try to sprint on sand. The north end of the house was now fully engulfed in flames, and he saw nobody else outside. He headed up the wide staircase that led to the second-floor deck.

April lay face-down on the floor, coughing and sobbing, disoriented by the noise and the heat and the smoke. She struggled to roll across the floor, but stopped when she could not be certain if she was actually moving toward an exterior door or closer to the blaze. She screamed, but discovered that screaming induced paroxysms of uncontrollable coughing. In total frustration, she decided to alternate rolling with screaming.

April's caterwauling hit Benjamin before he hit the door. He burst into the house and ran through the entry way. *Stop, drop, and roll*, he thought as he approached the smoke-filled living area near the center of the house. *Wait, that's not it. Maybe just the 'drop' part.* He fell to his knees and crawled into the inferno, homing on April's piercing, intermittent screams. He careened into what he thought was a rolled-up carpet, until it coughed in his face. *Carpets don't do that.* Then the carpet shouted "Help me!"

Ben assumed a crouching position and attempted to lift April to evacuate her using a fireman's carry. In life-or-death situations, humans will often experience a rush of adrenaline that enables them to perform extraordinary physical feats – feats that would otherwise seem impossible – to save the life of another person. That did not happen to Ben. He struggled to lift April, and failing, he resorted to a healthy rationalization. *We'll both be safer closer to the floor.* He hit the floor again, located April's ankles and realized they were tied. He grabbed the rope and proceeded to drag her feet first out of the fire, out the door, and onto the second-story deck.

April squirmed, sooty and sobbing and hacking, eyes shut and oblivious to the fact that she was now safe from the burning house. Ben, still on his hands and knees, caught his breath before attempting to untie her ankles.

"Hold still!" April's eyes popped open. She was still sooty, and sobbed and hacked, but she stopped squirming enough to allow Ben to untie her. After pulling the rope from her ankles, Ben stood and helped her to her feet, supporting her as they made their way down the stairs and into the yard. When she collapsed in the sand, Ben sat next to her and started to untie her wrists. "My name is Ben. I'm a friend of Peter's."

"I'm," April said, parsing her words between tears and snot bubbles and coughs, "April."

"I know. Where's Peter?" She slid her hand from

the now loosened ropes and pointed to the refinery fire where a house used to be. She broke down and rolled face-first onto the sand, sobbing uncontrollably. Ben welled up controllably, then removed his glasses and wiped his eyes with his shirt tail.

Benjamin called 911 to report the kidnapping, murder, and attempted murder. He neglected to mention the massive fire that he had just escaped, but that was inconsequential. Someone had already seen the smoke and notified the Dare County Volunteer Fire Department. An engine had been dispatched, but the house was fully involved by the time firefighters arrived. Ben and April watched from a distance while the firemen aimed streams of water over what was left.

A sheriff's deputy arrived and questioned April, who stood shivering due to the chilly October air, her baseline anxiety, and the bonus anxiety induced by the deputy's initial accusation that she and Ben were somehow directly responsible for burning down a perfectly good beach house. When Ben showed him Brooks's cell phone to prove they were the ones who called 911, the deputy allowed April to recount how she had been held at gunpoint by Dirk Reger at Dionysus headquarters, kidnapped by Martina and her associates, and then held hostage in the beach house until Peter came to rescue her.

"Then they put us in a room full of gasoline, and fired a rocket into it," April said. "Peter helped me get out...but he didn't make it."

The deputy realized that a complex time-consuming case involving kidnapping across state lines, murder, and arson fell under the jurisdiction of the FBI and inconveniently close to duck-hunting season. He notified the FBI. The nearest field office was ninety minutes away in Norfolk, but according to the receptionist, everyone was out of the office for the annual canoe trip. The deputy called the Atlanta field office directly, and arrangements were made for April to be interviewed there when she got home.

April looked horrible for someone who had just spent a couple of days at a luxury beach house, but above-average for someone who had almost been incinerated in a burning luxury beach house. The sheriff's deputy offered to call an ambulance to transport her to the nearest hospital, but she refused, promising to seek medical attention when she returned to Atlanta. Her shoulder throbbed (probably from her lack of foresight in not donning shoulder pads before being catapulted from the stairs) and she looked like a depression-era coal miner, but she had no other obvious injuries. The deputy relented, and told Ben and April that he would give them a ride back to the Winnebago after he wrapped up a couple of loose ends.

While they waited for the deputy, Benjamin called Brooks, handed the phone to April, and listened to her half of the conversation.

"Daddy, it's me. I'm okay. No, I'm fine, really." She wiped the tears with the back of her hand and turned to Ben. "Where are we exactly?"

"Outer Banks, north of Nags Head."

"Daddy, we're on the Outer Banks. There's police and firemen here. *No*, I didn't start smoking again. We'll be leaving here soon. Ben will drive us back." There was a pause. "No, Daddy, he didn't make it. Me too. It was Dionysus, Daddy. Yes, I've already told them. Okay. I love you too." She ended the call and handed the phone back to Ben. They stood and stared at the ocean and said nothing for a while, but despite the late fall breeze April felt cozy warm. For the first time she became aware of the blanket that had been placed over her shoulders. The deputy called to them from a distance, and they turned and started for his car.

"Thanks for the blanket," she said to Ben.

"I have no idea where that came from."

THIRTY-SIX

On that cool, sunny October day there was crispness in the air that underscored the keen anticipation brewing among Atlantans. That sense of anticipation was most acute in the beer-drinking demographic of men aged 18 to 54, and was created by an upstart brewer called Old New Hampshire Brewery.

The Old New Hampshire Brewery struggled in recent years with lackluster sales of it only product – cranberry beer. After a particularly disastrous advertising campaign that highlighted the product's ability to fight urinary tract infections, ownership brought in a new management team with a fresh focus. They scrapped the cranberry beer entirely, and set about developing a new ale that promised to "Be the best beer in the world with the word 'Old' in its name." The marketing department was given carte blanche, and a massive promotional campaign for Old New Hampshire Ale was rolled out with Atlanta as the test market. Expectations were high, as daily advertisements encouraged (some say warned) Atlantans to prepare for a blockbuster promotional event at the end of the month.

So when a massive, onyx-black New Hampshire-shaped object appeared one morning in the clear blue skies over Atlanta, nobody panicked. At first. The presence of the Charpaq battle cruiser did have two immediate consequences: it provided a modest spike in sales of Old New Hampshire Ale, and turbulence from a Charpaq landing craft caused the Old New Hampshire Ale promotional hot-air balloon to collapse and plummet to earth. At the end of the day, both of these events were seen as unfortunate.

The shuttle craft parked on Brooks's driveway, and a dozen Charpaqs – led by Commander Brasher – marched to the front door. Brasher rang the doorbell and waited. Brooks opened the door and was taken aback by the presence of a dozen extraterrestrials at his doorstep. After gathering himself, he boldly assumed that good etiquette was universal – even for creatures that from a distance could be mistaken for a small man riding a buffalo.

"May I help you?"

"I'm Commander Brasher of the Charpaq Fleet. May we enter?"

Brooks invited the commander in along with two or three of the troopers, but politely suggested – because space was limited and he had no furniture suitable for livestock – that the others should wait outside. Brasher and three troopers went in while the others milled about outside, unnoticed except by one neighbor who (for the second time that week) called the HOA president to lodge a formal complaint.

"I won't take much of your time," Brasher said as he stood in the living room, "but I'm here to find Peter."

"I was afraid of that," Brooks said. He was visibly distraught and spoke haltingly. "I just learned this morning that Peter died. He was killed while rescuing my daughter. I owe him my life, and now hers, too." He stood with his hands in his pockets and stared at the floor.

"That's so Peter," Brasher said. He looked at the other Charpaqs and they all nodded solemnly. "Tragic that he had to die in an accident like that."

"It was no accident," Brooks said. He looked Brasher straight in the eye. "He was murdered. By a jerk named Dirk Reger. He and his associates at Dionysus Pharmaceutical conspired to steal the BAT from Peter and kill him." Brooks felt a little better after venting, but worried that by divulging too much to the Charpaqs – an alien race he'd just met and didn't really know – that he might have just put every human on Earth at risk for retaliatory Armageddon. He decided to play the courtesy card again. "Can I get you some iced tea?"

Before Brasher could answer, a trooper burst through the front door. "Sir, we have a message from the ship. They're picking up a signal from the BAT."

"My apologies for the interruption, Mr. Robinson," Brasher said. He shot a look at the ill-mannered trooper. "I'm afraid we'll have to decline your kind offer – duty calls. I do thank you for your time. You have been more than helpful." Brooks walked them to the door and watched as they trotted back toward the landing craft.

On the way to the shuttle, Brasher chastised a trooper for standing on the grass. Brooks breathed a sigh of relief. Anyone who expressed genuine concern about his front lawn would probably not be inclined to vaporize an entire planet. "If you see Dirk Reger," Brooks shouted to Brasher, "tell him I sent ya." The commander turned and gave him a "thumbs up," a gesture that meant "I can't hear you" on Huull 4. As the landing craft lifted off from his driveway,

Brooks looked out over the trench marks in his yard and wondered where his old Impala was and where Cyril was – but mostly he wondered where his Impala was. Then he went back inside and waited for April and Ben.

Are you *sure* he's not in?" the FBI agent asked.

"I'm just a temp, but the scuttlebutt is that he almost never gets in before ten," Matt said. "But you're welcome to wait."

The FBI agent had few options. Along with his five helmeted, goggled, and armed SWAT team members he had already searched Dirk Reger's home and come up empty-handed, unless you counted a disheveled, bitter trophy wife holding a mostly-empty wine bottle. She wondered where Dirk was, too. As the agent questioned Matt, his colleagues milled about Dirk's office waiting area, antsy to make loud noises or smoke or someone cry. "Isn't that his office?" The agent pointed at Dirk's closed office door.

Matt turned to look at the door. The only door in the room. A door with Dirk Reger's name on it. "I think so."

"Mind if we have a look?" Before Matt could answer, one of the agents produced a steel battering ram, and with an arcing swing slammed it against the door and smashed it open. The *crash* and the splintering wood were intoxicating, and he paused to savor the moment while the others charged into Dirk's office.

Matt stormed in behind them. "What the hell, guys? It wasn't locked." One of the agents shrugged. After ascertaining that Dirk wasn't there and taking turns on the indoor putting green, the agents sauntered back to the waiting area to put it to its intended use.

Six miles away from Dionysus headquarters, an Atlanta police officer pulled over a black SUV, ostensibly for making an illegal lane change. He checked the driver's ID, and then asked him to step out of the vehicle. The officer walked back to his car and returned with a middle-aged woman who wore a white blouse and a lavender skirt and jacket. Jason did not recognize the woman, but something about her seemed familiar.

"Sir, please state your name," the officer said.

"Jason. Jason Inkster."

"That's him!" The woman took a step back and pointed a finger at Jason, who in a flash felt like his lower GI tract was in a revolving door, and he wasn't. This probably wasn't about the illegal lane change. "I recognize that voice anywhere. He's one of the ones who kidnapped me."

Jason now recognized Loretta, and without thinking he nodded a little. "Oh, yeah..." The officer arrested Jason. At Jason's suggestion, the officer also arrested his passenger. Loretta recognized his voice too.

"That's Brian!" Loretta said. "He's the one that was asking me all the stupid questions. You need to lock him up too!"

"Yes ma'am," replied the officer.

"I mean it. And don't just haul them off in handcuffs. You need to duct tape their mouths, tie a bag over their heads, and throw them in a big black bag, 'cause that's what they did to me. What's sauce for the goose is sauce for the gander."

"Yes ma'am, but -"

"They broke my front door," she continued. "And left tire marks in front of my house. My neighbors thought I did that. It's hard to live that kind of thing down."

"Yes ma'am, I'm sure that -"

"And that new door still don't close right. And I've been having nightmares – not about the door, but about the kidnapping. There's this one where a giant black spider traps me and starts..."

The officer had originally planned to drive Loretta home while a backup unit transported Jason and Brian downtown for questioning. "Excuse me," he said while Loretta was still talking, then he escorted Brian and Jason to his squad car, put them in the back, and drove off.

It was immediately clear to detectives that Jason and Brian's level of sophistication would make it challenging for them to plan and carry out bathing a dog, much less kidnapping a Loretta. They offered Jason leniency for his cooperation, and in turn he told them about Loretta's kidnapping, Peter's abduction, the failed attempt to steal the BAT, the conspiracy between Persona and Dionysus executives to kill Peter, and how Brian had yellow post-it notes in his apartment that looked suspiciously like the ones in the office supply closet at Persona. Jason decided to leave out the part about extraterrestrials and space vehicles for now – he was saving that card for an insanity plea should the police renege on their end of the deal.

Warrants were issued for Tor Kinney and Dirk Reger. The Atlanta police descended on Persona headquarters and took Tor away in handcuffs. As he was escorted from the building to a patrol car, Tor drew his jacket over his head to avoid embarrassment and negative publicity. This wasn't really necessary, since most Americans would have considered a health insurance company executive's arrest for kidnapping and conspiracy to be significantly less abhorrent than just being a health insurance company executive. Besides, on this particular day the attention of almost every Atlantan was diverted by what they thought was an overwrought publicity stunt promoting Old New Hampshire Ale.

Dirk was still nowhere to be found. A half-dozen Atlanta police officers stormed his house, but found only disappointment and resentment that the FBI had been there first. After commiserating with Mrs. Reger about what it's like to be in a loveless relationship where you're doing all the work and yet you get nothing in return but ignored and disrespected, they went to Dirk's office.

"We have a warrant for the arrest of Dirk Reger," said the police officer. He stood only a foot in front of Matt's desk, but he projected so that the FBI agents in the waiting area behind him could hear. He wanted to be assertive without being confrontational. It didn't last.

"For the love of God, they've already smashed the door open," said another officer before Matt could respond. "We didn't even get to smash the door." He stood and shook his head, then wiped his eyes. After some shouting and harsh words about jurisdiction and who makes more of an effort to communicate, the Altanta police officers declared that they were happy that the FBI agents didn't mind waiting there for Dirk. "It frees us up to pursue more interesting arrests," said one officer, and with that the police left the building and the FBI agents waited for Dirk.

Dirk and Martina stood in the lab, gazing at the BAT. After they had left the beach house, Dirk drove to a nearby airfield where a private jet was waiting.

In less than two hours they were back in Atlanta, where they took the BAT to the Dionysus research facility. Dirk, hiding the device behind his back, magnanimously announced that all of the employees could take the rest of the day off. None of the employees suspected anything untoward, except the possibility that Dirk was having an affair with Martina. Feeling a little sick to their stomachs, the employees went home. Dirk called Frank Francis and told him to meet him there.

The BAT was a little worse for wear; the LCD screen was cracked, it was dented and smudged, and it seemed to emit a protective shield of atrocious foot odor. But Dirk could overlook all of that. The BAT was a technological marvel, the likes of which had never before been seen on Earth. With the push of a couple of buttons, it could render any living creature disease-free in a matter of seconds, with no side-effects or lingering aftertaste. Not only could it profoundly alter the life of one individual, but it could be the spark, the genesis, for a new and improved planet Earth. Unfortunately, Dirk could overlook all of that, too. It was now his personal cash printing press, and he couldn't wait to replicate it. Because maybe, just maybe, the sound of several machines churning out money would drown out the voices in his head that, for some reason, kept shouting "Be nicer to others!"

Martina had had enough of just gazing at the thing. "Why don't we try it out? I know how."

"Why don't we?" Dirk said. "I can't for the life of me imagine anything bad that could come of it."

"I'll do you first," Martina said. "Stand back a couple of feet." She picked up the BAT and activated the diagnostic scan.

"That wasn't so bad," Dirk said. "Pretty light."

"That was just the diagnostics," Martina said. She activated the therapeutic scan. "All done. Now you do me." Martina showed Dirk how to use the device, and after he scanned her they set it back down on the counter and resumed gazing at it.

After locating the source of the BAT signal, the Charpaqs flew the landing craft to the Dionysus research facility and landed in the empty parking lot. The research facility was an unremarkable white two-floor free-standing building with rectangular windows and a large entryway under an awning in the front. The Charpaq troopers were antsy to make loud noises or smoke or someone cry, so they grew a little cross when Commander Brasher found the front door unlocked.

Martina and Dirk heard a clatter in the hallway and at first assumed it was Frank.

"Did Frank get a new herd of goats?" Dirk asked. No sooner had he completed his sentence, the lab doors burst open and the Charpaqs rushed in.

"Don't move," bellowed Brasher. The troopers behind him brandished their plasma guns. Bug-eyed, Dirk and Martina backed up against the counter. Dirk made it a point to stand in front of the BAT; he hoped against hope that they were here for Martina. "Are you Dirk Reger?" Martina breathed a sigh of relief.

"No!" lied Dirk. "I'm his brother," his eyes darted to the lab equipment as he tried to come up with an alias. "Erlenmeyer." Martina rolled her eyes.

"Well, Erlenmeyer," Brasher said. "We're here for the BAT. I know you're standing in front of it, I know it does not belong to you, and I know that if we did not take it from you, you would just misuse it and make an appalling mess of things. At least on this planet."

"Just give it to him," Martina said.

"No," Dirk said.

"Look," Brasher said. "We can do this the easy way, or we can do this the slightly less easy way. You can just turn around, pick it up and hand it to me or -"

"Or what?"

"Or one of my men could shoot you with his plasma gun, and I could just reach through the bowling-ball sized hole in your torso and get it."

Dirk was beaten. He slumped, turned slowly, picked up the BAT off of the counter, and handed it to Brasher. When he broke into tears, two of the Charpaq troopers high-fived. Brasher clutched the BAT as he and his men marched out of the lab and back to the shuttle. From there the shuttle lifted off and headed for the gigantic New Hampshire-shaped hole in the sky.

Martina attempted to console Dirk in any way she could without actually having to touch him. When he finally gathered himself and stopped sobbing, she spoke. "Look on the bright side. We got to use it on ourselves. We're totally healthy, and who knows? We might actually live forever."

Dirk was surprisingly reassured by her words. He looked up at her and gave a weak smile. "Yeah. At least we've got that."

At that exact instant Frank Francis pulled into the parking lot and a massive white beam of light shot vertically from the Charpaq battle cruiser and vaporized the Dionysus research building. A deafening thunder hammered Frank's eardrums, followed by an intense blast of air that shoved his car back toward the street. When the wind and the noise subsided and the smoke cleared, nothing remained.

Frank got out of his car and walked across the

parking lot to survey the damage. Where the research building once stood was now a perfectly round six-foot deep smoldering crater. Frank bowed his head, then turned his eyes up to the sky, raised his fist, and shook it violently. "Somebody at Old New Hampshire Ale is going to pay for this!"

Under questioning at police headquarters, Tor Kinney implicated Taryn in the conspiracy to kill Peter in order to obtain the BAT. The Atlanta police sent officers to her home, and while they were relieved that – as best as they could tell – the FBI had not been there yet, they saw no signs of Taryn. Someone thought to call her cell phone and ask her where she was.

She answered with a terse "What?" and informed them that she was currently in the board room at Persona headquarters, and that they had better not bother her again. She had spent the last several hours with a black marker and a dry-erase board diagramming a twisted and convoluted plan to acquire all rights to the BAT, even if Dionysus managed to get it first. Taryn did not realize it at the time, but she was the only person in the Persona tower at that moment. With their CEO under arrest, every Persona employee thought to themselves "What the heck?" and took the liberty of knocking off work early, their interest in the celebrated Old New Hampshire Ale promotional stunt playing no small part in their decision to leave the office.

When police returned to the Persona Tower they called Taryn back, informed her of the warrant for her arrest, and asked her to surrender and to come out quietly.

"Give me ten minutes to consider your offer," she barked. She ended the call, and with a heavy heart set about erasing all of her hard work from the dry-erase board. She toyed with the idea of a daring escape; with one phone call she could have a helicopter on the roof, and within hours she could start a new life in another country – preferably one without extradition. *Croatia, Kazakhstan, mainland China – my name sounds vaguely Asian, so that might work.* She told herself that she could build a business empire from scratch – she had done it before. After a couple of minutes, Taryn came to her senses. *With my resources and connections, there's no way I'll do time. I'll be back in the game in a week.* She picked up her phone and called the police back. "I'm coming right down." Taryn held her head high as she walked onto the elevator. She pressed the button for the lobby, and then called her attorney as the elevator dropped.

What happened next has been the subject of intense intergalactic speculation. Some suggest that Cyril might have mentioned to the Charpaqs in passing that Persona Insurance (specifically, Tor Kinney) was involved in the pursuit and abduction of Peter. Others suggest that the Persona Tower itself bore a striking resemblance to a Lepketrian battle cruiser – the Lepketrians being the arch enemies of the Charpaqs ever since the War of the Awkward Trading Route Misunderstanding. And still others insist that the Old New Hampshire Brewery was a front for a government-backed shadow organization that was dedicated to the destruction of capitalism and buildings over 40 feet tall.

Whatever the cause, as Taryn's elevator car passed the 13th floor a solid white column of light erupted form the hull of the C.S.S. Lewis and bathed the Persona Tower in a beam of instantaneous destruction. As the tower vaporized, a wave of screaming thunder washed over the city, followed by hurricane-force winds that shattered windows for blocks. A pillar of gray smoke rose vertically, then dissipated on the upper atmospheric currents. Car alarms sounded throughout the Atlanta metropolitan area – but that had nothing to do with the Persona Tower suddenly not being there.

"Nice crater!" gushed Vice-admiral Perch. Everyone on the bridge nodded in agreement. Even Cyril. Perch swirled his chair to address Lieutenant Daan. "So you've confirmed that the BAT is now securely on board?"

"Yes sir," said Lieutenant Daan, giving a short bow.

"And it is with a heavy heart that I am compelled to ask – have we confirmed the death of Peter of Blutaark?"

The lieutenant nodded with solemn dignity. "Yes sir. According to Commander Brasher's report."

"Very well." Perch rotated his chair briskly to address every crew member on the bridge. And also because he never tired of the sensation of being moderately light-headed. "Each and every Charpaq shall be eternally grateful for what Peter has done for us, but our job here is done. We're heading out." As Perch watched Earth shrink away on the omni-screen, two hazmat-clad security personnel entered the bridge and settled in next to the lieutenant. Cyril could not believe his ears. *The BAT is on board? Peter's dead? Clearly my luck is turning*, thought Cyril. He realized that he would need time to locate the BAT and formulate a plan to steal it before escaping in the *Rev 9*. He dug deep for what little charm he possessed and turned it on.

"You know, lieutenant – it would be boorish of

me to leave at a time like this. If it's not too much of a bother, perhaps I could stay on board for another fortnight or so?"

"I insist on it," said Lieutenant Daan. He nodded to security.

"Oh, *thank* you lieutenant," Cyril fawned. "If you'll just tell me where the guest quarters are, I'm certain I can find my way."

"Cyril, your background check revealed a number of unpaid tickets from the jurisdictions of Tintagel Gamma and Clovelly 3. Mostly for parking offenses, but there were a couple of moving violations, and one for general unpleasantness. A tad bit surprising that there's only one for general unpleasantness, but that's irrelevant. The point is, you're under arrest. These unlucky men will deliver you to the brig."

"Noooooooo!" bellowed Cyril as he slobbered, stamped his feet, and thrust his shoulders back and forth. Security subdued him and dragged him off of the bridge, and just before the doors slid shut he shouted back into the compartment. "That last crater really sucked!"

"They're taking him to the brig, right?" Perch asked.

"Yes sir," replied Lieutenant Daan.

"On the way," Perch said with a gleam in his eye, "have security stick him in torpedo tube #1 for a bit. If that doesn't shut him up, then maybe the vacuum of deep space will."

THIRTY-SEVEN

After leaving the Outer Banks, Benjamin drove the Winnebago back to Atlanta, stopping only once for a late lunch. April spent most of the trip asleep in the back. When they were close to Atlanta, Ben called Brooks to let him know they were almost home. Brooks was standing in the front yard waiting for them when Ben drove up over the curb, over the mailbox, and onto the driveway.

"I haven't quite got the hang of this thing yet," Ben said as he climbed out, but Brooks was oblivious to Ben and the cumulative damage to his front yard. Brooks was already embracing April, who had opened the door, bounded out of the RV, and dashed across the yard before Ben had brought the Winnebago to a complete stop.

Brooks had prepared a sumptuous home-cooked dinner. As they sat together at the small dining-room table, April devoured her food, prompting comment from her father about how her barbaric captors must not have fed her anything at all.

April nodded, and after swallowing said "Yeah. That's it. Any dessert?"

After dinner, they sat at the table and talked about everything except Dirk, Peter, and April's kidnapping. Only once did Brooks broach the subject of Dionysus. Before Ben and April returned, he had watched the local six-o'clock news, which reported on the curious destruction of the Dionysus research building. International experts on sudden building disappearances were at a loss as to what happened, but the news anchor opined that it was "probably a sinkhole." One reporter also mentioned that the CEO of Dionysus, Dirk Reger, was mysteriously missing, but the reporter somehow failed to connect that fact with the fact that his building was missing, too. Brooks simply told April that she probably didn't need to go into the office tomorrow.

Ben slept on the sofa and didn't wake up until almost noon. He had not realized how sleep-deprived he had been, and chalked it up to being around Peter's frenetic drive and the excitement surrounding April's rescue. April slept in her old bed in her old bedroom, and despite all the sleep she got in the RV the day before, she also slept until just before noon. She chalked it up to really enjoying sleeping a lot. They ate breakfast at noon, after which April decided she wanted to go back to her apartment to shower. Benjamin thought it best that she not go there alone, and volunteered to drive.

"Why don't you take my pickup instead of the RV?" Brooks said.

April was as thrilled with the absence of menacing black SUVs in her parking lot as she was to be home. Benjamin unlocked her door and went in. April followed. Benjamin stood with his hands on his hips and surveyed the apartment. "I'm so sorry, April. Looks like they ransacked this place looking for the BAT."

"Yeah. That's it." She excused herself to shower, freshen up, and find some clothes that weren't on the floor. Afterward, she decided to start the new job search by updating her résumé – but first she would tidy up the apartment. Ben pitched in.

"Which bookshelf does this go on?" he asked, holding up a copy of *To Kill a Mockingbird* that he'd just picked up off of the coffee table.

"I alphabetize by author," April said. She walked over and took it out of his hand and started flipping through the pages. It reminded her of Peter, and the security question Martina had asked her to come up with. *What literary character are you like?* April was on the threshold of bursting into tears when a slip of paper fell from the book and fluttered onto the floor. She froze, and looked up at Ben.

"Do you want me to get your bookmark?"

"I don't use bookmarks." Ben bent over and picked it up and unfolded it and handed it to her. She read it to herself. Then she re-read it. Goggle-eyed and mouth agape, she handed it to Ben. "What do you make of that?"

"Looks like a piece of paper with words on it. I can tell you more right after I read it." She was too shocked to respond to Ben or notice that he was being kind of a jerk. Judging by her expression, it wasn't clear to Ben that she understood what she had just read. So he read it aloud.

April,

I'm hoping this letter finds you safe and well. I wanted to thank you for everything you did for me during my visit. You're bright, honest, and kindhearted, and it's people like you who make a significant majority of alien races not want to blow up your planet just yet.

In return for your generosity, I have decided to bestow upon you a pretty neat gift. You're one of the only humans I met who has the intellect and good judgment tempered with the compassion and generosity necessary to fully appreciate this gift. Oh, and technically, it's not mine to give you - but let's let that be our little secret. Besides, the Universe will be a much better place if you have it, and everyone else doesn't.

Sincerely,
Peter

P.S. I suppose I should tell you where it is. You'll find it in an auto salvage yard outside of Birmingham, hidden in a vehicle in a row near the front and not far from the side fence. You'll know it when you see it. The junkyard is close to where Brooks found me. Take a knife, and maybe a tote bag to keep it in. And take this note with you.

I know exactly where he's talking about," Benjamin said.

"Let's go," April said. "First thing tomorrow!" Ben saw something in April that he had never seen before. Granted, in the few hours that he had known her, she had been either screaming or crying or sleeping. It was an exuberance and optimism that one only sees in the face of the rare child who actually got what he wanted for Christmas and then did not break it right away. And it was contagious. "What else do you have to do?"

"Well, my practice still thinks I'm in rehab," Ben said. "So why not?" Ben reflected that he had already been to that salvage yard twice, and both times it was a horrible, if not life-threatening, experience. *Maybe third time's a charm.* They made plans to leave first thing the next morning. April packed light, remembering to put a tote bag and a Swiss Army knife in her suitcase. Not packing reminded Ben that he had pretty much lost everything over the last several days: his car, his job, his Chevron credit card, and his reputation as someone who would never, ever shoot an alien. Despite everything, he was looking forward to the trip.

Thursday morning Ben and April picked up her car from the Dionysus parking garage and returned the truck to Brooks. Not wanting to worry her father, April told Brooks that they were going to the beach for the day, and if the police or FBI called to just take a message. Brooks told her about the latest news report; Dirk and Martina were missing and presumed dead, due to their being inside of a building that was suddenly a smoldering crater. *Could this day get any better?* thought April. They took off in April's car, and two-and-a-half hours later they pulled up in front of the salvage yard.

As best as Ben could recall from his panicked escape a few days earlier, the junkyard had not changed save for the smoldering ruins where the office used to be, a crushed fence, miles of yellow police tape draped around the perimeter, and the absence of two redneck meth dealers. They got out of the car, ducked under the tape and traipsed over a crumpled gate. Ben brought April directly to the *Rev 2*.

"This is it," he said with a fresh sense of wonder. "Peter's spaceship. This is the first time I've been able to take a good look at it without being threatened or shot at."

"Awesome. So where do we start?" April asked.

"Not sure. The trunk is already open. Might as well check it out first." They searched the trunk, looked under the lid and inside the entire compartment, and found nothing. "Let's pop open the cockpit." The canopy had not been completely shut (probably an oversight due to all of the attempted murder that was going on at the time) from the last time the vehicle was searched. Benjamin lifted it and then scanned the junkyard to make sure no one was taking aim at them.

"May I help you?" They both jumped back. April looked around, trying to locate the speaker. Ben remembered the on-board computer.

"Peter sent us," Ben said. "April is a friend. My name is Ben."

"Is April able to communicate?" asked Soledad.

"I am," April said. She leaned in to watch the flashing lights and dials on the instrument panel.

"April, my name is Soledad. I have been having kind of a difficult week. It is not so much getting pried open and shot at and having to associate with these ghastly Earth vehicles – no offense. It is just that I miss Peter."

"Me too," April said. Everyone was quiet for a minute.

"You said Peter sent you?" Soledad said. "For what purpose?"

"He said he left something here for me. But we can't find it."

"You may look about the cockpit if you wish." Benjamin and April searched in all compartments and under the seat, but found nothing. April sighed. Then Soledad spoke again. "Did Peter give you a written note?"

"Yeah, he did," April replied.

"May I see it?" April took the note from her pocket, unfolded it, then held it inside of the cockpit. Soledad scanned it. "Thank you. Is Peter -" Her tone was somber and distant. "Never mind. What you are looking for is inside the pilot's seat – on the right side, just above the arm rest. You will need to cut open the seat to access it. I trust you brought a knife. Be gentle."

April retrieved the pocket knife from the tote bag and handed it to Ben. "You." Ben opened it, reached in, and cut a vertical slit in the seat. He wanted to tell Soledad that she was being very brave, but told himself that he was being very silly. He folded the knife and reached into the opening. He dug around the gel padding until his fingertips met something cold, metallic, and cylindrical. He wrapped his fingers around it and pulled it out.

April gasped. "It's the *BAT*!" Ben rolled it over in his hands and examined it, and then grinned like a kid who just got the toy he wanted for Christmas. He hoped it didn't get broken right away.

"It is *a* BAT, but it is not *the* BAT," Soledad said.

Though not known for being innovative, the Glingecurds of Gyllenhaal 6 are very adept at replicating consumer goods (and even highly advanced technical instruments) that they themselves did not invent or have legal rights to. Their skills are so perfect and sublime that the demand for their high-quality low-cost knock-offs collapsed the economies of two entire galaxies. Fortunately, the subsequent centuries-long litigation that followed resulted in full employment after every resident of those two galaxies earned a degree in intellectual property law.

Peter understood the power and significance of the BAT, perhaps more so than his brethren on Blutaark who conceived and developed it. He was also well aware that having a spare could be infinitely convenient in light of the fact that bounty hunters, intergalactic police, and misguided capitalists might do unpleasant things to separate him from the BAT – including but not limited to separating him from other parts of his body.

"Peter had a functional copy made on Gyllenhaal 6 and hid it here," Soledad said. "Just in case something happened to the original...or in case something happened to him." Ben took another look. At the bottom, just above the power module, it read: *a product of Gyllenhaal 6. No rights reserved.*

"I can't thank you enough," April said.

"Judging from Peter's note," Soledad said, "he expects a lot from you. You should go now. I will just wait here. Godspeed."

April turned and looked at Ben, and with a plaintive expression mouthed the words "Can we keep her?" Benjamin looked at the *Rev 2*, and then looked at April's two-door Honda with a bicycle rack, and shook his head 'no.' "Take care, Soledad. We'll visit, I promise," April said.

April and Ben walked back to the car and got inside. "I believe this belongs to you," Ben said. He handed the BAT to April and she clutched it to her chest with both hands.

"I watched Peter use this," April said. "It's mind-boggling. But it's frighteningly less mind-boggling than the fact that he entrusted me with it. I feel like I could use some help. Like a mentor. You know – someone with not a liberal arts degree, and less anxiety."

"I have not a liberal arts degree," Ben said. "And less anx – well, I've got not a liberal arts degree, and nothing better to do. So now what?"

"We go back to Atlanta. And do amazing things."

THIRTY-EIGHT

"No, no, no," insisted the young man with dark hair, piercing eyes, and a trim beard. He had driven past the odd-looking hitchhiker four hours earlier just outside of Roanoke, Virginia. Despite the fact that he had never before picked up a hitchhiker, something compelled him. Rivers pulled over and parked his VW and waited for the stranger to catch up.

Rivers was pleasantly surprised, not only because the stranger didn't stab him right away and take his car, but because he turned out to be an engaging conversationalist. Over the next four hours they discussed topics as diverse as political science, astronomy, biology, literature, live theater, and bad dates. Rivers was skeptical of his story explaining the anomalous appearance of his fingers and forehead, but he thought it best to drop the subject; it *had* been a rather personal question, and Rivers had never spent any time on a farm. He told the stranger he could take him as far as Knoxville. When they passed the Knoxville City Limit sign Rivers wondered where the time had gone. *This was awesome,* he thought. *I should really pick up hitchhikers more often.* He had asked the stranger if he'd like to stop at a pub for a couple of drinks before parting ways.

"You just don't kill off the hero at the end of a novel," said Rivers. "It's a downer, and you'll lose your audience."

"It's done all the time."

"Yes, but not well."

"Sure it is."

"Then give me some examples," Rivers said.

"Hamlet."

"Technically, that's a play," Rivers replied. "A tragedy, not coincidentally."

"Fair enough. What about *Stranger in a Strange Land*?"

"Well, technically, Smith is killed at the end," Rivers said. "But he reappears in the afterlife. That's sort of not being completely dead, don't you think?"

"Perhaps we'll come back to that one. It would be nice to have a Fair Witness for this discussion, don't you think?"

"Ah," Rivers nodded and took another swig of beer. "Something we can agree on."

"What about *The Great Gatsby*?"

Rivers sat quietly for a few seconds. "Okay, you're right about that one." Rivers paused in thought. "Why do you think Gatsby had to die at the end?"

"Perhaps Fitzgerald was attempting to underscore the carelessness of the truly rich. Gatsby is drawn in by Daisy, but she ultimately rejects him. Between her betrayal and Tom's machinations, he's destroyed. Literally and figuratively. It happens to the powerless, those without. I've seen it time and time again, on an even more tragic scale, on dozens of planets."

"Planets?" Rivers raised an eyebrow.

"Sorry. It's this wretched Old New Hampshire

Ale. I meant continents."

"There are only seven continents," Rivers said.

"I meant seven."

"But not all continents are...it's not important. So you came up with one good example," Rivers said. "But my point was that it's rarely done well. In the vast majority of cases it's carried out in a heavy-handed manner by a hack writer looking for a quick thrill. It's like when the hero's in dire straits, and escapes by some completely implausible set of circumstances."

"I'm no hero, that's understood. But that has happened to me."

Rivers said nothing, but took another sip of beer and leaned in closer, as if the hitchhiker were about to reveal the secret to choosing winning lottery numbers. Had Rivers asked, he could have divulged that the computers of Amiplat could consistently provide winning numbers. The stranger detailed how he had been held hostage with a young woman in a third-floor room of a beach house. They were tied to chairs placed next to three marine tanks filled with gasoline. The kidnappers used an RPG launcher to fire a rocket into the room through an open window.

"How are you still here?" Rivers asked.

"We put the backs of our chairs together, and I untied her. She was able to escape first. I was secured to my chair, but by lunging I was able to move it forward – toward the opposite open window. I dropped eight meters onto the sand below as the blast demolished the house."

"At least the sand broke your fall," Rivers said.

"Actually, the sand broke the chair's fall. The wooden chair broke my fall. Just an unfortunate twist of physics, but the mass and acceleration of my body broke it apart, so I was at least free of the chair.

I found a tool box that the kidnappers had tossed outside, and I used a boxcutter to free my wrists and ankles – all of this while the house was incinerating. I hid under a boardwalk until the coast was literally clear. Then I just walked away, down the beach."

"Wow." Rivers wanted to carry on with the stimulating conversation and the mind-dulling alcohol intake, but he was only a college sophomore and wasn't accustomed to all of the stimulating conversation. "I'd love to hear more, but I really need to get going. Sorry."

"I understand. Thanks again for the ride."

"Where are you headed?" Rivers asked.

He explained how he was headed south to Birmingham, where he had a vehicle that needed a little attention, and a friend named Soledad who probably needed more. Then he planned to travel. He had some unfinished business. Rivers smiled, they hugged, and Rivers told him to take care. He was halfway to the front door of the pub before he realized he had never asked the hitchhiker his name, and when he went back to ask, he was gone.

About the Author

Douglas Lewis grew up in Fort Worth, Texas, where his sense of humor was honed by being raised in a middle class family, attending public schools, and being told at a very young age that his hometown was #3 on the list of Soviet nuclear targets. He was first published in high school, where his dark, ironic, angsty poetry was included in Insight, the school's yearly literary magazine. Flush with royalty money, he attended Texas Christian University, where he graduated in 1984 with a degree in biology, a minor in philosophy, and unwarranted optimism. Four years later, Douglas graduated from The University of Texas Health Science Center at Houston – internationally recognized as a medical school with a name that seems a bit too wordy. For well over four years, he has written and performed stand up comedy. By 2012 his three children had more-or-less reached adulthood and, takin advantage of the time he used to spend fielding calls from ups school administrators, he began writing *To Cure the Huma* He lives and works in Austin, Texas, where he can still occasionally found onstage performing stand up. When the him.

* 0 0 0 5 6 *